S O U T H E R N

B O O K

Secret
Tides

G A R Y E . P A R K E R

HOWARD
PUBLISHING CO.

Our purpose at Howard Publishing is to:

IF
P2394se
Bee

- *Increase faith* in the hearts of growing Christians
- *Inspire holiness* in the lives of believers
- *Instill hope* in the hearts of struggling people everywhere

Because He's coming again!

Secret Tides © 2004 by Gary E. Parker
All rights reserved. Printed in the United States of America
Published by Howard Publishing Co., Inc.
3117 North 7th Street, West Monroe, Louisiana 71291-2227
www.howardpublishing.com

Published in association with the literary agency of Alive Communications, Inc., 7680 Goddard Street, Suite 200, Colorado Springs, CO 80920

05 06 07 08 09 10 11 12 13   10 9 8 7 6 5 4 3 2

Edited by Ramona Cramer Tucker
Interior design by John Mark Luke Designs
Cover design by Kirk DouPonce, UDG | DesignWorks
Cover images by Robert Papp

Parker, Gary E.
    Secret tides / Gary E. Parker.
        p. cm — (Southern tides ; bk. 1)
    ISBN: 1-58229-359-7
        1. Plantation life—Fiction. 2. Southern States—Fiction. 3. Accident victims—Fiction. 4. Young women—Fiction. I. Title

PS3566.A6784S43 2004
813'.54--dc22

2004040523

Scripture quotations are taken from *The Holy Bible*, King James Version.

Dedication

A long time ago, when I was a history major at Furman University in South Carolina, my dad told me, "Son, you can't make a living with a history major."

Well, to some extent, he was right. Yet if I hadn't majored in history, I don't think I ever could have written a story like the one you'll find here. Being a history major gave me an interest in the large canvas of the human story, and that interest in the human story keeps me ever curious. It seems to me that without that curiosity, life gets pretty dull. With it, however, life takes on rich meaning.

So I dedicate this to all the history majors out there. Maybe you can't make a living with it, but perhaps you can make your life and the lives of those around you a little bit fuller, more colorful, more worth living.

Acknowledgments

Although this is a work of fiction, the social culture of the South Carolina lowland rice plantations just before the Civil War certainly wasn't fictitious. The men and women—both black and white—of this time and place lived the lifestyle reflected in these pages. Books such as *A South Carolina History* by Walter Edgar, *Mary's World* by Richard Cote, *An Antebellum Household* by Anne Sinkler LeClercq, *The History of Beaufort County* by Lawrence Rowland, Alexander Moore, and George Rogers Jr., *Roll Jordan Roll: The World the Slaves Made* by Eugene Genovese, *Within the Plantation Household: Black and White Women of the Old South* by Elizabeth Fox-Genovese, *Them Dark Days: Slavery in the American Rice Swamps* by William Dusinberre, and *Diary from Dixie* by Mary Boykin Chestnut gave me both information and context for the telling of the story. Any historical inaccuracies in these pages reflect on my failings, not those of these eminent researchers and writers.

In addition to the books that gave me confidence I was telling the story correctly, I also need to acknowledge the men and women at Howard Publishing for their enthusiasm for this project, especially Philis Boultinghouse. Ramona Tucker, editor, also deserves appreciation for her diligent approach and eager attention to detail and schedule. Her sharp eye made this work better.

Finally, as always, I express gratitude to my wife, Melody. She keeps the world around me humming so I can have the time to do fun things—like sit down to read, research, and then write the stories of the people you'll find in these pages.

Note to the Reader

The years between 1858 and the beginning of the Civil War were tumultuous ones for the South. Rumors of war abounded—a war that would forever change life for everyone, slave and plantation owner alike. Old institutions crumbled, and the system that had kept everyone—socialite, poor white, and servant—in their places disappeared.

In the effort to accurately reflect the time frame in which this historical fiction is set, I have used certain terms in this work that are offensive to me, personally, and that aren't reflective of modern speech and attitudes. Particularly is this true in reference to the men and women held in slavery on the plantations depicted in this novel. Please know that when terms like *darky*, *blackey*, *coloreds*, and *Negro* are used, they are reflective of this time frame and not meant as any offense to today's African-American community. Other terms that referred to the slaves, among them the most offensive, are not used in spite of their common uses in the period written about in this project.

Thankfully for all of us, the evil of slavery in our country disappeared during the Civil War, and many of the unfortunate racial terms and attitudes associated with it began to disappear from the American scene. There is no way to estimate—or apologize for—the physical, emotional, and spiritual damage inflicted upon generations of African-Americans through the travesty of slavery. The truths of God teach us that all people are equal, regardless of race. May the day hasten to come when we all fulfill God's will in this crucial arena of human relationship.

GARY E. PARKER

Part One

There is a tide in the affairs of men,

Which, taken at the flood, leads on to fortune;

Omitted, all the voyage of their life

Is bound in shallows and in miseries.

On such a full sea are we now afloat,

And we must take the current when it serves,

Or lose our ventures.

—WILLIAM SHAKESPEARE

Chapter One

The Oak Plantation, 1858

A band of thunderstorms hit the beaches of the South Carolina lowlands the day Camellia York accidentally killed the father of the man she hoped to marry. The storms didn't come ashore all at once, though. No, they gradually made their way inland, slowly eroding the blue sky of the early November day with dark clouds.

As the storms approached, Camellia stood barefooted about midway down a long wood table in a plantation cookhouse about three miles from shore. An old black woman, so stooped she looked like she'd carried a rock the size of a washtub on her neck for a long time, worked on the opposite side of the table. The woman's skin was so inky black that folks often said, if not for the whites of her eyes, they'd never see her after night fell. Camellia's skin was a soft white, and her hair hung in rich brown waves past her shoulders. The black woman wore a green bandanna, but it did little to contain the gray sprigs she called hair. Camellia's lips were full; her teeth were even and whiter than most. The lips of the black woman seemed to sink in around her mouth, and most of her teeth had long since disappeared. A dip of snuff filled her right cheek.

Flour covered the hands of both women. Camellia wiped sweat off her brow, leaving a smudge of the flour between her blue eyes.

The black woman grinned and pointed at the flour spot. "Miss Camellia makin' her sweet young face a mess. Lay on a mite more flour, and you be lookin' like a swamp ghost."

Camellia laughed and bent forward. The older woman grabbed a rag and wiped off the flour.

3

"There's not enough flour from Beaufort to Charleston to make *you* a ghost," drawled Camellia.

"That be true," said the black woman, chuckling. "Stella be black as the ink in Master Tessier's pen, oh yes I am."

The wood floor under the two women's feet creaked as they worked. Flies buzzed in and out of the open window to their right. The air hung heavy and hot in spite of the ominous clouds gathering outside. A low rumble sounded in the distance. A fireplace as wide as a wagon covered the room to Camellia's left, and the fire in it made the cookhouse even hotter than the outdoor temperature. Camellia faced the window and hoped to catch a breeze, but none came. She glanced around the room— a rectangular space about twenty by forty feet. Pots and pans and all manner of other cooking utensils hung on nails on the walls. Shelves on two of the walls contained flour, sugar, salt, and vegetables they'd put up in jars and cans. Barrels in the corners held cornmeal, rice, and wheat.

Camellia picked up a clay jar, poured flour into a bowl, took a touch of lard from a pail, and dug her hands into the flour. Stella did the same. Her hands turned as white as Camellia's. A strange notion seeped into Camellia's head. Could it be that all people were the same color, under their skin? she wondered. She held up her hands, covered with flour. "Look, Stella. Our hands look the same."

Stella spit into the snuff cup she always kept close by but said nothing.

Camellia wiped her hands on her apron, then scrutinized Stella. "Our clothes are about the same too."

Stella shrugged, obviously not catching Camellia's meaning.

Camellia started to say more but then decided if she explained it, Stella would just look at her as though she'd lost her mind and wave her off. So Camellia went back to her dough, massaging it steadily as her mind stretched with the realization of how much like Stella she truly was: An apron covered her plain brown dress, just like an apron covered Stella's plain gray dress. They both went barefooted except in winter or on the rare times they had traveled to Beaufort, close to thirty miles away, to attend church. They both labored from sunup to sundown on The Oak, a rice plantation of almost 3,000 acres and 325 laborers.

Camellia blew a loose strand of hair off her cheek as sweat rolled down between her shoulder blades. She patted out a biscuit and laid it by the ones she'd already finished. Stella dropped one beside hers. Camellia studied the wrinkles in Stella's hands—although nobody knew for sure, most folks figured Stella close to seventy. Camellia's earliest memories brought Stella's face to mind instead of a mama's or papa's. Stella had given Camellia a piece of peppermint—the first she'd ever had as a young child—and the girl had seen Stella every day since. That, maybe more than anything else, had stamped Camellia like a branding iron marked a horse. Now, except for her color, a little more refined speech, and the fact that nobody owned her, Camellia saw herself as real close to a darky.

The thunder rumbled again, this time closer, and Camellia hoped it would rain and break the heat. Although they'd finished the harvest a week earlier, the coastal lowlands often stayed warm right up to nearly December. Right now the day felt as hot as July—a sticky suffocating blanket that made the dogs stay under the porch of the manse and slowed everybody's labor to a crawl.

The thunder sounded once more. Camellia left the table and walked to the window. Low black clouds put a mean face on the eastern half of the sky. To the west the horizon remained blue, except for a few white clouds. Camellia scanned the yard. The manse stood on four-feet-high stone pillars a good rock throw away, a stately two-story white house with four columns on the front. Porches wrapped both the front and back. An oak tree, at least a hundred years old and so wide it took four people to get their arms around it, stood to the right of the front porch. From this ancient oak, with its moss-draped branches, the plantation had taken its name. About a half-mile to the left of the manse, snaking its way toward the Atlantic Ocean, the slow-moving Conwilla River created the current that made rice growing possible. A gravel drive, bordered on both sides by twenty-five moss-draped oaks, connected about a quarter-mile away to a wide dirt road that ran from Beaufort to Charleston.

Camellia wiped her hands on her apron. Although she owned none of The Oak and labored as hard as any of the coloreds that made it run, she loved the place. She loved the sandy soil that shifted under her feet;

loved the crash and spray of the ocean she visited almost every Sunday afternoon because she lived too far from Beaufort to walk to church; loved the sounds of the frogs, birds, and insects that made every summer night a throaty concert; loved the flowers that bloomed almost year-round, their smells and color keeping everything alive. Mostly though, she loved The Oak because she loved—

Lightning cracked the sky. Camellia jerked away from the window, her daydreaming ended. Thunder rattled the cookhouse as she turned to Stella. "That thunder sounds mean. Like it's got something hurtful to say but no words to speak it."

"Maybe it'll bring us some wet," said Stella. "Cool us down a mite."

"It sounds angry, not wet." Camellia eyed the odd sky—half of it blue, half black.

Stella grabbed a handful of potatoes and started peeling them. "What you know about angry thunder? A child your age don't know such things."

"I'm eighteen now." Camellia picked up a stack of the potatoes. "I can tell if a storm's got rain in it. Just open your nose and smell—that's all you got to do. And when it don't, it gets mad, you know that. Wants to take out the anger on somebody."

"You talk like a slave mammy," said Stella. "Readin' the storms."

"A white girl can read storms," Camellia claimed. "And this storm"— she looked at the window again—"I don't know . . . feels frightful . . . like it's a portent of something rough." The thunder mumbled again, and she shivered.

Stella stepped to the window, peered out, then moved back to her potatoes. "Got some blue sky left. Maybe the storm won't even get us."

Camellia wiped her brow.

"Not sure which is better," continued Stella. "We need the rain, but the wind and the blow might do some damage."

"That's the way with storms," said Camellia. "They bring the good and the bad, one in hand with the other."

Stella smiled. "There you go again with your philosphizin'."

Camellia shrugged. "Just thinking. I mean, just look at that sky. Part blue, part black. Which side will win? Which way will it go? And which is better? We do need the rain. But what if the storm whips up a bad wind, enough to tear up a house or two? So which is better? Storm or no storm? Hard to know beforehand, right? You think one thing is better but can't know for sure for a long time."

Stella kept at her potatoes. "You're a smart girl. Too bad you ain't had a chance to get some learnin'."

Camellia didn't reply, but her hands peeled potatoes even faster. The fact that a girl of her station had no chance for an education made her sad. But she knew no way to change the matter, so she wouldn't complain.

"When is Captain York gone be back?" asked Stella.

"Tomorrow," Camellia said, thinking of her pa, a former cavalry officer during the Mexican War. "He and Mr. Cain are hauling a couple wagons full of supplies back from Charleston."

"You reckon he'll bring back the blue calico you been wantin' for that new dress? If he does, I'll make a pretty one for you, just like you ask."

"Pa's not always dependable these days," Camellia said, frowning. "You know that. It's like he can't keep his head on real straight sometimes."

"He's got a lot on him, runnin' this big place," Stella put in. "The Oak is an armful, that's for sure." She sliced her potatoes and dumped them in an iron pot.

Camellia cut the last of hers and dropped them on top of Stella's. Captain York, her pa, served as overseer for Mr. Marshall Tessier. He managed the work of all the Negroes, plus a couple of white men who helped him. Every night he came home worn out and hungry. As the oldest child and only female in the house, the duties of cooking, cleaning, and keeping house fell squarely into her lap, in spite of the fact that she'd worked all day on the same plantation her pa had run for as long as she could remember. Sometimes that seemed strange to her, but since everybody in her world had their place and didn't usually squabble about it, she just squared her shoulders and kept quiet.

"That woman over in Beaufort said she didn't want him courting her," Camellia said. "He took it hard."

"That was half a year ago," Stella commented sharply. "He ought to be over any hurt she caused. She was a loose woman anyway."

"He's worse, if anything," lamented Camellia. "Like a barrel rolling downhill, busting up more and more as it bounces toward the bottom."

"How's he worse?"

Camellia wiped her hands. "Oh, you know, his drinking. And he spends most of his off time gambling somewhere. Cockfighting, horse racing, card games . . . anything he can find to make a wager. He hardly ever stays home, even on Sundays when he's not at work."

Stella's hands stilled as she swiveled toward Camellia. "Look at me, child."

Camellia obeyed.

Stella took both of the girl's hands. "Your pa got a lot of barky edges. Always had them. That woman in Beaufort, even as loose as she was, kept him with some calm. Now that she's gone, his mean ways have bucked back up. I seed it happen lot of times. A woman puts away a man, and he just goes off wild."

"Was he better before Mama died?"

Stella licked her lips. "That was a long time ago, child, back afore you got any memory. No use castin' your head back to them days."

As usual, Camellia thought, nobody seemed willing to talk about her mama. In her earlier years, Camellia had asked about her lots of times, but her pa always shook his head and told her there wasn't much to say. "She's dead," he'd state. "Typhus got her a long time ago." Gradually she'd let it drop. But the mystery still haunted her sometimes.

"Pa's got three of us left," said Camellia, changing the subject. "I can abide his crazy ways, but my brothers need a steady hand. When do you figure Pa will settle again?"

Stella lowered her eyes. "I wish I could promise you he's gone do that. But I reckon you and Chester and Johnny deserve the truth. Maybe your pa will, and maybe he won't. I seed it go both ways."

Thunder rattled the floor this time, and Camellia again moved to the window. The black clouds now covered three-fourths of the sky, growing larger and darker as the wind blew them closer. Lightning dropped and hit the ground a couple of miles away. Camellia suddenly felt weak, as if something as dark as the gloomy sky loomed over her. She wanted to cry.

For as long as she could remember, she'd tried to take care of her pa and brothers—Chester, now sixteen, Johnny, just over a year younger—even as more and more duties had fallen her way. But now it all felt too heavy to carry. Her heart sagged, and moisture glistened in her eyes. But then her stomach steadied. Giving up never did anybody any good, she knew, so she might as well not start now. She wiped her hands and took heart. One of these days, maybe soon, she'd get married and everything would turn out fine.

Trenton Tessier's face flashed into her memory, and she smiled. Master Marshall's nineteen-year-old son loved her. Hadn't he said as much this past Christmas when he came home from boarding school in Charleston?

Camellia remembered the best night of her life.

She and Trenton had taken a walk on the beach that Christmas Eve. Oh, she knew she ought not to have gone with him without a chaperone. But sometimes society's rules needed some bending. Besides, the fancy rules of courting that governed Charleston didn't really fit their situation, since they'd known each other since childhood.

The stars twinkled like pieces of broken glass that night. The ocean splashed gently toward shore, filling the air with scents of wet sand and salt. She and Trenton, so handsome in his tan frock coat, black pants, and calf-high boots, stopped about twenty feet from the water, and he took her hands in his.

"We've known each other most of our lives," he began.

She lowered her eyes, afraid to speak lest he notice her unpolished words and realize she didn't deserve him.

"I've missed you every day these last three years I've been away at school," he continued.

"I've missed you more." She looked up at him now, her shyness put aside to make sure he knew of her affection.

"When I come back to The Oak for good," he promised, "we'll have big decisions to make."

As the night grew chillier, she shivered, and he pulled her shawl tighter around her neck. Then he took her in his arms and held her for a long time. He kissed her and she trembled.

Although he'd not exactly asked her to marry him that night in December, he'd come real close, so close that she had no doubt he'd ask her pa for her hand as soon as he finished boarding school and came back to The Oak to assume his rightful position. Then she'd have all she needed—Trenton Tessier, a man of charm and strength and fine manners. That's all she truly wanted from life: Trenton to hug her every now and again, to tell her he loved her more than anybody in the whole world.

"You be daydreamin', child," said Stella, bringing Camellia back to the present. "Let's finish this supper. I don't want to haul it to the manse once that lightnin' moves closer."

Camellia hurried back to the table.

"You be thinkin' about Mr. Trenton, I figure," Stella said bluntly.

"You're right about that."

Stella spit into her snuff cup. "That boy ain't good enough for you."

Camellia ground her teeth. She and Stella had argued over this a lot. "I know he's got his faults," she began. "Sometimes he thinks too high of himself, spends too much time worrying about his clothes, the cut of his hair. And, yes, he puts too much store in his hunting skills. But what man of his quality and wealth don't have a bit of the barnyard rooster in him?"

"Money don't give a man the right to look down on folks," argued Stella. "I know it ain't my place to say it, but he's trouble, that one. You mark my word."

"You just don't know him. He's sweet and refined—as finely educated as any man in the whole country. He's charming too, you have to admit. Enough to melt the heart of any girl in Charleston. What right do I have to think less of him just because he's aware of his outstanding traits?"

"I'm just tellin' you what I think. Take it as you like. But one thing I know: You be pure in heart and he ain't. And you know it."

"When we marry, I can help him," insisted Camellia.

"A woman ought not marry for what a man can be," said Stella. "She be playin' a losin' game doin' that. Best marry a man for what he is, for that's mostly who he's gone stay."

"He said he'd go to church with me when we marry," Camellia answered, pouting.

Stella grunted. "Won't matter. He's like his pa. Reckon even the good Lord will have a hard time changin' that."

Camellia's face flushed at the mention of Marshall Tessier. A touch of anger ran up her neck. How dare Stella speak so ill of Trenton? She started to argue more but then thought of how Stella saw her beloved Trenton. He did treat the coloreds poorly sometimes, so no wonder most of them held him in low regard. But he wasn't the only white man with that fault. If she waited until she found a man who handled the Negroes gently, she'd never marry anybody. Besides, the darkies needed a strong hand to keep them steady with their work; everybody knew that.

After she and Trenton married, she'd tell him to give the servants more respect; she'd help him see how they kept The Oak thriving the way it did. She smiled as she imagined the days after her marriage. So much would change. She'd get a tutor and learn to read. Buy nice clothes so she could dress up and make Trenton proud. Take him to Saint Michael's in Beaufort, where they could sit in the front row and listen to the parson teach them the Word of the Lord.

Lifted by her dreams, Camellia turned to her potatoes once more. Thunder rumbled directly overhead, and the room turned dark as the sun disappeared completely. Footsteps clomped on the cookhouse porch. *Just who would come out in this storm?* Camellia wondered.

Then the door swung open, and Mr. Marshall Tessier, master of the plantation, pushed his bulky frame into the room. He wore shiny black boots and tan riding pants. A brown ruffled shirt was open at the throat, and his eyes looked bright, as if they had too much fire burning in them. He smelled like old tobacco and stale ale. Camellia's heart began to race.

"Mrs. Tessier wants you to come to the manse," Tessier told Stella without looking at her.

"I got potatoes left," Stella said, her eyes down. "You reckon I might finish them afore I go to Mrs. Tessier? She wants supper on time, I expect."

Tessier glanced at Stella only for a moment before focusing on Camellia again. "You go like I said," he snarled. "No uppity smart mouth either."

Stella muttered softly.

11

"I said git!" Tessier demanded. "Unless you want a switch on your old hide!"

Camellia caught Stella's eye and tilted her head toward the door. Although she hated to face Tessier alone, she didn't want Stella to be punished. She'd seen him switch slaves before, and he was merciless.

"Be back soon as I can," Stella told Camellia as she reached the door.

"I'll finish up the potatoes," said Camellia.

As soon as Stella left, Tessier stepped closer. "You fill out that dress most amply," he said, inspecting her head to toe.

Camellia's skin crawled. Tessier had said such things a number of times over the last year or so. Frightened by his attentions, she'd told her pa about it a couple of months ago. But Captain York had laughed off her concerns. She would never forget their conversation.

"You're a strikin' woman now," her pa said when she confided her fears. *"Got to expect men to take notice."*

"But Mr. Tessier is a married man!" she protested. *"And he's old too— got to be near sixty!"*

Her pa rubbed his neatly trimmed black beard. "You handle this easy like," he finally said. "You can't trifle with a man like Tessier."

"I'm not the one doing the trifling," she argued, *a low anger rising as she realized her pa, always so strong, might not stand up to Tessier like she thought he should.*

"Tessier pays the wages," her pa continued. *"Got to give the man with the money a little rope. He's just havin' a bit of fun with you; nothin' to fret over."*

"You defending him?"

Her pa straightened then. "No. You're my girl, and I won't let him hurt you. But you've got to keep steady here, understand the ways of the world. Everythin's not as pure as you see it. You've blossomed this past year but still aren't used to handlin' men's coarse ways. Remember that Tessier can put me off this place at any second . . . and you too. Just stay out of his way."

"I'm trying," she said. *She wondered if she should tell him about her plans with Trenton. Her pa, of course, knew they spent time together when Trenton*

came home for visits. But so far nobody had said anything about any romance between them.

"But he's . . . Trenton's father," she finally stammered.

"What's goin' on with you and Master Trenton?" he asked curiously. "He treatin' you proper?"

She shrugged. "Trenton says we have big decisions to make when he comes home."

"A rich boy like Trenton is liable to play with a girl like you," her pa said sternly. "But he ain't likely to marry you."

Camellia pouted at the stinging words. She knew her station in life, how the classes stayed separate—owners at the top, darkies at the bottom, white trash who didn't work just above the darkies, white folks who did work on the rung above them. But Trenton would overlook all that. She felt certain of it.

"Trenton will marry me," she said, chin lifted just a bit. "He loves me."

When her pa grinned, she saw that he liked the idea of a marriage between her and Trenton. Although strong in a lot of ways, Captain York had a weakness for money, and he tended to give wealthy folks more respect than he did anyone else.

"I hope you're right." He beamed. "So stay away from his father. That's the best thing for everybody."

Camellia had tried to do just that, and it had worked for the past few months. Now she hoped she could escape again. She tried to move around Tessier, but he stuck a boot between her feet and blocked her escape.

"I've had my eyes on you," he said.

"You've been with a bottle," Camellia said, her voice stronger than she felt. "Smell like whiskey."

"I won't hurt you," Tessier said softly. "Just want a little kiss."

Camellia relaxed a little. Tessier had said similar things in the past, but she'd always managed to keep him at bay.

"I'm not . . . not experienced in the ways of the world," she said, backing up slightly. "You can find better than me to kiss."

"I can make amends for that." He moved a little closer. "I can teach you how to please a man."

Camellia's eyes searched past Tessier, looking for a way out. If she could get to the porch, she could run, and Tessier, in his drunkenness, probably couldn't keep up with her. The room darkened even more as the clouds finally took over the whole sky and wind whipped through the windows. Tessier stepped still closer, until she could feel his breath on her cheek.

"I can give you anything you want," he coaxed. "I can send you to the best schools in the East, make a proper woman of you, clothe you in the fashions of Europe, provide you with manners, culture—all the things you surely want."

"That's a kind offer," she said, still trying to stay polite. "But I have no desire for such as that."

"Money then; is that it? I have more than I can ever spend. You give me what I want, and I'll take care of you." His fingers snagged her hair. "Such luscious brown hair," he whispered. "And skin as soft as a swan's feathers."

Camellia's stomach rolled, but she kept her voice even as she spoke. Maybe she could still get out of this without any real harm. "What about your wife?" she managed to ask.

Tessier chuckled. "She's no concern of yours." He touched the back of Camellia's neck and then bent to kiss her.

Camellia almost panicked. Master Tessier had never gone this far! What would happen if she let him kiss her? Would that be the end of it, or would he want more? Unable to tell, she began to pray for something—anything—to end the unpleasantness. When Tessier's lips touched her cheek, she twisted away. He tried again, but she pushed him off.

"You reject me?" he bellowed, his face bunched in rage.

"Your son!" she cried, her voice now desperate. "He and I are—"

He laughed at her objection. "Trenton is a boy! He has no idea how to treat a woman like you!"

"Just let me go!" she pleaded. "I won't tell anybody." She tried to back up more, but the worktable stopped her.

"You think I care?" he yelled. "I'm the master of this place, understand that? You, your father, my wife, or anyone else has no power here!" He grabbed her by the shoulders and dug his fingers into her flesh.

"You're paining me," she whimpered.

As he twisted her face to his, rain started to pound the roof. Thunder roared. In her fear and disgust Camellia almost collapsed. Then a bolt of lightning struck close by, shocking her heart into pounding again and sending a reserve of strength she didn't know she had rushing through her bones. She wouldn't give in to such unwanted attentions without a fight, she decided. She wouldn't let Tessier kiss her, wouldn't let him treat her as if he owned her! No one owned Camellia York!

As Tessier again bent to kiss her, she kneed him in the stomach. Doubling over in pain, he backed up. Camellia rushed toward the doorway and almost made it out before he caught her by the hair and jerked her back. She twisted and punched at his face but missed. Wrapping his arms around her, he locked his hands at the small of her back and squeezed.

"You're a woman of fire!" he bellowed. "Just what I like!"

Seeing no choice now, Camellia reared her head back and thrust it into Tessier's nose. He screamed, let her go, and stumbled backward. Camellia ran again, but he grabbed her once more, this time by the back of the neck, and spun her around. His hands tightened like twin vises against her windpipe, and she fell back against the worktable. She tried to scratch his face, but his grip increased until she couldn't breathe! Her lungs felt like they'd pop at any second! She tried once again to kick him, but her legs couldn't move. When her eyes began to blur, she knew she'd reached the end of her fight.

"Pl . . . please," she gasped.

"You made me do this!" Master Tessier panted.

Camellia tried to fight more but had no strength. Her body went limp. She closed her eyes and prayed to die, hoped to die, wanted to die to avoid the humiliation of what she feared Tessier would do to her.

She heard footsteps on the porch and opened her eyes just as Stella rushed in, her head soaked from rain. Stella's return gave Camellia renewed courage. Raising both hands, she raked at Tessier's eyes. He cried out, let go of her neck, and staggered against the wall.

Stella grabbed the potato pot and threw it at Tessier. The potatoes spilled to the floor. The pot hit Tessier in the chest, but he knocked it away. Still fighting for breath, Camellia searched for a weapon, and her fingers closed on the peeling knife. Holding it like a dagger, she yelled, "I'll use it!"

"No you won't!" Tessier rushed at her, and she backed up. But he kept coming. Feeling the table at her back, she stopped, poised to defend herself. Just then Tessier lunged for the knife . . . but his feet slipped on the spilled potatoes. Off balance, he fell forward. Camellia jerked out of his way, but he grabbed at her as he toppled over. His right hand closed on the knife blade as his head hit the table with a sharp *thwack*. His body sagged; his face fell into the potatoes. He rolled over and tried to rise but fell again. His eyes rolled back, then closed. A knot the size of an apple appeared over his left eye, just past the temple. Blood dripped from a cut in his skull and from his hand where he'd fallen on the knife.

Stella squatted and lifted his head. Outside the thunder and rain suddenly stopped, as if listening to hear what would happen next. Tessier's breathing sounded ragged and shallow.

Camellia grabbed a rag, wet it from water in a barrel, and dropped to her knees.

"Is he all right?" she asked, rubbing the rag over his face.

"Reckon not," said Stella, laying his head on the floor. "Busted his skull right good." She pointed to the blood seeping out.

"We have to help him," said Camellia frantically as she held the rag to his head.

Stella bent to his chest and listened to his breathing. "It ain't good."

"We best go for a doctor!" pleaded Camellia.

Rising up, Stella took Camellia's wrists into her hands. "Maybe he be past our help. Or a doctor's. Maybe the good Lord gone call him home."

Camellia struggled against Stella's hands. "We have to try!" she urged. "Go for aid!"

"Give me one good reason why."

"Because it's the right thing to do!"

Stella let go of Camellia's hands and pointed at Tessier. "That man was goin' to have his way with you. That be the right thing to do?"

Camellia shook her head.

"And what if he should live?" asked Stella. "He'd put you and your family right off this place. Me too. After he whipped me, he'd sell me fast, like a horse he don't need." She stood and toed Tessier in the chest.

The wind whipped through the window, blowing Camellia's hair. Rain started falling again, but gentler now. Tears streamed down Camellia's face. She bent to Tessier again. "We just let him die?"

Stella patted her back. "He'll live or die on his own. Not up to us."

Tessier took several shallow breaths.

"I did this," said Camellia.

"*He* did it," Stella countered. "You and me both know it."

Camellia thought of the doctor again and started to stand. No matter what Stella said, she couldn't just stand by and watch a man die. But then Tessier heaved one last big breath and lay still.

Stella shook her head. "Not ours to worry about. He be gone."

Camellia touched his chest. It didn't move. She looked up at Stella. "How will we explain this? They'll accuse me of killing him, and they'll be right."

Stella grabbed a rag, handed another one to Camellia, and started cleaning up the potatoes. "The man be drunk," Stella said, as if talking about the weather. "He come to check on supper, see what we was fixin'. He tripped on this stool." She took a two-step stool from beside the fireplace and laid it by Tessier's feet. "He tripped on this stool and fell into the table. That's all we got to say."

"What about the cut on his hand?"

"A man falls, he grabs for the table, and his hand catches on the knife. He cuts the hand as he falls. A simple thing to happen."

"You think folks will believe us?"

"If we stick to our stories, they'll let it stand, I reckon. How else they gone say it happened? Two women knocked him on the head? What sense that make? Just say the story over to me; I'll say it over to you. Then we take it to Mrs. Tessier."

"But we're lying," said Camellia.

Stella took Camellia's face in her hands. "Listen to me, child. This is the way it gone be. Mr. Tessier tripped on a stool and busted his head.

That's my story, and it best be yours. Any other way, and we both gone be messed up for the rest of our lives. You got that?"

Too shocked to think of a good argument, Camellia nodded blankly.

"Now repeat the story to me," ordered Stella.

Camellia started to protest. The notion of lying cut against all she believed. Yet, Stella told it right. Mr. Tessier had caused this by trying to take advantage of her. If he hadn't made his shameful approach, he'd still be breathing. He carried the weight of what had happened, not her. Why should she hand over her life for a bad man's sins? And what about Stella? If anybody ever heard the whole truth, they'd hurt Stella too, put her off The Oak. Where would she go at her age? What would she do?

Outside the thunder rumbled as the last of the storm died away. Like the storm had fought with the clear sky to see which would win, now Camellia fought within her soul. What should she do? She wanted to tell the truth but knew she had no choice but to lie.

"You done no wrong here," Stella whispered. "Mr. Tessier brought this on. Just tell the same story, over and over. Nobody will ever know the difference."

Camellia stared at Stella.

"We best go to the manse," said Stella. "Tell your pa and the others what happened."

"I'm fearful," Camellia said.

Stella nodded wisely. "I been fearful all my life, child. But I got words for you. You get used to it."

Chapter Two

The storm that hit The Oak that day missed Charleston, and the sun, a strong steady heat that seemed as though it wanted to bake everything to a crisp, never let up. Underneath that sun in Charleston, a crowd of close to fifty people stood around a raised wood platform about a half-mile from the ocean, not far from the center of town. Most of the people in the crowd were men—rough men, fancy men, men in hats with tobacco in their cheeks, men in frock coats and ruffled shirts—all kinds of men from the best to the worst that South Carolina and its neighboring states had to offer. The smell of sea air and poorly washed bodies drifted in and out as a light breeze rose and fell. A variety of dogs mingled in and out with the men.

A line of nine coloreds stood on the platform—seven men and two women. The men wore chains on their ankles; the women were unshackled. A bald, stocky white man in a blousy blue shirt stood slightly in front of the darkies, his booming voice chattering constantly as he tried to jack up the prices on the men and women he wanted to sell.

The two women stood at the end of the line, the last of the coffle for auction that day. The taller of the two women, a buxom girl with skin the color of butterscotch, kept her head up and her eyes straight, almost as if she dared any man to make too low a bid on her.

The man in the blousy shirt moved to the first darky, explaining all his fine qualities. The taller woman at the end of the line tried hard not to hear. Her lips pouted; she wished she had a last name other than one stuck on her by a white man. People with their own last names didn't get sold off when the fever burned through their plantation in late summer and killed off their master and two of his children. But since she didn't

have a true last name, the banker man had come to the Rushton plantation about a day's ride from Richmond only a month after the fever and
poured out some harsh news. She could remember it all, as if it were yesterday.

*"You got to raise some quick cash money," the banker had told the widow
Rushton, his face all scraggly with a sorry gray beard. "Mr. Rushton owes the
bank a note you can't pay without doing so."*

*Lady Rushton glanced around the room, her round face flushed, her brown
eyes wide. "Bring me some water, Ruby," she ordered her house servant.*

*Ruby had obeyed quickly, her heart pounding with the tidings the
banker had brought. Having served in the house all her life, she knew the
chunky Mrs. Rushton didn't know much of anything about the business of
a plantation.*

*"How much money does your bank require?" Mrs. Rushton asked the
banker after Ruby handed her the water.*

"About twenty thousand," said the man.

*"Can you wait for the harvest?" she asked. "I expect we could raise that
much after we get the tobacco crop sold."*

When the banker rolled his eyes, Ruby decided she didn't like him much.

*"You never know about crops," he said. "Maybe they earn something,
maybe they don't."*

*Mrs. Rushton wiped her wet eyes. "I am not good at this," she admitted.
"I wish Junior was older."*

*Ruby nodded her understanding. Mrs. Rushton's oldest boy had barely
reached twelve years.*

*The banker picked at his beard, as if digging for lice. "There's one sure
way to raise some money. Faster than anything else I know."*

Mrs. Rushton looked up at him. "How's that?"

"You can let go a few of your coloreds."

*Ruby held her breath. In all her twenty years, the Rushtons had only sold
one of their servants. That man, a squatty field worker with no left hand, had
run off at least three times before they got shed of him.*

*"I'd rather sell a Negro than whip one," Mr. Rushton had told his over-
seer the day they caught the one-armed runner and whipped him for the third*

time. "Just go on and get what we can for him."

That had happened seven summers ago. But now Master Thomas Rushton lay six feet under the dirt on a high spot about five minutes away from the house, and his missus needed fast money.

"I am not happy with the notion of selling," Mrs. Rushton told the banker.

"I don't see where you got much choice," said the banker. "Not unless you want to sell off some of these fine furnishings." He waved his hand over the room.

Ruby's eyes followed his hand. Soft rugs the color of a dark red apple lay on the floor, and matching drapes hung on the glass windows. The sofa, hauled in on a wagon from Philadelphia, had legs that curved all the way to the floor. Ruby had heard Mrs. Rushton brag more than once that it looked like the sofas they made over in a place called France. Tall chests, fancy chairs, and well-smoothed wood tables covered with fine oil lamps and carved glass figures completed the décor in the sitting parlor.

A sudden chill rolled through Ruby. Mrs. Rushton loved her pretties far more than she did her coloreds.

"How many will need to go if we do it?" asked Mrs. Rushton.

The banker smiled. "No more than ten to fifteen, I expect. Depending on their value, of course."

Mrs. Rushton wiped her eyes again.

"You'll need to make a list for me," said the banker. "Which ones you want to sell, which ones to keep."

Mrs. Rushton waved him off. "I can't do it. Work it out with Mr. Landers."

"He's your overseer?"

"Yes, do whatever he says."

Ruby shivered when she heard that. Landers had no use for her because he knew that Mrs. Rushton's oldest child, Donetta, had taught her to read and write.

"It's not helpful," he'd complained to Mr. Rushton the day two years earlier when he'd hauled Ruby to the master's chambers after he caught her reading late one afternoon on the front porch. "Keeps her from doing proper work."

"But I done all my chores for the day," pleaded Ruby.

Master Rushton stared at Ruby. "Donetta taught you, didn't she?"

Not wanting to get Donetta into trouble, Ruby kept quiet, her eyes on the floor.

"Don't matter who taught her," said Landers. "If I'm gone keep this place runnin' right, I can't have all the darkies sittin' around readin' books on me, now can I? Besides, it's against the law."

Master Rushton looked from Ruby to Landers. "What do you want to do with her?"

"Maybe we should make an example of her," Landers said, narrowing his eyes.

Mr. Rushton appeared to be considering the matter. Then he shook his head. "Leave it alone. You know I don't take to whipping. Just makes everybody glum and hateful. Besides, my own girl did the teaching. How can I whip Ruby without doing harm to my own girl?"

Landers started to protest, but Rushton held up a hand. Landers cursed under his breath and left the room.

"Stay clear of him," Master Rushton warned Ruby after Landers had disappeared. "And keep your reading to your room."

Boss Landers had not liked her since that day. So when the chance to get shed of her showed itself, he snapped it right up, picking her as one of the thirteen hands to haul away for auction to satisfy the banker.

Ruby had tried to talk Lady Rushton out of selling her, but the silly woman had just covered her face and let it happen. With Donetta off at boarding school, Ruby had nowhere else to turn, so Landers had shipped her and the rest of the coffle over to Richmond. Four field hands got sold off there, each of them going in a different direction. Four good men and women she had known and loved now were scattered out like thistles on a breezy day. The others, Ruby included, had been shipped by boat from Richmond to Charleston.

"Better prices in the South," Ruby had heard Landers say to the ship's captain as he led them aboard. "More need for the blackeys way down in the land of cotton."

Ruby ground her teeth and wished she could put her hands to Landers's throat. A man like him needed somebody to squeeze his breath out, to make his tongue turn black with death from lack of air. But she, of course, a woman with no name of her own, had no way to harm Landers. So she had shuffled onto the tall sailing ship; had taken her spot on the deck where they put her and her fellow coloreds; had slept under the small canvas tent they had given them to cover their heads from sun and rain.

Now, less than a month later, she stood on the platform in front of the sweaty white men, her right ankle rubbed raw by the chain she had worn since she left Virginia, a chain that had scraped her smooth skin until it peeled and bled. To her back, a light but hot breeze blew at her head. She'd spent the night in a building one street over from the ocean, just two streets from where she stood. She listened to see if she could hear the waves washing in but didn't hear anything. She wished the water would reach all the way to where she stood, that it would come in one large wave and wash her away forever. It didn't matter if it drowned her; in fact, that would please her greatly.

Her mouth set with anger, Ruby examined her brown dress and tried to put the whole matter out of her head. Although still clean, the dress had a tear near her left shoe and more than a few worn-out places. She glanced at the others on the platform. Some were as black as cooking skillets; others almost yellow-brown. The tallest man stood as high as a horse's ears, the shortest no higher than three washtubs stacked on one another. The other woman wore a stained cloth on her head and had only three fingers on her right hand. She wouldn't bring much. The blousy-shirted man pointed at the crowd, his tongue moving like a lizard in and out over his lips.

Ruby glanced at Markus, the tallest of the black men. The two of them had taken each other to marry six years ago. Part of her dared to hope she and Markus would end up at the same place, but the other half knew better. The chances of it didn't add up to much. People with no last name got split up all the time—no matter that they had spent lots of nights on a pallet together, and in spite of the fact they had made a living baby out of their union.

Ruby thought of her boy, Theo, the only thing she loved as much as she did Markus. Though she had wailed and pulled her hair until it came out in clumps, Mrs. Rushton hadn't seen fit to send Theo with her and Markus.

"Mr. Landers says he won't fetch much, since he's so young," Lady Rushton had said as Ruby begged her to let her keep her five-year-old boy. "Best leave him with your mammy."

The auctioneer started the bidding on the shortest darky. Ruby wiped sweat off her face and pictured Theo. Born with an empty socket where his right eye should have been, Theo's growing had stalled out real fast, like he didn't have enough skin for his bones. Boys his age already stood half a head taller than him, and from what she could see, he wouldn't ever reach too much higher than just about bosom level with her.

At first she had felt grieved over the boy's smallness—sorry that he'd taken such a strange turn. But then she noticed how good he talked, like his lack of growth had left some extra power for his head to use. A short but wise child with a round face and a mouthful of teeth, he sounded grown up almost from the day he started speaking. Her mammy, Nettie, said the Lord had made Theo special; had taken his eye so as to give him a different kind of seeing . . . visions that most folks never spied. Since Ruby didn't really believe in the Lord, not after what she'd been through, she wanted to argue with her mammy. But since she knew that nothing could shake Nettie's stout faith, she let it go.

"I will take care for this baby," Nettie had said as Ruby made ready to leave the Rushton house. "I will keep him till the day you come back and claim him again."

Theo hugged Ruby, then took a spot in his mammy's lap.

"Don't reckon that day will ever come," said Ruby, her brown eyes wet and red. "Reckon I won't see my baby again in this old world."

"Don't be grievin', Mama," said Theo. "I'll set eyes on you again. I seen it."

Ruby knelt and took his tiny hands in hers. He believed what Mammy Nettie had told him; that the Lord had gifted him with the power to see what others couldn't. How could she argue with him against that notion?

"You watch out for your mammy," she said, not daring to tell him that his mammy's crazy notions had never helped anybody. "Do what she tells you."

Theo touched her cheek, as if he were the adult seeking to comfort her.
"You be comin' back someday. I seen it."

"I hope you see it right," she said.

"I do," he stated. "Sho as a dog likes a bone, I seen you comin' for me."

After hugging him one more time, Ruby had turned away and left.

Now, as she was about to be sold, she wiped her eyes and pushed Theo and Markus out of her head. Unless some true miracle took place—and she saw no reason to expect one—they were dead to her, dead and gone forever.

The auctioneer sold off the shortest man and called up the next man. "See these good features," said the blousy-shirted man. "A strong back, thick biceps and thighs, clear eyes—all the things you want in a field hand. What's the opening price for him? Don't try to low bid me either. This is a good hand, and you all know it."

A man made a bid, and the auctioneer took off yelling. Sweat soaking through the back of her dress, Ruby kept her head down. The afternoon moved slowly, and Ruby's back ached. The auctioneer kept on working. People made bids. Men stepped in and out, buying and leaving, shouting and spitting streams of tobacco and snuff juice into the cobblestones under their feet. Ruby wished she could go on and die. Shame made her sad and hopeless. She lost track of time. The blousy-shirted man kept things moving.

"Now, just look at this," he said, turning a fat Negro around so his back faced the crowd. "He ain't ever been whipped. That means he ain't a runner, no sir, no chance of that." He told the darky to take off his shirt, then pointed to his back. "You see any stripes there? No, you don't. He's a gentle man, yes he is." He twisted the black back around.

"I'll go seven hundred," yelled a man from the left of the crowd. The auctioneer nodded, and the bidding started again. Before long he sold that man, then another, and finally came to Markus.

Ruby stared at her man. Markus had shoulders like an ox and wide clear eyes. He knew how to keep horses and fix wagons and such. Markus tried to look her way, but the auctioneer grabbed his chin and squeezed it until he turned back to the crowd. Ruby saw Markus's muscles tighten.

She knew if he got the chance, he would pick up the auctioneer, bear-hug him, and crack his back like snapping a twig.

The bidding started at nine hundred dollars. Within a few minutes a man with a curly mustache ended it all at the price of eleven hundred.

Ruby listened hard to see if anybody mentioned the man's name or where he lived, but nobody did. She ached to follow Markus as they took him away but knew she couldn't. A man in the back would take the dollars from his buyer and write up the papers that sent her man to his new master. She wondered how far away from Markus she would end up. If they lived close enough, maybe he could get a pass every now and again and come see her on Sundays when they rested from their labors.

Only one more Negro stood between her and the blousy-shirted man. She wiped her face, then brushed down her hair, straighter than most of her people and not nearly as coarse. The auctioneer finished quickly with the last Negro man, moved him off the platform, and turned to her. She kept her eyes on her bare feet.

"Now look at this one," said the man, pointing to the spot where he wanted Ruby to stand. "She's straight from the house of Mr. and Mrs. Thomas Rushton outside of Richmond, Virginia. She's named Ruby, and she was raised for the house: for cookin', cleanin', sewin', and tendin' children."

Ruby moved to the spot where he pointed. She felt the crowd studying her, felt the men's eyes moving up and down her body. Her skin seemed alive, like ants crawling on her arms and legs. She hated the way the men looked at her. It didn't seem right somehow. Why should a man get to study a woman this way? Look her over as if she was a prize cow he might want to purchase?

At least five men had come by her stall that morning, walking one at a time into the small space where she'd slept last night. The men had made her stand up, had made her open her mouth so they could see her teeth, had made her pull up her skirt so they could see her feet and legs.

Ruby had glared at each man and wished she had a pistol to shoot them.

"She's twenty," said the auctioneer. "Took care of the Rushton's babies since they first drew breath."

"Why'd they get shed of her?" yelled a man from the middle of the crowd. "Mr. Rushton set his eyes for her and his missus take offense?"

The crowd laughed, and Ruby wanted to shrink up and disappear. Although Master Rushton had always acted the gentleman, a few other white men had tried to make advances on her since she first got her womanhood nearly seven summers ago. Donetta had warned her about such things; had told her that her light skin and curvy figure might prove a strong enticement to menfolk of all colors.

"Best marry up fast," Donetta had advised when Ruby was near her fourteenth birthday. "That won't guarantee a white man won't come for you, but it'll give you some protection. Least on our place it will."

Her marriage to Markus had followed soon after, and so far she'd escaped any white man's advancements. But now, with Donetta out of her life forever, who knew what might happen?

The crowd's laughter died away. "She's a clean woman," said the blousy-shirted man, making sure to get the selling points stated early. "No diseases, no scars of any kind. I got the papers to prove it. She got sold when her master died. The family needed money."

The men nodded with understanding.

"Who'll start the biddin'?" asked the auctioneer. "Openin' price is eleven hundred."

"I'll go twelve," said a man Ruby recognized from her stall earlier in the day.

"Make it thirteen," said a second man, this one to her right.

"Fourteen," shouted a third.

A stir ran through the crowd. "Fifteen," came the bid.

Ruby bit her lip in anger. A trickle of blood showed. People with a last name never got bid on.

"Sixteen hundred."

"You're not wantin' her for cookin'!" somebody yelled to the last bidder.

The men roared. Ruby's eyes blurred. She hoped the man who had bought Markus would make a bid, but she didn't see him anywhere.

"Eighteen hundred."

Ruby glanced up and saw that a new bidder had made an offer. This tall, broad-shouldered man wore a gray hat that appeared almost new. The bidding stopped. The tall man strolled toward the platform with an easy gait, like a racehorse sliding over the ground. When people stepped back to let him pass, Ruby saw a mixture of fear and grudging respect in their eyes. A well-trimmed black beard covered the man's face. Another man walked beside him, this one a couple of inches shorter but equally thick in the shoulders. The second man wore a hat too, but his was a floppy thing that the sun had baked on for at least a thousand days.

"Any other bids?" shouted the taller man, now facing the crowd as he reached the platform. The crowd took a breath. He faced the milling group, his posture daring the others to bid against him. He spat tobacco juice to the ground, like he was a lion marking his territory.

"It's Captain Hampton York!" somebody called. "From The Oak."

Ruby studied the man's back. His black hair fell over the collar of his tan shirt. He looked late thirties, maybe forty. He hadn't come to her stall. For that she was grateful.

The auctioneer tried to up the bid one more time. "Are we goin' to give her so cheaply to Captain York? Just let him walk in here and claim her away from us?"

"He works for Marshall Tessier!" shouted a voice from the back. "Tessier has more money than all of us put together! York wants her, he gets her; we all know that."

Ruby held her breath.

"Then I reckon she's sold!" yelled the auctioneer. "To Captain Hampton York for Marshall Tessier, master of The Oak!"

The auctioneer pointed to his left, and Ruby moved off the platform and down the steps. Hampton York and his companion moved to her side, and she stopped. York's eyes roamed up and down her body. She wanted to scream and tell him to stop looking at her, but she knew she didn't dare.

"You likin' what you see?" she finally asked, her eyes bolder than proper for a darky.

"You truly healthy?" York asked, his voice as deep as tree roots.

She glared at him for another second, but when he didn't blink she averted her eyes. York took her chin and jerked her face up. His companion tightened his lips and looked away.

"You've had a man, I reckon," York said. "Nobody I know keeps a purty one like you around without some babies."

"I took a man named Markus," she replied.

"I saw him earlier. Robertson bought him."

"His place close?"

York spat on the ground. "Not your place to ask no questions."

She pulled her chin away, and he dropped his hand.

"You had babies?" asked York.

"It don't matter if I do," she said flatly. "Don't got them now."

"The Oak is a good place," York said. "Surely finer than the one you come from."

"I reckon I'll be the one to judge that."

York grabbed her chin again, his hand rougher this time, his eyes daring her to pull away again. "You're accustomed to good treatment, is that it? Never sold before, I'll wager on that."

She ground her teeth.

"You belong to Marshall Tessier now," he growled. "I run The Oak for him. You do what we tell you, and you'll fare well. If not, I promise it'll go hard on you."

Ruby glared back at him, but inside her stomach she felt quivery. York's tone left no doubt that he wouldn't take easy to anybody crossing him.

"I'll see to her," York's companion said, stepping closer to touch York's shoulder. "You go settle up in back."

York glanced at the shorter man, then dropped his hand and walked away. Ruby stared at the man beside her.

"I'm Josh Cain," he said quietly. "Sorry about your man, your babies, if you have any."

Ruby shook her head, her lips tense with anger.

"Look," Cain continued. "I know you're agitated. But you're going to a good place, and that's the truth. Don't mind Mr. York. He gets upset when somebody challenges him."

Ruby shrugged. "It don't really matter. I got no last name."

"What?"

She shook her head. "A white man can't understand it. But I got no name. I belong to somebody else. Whether it's a good place or a poor one, I got no say over it. That's all."

Cain took a handkerchief from his back pocket and handed it to her. "It's clean, and I have water in the wagon." He pointed down the street. "You can wash up there."

Ruby took the handkerchief and scrutinized Cain. Blond hair poked out from under his wide-brimmed brown hat. His blue eyes looked kindly, as if he saw the good in people more than the bad. He had white teeth, no sign of tobacco of any kind on them. His speech sounded a little more educated than York's—not as coarse.

Deciding Josh Cain might treat her fair, Ruby softened a little. "Can I ask somethin'?"

"Sure."

"Mr. York said a fella named Robertson took Markus."

"Yes."

"Where this Robertson live?"

"Too far for a pass, if that's what you're thinking."

Ruby dropped her head. "Even so, I still want to know."

Cain sighed. "Okay. Robertson grows cotton between here and a town called Columbia. It's inland a good ways, maybe ninety to a hundred miles."

Ruby looked up. "Markus be my man. We pledged love forever."

"You have to forget that," Cain said. "No good thing can come of it."

Ruby's eyes brimmed as the hopelessness of her situation fully hit her. "I got a boy named Theo, back with my mammy in Virginia. I lost two other babies before they ever saw light. Theo's the only one left."

Cain's face clouded, and Ruby thought she saw mercy in his eyes. She spoke before she could stop herself. "I plan to see them again someday. Theo and Markus. Theo said he seen it."

"Saw it?"

"Yep, he got the vision."

Cain's jaw firmed. "Don't think crazy," he advised. "Woman or not, York won't stand anybody running. That'll get you whipped—or worse."

Ruby nodded. "I know my place. But who knows what time will bring?"

"Let's get you ready to travel," said Cain, ending the talk and pointing toward the wagon. "We leave for The Oak in a little while. Have close to forty miles to travel between today and tomorrow."

Headed to the wagon, Ruby wiped her face and made a vow. One of these days she would see Markus and Theo again. No matter what it took, no matter what it cost her, she would not let go of that hope. To do so meant she might as well go on and die. Yes, she belonged to The Oak now, to a man named Marshall Tessier. Maybe he would treat her right, maybe not. No way to tell about a white man, she knew that. But either way, it didn't matter. She would do what she had to do to keep her pledge to her baby. That pledge was the only thing that gave her enough strength to go on living.

Chapter Three

The sun came up steamy the next morning and baked Josh Cain from overhead, causing sweat to roll into the collar of his brown shirt as they made their way toward The Oak. A wagonload of supplies—flour, cloth, nails, whiskey, salt, and a whole lot of other provisions—made the four mules that pulled his wagon strain against their traces. Ruby, the newly purchased house servant, sat on the back of the wagon, her long legs swinging with each jolt down the rutted dirt road. Hampton York rode nearby, on a dappled gray horse. Except for York, Josh, and Ruby, the trail was deserted. The three had spent the night in a field about fifteen miles out of Charleston and hoped to make the rest of the trip before nightfall.

Josh wiped his brow, then pulled a book from under the wagon seat, opened it about a third of the way, set the traces in one hand and the book in the other, and started reading.

York edged his horse closer. "You readin' again, I see. Takin' up more new words."

"So what?" Josh asked, not looking up. "A man can try to improve, can't he?"

"I won't argue that with you," York said. "But this is me you're jabberin' at, remember? Your brother—at least half. Managin' to read a little won't raise nobody's station in this world, and we both know it. So you might as well stop tryin' to speak so fine, like a boardin' school boy."

"I try to educate myself. Nothing wrong with that."

"It'll do you no good, that's all I'm sayin'."

Josh clicked at the mules, but they ignored him. "I expect we're talking about two different things," he suggested to York. "You say learning will do me no good. If you're thinking about making more money or raising my 'station' as you put it, then you're probably right. But that's not my meaning."

York shook his head as if to dismiss a child. "You don't want to better yourself?"

"Well, sure I do, but I don't stay awake at night figuring how to become a rich man. I see other matters as more worthy than that."

"Yes, you jawed this nonsense to me more than once."

Josh wiped his brow again. York was right. They *had* plowed this ground lots of times. But Josh wanted different things than York. He wanted a strong family; wanted folks to know him as a man of integrity and faith in the Lord. Things like that didn't show up in any account ledger anywhere, but he didn't care. With his wife, Anna, and his children, Beth, Butler, and Lucy, he felt like he had just about as much as any man could want.

York adjusted his hat. "A man's got to have dreams. Some desire to pull up from his origins. But it ain't a matter of knowin' a few fancy words. If a man's goin' to better his prospects, he's got to make it happen, that's all. Take a chance when the opportunity comes."

"What kind of opportunity?"

"Hard to say. But you'll know it when you see it."

"Sounds like you're talking about pure luck."

"Thought you put your faith in the Lord; didn't believe in luck."

"I don't. But you do," Josh shot back.

York grinned. "Well, call it what you want. But if good fortune comes, you got to do somethin' with it. It's one thing to get dealt a good hand; it's another altogether whether you take advantage of it. That part depends on the man. When the luck shows up, will he take it by the throat . . . or let it pass?"

"Guess it depends on whether the man sees it as something that'll lead to good or not."

York wiped his face. "You make it too hard. Do too much figurin' before you act. Maybe it's 'cause you were the baby, not forced to take care of yourself."

Josh grunted. "I've done my share of taking care of myself. Remember a time or two I took care of you as well."

York pulled off his hat and fanned his face with it. His horse pranced, as if it wanted to rush off, but he held the reins tightly. "Yep, well, that was over eleven years ago, war and all. Shot up like I was, I couldn't do much to help myself."

Josh remembered the episode, during their adventures in the army near the end of the Mexican War. He'd been eighteen at the time, York just thirty. Josh hung his head and pushed away the memories. He'd learned a lot in that war, a lot of it too painful to recall.

York put his hat back on. "It's truly surprisin' that two men with the same sire can turn out as different as you and me."

"Yes, me handsome and you ugly," Josh threw in. "I got it from my mama."

York shoved his hat low over his eyes and spurred his horse, leaving the wagon behind.

"Didn't mean any offense," Josh yelled, realizing he'd upset York by unintentionally reminding him that their pa had never married York's mama but had married his, thereby giving them different childhoods, as well as last names.

York waved him off.

Josh clicked at the mules, then glanced back at his book, a tattered copy of *Pilgrim's Progress*. The wagon bounced along. The sun burned hotter. Josh flicked the reins at the mules every now and again, but they didn't speed up any. He didn't blame them. Nothing moved too fast under the weight of such sticky conditions. As the mules gradually covered the miles along the dusty road, the sun rose higher. Josh squinted up from his book from time to time. York rode a good thirty feet ahead, his body low in the saddle, almost as if dead. Josh knew better, though. Hampton York possessed more fire in his body than most any man Josh knew. But sometimes that fire got York in trouble. Josh shook his head as he remembered the times he'd paid to get York out of jail when he got in fights after drinking too much.

The mules sped up a little when they reached a slight downhill stretch. Josh glanced back at Ruby; she hadn't moved. He felt bad for her, the way the Rushtons had split her from her husband and son. A lot of times an owner refused to sell a servant family unless they all went together. Josh hoped her pouty ways would end soon. York didn't like a darky with an angry temperament.

The mules slowed as the downhill ended, and he peered at his book again. But for once he didn't feel like reading anymore. Every time York bought a new servant, Josh felt bleak. The whole slave business made Josh squeamish—like he knew he'd swallowed poison but didn't have any medicine to make it better. It didn't quite square with what he knew of the Lord that any human should claim another as his own. He stared at York's back and wished he could talk to him about it. But Josh knew it wouldn't do any good. York had no such qualms about owning darkies; saw it as absolutely necessary for a place like The Oak to operate. And Josh knew that, no matter what it took, York would do that very thing to make The Oak prosperous.

Josh thought of Marshall Tessier and frowned. Truth was, he didn't like the man—didn't trust him and didn't like the way he treated his servants either. Yet Tessier paid good wages and left Josh alone to do his work. What more could a man ask from his boss?

Josh turned his attention back to his book. Slowly the morning ended, and the mules turned left at a fork in the road. A few minutes later Josh steered them off the dirt path into the shade of an oak grove. Heavy moss draped the trees like loose gray sweaters. The mules moved more quickly as they neared Mossy Bank Creek, about fifty yards away.

York was already there and off his horse. "Waterin' hole," he said as he did every time they stopped at this spot.

Josh turned to Ruby. "We'll take some rest here. Let the animals drink."

Ruby hopped down as the mules reached the water. Josh jumped out, unhooked the mules, then led them down the shallow bank where they could drink. York took off his hat, fell to his knees, and plunged his face into the creek. Josh dipped his hands in the clear water and then washed his head and neck. Flies buzzed at his eyes, but he brushed them away. He drank deeply. When he looked up, he saw Ruby downstream, her face also in the water. His squeamish feeling returned. Servants always drank downstream of white folks, lest their spittle mix in the water and float down to where their betters drank. But what made one person better than another? Didn't the Lord love all folks equally?

He took a deep breath. "Some food is in the wagon under the seat," he called to Ruby. "I'm sure a biscuit with a piece of ham would taste fine right now."

She stood and walked toward the wagon. Josh joined York on the bank. York took out the last of his store-bought tobacco, put the chaw in his mouth, and tossed the wrapper to the ground. A couple of minutes later, Ruby brought them biscuits and ham. Josh took some, handed some to York, then gave the rest back to Ruby. She sat down under a tall pine some distance away.

For several minutes Josh and York rested and ate under the thick branches of an oak that partially hid the sun. When Josh's eyes grew heavy, he decided to take a short nap. Finding a shady spot just up from the creek, he stretched out on the loamy soil. His eyes stared into the creek. Even the water moved lazily. Josh yawned and almost closed his eyes, but then a piece of paper floated by. Josh blinked in surprise; it looked like money!

Josh glanced at York to see if his half brother had noticed, but he hadn't. When Josh looked back at the creek, he saw a second piece of paper close behind the first. He stood and waded gently into the water, his boots filling with the warm liquid.

Bending, he picked up both pieces of paper. They were two five-dollar bills, issued from the Bank of Columbia, South Carolina.

Josh checked York again. He was still resting, his eyes closed. Josh scanned the creek but saw no more money. He started to go back to shore but then heard a low moan.

"You hear that?" he whispered to York.

York stirred but didn't speak. Another moan sounded. Josh eased toward the sound, careful not to splash. The creek bent left about ten yards away, and Josh peeked around the edge. The undergrowth grew thicker here, and the sun seemed distant. Josh bent lower. Then he saw it—a man's body—a short distance away, his lower half in the water, his face staring at the sky! Josh almost called for York but then grew cautious. What if somebody had harmed this man and now lurked nearby?

Wishing he had the pistol he kept under the wagon seat, Josh moved quietly through the creek and reached the unmoving form by the bank. The man wore a collared brown shirt and a belt with a carved silver buckle. A sandy beard covered his face, and his hair looked freshly cut. One of his hands lay palm up, as if expecting somebody to put something in it.

Josh squatted to search the man for signs of injury but saw none. The man's eyes remained closed, and a soft groan again escaped his lips.

"Hey!"

Josh looked up and saw York coming his way, his angular body sloshing through the water. Josh threw up a hand to signal for quiet. York slowed, but not much; he reached Josh in a matter of seconds.

"What you got here?" York asked, squatting by Josh. "Looks like a fancy man."

"He's hurt," said Josh. "But I see no injury."

York grabbed the man and propped him in a sitting position against his side. Josh's eyes widened. Blood covered the man's lower back and had seeped into the ground beneath him.

"Back shot," said York as calmly as if announcing he wanted apple pie for dessert. "Not long ago from the looks of it." He laid the man down.

"How bad you think it is?" Josh asked.

York stood without answering, his eyes searching the brush that hemmed them in. Josh stood too and peered up and down the creek bank.

"Spread out," ordered York. "See what you can find."

"What about him?" Josh pointed at the injured man.

"We've both seen that kind of wound. He took a shot from the back, and it got somethin' vital, liver maybe. He ain't long for this world, I'm figurin'."

"We ought to stay with him," Josh said.

"Do what you want. But I'm thinkin' the man who shot him might still be around here. If he is, I want to know it."

Josh stared at the wounded man while York eased away. Josh bent and gently opened the man's eyes. They showed white. "I'm Josh Cain," he said softly. "I'll sit by you."

The man's eyes flickered but didn't open.

"You got any words?" whispered Josh. "Anybody I ought to see for you?"

The man's mouth moved as if he wanted to speak. Josh lowered an ear.

"Ru . . . ," the man muttered.

"Go ahead."

"Ru . . . Ruth."

"Ruth?" Josh repeated.

The man tipped his head slightly as if to say more, but then his neck relaxed. Josh knew the man had died. He ground his teeth as bad memories of the war flooded back. He'd hoped he'd never have to see another man die. Gathering his emotions, Josh folded the man's arms over his chest and checked for York, but he had already disappeared around the bend. Josh stood to go after him, but something to his left caught his eye. A piece of white paper peeked out from under a thick stack of driftwood a few feet away. He pushed back a bit of brush and pulled out the paper; it was another five-dollar bill. Confused, he brushed it off, looked back at the dead man, then once more at the driftwood. His curiosity getting the better of him, he dropped to his knees and cleared away a few more limbs, twigs, and leaves. Then he saw the hole. Quickly Josh scanned the area. Had the dead man tried to bury something, then cover it up with driftwood?

Josh scooped out handfuls of the soft dirt. After a minute or so his fingers hit a solid object. He dug faster and, within seconds, found a wooden box the length of a hammer handle resting in the dirt. After brushing off the top, Josh hurriedly opened it and saw two stacks of money. He glanced around again, then focused once more on the box. Several layers of money lay inside—fives, tens, and twenties, even a few hundreds. His eyes rounded as he touched the money, more than he'd ever imagined, much less touched!

Josh rocked back and sat down, his hands full of cash. He tried to figure what had happened. Obviously, the dead man had buried this money. Just as obviously, somebody had killed him while trying to find it. He and York had interrupted the thief's efforts. But who really owned the money? Had the bearded man taken it from the man who shot him, and that man was simply trying to get back what was rightfully his? Or did the money belong to the bearded man, who had fallen into the hands of a thief?

Unable to answer, Josh started counting. When he reached three thousand dollars and still had more to go, he stopped. A sense of disbelief hit him. Who carried this kind of cash? Not even the wealthiest of plantation owners possessed this much loose money.

Then a shot rang out. Josh forgot the money and jumped to his feet. Another shot sounded.

"Josh!" The yell roared down the creek bed.

Josh shoved the money back into the box, hid it back under the driftwood, and rushed back into the creek, toward the yell. Another volley sounded. Josh tripped and fell, got up, and ran harder. Water spilled down his face and chest. When Josh rounded the bend, York was standing in the middle of the creek, his pistol pointed toward a mammoth oak on the bank. Josh sloshed forward, forgetting caution as he reached York. "You see anybody?" he shouted.

"I might've shot him!" panted York.

"You okay?"

York spat tobacco juice and ran toward the oak without answering. Josh followed, and together they reached the oak. Blood drops stained the tree's roots, and Josh dropped to a knee to inspect them. York ran past him, pistol ready. Josh checked the blood once more, then followed York into the woods. He found York about fifty yards in, leaning against a tree, panting.

"He's gone," said York.

"You get a glimpse of anybody?"

"Nope, not really."

Josh saw blood on York's fingers and realized he'd been shot. "How bad are you hurt?"

York twisted and showed Josh a wound in his left bicep. "The ball cleared the flesh. I'll clean it. Be fine."

"Should we go after him?" Josh nodded toward the woods.

York shook his head. "Reckon not. This ain't really our business. We got materials in the wagon that need deliverin'. We'll go into Beaufort after we get home. Tell the sheriff. He'll handle it all."

"Guess he's got a murder to figure out."

"Your man die?"

Josh nodded.

"We'll take him to The Oak," said York. "See what to do from there."

Josh thought of the money. *What if . . . ?* No, he wouldn't even consider that. The Good Book said the love of money was the root of all evil. Yet that much money could change a man's life. Send a man's kids to a fine school; buy a man a piece of land for his family. Give him freedom so he didn't have to work for somebody else.

Josh tried to lick his lips, but they felt glued together. He and York started back toward the dead man. Josh wondered if York would notice the spot under the driftwood. If not, he could just leave the money for now, come back in a day or so to pick it up. But what if the other man returned and found it first?

When they rounded the creek bend, Josh saw Ruby kneeling by the dead man. York sloshed toward her, Josh behind him.

"This man be dead," Ruby said.

"We know," said York, reaching her. "Somebody shot him, then ran off. We went after him."

Ruby stood and Josh knelt by the man. His eyes darted to the hidden money, and he thought again of keeping it. Yet Josh Cain had never stolen before. He never cheated, didn't use swearwords, didn't even drink. None of those vices faintly appealed to him. Then why did the notion of stealing the money claw at him so hard? He wiped his hands on his pants, then focused on his fingers. They looked clean, but he knew otherwise. They'd touched another man's money and now wanted to keep it.

He dipped his hands into the water and rubbed them hard together, hoping they'd feel cleansed. As the sun peeped through the trees and reflected off the water, Josh stared into the creek and thought of his mother who had raised him close to a creek just like this one. They'd taken fish from that creek, bathed in it, played in it, drunk from it. His mother's fine features seemed to rise up from the wet, a question in her eyes.

Josh wiped his face. His mother, now deceased, had worked as a schoolteacher all her life, never owned much of anything except her dignity, good character, and her unfailing faith in the Lord's goodness, despite hard times. Since his father had died before Josh knew him, his mother had taught him everything he knew—how to read, how to deal with honor with other folks, how to labor hard. What would his mother think of his desire to keep this money?

Feeling ashamed, Josh let go of the notion. No matter how much his family needed it, he wouldn't do such a terrible thing. He'd done enough wrong in his life; there was no reason to add more to it. He stood, moved to the driftwood, and uncovered the box.

"What's that?" asked York as Josh lifted out the wood container.

"A box full of cash," Josh said, handing it to him.

York opened the box, and his eyebrows arched. "Go to the wagon," he ordered Ruby.

She dropped her eyes and did as she was told at once. York waited until she'd left, then pulled out a wad of the money and started counting it.

"It's over three thousand," said Josh. "I counted that much before I stopped. There's more under that."

"You counted it?"

"Not all."

York put the bills back in the box and stared at Josh. "You could have kept this secret . . . and the money all for yourself. Why didn't you?"

"I considered it," admitted Josh. "But . . . I'm not a man given to thievery, I guess."

"But he's dead," said York, pointing to the body. "You'd not be thievin' from him."

"But from somebody."

York closed the box but didn't give it back. "We could keep it. The two of us split it half and half."

"I'm not disposed to do that," said Josh.

"Why not?"

"Because it belongs to somebody else."

"You find any papers on him?" York indicated the dead man.

"Didn't take time to search."

York quickly checked the man's pockets but found nothing. "He's got no papers," he said, as if expecting it. "So he's not from any proper authority."

"Maybe somebody took his papers."

"That's possible, but we don't know that. So far as we know he's a thief himself, maybe a gambler."

"Men don't gamble that kind of money."

York spat and grinned. "You don't know much about gamblin' if that's what you think."

Josh shrugged.

"Tell me what you want to do," said York.

"We should carry him to the sheriff—in Beaufort or back to Charleston, either one."

"And do what?"

"Leave the body and the money in the law's hands."

York held up his arm. "I'm shot," he said. "The authorities are likely to believe you and I killed this man, and that I took a wound doin' it."

Josh rubbed his face. York spoke a truth he hadn't considered. Josh thought about the name the dead man had spoken; he wondered if he should tell York. But then he realized that in a place as large as Charleston, even Beaufort, it might take days to find a woman named Ruth. And what if this Ruth didn't live there? What if the dead man hailed from Columbia or Savannah or somewhere else Josh had never even visited? He couldn't just leave The Oak and go traipsing all over the country to look for somebody he'd never met. Besides, if he did do that and actually found the woman, what would keep her from accusing him of killing the bearded man?

"We should go on to The Oak," Josh finally said. "Take the body and the money to Mr. Tessier."

York laughed. "I'd rather go to Charleston. Tessier's a rascal. Likely to just keep the money. You know I ain't lyin'."

Josh shrugged again. York said it right. Although both of them worked for Tessier, neither of them trusted the master. "What's your plan, then?"

York's gray eyes sparkled. "I say we keep it. We bury this man right here and split this money right down the middle. Who'll know the difference? That's as sensible as anything you said, and you know it, so do I."

Josh took off his hat and scratched his head. The temptation reared up again. But he'd already beaten it once, so he put it down a little faster this time. "I can't do it."

York smiled. "I figured on you seein' it that way, Brother. So I'm willin' to make it easy for you."

"What do you mean?"

York pointed at the dead man. "First, we'll put him in the ground, as is proper. Then I'll hold on to the money until I can figure the best thing to do with it."

"It's not yours to hold," argued Josh.

Josh saw York's mean streak rise in his glare.

"You're buckin' me on this?" York challenged.

"It's not right," said Josh. "Bad will come of it. It always does."

"It'll be on *my* head," York fired back heatedly. "Nothin' to sully your lily-white heart."

"That's not what I'm worried about."

York spat tobacco juice into the creek. "Look," he said, softening his tone. "I don't want us to get at each other over this, but at least let my arm get better. We go now, and the law'll get suspicious real fast. You know I've had some rough dealin's there. I take a dead man in, and I'll get the blame for sure. You don't want that, do you? How'll that do any good?"

Josh wanted to argue more, but York's reasoning sounded solid. If he went to the law, he might get his brother in trouble, and he didn't want that.

"Let's bury him," said York.

"Okay."

York headed to the wagon, and Josh followed. At the wagon, Ruby raised a questioning eyebrow but didn't make a sound. York pulled a shovel out and hurried back to the body, Josh right behind him. They took turns digging, York's face tightening in pain every now and again from the wound in his arm. After burying the man, Josh took a couple of straight, knee-high sticks he found, tied them together like a cross with a piece of cord from the wagon, and stuck the marker in the ground at the man's head. Then he took off his hat and stood over the grave. "We ought to say a few words."

"Go on then," York said. "You're closer to heaven than me."

Josh looked at the sky, his mind in a swirl. "We don't know this man, Lord," he started, "but you do." He paused over what to say next. He tried to think of some scripture; after all, he read the Good Book almost every day. Then, after a minute, the words of Jesus from John 11:25 rose in his head, and he softly spoke them. "I am the resurrection, and the life: he that believeth in me, though he were dead, yet shall he live."

Josh chewed his lip once, then continued. "We don't know if this man lived well or not, Lord, but he's come to a bad end. I pray he made his soul right with you, even at the last moment. So bless him now. Receive him into your strong arms and keep him forever. That's my prayer for this man we don't know. In the name of Jesus, amen."

Josh and York both put their hats back on as they left the grave and walked back to the wagon. York tied his horse to the back, shoved the money box under the wagon bench, and climbed into the wagon with Josh. Josh took the reins again, and Ruby sat in the rear, her back to them. York tied a handkerchief around his arm to stop the bleeding. A couple of minutes later they reached the main road again. Josh's mind was still whirling. A couple of miles passed. The afternoon sun continued to bake them.

Then York swiveled suddenly toward Ruby. "Turn around, woman," he ordered sternly. "You will forget what you saw today. That clear?"

Josh wished once again that York didn't act so hard with the servants.

"I know my place," Ruby said. "What white folks do ain't no business of mine."

"Exactly," said York. "Just keep it that way." He spat off the side of the wagon.

Ruby jumped from the wagon and moved to the roadside, where the trees offered some shade. There she stopped until the wagon had moved several paces ahead. Then she started walking again, her pace just fast enough to keep up with the wagon.

Josh faced forward as York settled back into his seat. Josh tried to calm his mind. At times like this he didn't like his half brother, didn't like how he put him in such a hard spot. Not wanting Ruby to hear, Josh leaned close to York. "You aim to keep that money, don't you?" he whispered.

"Least for now, I do," York said. "I already said that."

"Your conscience won't gnaw at you for it?"

"I suppose it might. But I can pay that price for the amount of money in that box."

"You expect me to keep your secret?"

York pushed back his hat and stared at Josh. "I expect so."

"What if I won't?"

"You're my brother," he said. "Friend too. Hate for that to end."

"Something like this can prove mighty hard to keep quiet. What if the man who shot you comes looking for that money?"

"He don't know who I am," said York. "And we don't know for certain he even knows about the money."

"But he could come."

"Yes, he could."

The wagon bounced down a slight hill, then started pulling up again. "This is one of those moments, don't you think?" asked Josh.

"What do you mean?"

"Like you said earlier. An opportunity. A time a man's got to grab or let go forever."

York grinned. "Yes, I see what you mean. It's like this just fell right into our laps. Good luck from the sky."

Josh licked his lips. "It's hard to pass it by. I got to admit that."

"You changin' your mind?"

"No, don't think so."

"You let me know if you do," said York. "Anytime you want your half, you got it. You know I won't cheat you. You want it, I'll hand it over."

Josh clicked at the mules, but they ignored him. He clicked again, more insistently this time, and flicked the reins on their backs. This time they actually sped up a little, and he breathed a sigh of relief. Maybe, if they moved fast enough, they might get him back to The Oak before he yielded to the temptation to join York in his plan to keep the money for himself.

Chapter Four

Leaving York with Ruby and the wagon about a half-mile from the manse, Josh split off and headed through a stretch of unplowed fields, toward his house. The sun had just about disappeared, and a slight nip hung in the air in contrast to the heat of just a few hours ago. He knew Anna would have supper ready by now but would hold it for him to return before letting anybody eat. He smiled as he thought of his family—the Lord had blessed him more than most men, men like York who had never found any luck with love or happiness with women.

Thinking of York, Josh tried to figure a way out of his current predicament. He'd feel guilty if he just let York keep the money. But how does a brother, even if just half, put another brother in trouble especially when that brother already had some struggles in his background that would make it even worse?

The heaviness of Josh's heart lifted a little as he neared home. Although it strained him with its demands, his labor on The Oak pleased his soul. Growing rice agreed with him, the way it took such a regular method to make it happen. The steadiness of it all—what to do in this season, what to do in that one—satisfied something deep in Josh. It matched up well with the nature of his mind, the order in things he liked to see.

The vast rice fields of The Oak lay along the banks of Conwilla River, the fresh water rising and falling with the flow of the ocean tide that pushed it in and out every morning and night. Banks of wood and earth about eight feet wide at the base and three feet high—what they called check banks—allowed him to flood the fields separately from each other on a regular schedule. The hard labor of the field hands built the banks with great precision and kept them up by constant care, clearing the ditches and drains with hoes and shovels.

During the winter, the servants plowed the fields and dragged them with a harrow to break up the earth and keep the field flat—a necessity for growing good rice. In April they sowed the seed for a new crop, pressing the seed into balls of wet clay and then drying the balls before putting them into the ground.

After the sowing, they immediately flooded the fields, keeping them wet until the seed pipped or germinated, a step that usually took somewhere between four to fourteen days. After that, they drained the fields, hoed them for weeds, and kept them dry until the young, needlelike rice plants formed rows across the field.

Then came the flooding again, a series of water flows that gave the rice protection from weeds and provided all the moisture it needed to grow strong. Finally, the harvest flow of water came—the flooding occurring in late summer, after the rice plants had grown to about fifteen inches. This flood supported the stalks until shortly before the harvest that started in late August and lasted usually until almost the end of October.

Everybody worked at a frantic pace in harvesttime—from sunup until late at night. A couple of days before the harvest, they drained the water from the fields and sent in the field hands to cut the stalks with sickles— rice hooks they called them. After they'd cut down the stalks, they left them in the fields to dry for a couple of days. Next they stacked the stalks in ricks about seven feet wide, twenty feet long, and as high as a man could make them. When all the rice was cut and dried, they hauled it away to a mill on a mule-drawn cart or a rice flat—a flat-bottomed barge. After milling the rice, they stored it in barrels made of pine and banded with birch and white oak hoops. Each barrel carried about six hundred pounds of rice.

Lots of things made the work hard—stifling heat, swarming horse flies, field rats and mosquitoes, the danger of malaria and yellow fever. For Josh, though, the sight of a smooth field of swaying rice in the middle of a gentle flood of water made it all worthwhile. He liked the ebb and flow of it, the way it connected to the ocean, the way it tied to all things natural. He could just see God smiling down upon it all.

Josh breathed in the fall air as he reached his front yard. About a half-mile from the manse, his house was a four-room square home with plank floors and one shuttered window on both sides of the front but none in the back. Oak trees surrounded the house on all sides, the moss off the branches, like an old woman's gray hair, almost touching the ground. Chickens darted across the well-swept yard as he walked up, and a brown cat with a missing left ear raised his head and meowed at him from the porch.

Josh stepped up onto the porch and scratched the tom behind the ears. "Evening, Copper. Everybody busy with supper?"

Copper didn't answer as Josh moved to the door. Noise erupted from inside the house at the sound of his feet. A couple of seconds later three kids rushed him as he opened the front door.

"Hey!" Josh called as he bent to pick up Lucy, the youngest of his children at six. Lucy wrapped her arms around his neck, and Butler grabbed him by the arm and tugged.

"Whoa there," said Josh, leaning against Butler, his seven-year-old. "Let me get in the door."

"Stella came over," said Butler, all out of breath. "Late yesterday. Said she got news."

"What news?" asked Josh.

"News from the manse," shouted Butler.

Josh eyed Beth, his eldest at nearly ten, who reached over to give him a hug. "What's going on?" he asked.

"It can wait," said Beth. "We got other troubles. Mama's got the headaches again. She's restin' on the bed."

Josh's face fell. Beth's brown eyes were dark and sad. A quick grief ran through him. Sometime in May of the past year, Anna had started suffering off and on from rough pains behind her eyes and over her ears. At first she tried to ignore the hurt and keep on working. But then the headaches got more regular and more painful.

"It feels like somebody put my head on a road and ran a wagon over it," she moaned to Josh one morning as he sat by her, a wet rag in hand for her head. "It hurts bad."

Josh did all he could to make her comfortable, but not much seemed to help. He got York to call in a doctor from Beaufort, but the doctor didn't know what to do about it either.

"Might be the heat," the doctor had said as he ran his fingers over her head, checking her temples and behind her ears. "Sometimes women especially can't take how hot it gets. She take any knocks on the head or anything?"

"Not that I know of," Josh said.

Anna shook her head.

The doctor peered into her eyes. "What goes on in the head isn't known to man or beast. A true mystery, that's what it is."

"But you've seen this before?"

The doctor shrugged. "People with headaches, yes. Some come pretty regular; a few people get them so bad they have to go to bed with them."

"What can we do?"

"Now that's the hard question," said the doctor. "One thing that works for one won't work for another. But here's what I'd try. Put her in a quiet place when the aches come on her, out of the light. Keep her real still and quiet. And give her a tablespoon of this when she first starts hurting . . . more if it helps." He handed Josh a bottle of dark liquid.

Josh took it, opened the top, and took a sniff. "What's in it?"

"Don't ask," said the doctor. "Let's just see if it eases her some." The doctor shook Josh's hand and walked out.

The next time the headaches came, Josh started Anna on the dark liquid. It did seem to help some, but to Josh's grief, it didn't completely cure the pain. And, over the last couple of weeks, the aches had gotten even worse. Now, as he stared at Beth, Josh wished he knew what else to do. Other than the dark liquid and his constant prayers to the Lord for help, he felt totally helpless.

"How long has she been down?" Josh asked Beth, walking with Lucy and Butler wrapped around his knees toward the back room where he and Anna slept.

"Since this mornin'," said Beth. "She rose, put out some food for us, and brought in the eggs. That was it. The headache hit her, and she headed to the back."

Josh patted Beth. "Sorry you have so much on you. I know it all falls on you when your mama's hurting—the cooking, cleaning, and caring for the young ones. I wish I could aid you more."

"Don't worry, Pa," said Beth. "You got your work. Not a lot of time to fret about mine here. I'm almost ten, old enough to help. We all pitch in, we'll get it done just fine, you'll see."

Josh smiled but only for a second. Beth had grown up fast. Guess that happened when a mama took sick and you were the oldest. Unfortunately, since the nearest school was almost in Beaufort, Beth hadn't received any education either, except for what little Josh had been able to teach her.

He reached the bedroom and peeked in the open door. Anna lay on the thin mattress of their bed, a wet rag over her face, one bony arm over her chest, the other across her forehead. Her thick hair, the color of a penny, lay spread out on the pillow, and her face, always thin, now looked drawn, as though somebody had stretched it past its going point.

"Go on now," he said to the kids, putting them down. "Let me talk to your mama."

"You gone kiss her, Pa?" asked Butler, a shy grin on his face.

Josh smiled at his boy and ruffled his hair. "I just might. I missed your mama. Need a kiss real bad. Now leave us alone so I can get that kiss in a proper way, without such an audience."

Butler grinned again, and he and Lucy shuffled away. But Beth stayed. Josh again saw the worry in her young eyes. He took her by the shoulders and pulled her close. "I know it's hard. But your mama will get well soon. It's probably just the hot weather. Now go on with Butler and Lucy. They need you." He squeezed Beth once more. She sighed and left.

Alone now with Anna, Josh sat down by her in a straight chair and took her hand. "I got home," he said quietly, "a few minutes ago."

She stirred, lifted the rag, and opened her eyes. A tiny smile crept to her lips before pain rode it. He knew she was in agony. "I'm glad you're home," she whispered. "You keep things lively around here."

He kissed her forehead. She handed him the rag, and he dipped it in a water-filled iron pot on the floor. Patting her face gently with the wet rag, he said, "Sorry the aches came again. You take the tonic the doctor left?"

"Some," she said. "But you know it makes me droopy, and I don't want to sleep too much. Can't keep up with the children that way."

"Beth takes good care of the little ones," he said, laying the rag on the floor. "You know that."

"She's still a little one herself."

Josh hung his head as Anna rubbed his hand. Anna's hands were so small, like the hands of one of the porcelain dolls he saw in a store window in Charleston almost every time he went there. He'd noticed her hands the first day he met her in Savannah back in midsummer 1848, right after he got back from the Mexican War. Josh remembered the months after he and York returned from the fighting. Although they'd ridden back from Texas together, they'd split up soon after, with York going to Charleston, and Josh to Savannah. Josh was the one who had insisted on the split.

"I came straight to you after Mama died in '46," he'd said in an effort to explain. "But now I need to see if I can make it on my own."

"But we ain't been together but a couple of years," said York.

Josh nodded. York's mama and pa had lived together without ever standing before a preacher, and she had died giving birth to him. His pa, a man who kept the livestock for a rice planter on a plantation near Georgetown, had married about four years later. Josh came from that union after his mama failed to deliver three other babies. By the time Josh was born, York was already twelve years old. When their pa passed on from the consumption four years later, York, almost seventeen at the time, left to seek his own way. Although half-brothers, they hardly knew each other when Josh's mother died and he went to join York just before the war. Now maybe they knew each other too well. York's gambling and drinking cut against a lot that Josh believed in, and Josh tended to stay too strait-laced for York.

Thankfully, York hadn't argued too much about them going their separate ways, and Josh was glad. York reminded him too much of the war, especially of the one thing that continued to haunt Josh with guilt in the dark of night. True, he was glad he knew his brother better now, but the war had caused Josh to do things he wanted to keep buried. With York around those things stayed alive.

He'd met Anna in Savannah after the war; had spotted her hands in the small store she and her pa and two sisters ran there. He had stepped into the store to buy some leather to make a new belt. Anna, a year younger than him, had cut the leather for him, her fine hands wielding the knife with more strength than he thought possible for such fragile features.

She had smiled at him and wished him a good day as he paid for the leather. After he'd stepped outside, he realized he needed to buy something else too, although he didn't know for sure what that was. Back in the store, he bought three buttons, not because he needed them, but because the buttons happened to be in the glass case right by the spot where Anna stood. After paying for the buttons, he decided he needed some flour. By the time he'd bought the flour, he'd somehow managed to find out her name and where she was from.

Over the next three months, he found a whole lot of reasons to go back and buy things from her store. By the time fall rolled around, he told her that if he didn't marry her soon he'd end up broke from spending all his money at her store! Since he didn't want to do that, would she please marry him so he could get out of debt?

To his great joy, she said yes, and they married three weeks later. Although not his first choice as a place to settle, Josh had taken work repairing ships in Savannah's harbor so Anna could stay near her folks. Over the next six years all three of their children were born. To everybody's sorrow, however, her pa died near the beginning of 1854, and the sisters got into a squabble about who got what of their pa's business. Discouraged by all the bickering, he and Anna agreed that maybe the time had come for a fresh start. Since York had asked him by letter more than once to come help him run The Oak, they decided they'd do just that. They moved there in the fall and settled in.

"The trip to Charleston go okay?" Anna asked, bringing him back to the present.

"Yes, we loaded up the wagons with provisions for the winter. Brought home a woman for Stella to train for the cookhouse."

"Stella's getting creaky. She could use the extra help. York stay out of trouble this time?"

Josh smiled. "I kept him close at hand, made sure he stayed sober."

Anna patted his hand. Josh started to tell her about the episode at the creek, to ask her what he ought to do. She always gave him such good advice. He wanted to ask her how to make York give the money to Tessier. Yet he feared bothering her, feared it would make her head hurt worse.

"Stella came out," she said, breaking his thoughts.

"Butler told me," he said, deciding to wait until she felt better before telling her anything about the dead man and the money. "What's the news?"

Anna closed her eyes again. "Tessier. He's dead."

Josh sat up straighter. "Marshall?"

"Yes."

"How in the world?"

"It's all a little fuzzy. But he took a fall somehow, hit his head. Killed him straight out. Happened yesterday, right before supper."

"He drinking?"

"Nobody said."

"Most likely, though."

Anna rubbed her forehead, her fingers digging into her skin. "Camellia and Stella were there. They saw it happen."

"Where was he?"

"In the cookhouse."

Josh's brow wrinkled. What was Tessier doing in the cookhouse? That didn't make sense. He started to ask Anna but stopped because he knew she'd have no answer. He stood and walked to the room's only window, an open square a few feet from the bed. "Grim news. It'll stir up lots of things, for sure." He stared out in the direction of the manse, torn about what to do. Although Anna needed him, he also knew he should go find York. At such a time York would need his help. To his relief, Anna brought it up for him.

"You ought to go see York," she said. "He'll want you close by."

Josh's heart filled with love for his wife. Anna read him better than he did himself. "You sure you're okay?"

"I'll take some more tonic. I'm fine now that I know you are home."

"I won't stay gone long," he promised. "Just need to find out what's happening."

"Do what you need. I'll get better soon. Always do."

He leaned over and kissed her on the cheek. Again he thought of the man at Mossy Bank Creek. The urge to say out loud what had happened pushed at his chest like a high river shoving at a dam. Somehow he knew that the longer he kept the secret, the harder it would be to tell it, the more difficult to let it out in the air. If he didn't get it said soon, it would harden in his throat like mud in the sun's heat. But when he started to speak, Anna interrupted him.

"Go on," she urged. "I'm fine."

Josh nodded. No reason to bother Anna right now, not while she hurt so much, and not while York needed to see him. Right now he had no time to go into the detail he'd need to explain if he told her all that had happened.

"I'll see you in a while," he said. "Just let me talk to York. Make sure he's doing all right."

She nodded, and Josh kissed her one final time. Then he left, his mind filled with troublesome thoughts.

Chapter Five

The fields were quiet as Hampton York turned the wagon up the gravel path that led the last two hundred yards to The Oak. He took a deep breath and glanced back at Ruby. "This here is the finest plantation in the whole state," he said. "We got close to eighteen hundred acres in crops. Not just rice neither. Corn, oats, beans, sweet taters." He waved his hand over the area. "Got at least seventy-five cows, about sixty horses, a hundred and fifty cattle, maybe seventy hogs." He grinned. "I run the whole thing. Mr. Tessier and me."

"You're a mighty big man, I reckon."

York narrowed his eyes at the uppity tone in her voice. But he felt too pleased to punish her for it. "We do close to fifty thousand bushels of rice a year. Over a million pounds. Got our own mill, bring in fifty to sixty thousand a year. You do that good at the Rushton place?"

"None of that my business," she replied.

York took out a chew of tobacco, slipped it into his lips. He gazed across the land. The sun had just about disappeared. York saw nobody moving about and heard no sound except a dog barking in the distance. He sat up straighter. Things were too quiet, even for this time of day. Concerned, he tapped the mules with the traces. By the time he reached the oaks bordering the road, he was sure something had happened.

Jumping from the wagon at the main barn, he ran the last fifty yards, his feet heavy in black boots. A stocky middle-aged black man about half his size met him a few feet from the manse, his toothless mouth set somber. "Put my horse up, Leather Joe," York ordered. "Take my saddlebags to my house." The servant quickly ran off, his bare feet kicking up dust.

Stella met York on the manse's front porch, her hands clutching her apron.

"He be dead," she said as she rushed down the steps. "Master Tessier fell in the cookhouse yesterday. Smashed his skull like a peach under a hammer."

"What nonsense you sayin'?" York demanded, not able to grasp what she had said.

Stella shook her head side to side. "It be the gospel truth," she insisted. "Mrs. Tessier took to the bed, her heart is so broke."

York grunted but didn't say a word. Stella knew as well as he that Mr. and Mrs. Tessier were anything but a happy couple. Although a man of great means, Tessier came from rougher stock than his lady, and there was almost twenty years' difference in their ages. She stayed in Charleston most of the time; had only come to The Oak in the last couple of weeks after the fever season had pretty much ended. But good marriage or not, this news would surely have knocked Mrs. Tessier off her feet.

"What happened?" he asked, still not moving.

Stella clucked her teeth and told him the tale. York raised his eyebrows as she spoke but didn't interrupt. When she finished, he tried to clear his head but found it hard. Such a thing shook up a man, no two ways about it. He spat tobacco juice, wishing Josh hadn't gone home yet. At a time like this a man needed somebody to talk things out with. Somebody he could trust.

"How's Camellia?" he asked.

"Okay, I reckon. Not perky, you know. Upset by seein' Tessier dead and all. But she be a strong young woman. Give her some time; she'll move ahead just fine."

York, recalling what Camellia had told him about Tessier's advances, started to ask Stella a question. But then he decided against it. No reason to raise a matter like that at a time like this. "Camellia at home?" he asked instead.

"Yep. Chester and Johnny are stayin' close to her. Me too, when I get the chance."

York considered going to Camellia. But since the boys were with her, he figured he could take care of a few things first. "Mrs. Tessier in her room?"

"Yep. I expect she be heavy-eyed, if you know what I mean."

York nodded. Mrs. Tessier took generous doses of laudanum—a mixture of whiskey and opium—almost every afternoon, even in good times. No telling how much she'd take to deal with this.

"You got servants with her?"

"A couple. Trenton be there too."

"Trenton? How'd he get here?"

"He was in Beaufort for somethin' or other, I don't know what. But Mrs. Tessier sent for him soon as it happened. He rode in last night. Been with her ever since, sittin' close by."

York took off his hat and scratched his head. A thousand thoughts ran through his mind. Although mean as a swamp snake, Mr. Tessier knew how to run a plantation, no doubt about that. He loved it too, wouldn't leave the place during the hot months of May through October, like so many plantation owners did. No sir, Mr. Tessier stayed on his plantation most all the time, worked as hard as anybody. It wasn't easy making one prosperous. Fact was, a lot of plantations, even some of the largest, lived right on the edge of hard times. With most of their value tied up in land, buildings, and darkies, a couple of years of bad harvests or low prices pushed most of them right to the edge of going broke. York knew because he and Mr. Tessier had come up against the matter more than once. Only a calm head, hard labor, and sharp dealings kept the place in business.

"It be all right," Stella said softly. "We get past this."

York looked sharply at her. "I don't know. Without Tessier around, all manner of things could break loose. You know Mrs. Tessier. She hardly lifts a hand around here and knows next to nothin' about runnin' a plantation."

Stella nodded. "She don't care much about The Oak, that's the truth. Just likes how it keeps her livin' the fine life, like those folks in Charleston and up in New Yawk or somewheres. No way to count on her if times get tough."

A second thought came to York, one that both pleased and frightened him. Without Tessier around, Mrs. Tessier would have to depend on him more than her husband ever did. No one else could handle the place! Yet, if anything happened, he'd get all the blame. With power came responsibility.

Vexed by his situation, he started up the steps to go to Mrs. Tessier.

"What you want done with her?" Stella asked, pointing at Ruby, who had quietly left the wagon and joined them by the steps.

York stared at Ruby. He'd completely forgotten about the new darky. "She's to help you in the kitchen—house too if you need it."

"I train her?"

"Yep."

"Step over," Stella told Ruby. Ruby obeyed, her eyes down.

"She be a fine lookin' child," said Stella, eyeing her head to toe. "Reckon Mr. Tessier be lookin' down feelin' right sad he didn't live to break her into the place just right."

"You mean lookin' up?" asked York, with a twist of his lips.

Stella chuckled.

York turned serious again real fast. "No time for foolishness." He headed up the steps. "Just take her to the back and leave her there. Tell Leather Joe when he puts up my horse to leave my saddlebags in the stall. Then get me a clean shirt and meet me inside. I got things to attend to."

Stella slipped away. York took off his hat and entered the house. A black man wearing a long gray coat, white shirt, and black pants met him in the entry, his wide shoulders almost filling up the doorway.

"Afternoon, Obadiah," York said.

"It's a awful bad day," Obadiah replied.

"You buildin' a box for him?"

"Yes, sir. I finish it up pretty quick. Will lay Mr. Tessier out in the parlor in the finest box anybody around here ever did see."

"Mrs. Tessier approve what you're plannin'?"

"Yes sir, I tell her, and she say go on and do it. She liked it that I'm gone cut prayin' hands right into the sides."

York nodded. Obadiah, a free man of color who lived about halfway between The Oak and Beaufort, handled wood better than anybody he'd ever seen. When not building boxes for the dead—white folks and black—he shaped other furniture—tables and cabinets and such. Folks said he could make wood of just about any kind come alive in his hands.

"I best get back to work," said Obadiah. "Got to finish up the box, then get a hole dug for it."

York nodded. Not only did Obadiah build the coffins, he took care of burying the dead too. "You know when the parson is comin'?"

"Nope, nobody said nothin' to me. But I be ready when the time comes, you know that."

York watched Obadiah leave. He'd known the black man ever since he came to The Oak. Close to forty now, Obadiah had gotten his freedom papers the year his pa—a white shipbuilder and land baron from Savannah—died. That happened every now and again: A white man who had taken up with a slave woman would let the offspring of the union go free once he had passed on. Obadiah's pa had left it in his will that all his servant children—four in number—would receive twenty acres of land, fifty dollars in cash, and papers of freedom ten days after he died. Nineteen at the time, Obadiah had immediately moved from Savannah, taken up residence on his new land, and started building boxes for the dead. He'd done well for himself.

York faced the entryway to the manse again. Although he'd worked over fifteen years with Mr. Tessier, he'd never entered through the front door. A large table with a tall oblong mirror sat to his left. A staircase with a shiny wood rail hugged the wall to his right, disappearing into the heights of the second floor. A number of smooth rugs—most of them a shade of burgundy or gold—lay on the hardwood floor. The ceiling, cut with a circular pattern in the center, loomed at least sixteen feet over-head. About halfway up the wall to the ceiling hung a mammoth full-length portrait of Mr. Marshall Tessier. He wore a red jacket with a black collar and gold buttons and a lacy white shirt, buttoned at the neck. Black pants and boots clean enough to eat off of glistened from the painting. A hound dog lay at his feet on a gold rug.

York took off his hat as if in reverence. What he wouldn't do to have his portrait hanging in the front room of a fine house like this one! It was about as high an honor as a man could get! A frightening idea hit him. Mrs. Tessier wouldn't stay a widow for long. With this kind of property, a line of men as long as a row of cotton would head to her house as soon as Mr. Tessier turned cold in the grave. Surely somebody would win her hand pretty quick. What would that mean for him? A new owner might bring his own overseer. Hampton York clenched his fists. How dare somebody come along who might boot him off the place!

As Stella stepped from the back of the house, he pushed away his ill thoughts. She tossed him an old but clean brown shirt. Without explaining, he slipped it over the one he wore.

Stella pointed to his arm. "You hurtin', I see."

"Nothin' to it," he said quickly. "Snagged it on some brambles."

Stella grunted but didn't argue. "I take you to Mrs. Tessier. But remember, she might not be too clearheaded."

"I'll pay my respects, then leave her alone."

Stella led him up the staircase. "Where that girl Ruby come from?" she asked.

"Virginia. A man died, and his wife had to sell some of their Negroes to raise cash."

"That not gone happen here, is it?"

"Reckon not," he said as confidently as he could muster. "We'll do just fine." Just then they reached the top of the stairs. "Never been up here."

Stella laughed quietly. "It's a purty place. Fancy as a Charleston hotel. Not that I ever seed one, mind you." She stopped by a double wood door. "I'll see if she's open-eyed."

York waited while Stella stepped into the room and closed the door. He peered over the balcony at the splendid house. What a man wouldn't give for a place like this! He let his mind wander. How much money did Tessier actually have? What had it cost to build this place? How did a man ever come to such a fortune?

The bedroom door opened, and he turned to see Trenton Tessier stepping out and closing the door. The boy looked tired; his brown eyes sagged.

"I'm sorry to hear of your father's death," York quickly said, his tone as proper as he could make it. "A shock to all of us. Have you sent for Calvin?"

Trenton nodded as York mentioned the youngest of Tessier's four children, the fourteen-year-old boy who attended the same boarding school that Trenton was about to finish. "I sent Uncle Bob for him and my two sisters," he said, mentioning the house servant who drove the family carriage. "They should arrive soon."

York thought of Martha and Miranda, Tessier's two daughters. They had married brothers from a banking family in Charleston and lived there now. They were two of the vainest, meanest women he'd ever known.

"How is Miss Camellia?" asked Trenton. "A shame she had to see this happen."

York eyed him hopefully. "I came straight here, so I haven't seen her yet. But I'm sure she's brokenhearted and will want to pay her respects to Mrs. Tessier as soon as possible."

"Tell her . . . tell her . . . " Trenton stopped and shook his head.

York shifted his feet. Trenton and Camellia had grown up together, played with each other like brother and sister. York knew Camellia had some hopes about their future. Even though he feared she'd set her sights too high, he wanted to help make the match any way he could. York dropped his eyes. Camellia deserved a better pa than him, a better . . .

"I'll inform Camellia that you've come home," he replied in the most proper English he could muster.

"I'll see her as soon as I can," Trenton said.

York changed the subject. "Your father was a fine man."

"He was a scoundrel, and we both know it," Trenton replied in a stony voice. "No use pretending anything else."

York started to protest, then hesitated. If young Mr. Tessier wanted to face the facts so clearly, then so be it. Yet he still felt cautious. What if this was some kind of test, a ruse to see where his loyalties rested?

"Every man has his faults," he said, deciding on a middle course. "Even your pa. But he knew a thing or two about a plantation. And he always treated me fair; his darkies too."

Trenton eyed him, and York returned the stare. Just past nineteen, Trenton was dressed stylishly in a ruffled green shirt, tapered mustard-colored slacks, and a wide-buckled black belt. A man of medium height, thin shoulders, and short-cropped brown hair, he needed only a few more months to finish his schooling. Then he'd take his place as a grown man in the finest of the South's society circles.

"I've come to see Lady Tessier," York said, deciding to get on with the matters at hand. "Express my sympathies; see what she needs."

"Mother is resting," Tessier said firmly. "Perhaps you should visit her after she's had time to settle some."

York noted the fine diction of the young master. Obviously, his schooling had given him a lot more polish than his dead sire. But did that mean he was kinder too? Less bent on his own way?

York recalled an instance from several years earlier.

At the request of Mrs. Tessier, Obadiah had shaped a bust of young Trenton, but Trenton had immediately disliked it. Hauling the offending carving before his father in his library, Trenton demanded that Obadiah receive a whipping.

"He made my shoulders as thin as a lamb's!" he railed.

Sitting by Tessier's desk, York thought the bust captured the young boy's body almost exactly. "You've not filled out yet," York said, hoping to calm the boy. "Wait a couple of years and let him do it again."

Trenton glared at him, then addressed his father. "I want him whipped," he repeated.

"You can't whip no free man of color," York put in. "Unless he broke a law."

Trenton quickly turned on him. "You've got no say in this," he snarled. "You just work here, remember?"

York glanced at Tessier, then looked away.

"He's right, though," said Marshall Tessier. "Can't whip Obadiah without the law involved."

Trenton threw the bust on the floor. "I want this thing burned!" he shouted.

"He got your face fine," his father said. "That ought to count for something."

Trenton eyed his father. "You want me to go to Mother?"

"What if we don't pay him for it?" Tessier asked slyly. "As much as he likes money, that'll hurt Obadiah more than a whippin'."

York started to argue, to remind him that all the darkies would hear about it if he didn't pay Obadiah and would no doubt find a way to take their revenge. But, not wanting to displease his master, he kept his mouth shut.

Trenton kicked at the bust on the floor. "Okay," he finally said. "Don't pay him."

Tessier turned to York, his palms up. "See to it," he told York.

So he had. Obadiah had received no money for the bust. When The Oak Negroes learned of the injustice, they slowed their pace for two solid weeks, their low output their way of standing against the wrong Tessier, Trenton, and York had committed.

Now York stood before the grown-up Trenton. He was still a slender man, never quite filling out as much as most his age. York tried to figure what to do. Should he go without seeing Mrs. Tessier? But she might see that as impolite, might wonder later why he hadn't come to pay respects the minute he returned from Charleston. Yet what would happen if he insisted on visiting her and displeased Trenton, the elder son who now stood to inherit the power of his father?

Although not sure, York decided to stand up to Trenton. If he didn't, the boy might see him as weak, never a good trait for the overseer of a plantation.

"I prefer to speak to your mother now," he insisted, but politely. "To assure her I'll take care of things, give her peace of mind about that."

Trenton glared at York but then relented. "Okay. But only for a moment."

York gave a nod.

Trenton stepped back and let York enter. Mrs. Tessier lay on a four-poster canopy bed under a white cover up to her waist, her head propped on two pillows, her eyes glassy, a handkerchief in her right hand. She wore a light blue robe over her nightclothes. A servant stood on either side of her and waved fans the width of shovels to keep her cool. Trenton moved to a corner behind York and waited.

York eased to the bedside. At first Mrs. Tessier didn't seem to see him. He inspected her face. Skin a pale white, like flour in a skillet. Eyes brown with thick brows that almost touched in the middle. A light mustache, but not so you could see if you weren't looking. A thick woman, but not overly so. Not a woman who would take your breath if you saw her standing in a parlor, but not unattractive either. Slightly above ordinary— nothing more and nothing less.

"Mrs. Tessier?"

She glanced at him, her eyes unfocused.

"I'm sorry this has happened. But please know I'll take care of everythin'."

She waved her handkerchief, as if none of that mattered.

He knelt as she put her handkerchief to her mouth and sobbed softly. He glanced at Trenton, then back at Mrs. Tessier, pondering what he dared to say. "I know The Oak," he said quietly, trying to speak properly. "I will make sure it continues to prosper."

Trenton took a half step his way. Mrs. Tessier nodded as if understanding. Without thinking, York lightly touched Mrs. Tessier's hand. "I'm at your disposal," he said quickly. "Anything you need, let me know."

Trenton moved again and York stood, his breath ragged. Perhaps he'd gone too far by touching her, but so what? The way he saw it, if Trenton and Camellia became husband and wife, his familiarity with Mrs. Tessier wouldn't matter. If not, he needed another plan, and if it had any chance of succeeding, he needed to start now. Yes, it meant some risk, but given his situation, why not take it? Who knew whether Trenton and Camellia would ever marry? Whether Trenton might want a new overseer? Whether he would even keep The Oak? Lots of young masters got rid of property left to them by dead fathers. The way York saw it, he had few choices.

He stood and faced Trenton. "Please know again of my sorrow," he said, his words as formal as he'd ever used. "I'm here to serve you and your mother."

Trenton clenched his jaw but stayed quiet.

York licked his lips. "I'll maintain the plantation as well as ever. With all you have on your mind, I don't want you to worry about The Oak."

Trenton pulled up to his full height, setting his shoulders as far back as their round shape would allow. "You need not fret about The Oak."

"I always fret about The Oak," York said. "Your father paid me to do so."

Trenton clicked his heels together. "I'm coming home to take care of The Oak just as soon as I finish school."

York decided to stay calm. "We'll look forward to that. You can follow in your father's footsteps."

Trenton snorted. "I plan to do much better than my father."

"It's good for a man to have ambition. I'll do all I can to assist you."

Trenton's mouth edged up at the corners. "You are a careful man."

"I'm loyal," said York. "Eager to do my job as best I can."

"You'll care for The Oak until I finish school?"

"I'll do for you whatever you wish."

Trenton smiled widely. "We'll bury my father as soon as we can get a parson. Then I'll go back to Charleston."

"Will your mother go with you?"

"I don't know. Maybe she'll go to Charleston, maybe Columbia. Time to decide that later."

York nodded. "Let me know what I need to do for the burial."

"I'll talk with you later."

"Anything else I can do to aid you?"

Trenton rubbed his chin. "One thing," he finally said. "I've sent someone to the sheriff in Beaufort. He'll want to talk to Camellia. Tell her to prepare for his coming."

"Certainly," said York.

"I'll stop by to see her soon."

"As you wish. Some notice would give her time to make herself presentable."

"She is always presentable, at least to me."

York raised an eyebrow and let his mind linger again on the possibility of a match between Trenton and Camellia. He'd run The Oak forever if that happened!

After Trenton pivoted and walked off, York headed down the stairs. When he reached the front porch, he stopped and looked out. The sun had completely set, but he could still see the outlines of the place. Close to thirty bunking houses for the Negroes sat over five hundred yards away and downwind to the left. Three different barns stood halfway between the manse and the bunking houses. Out of sight past all that lay the rice fields.

York lifted his eyes to the moon. He'd worked for somebody else most of his life; had bent his ways over and over again to please them, to do their bidding, to make their plantations profitable. He'd accepted his place in the world. But now another change had come, and this one threatened everything. If Trenton turned against him, he'd lose his job and end up on the road with nowhere to go. After managing The Oak, anything else would feel like failure.

York remembered the money in his saddlebags. If he wanted, he could take that money and buy some property. Not much, but a little. But if he got anything close by, people would be real suspicious about where he'd gotten enough money to go out on his own. Most would figure he'd stolen it from Tessier, probably after his death. They'd think he'd taken advantage of Tessier's widow to line his own pockets. Young Trenton might even come after him and demand he return the money.

York put in a new chew of tobacco. If he kept the money, he'd have to leave the lowlands to spend it, no question about that. That notion didn't appeal to him, but what choice did he have? He thought of Josh and wondered what he'd do. He'd give the money back. But to whom? Young Tessier? That made no sense. To the sheriff in Beaufort? But what about the dead man? They'd surely accuse one if not both of them of killing him. That would lead to all kinds of problems.

As he stepped off the porch, York knew he needed time to think. For now he'd keep the money, run the plantation, and try to please Mrs. Tessier. After young Trenton returned, who knew how things would unfold?

Set on his course, York let his mind run. Trenton seemed mighty concerned about Camellia. What did that mean? Better yet, how could he use that to make sure he protected what he had worked so long to attain?

Chapter Six

Josh met York on the front steps of his house, where he'd waited for the last few minutes. Dark had completely fallen, but he could still see the worried look on York's face as he walked up and shook his hand as if he hadn't seen his half brother in a long time.

"An eventful day," he said, noting York's saddlebags across his shoulders. "Your arm okay?"

"Yep. Stella got me this shirt."

"Hard to think how fast things can shift on a man."

York took off his hat and led him inside the house. Camellia stepped from the kitchen. York dropped his saddlebags on the floor. "Rough couple of days, huh?" he said to her. "You doin' okay?"

Camellia looked at her feet. "I'm upset."

"Where are the boys?" York asked, his attention already shifted.

Josh's hands tensed. York needed to pay more attention to Camellia! She needed a time to sit down, to tell everything that had happened to her.

"They're still working, I guess. I saw them midday, when they stopped at the cookhouse for food."

York shuffled, and Josh wanted to smack him. Camellia needed somebody to listen to her, somebody to get her a cup of coffee and pat her hand and give her comfort. But York did nothing of the sort, and Camellia glanced back up, her face sad.

Josh caught her eye and smiled as warmly as he could. "Anything I can do for you?"

She nervously wiped her hands on her apron and shook her head.

"You let me know if I can help in any way," he said. "Any way at all."

Camellia smiled thinly. "You two need something to eat. Go on and sit down. I'll fetch you a bite."

Josh wanted to argue, but she left before he could say anything. Although the two of them didn't do a lot of talking, they saw each other almost every day. He respected the way she took care of her family at the same time she labored on The Oak. No telling what York and his boys would do when Camellia took on a husband, and surely that would happen soon. Every eligible man within twenty miles seemed sweet on her. He suspected that the only thing that had kept her from marrying already was the dream of Trenton asking for her hand.

York pointed to a chair by the fireplace, and Josh took a seat. York threw a log onto the low fire that was already burning, then fell into a seat across from Josh.

"Anna told you about Tessier, I reckon," York began.

"Yes, soon as I got home. It's an unpredictable world, that's for sure."

York took off his hat and hung it on his knee. "I saw Mrs. Tessier."

"She heavy-eyed?"

"Not as bad as I thought."

"She's not your typical plantation lady, for certain. It's a wonder the manse runs as smoothly as it does."

"Stella keeps it in order. That's the only way."

"When do you think we'll bury Tessier?"

York picked up a spit cup from by his chair. "Soon as the parson can get here. A body won't keep long this time of year. Anna tell you how it happened?"

"Said Tessier was in the cookhouse, slipped on some spilled potatoes, hit his head. Curious, if you ask me."

"How so?" York spat into his cup and stared at him, his face wrinkled.

"Well, I don't mean to raise any questions if none should get raised, but what's Tessier doing in the cookhouse? Cooking isn't exactly the responsibility of the master of a plantation."

York stroked his beard. "That's a mystery, for certain. But only Mr. Tessier would know, and he's dead and can't tell us."

Josh shrugged. "Just curious, that's all."

"What else?" asked York.

"Anna said he cut his hand on a knife."

"Yep. When he fell, he grabbed on to one."

Josh stared into the fireplace. A single flame darted up, flickering against the stone. He wondered what more to say, pondered whether to mention what he'd been thinking. "You remember what you told me a few weeks ago?"

York stayed quiet.

"You told me that Mr. Tessier had made some advances toward Camellia," continued Josh. "You tell that to anybody else?"

York's face darkened. "That had nothin' to do with this!" he growled. "How could it? You thinkin' maybe he come at her, she cracked him on the head?"

"No," soothed Josh. "Nothing like that. Just want to make sure you didn't tell the story to anybody else. Cause anybody to get suspicious."

York spat into his cup. "My mind ain't thinkin' straight right now. But you're the only one I told. I know that for a fact."

"Look," Josh said, "a lot has happened today—more than we can handle real easily. Just stay steady, okay?"

York nodded. "Camellia was just there. Nothin' else to it. She and Stella said the same thing. Folks will believe them. No reason not to."

"They send for the sheriff?" asked Josh.

"Yep, Trenton did."

"Master Trenton is here?"

"Yep, he was in Beaufort, and Mrs. Tessier sent for him."

Josh stood and moved to the fireplace. "You think Trenton had any notions about his father's advances on Camellia?"

York quickly shook his head. "Not unless somebody else told him. And who would?"

"Camellia maybe?"

"No, she wouldn't do that. Camellia's a quiet girl, not one to bring out such a thing if she don't have to. She wouldn't tell Trenton such a bad thing about his pa."

"I suppose not." Josh rubbed his face and turned his thoughts to other matters. "You still got the money?" he asked softly.

York pointed to the saddlebags. "Stopped by the barn before comin' here. It's all right there."

"What do you plan to do with it?"

"Don't know. Too much happenin' right now to give that much thought."

"You could give it to the sheriff when he comes. Walt's a good man."

"No reason confusin' one man's death with another. Liable to make Walt real suspicious about both. We already made our decision over this."

Josh clenched his fists. Although York held the money, he still felt responsible for it. "I think we ought to get shed of it. Feels like it's got meanness on it . . . that it'll bring us bad luck."

York chuckled lightly. "There you go again, a man of the Lord talkin' about luck. No such thing accordin' to the parson, least what little I've heard from him. It's all the Lord's will, ain't it? Everythin' that happens?"

Josh refused to take the matter lightly. "This might not be the time for a religious talk."

"You surprise me, Brother Josh," teased York. But his voice had a slight edge to it. "Seems to me a man of the Lord should want to talk religion just about anytime."

"And you surprise me, Brother York, raising questions about the Lord, you being a touch standoffish when it comes to matters of faith."

"I can ask a question or two, can't I?"

Josh tilted his head. Did York really want to talk about faith, or was he using the question to keep from focusing on the money? "Questions are good," he said. "Talking and all. But I guess I like to *do* my religion more than just talk about it. Seems that's the best kind of belief anyway."

York stopped teasing. "So you don't think all this is the Lord's will? Us findin' that money? Tessier dyin' all of a sudden?"

"*I* found the money," Josh said firmly. "Not *we*. And whether or not it's the Lord's will, I have no way to say. What I can say is this—it's not the Lord's will for anybody but the rightful owner to keep that money."

"But what if we don't know the rightful owner? Is it our duty to go lookin' for him?"

"Don't know the answer to that one either."

Camellia stuck her head in the room. "Got food on the table. Come on back and wash up."

"Give us another minute," said York. "Be right there."

Camellia turned back to the kitchen.

Josh moved to the saddlebags and lifted them from the floor. "The man mentioned a name," he said, facing York again.

"So?"

"Mentioned the name Ruth, like it meant something to him."

York dropped his eyes. "Maybe that's his wife. Or a sister. Or maybe he was tryin' to say one of your big words, like *ruthless*, but didn't get it all said. Nothin' we can do with any of that."

"I thought maybe I'd ask around some, maybe in Beaufort or even Charleston the next time I'm there."

"Good luck with that. What about Savannah? Maybe he came south to north. Then Columbia. Why don't you just give up your work and your family and ride all over the state seein' if you can find Ruth?"

"I know it's unlikely," said Josh, angry at York's mocking tone. "But I have to try. Can't just let it go."

"Sure you can. You won't find anybody anyway, I don't expect."

"I'm sure you're right, but I need to try."

"I'm sure you do." York pointed out the room's only window. "All this is up for grabs now," he said, sweeping his hand across the expanse of the plantation. "Mrs. Tessier will surely marry again. Some new master will come in and take over this whole place."

Josh moved to his side. "That's beyond the two of us. We just work here."

York spat into his cup. "It don't have to be that way. Not if we play our cards right."

"What do you mean?"

York faced him, his eyes bright. "You know how Master Trenton and Camellia grew up together."

"Yes, they've been friends for a long time."

"He may have leanin's toward her."

Josh glanced toward the kitchen, slowly shaking his head. When he spoke, he took care to make sure Camellia couldn't hear. "Even if he does, it's not likely they can end up husband and wife. You know how things work. A man of his station doesn't marry down. It's not proper."

"No law against it."

"Oh, there's a law, all right. It's just not on the books anywhere."

"No punishment if it happens."

"You're wrong again. Plenty of punishment . . . for them and their kids. All the society people in Charleston, Beaufort—you know how they'd act. Oh, they'd speak nice to her face and all. The Tessiers hold too much money for them to do anything else. But behind her back they'd say awful things. No matter what she did, they'd look down at Camellia the rest of her life . . . and her children, too, when they come. They'd treat them like mongrel pups."

"If she and Trenton love each other, they can get past all that."

The conviction in his half brother's voice, the tone that said this not only *could* happen but absolutely *had to* happen gave Josh pause. Although he didn't want to think it, Josh suddenly realized that York wanted this marriage as much for his own purposes as for Camellia's happiness. In fact, even if it might not end up best for Camellia, York wanted this anyway. A marriage between Camellia and Trenton guaranteed York's position.

A bitter taste rose in Josh's mouth, reminding him again of the thing he disliked most about his half brother: the extra dose of ambition that lay in his gut, the selfishness that put a hard edge on him. Part of Josh wanted to say all this to York, to lay it out plain and hope that by speaking it he could give York a chance to see it, to fight it, and to destroy it forever. But how do you say that to somebody you love? How do you tell a person that he's got a heart of stone when it comes to wanting something even if it hurts someone else? Especially when that person has cared for you when you figured nobody else would?

"Maybe love can get past all that," Josh finally said.

"I'll run this place for them after they marry," said York. "Make it the finest plantation in the South."

Josh put a hand on York's shoulder. "You shouldn't get your heart set on this. What if it doesn't come to pass?"

York stared at Josh with a shimmery look in his eyes. "I got no doubt it will happen. But even if it don't, I'll come up with some other notions."

"What notions?"

York shook his head. "I'll keep those to myself for now. A man of the Lord like you might not think them too Jesus-like."

"We don't keep much from each other," said Josh.

"That's right, but maybe this time it's for your own good."

Josh tried to read York's mind but failed. Sometimes York thought in ways that he couldn't match.

"Let's wash up," said York. "After supper, we got a lot to do."

"It'll be confused around here the next few days," said Josh.

"Yep. Got to get the old man buried."

"What do you need me to do?"

"Don't know yet. Just stay close."

"Anna's not feeling well, but I'll do all I can."

They walked toward the kitchen.

"Headaches again?" asked York.

Josh nodded. "Puts her in bed a lot of afternoons, with rags over her face to keep out the light."

"Sorry to hear that."

"You talkin' about Aunt Anna?" asked Camellia, reaching for a coffeepot as they entered the room.

"Yes," said Josh, taking the pot and setting it on the table. "Bad headaches."

"Tell her I'll check on her," said Camellia.

"She'll be glad to see you."

Josh washed his hands in the wash pot by the back door, then took a chair, his mind on Anna. She held his world together. When she hurt, he did too. He thought of Tessier's sudden death, the way everything had changed all at once. A chill ran through him. What if something happened to Anna? How would he survive? He pushed out the notion, took the coffeepot, and poured a cup. Footsteps sounded in the front room.

"Sounds like Chester and Johnny," said Camellia, headed toward them. "I'll tell them supper is on."

Josh faced York as she left. "You best not hitch your wagon to Camellia and Trenton marrying up," he whispered. "Nor to any other notion either. Nobody knows what'll happen next."

"I'm an optimistic man," said York. "Nothin' wrong with that."

Josh poured York a cup of coffee. "You haven't told her yet, have you?"

"Nope," York answered. "Never saw reason."

"She's old enough to know."

"That's the truth," York replied. "But it just don't seem right, least not now."

"You're afraid of telling her, that's the thing."

York nodded. "I know what you're figurin'. You think I'm holdin' back because I'm hopin' for her to marry Master Trenton. That I'm just watchin' out for myself."

Josh wiped his hands on his pants. He knew his agreement with York was written plainly on his face.

York spoke again. "You're some right, but I ain't afraid just for me. I'm fearful for her too—what she'll feel when she finds out that her mama bore her out of wedlock. That she . . . "

As York's words trailed off, Josh saw the hurt in his eyes. Josh knew that despite his faults, York truly loved Camellia and her brothers.

"Camellia's not your real daughter," said Josh. "No matter how much it hurts her, she needs to know that someday. She needs to know you stepped in and married her mama, even though she already had Camellia and came up expecting a second baby by another man after you married her. You took care of Camellia and Chester like you had sired them, even when her mama didn't stay true to you."

"I don't know how that will do any good for anybody. You're not plannin' on tellin' her, are you?"

"It's not my place," said Josh.

"I reckon it's not."

Camellia came back, her brothers stomping in behind her. They were tall boys, like York, with dark features, loud voices, and ready tempers. Also like York, they worked hard and didn't like anybody who didn't. Josh wondered how Camellia's softer temperament managed to mix with such a rowdy group. Somehow she managed it.

York drank his coffee. Josh hung his head, his emotions torn over York's dilemma. Although he'd not been with York when it all happened, York had told him the secret story. Camellia's mama had not lived a virtuous life. A finely featured young woman, she'd grown up an orphan and had taken to living with a man after she got out at the age of sixteen. Camellia had come out of the union with that man before marriage, Chester after her. Sadly for her mama, though, that man hadn't done well making a living for them. So when she met York, she left Camellia and Chester's father and took up with York. He loved her, he said, when he got on his knees to ask for her hand in matrimony. It didn't matter to him that she'd fallen short in the realm of chastity. So long as she stayed true to him after the marriage, he wouldn't hold her past against her.

The marriage lasted almost two years, just long enough for them to have York's boy, Johnny, but not much more. Camellia's mama had run off in April that year, 1844, without warning or explanation. Nobody ever knew where. York tried to find her for a while, but she never showed up. Most figured she'd run off somewhere out of state, a long way from The Oak. Just over two years later, after Josh's arrival at the Oak, York heard from her one final time when a box reached him in the mail. The box contained her last belongings: a pair of earrings, a Bible, the red dress she wore the day they wed, and a navy blue cape. A short letter, written in a scraggly hand, came with the other things.

Hampton, I am sick with the typhus. Will not make it, I expect. Sorry I was not a good woman for you, not a good mother to my children. I am a sinner. May the Lord forgive me. If you see fit, give Camellia my things and tell her and the boys I have sought to mend my ways. Asking mercy . . .

Then she had signed her name.

After showing Josh the letter, York had torn it up and burned it in the fireplace. As for the rest of the things, Josh didn't know what had become of them. Knowing York, they were probably destroyed long ago.

"We will not speak of her ever again," York had told Josh a couple of days after burning the letter. "She is gone forever."

They had pretty much kept true to that decision. Only when Camellia or one of the boys asked did York ever say anything about her. Even then, his words were sparse. "Your mama died of typhus," he said simply. "She was a beautiful woman. Camellia looks like her."

All that was true. Why York left out the fact of her unfaithfulness, Josh didn't quite know. Was it to spare the children the hurt of knowing their mama was a tart . . . or to protect York's own pride? With York, a body could never really know.

Josh wiped his face. Was York right? Was it best to keep from Camellia the secret that she'd come from a mating between a pa and a mama with no virtue? Or should York tell her the truth?

Josh shook his head. *Too many secrets,* he thought. *Too many unsaid truths.* Somehow, he figured, the secrets would get out. And when they did, who knew what unexpected things they might shake loose?

Chapter Seven

When the parson showed up from Beaufort two days after Tessier's death, everybody gathered in a high spot among some thick trees a long way behind the manse to pay their respects to the dead man. The parson, a bald cleric as round as a barrel in a long black coat that didn't meet in the front, quietly called everybody to order. The day turned out breezy and cool, with the first true feel of fall in it. Thick white clouds built up overhead. The parson wiped his brow in spite of the chill and started in on what a good life Marshall Tessier had lived, how he'd generously given most of the money to pay for a new section of the Episcopal church in town.

"Although he never had much time for churchgoing, given his steady work here at The Oak," said the parson, "Mr. Tessier helped make it so everybody else had a fine house of worship where they could meet. The Lord's now made a place for him, a place better even than the beautiful manse of The Oak."

Sitting by his mother in a wood chair near the head of the casket that Obadiah had built, Trenton Tessier found his thoughts drifting from the parson's words. He wondered what would happen to The Oak; whether he should go back to school or not; how his mother would cope with all this. Trenton shrugged. His mother and father weren't exactly a well-matched set. Truth was, he suspected if his mother could find a man to run the plantation and keep the money coming in, she might not even miss her deceased husband. Trenton considered the notion of her taking another husband. She was young enough. Why not? But how would that affect him?

Trenton glanced over the crowd, over seven hundred people he guessed, counting the Negroes. The burial of a man as wealthy as Marshall Tessier brought folks from all over. He eyed his mother. A black lace veil covered her face. The veil matched her dress and gloves. Although he couldn't see her eyes, he knew they were clear today, off the laudanum for this occasion. That surprised him a little, but then again, maybe this would shake her up some, cause her to shoulder some of the load for a change.

Calvin sat by her, his hands busy going in and out of his coat pockets. Trenton reached for his mother's hand and hoped the parson would speed things up. His father had never claimed anything more than a facade of religion, and everybody in the crowd knew it. No reason to pile the hypocrisy on too heavy. The parson read the Twenty-third Psalm.

"The LORD is my shepherd; I shall not want. He . . . "

Trenton's eyes moved to the edge of the crowd. It took him a couple of seconds before he found her, standing near the back, her brown hair shimmering as it fell beyond her bonnet and then onto and past her shoulders. She wore a simple blue dress, clean and obviously pressed for the occasion with hot bricks. He tried to catch her glance, but she kept her head down. The house woman Stella stood by her, one arm around her waist.

Trenton wiped his brow with a starched white handkerchief and focused on the parson again. Hickman—that was his name, Reverend Donald Hickman, parson at Saint Michael's. The parson moved to a new passage of Scripture.

"Let not your heart be troubled: ye believe in God, believe also in me."

Trenton stared at his father's casket, realizing that life could change in a hurry. One day he was off at boarding school with not a care in the world; the next day his father was dead, and he now carried the responsibility of caring for a family and one of the largest plantations in the South. Trenton scrutinized his sisters, Martha and Miranda, both of them dressed like his mother. Their husbands, Gerald and Luther, stood behind them—their tall black hats perched carefully in their hands and their faces blank. Although he didn't particularly like either of the men, he did appreciate the fact that they took care of his sisters.

The preacher continued to read from the Scripture. "Behold I shew you a mystery . . . "

A dog barked. Trenton considered the parson's words. *Will we all be changed?* he wondered. Will a man of faith in the Lord receive a new body, an incorruptible one made for the heavens? But what about a man with no faith in the Lord? A man like his father, a man who put his faith in the product of his own hands, in the fierce effort of sweat and heart? What happened to a man like him when they laid him out horizontal in the ground? Not given to thinking too often or too long about such matters, Trenton had to admit he didn't know.

The preacher asked everyone to pray. Trenton bowed his head. While the parson prayed, Trenton pondered his future. What should he do now? What did he want to do? Did he want to come home and run The Oak, or did he want to talk his mother into selling the place? Camellia's face rose in his head. Since childhood, they'd talked about marrying someday. Should he do that now that he'd become the man responsible for his father's businesses? Oh, he knew what his mother would say. "She's beneath you," she'd point out. "Not quality." He knew that of course. As he'd gotten older he'd learned what he never knew as a boy. Men of his status married within their class; anything less than that caused scandal of major proportion. But no girl matched Camellia's beauty—not any he'd seen in Charleston or anywhere else. Besides, what right did his mother have to tell him what he should or shouldn't do? If he wanted to marry Camellia, he'd do it—no matter what she said.

When the parson finally said "Amen," Hampton York and Josh Cain nodded. Four of the darkies stepped forward and lowered the casket into the hole already dug. The parson took Trenton's mother by the elbow and helped her from her seat as she walked to the casket. The parson gave her a handful of dirt, which she dropped on the casket. Trenton, Calvin, and his sisters then joined their mother. The parson handed a shovel to Trenton, and he lifted a shovel full of dirt and dropped it into the grave. Calvin did the same, then his sisters.

With his mother on his arm, Trenton left the grave and headed back to the manse. Before long the rest of the crowd followed and started in on the food that the servants had laid out in the yard on wood tables. Trenton led his mother to her bedroom and helped her lie down under the canopy of the bed. A couple of minutes after he got her situated, someone knocked on the door.

Trenton opened it, and Stella stepped in, Ruby beside her. "We come to aid Mrs. Tessier," said Stella.

Trenton nodded and Stella pulled off his mother's veil and gloves. He turned his back while his mother slipped out of her dress and petticoats and lay back on the bed. When he faced her again, Stella stood over her on one side, Ruby on the other. Stella wiped her face with a damp cloth while Ruby fanned her with a large fan.

"It be a hard day on you," said Stella. "Wonder you don't just pass right out. Thank the Lord the heat broke some, that's all I got to say."

Mrs. Tessier glanced at Trenton and patted the bed. Trenton moved to her, and Stella and Ruby stepped away. Trenton took his mother's hands. He noticed her eyes, dry as dust and far clearer than he expected. He wondered why she hadn't already called for a dose of the laudanum, then hoped she wouldn't. Sometimes a thing like this shook people up so much they changed some habits—for better or for worse.

"I'm glad that's over," Mrs. Tessier said.

Trenton nodded. "Lots of people came—from Charleston, Beaufort, even Columbia."

"Your father had business in a lot of places."

Trenton considered Stella and Ruby as they waited in the corner. Their eyes seemed a long way off, seeing something he couldn't. He considered the strange world between whites and blacks. Although the house servants saw, heard, and knew everything that happened with their masters, they knew to keep it quiet if they wanted to keep their place in the house. They acted like deaf and mute beasts in a way, unable to speak what they experienced.

He faced his mother again, wanting to speak truthfully of some things he'd long wanted to express. Although fearing he should wait, he didn't really like that notion. As the elder son, he carried the authority to speak what he really wanted to say.

"I know you and Father kept separate rooms the last few years," he said, deciding on the straight talk. "I know he traipsed around with other women."

"We understood each other," she said, expressing no surprise at her son's bluntness. "He provided things I needed; I provided things he needed. Not exactly happily ever after, but we stayed together."

"Did you ever love him?" he asked wistfully, hoping for a positive answer.

"I married him at twenty. He was forty, a widower. You know that."

"Yes, his first wife died of fever, without giving him children."

"I needed to marry for my family's sake," she said. "No reason to lie about it. We were an old Charleston shipping family, but down on our luck. Had lost a couple of ships to storms; another to piracy. Your father came along, and I knew him from other times, parties and socials. He courted me for a while. He was a handsome man, well-dressed, even if a bit forward at times, rough with speech and liquor. After four months or so, he approached my father. They made a deal. I'm not the prettiest of women, and I'm not afraid to say it. I didn't have that many suitors at the time. So I agreed to the arrangement, liked the life your father promised, the fact he could provide for me better than anyone I knew. We married. I'm not sure love had a lot to do with it. But a lot of marriages happen that way, not just mine and your father's."

Trenton stared toward a window. "I want to marry someone I love."

Mrs. Tessier pushed herself up higher on the pillows. "I want that for you too. But it may be hard to find. Not that many girls of your station available."

"I've already found it."

"What?"

Trenton held his breath, not knowing whether to press ahead or not. Maybe this wasn't the best time for this. Yet he'd already started, so he might as well finish.

"Tell me what you're saying," insisted his mother.

Trenton stood and walked to the window. Crowds of people milled about below, many of them busy with the food, others sitting about in chairs. The lace curtains on the window hung straight and still.

"I plan to marry Camellia York," he said quietly. "Just as soon as I finish school."

Silence fell. Trenton looked for Camellia in the crowd but didn't see her. Probably in the cookhouse, he remembered, working like a darky. He'd change that for her, he decided fiercely. Dress her in the finest clothes, make her the lady of the plantation after his mother passed, treat her like the queen she deserved to be.

"You're a romantic," said his mother. "I'm glad for that. But you can't marry Camellia York, and you know it."

Trenton faced his mother again. "Why not?" he asked, although he knew what she'd answer.

"She's barely above white trash. Her stock is too low. She's not schooled, has no refinement, no quality. People would laugh us right out of Charleston."

"I don't care about people in Charleston," he claimed. "Let them laugh all they want."

"They'd never accept her," his mother continued. "Her children either, your children, my grandchildren."

Trenton moved back to the bed. His mother touched his face.

"You're not even twenty yet," she said. "You grew up with Camellia; she's the best friend you ever had. I can understand your attachment to her. But that doesn't mean you love her. You're so young—give yourself some time. You'll meet the right woman. A lady you can love who's equal to you."

"I've lived almost four years in Charleston," he said. "I've met girls from all the society families. They're all empty-headed; care for nothing but the next dance, the latest fashions from Europe, the step of the horses that pull their carriages. I want a woman of substance, somebody who knows how life really works, a woman of beauty and depth. Camellia is all of that and more."

Mrs. Tessier smiled ingratiatingly. "I'm not asking you to give up your romantic notions. Your father had them too, surprisingly enough. All young men do. I find such notions . . . charming. But don't rush into this. Finish school, then see what you want. You *can* have love, but not with Camellia York."

Trenton shook his head. "I plan to ask her before I go back to school. With Father's passing, I want that settled, want her by my side when I come back to run The Oak."

"Now isn't the time to deal with this," said Mrs. Tessier more severely, now sitting on the bed's edge.

"It's exactly the time," argued Trenton. "Everything changed when Father died."

"Then I say you can't do it," said Mrs. Tessier. "I won't abide it. I need you too much, need you giving all your attention to your father's business interests. You're the heir, the one trusted to keep things running right."

Trenton eyed his mother. She stared at him for several seconds, then dropped her stare to the floor. Her posture told him she had more on her mind than his plans with Camellia. For the first time he realized she had some fears about her own future. He sat down next to her and put an arm around her waist. "What is it, Mother?"

She shook her head. "I'd rather not say."

"You're asking me to give up a woman I love. You have no choice but to tell me what's bothering you."

She dropped her head to his shoulder. "It's The Oak. You know the yield's been down some the last few years."

"Yes, but I'm surprised you know it."

She smiled briefly. "I'm not as dull-headed as some think. I pay attention. Besides, your father told me more than most suspected. He knew that when it came to matters of finance, I was a most interested party."

"So the yield's been down. What about it?"

"Your father said he feared the land was played out—too much growing and not enough lying fallow. He was thinking about buying some land farther inland, starting some cotton maybe."

Trenton weighed that idea. "Nothing wrong with that. If we have to do it, we can. But maybe we'll switch off some fields here for a few years and see if that helps. We've got enough land to do that easily enough."

Mrs. Tessier stood and moved to her dresser, then sat down heavily, indicating to Stella that she should brush her hair. "It's not just the land," Mrs. Tessier said. "Your father also owns my family's shipping company."

"I know."

"We lost a ship to fire last year, before it even got finished. They were building it up in Philadelphia when a dock fire spread. Burned our ship and three others to ashes."

"So what? Losing one ship won't break us."

"It won't break us, but added to low rice prices and poor yields, it does cause us some concern. A few more strokes of such ill fortune and we could face some deep troubles."

Trenton wiped his face. "You're telling me I shouldn't marry Camellia because I might need to marry a girl of means? Is that it?"

Mrs. Tessier's eyes, reflected back from the mirror, fixed intently on his. "I'm telling you I want you to marry for love. But it would be helpful if the woman you love also brings some dowry to the altar, some standing in the community as well, some education and refinement—all the things a man of your breeding deserves."

Trenton paced to the window again. This time he saw Camellia as he stared out. She set down a plate of food on the table and took a seat. Her hair glistened in the sunlight. He considered all his mother had said and knew she hadn't lied. Although he'd spent years away from The Oak, he'd not seriously courted many girls, not spent much time with anyone except Camellia. How did he know he loved her? Had he ever tried to love anyone else?

He raised his eyes past Camellia, out to the land and property beyond. He loved this place, he realized, all it stood for and the power that came from being the older son of its owner. He couldn't stand the thought of losing it. How could he live if that happened? How could he face other people? If marrying Camellia meant he couldn't keep The Oak . . . ? But how could he not marry her? He'd hoped for that since his boyhood, and the notion of giving her up because his mother said he should galled him to no end. He didn't like anybody forcing him to do anything, especially his mother. Women shouldn't tell men what to do or how to do it, mother or not. His father had shown him that; had taught him that men ruled, always had and always would. He'd accepted that teaching the same way he'd learned to shoot a rifle, without question or reflection. A man got to choose his course in life, and everybody else in the family had to follow what he chose.

He drew his eyes back to Camellia. She looked so lovely, so soft, so . . .

Trenton faced his mother again and felt tired all of a sudden, as if someone had dropped the weight of a barn on his shoulders and made him carry it for a long time. He wanted to run from his mother, run from The Oak, take Camellia and run until they reached a place where no one knew them, where no one placed any expectations on them, where no one wanted anything from them.

"I don't know, Mother."

"I'm counting on you, Trenton. You'll do the right thing. I know you will. Just don't rush your decision. Go back to school and give yourself some time to ponder matters."

Trenton took a deep breath.

"Leave me now," said his mother. "All this has wearied me."

Trenton nodded, kissed her on the cheek, and headed outside. Standing on the porch, he wanted to go to Camellia, but knew he couldn't until he figured out what he would do. To go to her now, while he remained so unsure of his course, might do more harm than good. He wiped his brow and hung his head. For the first time in his life he felt like a grown man, and he wasn't sure he completely liked the feeling.

About half a mile away from where Trenton stood, Hampton York eased to the ground and leaned up against a massive oak tree. Birds chirped overhead, but he barely noticed. A creek running toward the Conwilla River trickled twenty feet to his left, but he paid it no attention. Completely alone for the first time since learning of Mr. Tessier's death, he placed the money box from Mossy Bank Creek between his booted feet and put a new wad of tobacco in his cheek. The sun splashed through the tree and bathed the box with a golden glow. York looked left and right to make sure of his privacy, then quickly opened the box and picked up a handful of the money that lay inside. His hands trembled as he counted the bills. When he finished the first handful, he put it to his side in a neat stack and started on the next. In seconds that stack joined the first one, and he grabbed the last fistful of money. His lips moved silently as he counted—four thousand, six hundred, seven hundred, eight hundred, nine hundred—an even five thousand.

He spat into the underbrush and checked the box again, as if expecting to find more. His eyes widened as he saw a tintype picture resting on the bottom of the box. He again glanced around, then, seeing no one sneaking up on him, lifted the tintype from the box and studied it with squinted eyes. The picture showed the clear image of a man with a swarthy face, a stern brow, a long handlebar mustache, and weathered eyes.

York ran his fingers over the image and cursed under his breath. Although he'd not seen the man in the picture for a long time, he had no doubt of his identity: Wallace Swanson.

York studied the image. What was Swanson's picture doing in this box? Nobody had seen or heard from him in years. Wasn't he dead? Since he hated Swanson more than almost anyone on earth, he sure hoped so; he hoped Swanson's sorry carcass was rotting somewhere in a grave, preferably one with no marker.

What did this picture mean? Why was the man at Mossy Bank carrying it, along with five thousand dollars? Maybe most important of all, what should he do about all this?

He spat again, laid the tintype back in the box, and nervously rubbed his beard. Five thousand dollars, a picture of Wallace Swanson, and a dead man made for some unusual happenings, that was for sure.

York's head hurt as he wondered if Swanson was alive. If so, where? No way to know, and he sure couldn't leave The Oak to go looking for him. York picked up the money and ran his fingers through it. Did the money belong to Swanson? If so, how'd he get it? The last time he saw the man he owned little more than the clothes on his back. But if it didn't belong to Swanson, why was his picture in the box? Was he a friend of the dead man? But what kind of man carried another man's picture around in a money box?

A light breeze blew across his face as York considered the possibility of asking around; maybe he could find out a few things about Swanson. But then he thought of the man who'd shot him at Mossy Bank. If he asked around and the man who shot him heard about it, he'd surely come looking for him, try to get the money from him. York checked the wound on his arm. At least it didn't hurt anymore.

After putting the money back in the box, York shut the lid and eased himself back up. Until he knew more, maybe he should keep things quiet; wait and see what happened. Who knew? Perhaps he'd never hear from anybody. If not, given a couple of years, he could probably start spending the money, a little at a time for sure, but better than not at all.

A squirrel darted to the ground about fifty feet away and chattered at him. York thought of Josh and quickly reopened the box, lifted out the money, grabbed the tintype beneath it, and put the money back. The dead man had said "Ruth" as his last word. What did that mean?

Too confused to think anymore, York put the picture in his coat pocket and closed the money box. Even if Josh came looking for the money, he didn't want him knowing about Wallace Swanson. No reason for anybody but him to know about Swanson. No reason at all.

Part Two

Wait, thou child of hope, for
Time shall teach thee all things.

—MARTIN TUPPER

Chapter Eight

The rest of November passed slowly for Camellia. Although she stayed plenty busy, she gave no real attention to her labors. She cooked almost every day, side by side with Stella and Ruby and two other servants, but she was numb. After Tessier's death, life seemed like a dream; she felt cut off from it all, as though somebody had put her in a trance. Not even a visit from Trenton and Walt, the sheriff from Beaufort, made any dent in her blank stare.

"I already asked the Negro about Mr. Tessier's death," Walt had said when he came to visit a week after the incident in the cookhouse. But Walt's round face and thin voice was blurry to Camellia's eyes and ears. "Thought I'd talk to you too. Why don't you tell me what happened?"

Camellia had repeated in flat tones the story she and Stella had rehearsed. Walt had watched her closely. Afterward she was sure he and Trenton could see through her lies. Yet, when she finished, Walt had said, "That's what the darky woman told us," and left her alone.

The only part of that awful day she remembered well was her conversation with Trenton, who had waited behind after Walt had gone.

"You feeling okay?" he had asked.

"As good as I can expect," she said, her eyes down. "Please know I'm sorry about your father."

Trenton waved it off. "He was a hard man to love."

"Just the same, he was your father."

"Yes, he was."

She waited for him to say more. He took her hands, but his palms felt cold and lifeless. He touched her chin and lifted her face. "I'll go back to Charleston in about a week."

"You'll finish your schoolin' this spring?"

"Yes. Then I'll return to The Oak for good."

"I know you will be glad to come home."

Trenton smiled and straightened his back like a rooster stretching. "Will you be glad when I'm back?"

Camellia pulled away and smoothed down her skirt, her feelings jumbled. She'd killed Trenton's father. He could never love her if he knew that. "You're my friend. Of course I'll be glad to have you return."

Trenton put his hands on her shoulders, but she drew back again. Chaste girls didn't let men take such advances.

"I've missed you," he said.

Camellia felt even more confused. How could she lie to Trenton, let him think so well of her when she knew better?

"We need to talk," he continued.

"It's too soon. Too close to all this." She waved her arm, taking in all that had happened.

"When I come home," he said, "then we'll say all we need to say."

"Yes," she agreed, hoping that would satisfy him so she could have time to clear her head.

After Trenton left her she'd tried to go back to normal life, tried to forget Tessier's death. But she kept seeing Mr. Tessier when she lay down at night; his face haunted her as she tried to sleep. The smell of his breath hung in the air everywhere she went, and the sound of his head cracking on the table sounded time and time again in her ears. Her eyes turned red from lack of sleep, and her feet shuffled like an old woman's as she moved from manse to cookhouse and home again. She lost weight, and her clothes hung loose on her thin bones. She wanted to talk to somebody about it all but didn't know where to turn. Her pa, never given to a lot of words, especially with her, seemed more distant than ever.

Camellia knew that Tessier's death had dropped a heavy load on him, but still she wondered why he'd withdrawn even more. Unsure of how to approach him, she decided to keep things quiet. Besides, what could her pa do if she told him? No way would he go to the law and tell them his daughter had caused Master Tessier's death. And, even if he did, what difference would it make? It wouldn't bring Tessier back to life.

After Trenton returned to Charleston, her pa started spending more and more time away, coming home hours after dark, eating quietly and falling straight into bed. Chester and Johnny managed to get him to talk some every now and again, but the talk usually stayed on matters of interest to men. Camellia felt more alone than ever. As the days got shorter and the weather colder, her spirits fell lower and lower. She wished more than ever for a close woman friend. She had Stella, but custom allowed a white girl to tell a darky only so much, no matter how close the two of them were. She considered going to her aunt Anna, a sweet woman if she ever met one, but Anna had three children and trouble with her headaches—Camellia didn't want to add to her load.

She traveled to Beaufort for church as often as she could and listened to the parson's sermons. She wished she could just stand up and shout out the truth to everybody about what had really happened in the cookhouse. Guilt ate at her like rust on a pot; she felt if she didn't confess her sin to somebody, she'd surely rot from the inside out. When she went to bed at night she tried to pray, but God seemed a long way off. She began to wonder if God even heard her stumbling words, and she became more and more silent, talking only when absolutely necessary. Her skirts hung on her like empty bags, and her hands turned redder and redder as she kept washing them over and over in the water pot in the cookhouse in a vain attempt to rid herself of guilt.

Her pa and brothers seemed ignorant of her sadness. So long as she kept their clothes washed and some food on the table, they didn't seem to notice anything about her.

Finally, Christmas came. But, unlike most years when the Tessier family all gathered at The Oak, Mrs. Tessier headed to Charleston instead, leaving Camellia's pa to hand out the presents to the darkies on Christmas Eve. Her pa gave everybody a new set of clothes and shoes, a jug of whiskey to each man and a piece of red ribbon for every woman. The children got cloth dolls, even the boys. The darkies killed enough chickens for everybody to get the piece they wanted, and a traveling preacher set up in the barn for a few days and gave a pretty good message about the baby Jesus. The servants got drunk afterward, and a fiddler and banjo player took out battered instruments and started to play. The party lasted three days, but to Camellia it didn't seem to have as much joy in it as usual. To her, everything seemed lifeless, hopeless, and useless.

With the new year, the weather turned wet and cold. One late afternoon, just after the day's cooking was finished, Stella caught Camellia as she hauled the last skillet of corn bread onto the table. "Put down that corn bread, child," ordered Stella. "We be takin' a walk."

"What do you mean?" asked Camellia. "We've got things to do."

"Those things can wait."

Too weak to care or argue, Camellia obeyed.

"Come with me," said Stella, handing her a shawl and bonnet.

"Where are we going?"

"You got to talk to somebody."

"What do you mean?"

"Look at you. Not eatin', not talkin', not sleepin'. You lettin' what happened chew you up. Not healthy to let that go on forever. You got to tell out your demons so they lose their teeth."

"Who you got in mind?" Camellia asked, trying to figure who she could trust to keep her secret.

"Just you wait and see. Put on that shawl, bonnet too."

Camellia again obeyed. Stella led her out of the cookhouse toward the back of the manse. A gray sky looked down on them. Camellia pulled her bonnet close and tried to make conversation to keep her mind off her fears. "I like Ruby. Seems to have a good head on her shoulders."

Stella smiled. "That be true. But she be better lookin' than is good for her. All the young men come strappin' around every Saturday night, Sundays too. She can't get no rest from them, Obadiah especially."

"He's coming most every week?"

"Yep, even though she don't pay him that much attention. He gave her a seashell necklace for Christmas. She won't wear it, though."

"She seems gloomy most of the time."

"Yep, and keeps her words pretty tight. About all I learned from her is she used to have a man named Markus and a baby boy, Theo."

"Must be hard on her, leaving them."

"Reckon so."

They rounded the back of the manse and headed down a trail the width of a wagon. Four small houses, including the one where Camellia lived, sat about two hundred yards down the trail. Two of them were empty, their front windows shuttered and vines covering their front steps. Camellia stopped as they reached the houses, all of them better than the servants' quarters, but none large or fancy.

"Why are you taking me home?" she asked. "I'm not going to tell my pa, if that's what you're thinking. He's got enough on his shoulders."

"It ain't your pa I got in mind," said Stella.

Camellia's brow wrinkled. "Who, then?"

"Just come on, child."

Camellia followed Stella toward the last house in the group. A row of cedar trees fronted the place, and a freshly painted white fence bordered it. The dirt yard was broom-swept smooth, and the house looked fresher than the others, even her own. Camellia slowed as Stella reached the steps of the house.

"Come on," said Stella. "Nobody here gone hurt you."

"I won't tell Anna. Although she's my aunt, and a good friend to me, she's not strong. I won't put worry on her head."

"I ain't thinkin' of Anna," said Stella. "Josh Cain, he's the one."

Camellia dug her heels into the ground. "He might tell Pa."

"I reckon not," said Stella. "He's a trustworthy man. I figure if you don't let out what you got buried in you, then it's gone block up your insides so much you can't even live. I don't want that to happen to you. So I been figurin' who we can tell. Not the parson in Beaufort; he owes too much to the Tessiers and would do anythin' to get some more. Not your father either, 'cause he might say somethin' when he be drinkin'. That leaves Mr. Josh Cain, a man solid as a oak. Got strong roots that won't tear up easy."

"But he's my uncle," said Camellia. "I shouldn't draw him into this."

Stella looked down. "Half-uncle. You know that. But he be different than your pa, in lots of ways. Mr. Cain's the only one I know we can trust to hear this and keep it to his heart."

Camellia weighed the matter. Josh Cain, her elder by ten years, had a knack for making people feel good. Lots of people, herself included, mentioned his eyes when they spoke of him—how they gave off a kind look, like they took you right into them and blessed you. But Mr. Cain worked close with her pa. What made Stella think Josh wouldn't go to York with her secret? Although she'd known him for a long time, she'd never really talked alone with him and didn't know how he'd take to such a thing as this.

She rubbed her head against the ache behind her eyes. Nothing seemed clear. If she told Cain, he might tell her pa. But if she didn't, she might as well go on and die.

"Okay," she finally said, gathering the shawl closer against the day's chill. "Maybe Mr. Cain can help me figure what to do."

Stella nodded sharply. "He said he would meet us before suppertime."

They walked up the steps and knocked. A second later Anna Cain opened the door. She wore a simple gray skirt, a green apron, and a black blouse, buttoned to the neck. Her copper hair, shorter than Camellia's, was parted in the middle. She looked pale . . . as if enough blood didn't pump through her veins.

"Welcome, ladies," Anna said, as if welcoming them to tea. "Josh is expecting you."

Camellia smiled briefly and followed Anna through the narrow door to the front room. The house, though sparsely furnished, smelled clean.

"The kids here?" Camellia asked as she sat down.

"Lucy and Butler are out playing," Anna answered. "Though I can't imagine why in such cold. Beth's in the kitchen."

"She's getting bigger every day," said Camellia. "Smarter too."

Anna beamed, and Camellia saw the love in her eyes. A feeling of kinship with Anna ran through her. Anna loved her husband and family; someday, after Camellia and Trenton married, she'd have a family she loved just as much.

"Josh is washing up," Anna said.

Camellia smoothed her skirt. Stella stood behind her. Camellia glanced around. A fireplace bordered the wall to the right. A blue curtain hung over the single window to the left of the fireplace. A picture of a sailing ship on the ocean hung by a nail on the wall by the window. The colors were bright and strong. Camellia pointed to the picture. "Who did that?"

"Josh," Anna replied proudly. "He draws one, hangs it a while, then tears it down and throws it out."

"He ought to keep them," said Camellia. "Got a real knack for drawing."

"He's never pleased with them," Anna explained. "Won't let me keep them."

Camellia started to stand to examine the picture closer, but the sound of footsteps stopped her. Josh Cain entered the room, his hair wet, his face still moist from washing.

"I'll get some water for everybody," said Stella.

"No, Stella." Anna held up a hand. "I'll do it."

Stella stopped and Anna left the room. Josh took a spot by the fireplace and stared first at Camellia, then at Stella, then back at Camellia.

Camellia took a good look at him. Blond hair, eyes as blue as a clear day, a scar on his chin. Not a tall man but with wide hands and long fingers for his height. His teeth were more even than most men she knew, and whiter too, probably because he didn't chew or smoke, at least not that she had ever seen.

"I understand you want to talk to me," he said gently.

Camellia tilted her head. His language was finer than her pa's—still not polished like Trenton's, but not nearly so coarse or uneducated as most men's. She suddenly felt nervous. Everyone knew Josh Cain as an honest man, and here she'd come to tell him she'd killed Marshall Tessier. Surely he'd want to haul her away to the sheriff. She wanted to run, to leave this house and never come back. But what would happen if she did? How would she live with herself?

"She all tore up inside," said Stella, filling in the silence. "Not sure she ought to say her mind."

Josh took a seat and put his hands on his knees. When he spoke, his voice sounded smooth, like a slow-moving stream. "Just take it easy," he offered. "Nobody here will repeat anything you say. Stella told me you wanted this kept secret. I promise you I'll hold it close, whatever you tell me."

"But you got no clue what I'm to tell."

"It matters not."

Anna reentered and handed them all a cup of water, her hands shaking slightly as she handed the last cup to Josh. Camellia noticed sweat on her brow and an even whiter tinge to her skin and lips.

"I think I best go rest," Anna said. "I'm not feeling well."

"Need anything?" Josh asked, concern evident in his eyes.

"No, you stay here. Give me a few minutes to rest, that's all." She left before Josh could do anything else.

"She be a fine woman," said Stella. "Not many white ladies be offerin' water to a darky."

Josh smiled at Stella, then faced Camellia again. She clenched her hands in her lap. If she couldn't trust him, she couldn't trust anybody. She decided she better speak in a hurry before she turned coward. "It's about Mr. Tessier," she started. "The way he died."

She quickly told the story, watching Josh the whole time, studying his reaction. His face was blank as she talked, and that gave her courage to say everything except the part about Stella coming back before Tessier slipped. When she'd finished, she sat back and unwrapped her fingers, her heart slowing some now that she had confessed her crime.

Josh closed his eyes. She could see him trying to measure what to say or do. She held her breath and waited, not daring to interrupt. After several minutes of silence, he opened his eyes, stood, and threw a log into the fire. He poked it with a long stick. When he finished, he faced her and Stella again.

"Sounds like you have no sin in this," he offered. "A man comes with advances on you, no matter his station or yours, you have a right to say no. If he presses his desires and something happens, that rests on his head, not yours."

"I don't know that the law would see it eye to eye with you," said Stella. "She bein' a woman of lower station than Mr. Tessier. You know good as me that a body's place makes all the difference with the law."

"You know about all this?" he asked Stella, his surprise evident.

"I be there when it happen," said Stella. "Miss Camellia left that part out."

Josh faced Camellia again. "You lied to the sheriff."

"I got scared," said Camellia. "Not sure what would happen."

"I made her keep her quiet," said Stella. "Blame me, not the child."

Josh sat down, hands on his knees. "Secrets are hard to keep. They'll eat you up after a while."

Camellia wondered if Josh Cain kept any secrets, then decided not. A man of his character didn't lie well.

"I believe you could convince a sheriff of your story," he said slowly. "A jury too, if it ever came to that."

"No!" Stella emphasized. "We not goin' to no law; you promised me you'd keep quiet whatever she told you. I wouldn't have brought the child to you if I thought you wasn't a man of your word."

"I did say that," Josh agreed. "But I didn't know how serious it was. A man is dead . . . the most powerful man in the area."

"All the more reason to keep our quiet," insisted Stella. "What good it gone do to say this now? Who's it gone help? Poor Mrs. Tessier? It gone be good for her if me and Miss Camellia tell out that her husband tried to have his way with this young girl? And Mr. Tessier? His name already not so good. Most folks will believe us, even if they throw us in jail for it. They know the truth. That man messed up a lot of girls, white and other, you know that. Why drag his name down in the mud any more than already? Then, last, what about Miss Camellia here?" She moved to Camellia's side and put her hand on her back. "She's barely a woman. Even if the law believes us and lets us go, she still gets a bad name for this, people whisperin' behind her back. What good that gone do?"

As the old woman pushed back a sprig of her frizzy hair, Camellia wanted to hug her. Although some might point out that Stella had selfish reasons for not wanting the truth told, Camellia believed she didn't really care much about any of that. Stella truly wanted to protect her, and that warmed Camellia's heart. She couldn't remember anybody else who had ever looked out for her interests first, not even her pa. She loved Stella for it.

Josh stood again, this time walking to the window. "You make a lot of sense," he said, looking out. "But I have to tell you it goes against my nature to leave things unsaid."

"Mine too," Camellia agreed. "Reckon that's why I don't sleep so good these days."

"A conscience can be a powerful thing," he said.

"Everybody got a few things on their conscience," offered Stella. "Expect even a man like you."

When Josh pivoted back and faced Stella, Camellia sensed something pass between them.

"Tell you what," Josh said. "Let me think some on this. I don't see any hurry about it, do you?"

Camellia shook her head.

"That be fine," said Stella. "You do all the thinkin' you need. Mr. Tessier be dead. No rush gone change that."

"Josh!"

The scream came from the back of the house. In spite of its shrillness, Camellia recognized Anna's voice.

There was a loud thunk, and Josh ran from the room, Stella and Camellia close behind. Camellia paused as she reached the bedroom door, but Stella kept right on going. Camellia followed her inside. Anna lay on the floor by the bed, both hands gripping her head, as if trying to squeeze her skull in a vise. Her cheeks were red, a sharp contrast to the pale color she'd had when she left them.

Josh knelt by her. "What, honey? Where does it hurt?"

Anna tried to speak but managed only a few low moans. Beth suddenly appeared by Camellia, who instinctively hugged the child.

"It be somethin' in her head," whispered Stella. "I seed this once, long time ago."

Josh glanced at her, freezing her into silence. "She'll come around after a few minutes."

Camellia hugged Beth tighter as Josh tenderly picked up Anna and tucked her into bed. Camellia took Beth and headed to the kitchen for some water.

"Mama gets the headaches," said Beth, handing her a clean rag. "We all help when she does."

"You stay here," said Camellia, wetting the towel in the water basin. "Let me go check on her. I'll come back in a few minutes, okay?"

Beth nodded as Camellia started back to the bedroom. She found Josh sitting by Anna and rubbing her temples.

Camellia handed the towel to Josh and stepped back. Anna stared blankly at the ceiling. Her mouth moved but no words sounded.

"Leave us for now," said Josh as he put the wet towel over Anna's eyes. "She needs quiet."

Stella shook her head and led Camellia from the room. "Go to the manse," Stella said. "Tell your pa about Anna. See that he sends somebody to Beaufort to find us a doctor man."

"You think a doctor can help?"

"Not for me to do no guessin'," said Stella.

"But you said you saw this once."

"Yes. A darky named Toby, no more than thirty years. Sittin' on his porch on a Saturday night. Healthy as a young horse. Grabbed his head and bellowed out somebody had stuck a pointy stick in his ear. A few minutes later, he kilt over, his eyes rolled back, and frothy wet came to the corners of his mouth. He stayed with us about four months, then passed right on to Jesus."

"You see this as the same thing?"

"Go on, child. Go to the manse. Send for a proper doctor; let him say what it is."

Not knowing what else to do, Camellia obeyed, hesitating only long enough to tell Beth bye and that she would pray for her mama. Heading to the manse, she wondered what Josh would do with what she'd told him? Nothing, she decided. At least not for a while. Right now Josh Cain had a whole lot more on his mind than what had happened to Marshall Tessier.

Chapter Nine

Ruby stayed mad a long time during that first winter on The Oak. Although Stella allowed her to stay in the two-room cabin where she lived near the manse, Ruby didn't even talk to the old woman at first. Why should she? Stella liked to boss, and Ruby didn't want to obey.

"You'll take care of the top floor of the manse when people are home," Stella directed. "Make the beds, keep the chamber pots clean, sweep up floors, keep fresh water in the basins in all rooms, wash clothes in the iron pot in the wash house. When they be not home, you'll take to the kitchen with me and Miss Camellia."

Although she mumbled a lot about the bad hand life had dealt her, Ruby knew better than to disobey. No use making Stella or anybody else mad, especially so close to Mr. Tessier's dying. White folks in the middle of hard things often treated their darkies poorly, taking out their bad feelings on somebody who couldn't do anything back. Besides, if she had any notions of ever getting shed of the place, she needed to stay quiet and study out the people, figure out who could help her and who couldn't. A colored gal raising a ruckus would attract too many eyes, eyes that might keep that gal from running off when the right time showed its head.

With Mrs. Tessier gone, the manse didn't need much cleaning during those winter months. So Ruby spent as much time alone as possible, not even talking to the other two girls, Lisa and Lydia, who worked with her in the house. She liked the aloneness in those early days. No reason to get too friendly, since she didn't figure on staying too long once the summer hit and she could run.

As the weather got colder, however, Ruby found her foul mood hard to keep up. Until the day that Mrs. Rushton had sold her, she'd always been talkative and happy; staying quiet all the time made her sad. To her surprise, she gradually found that she wanted some company, at least part of the time, and turned to Stella. In spite of the fact that Stella liked to bark her orders, Ruby sensed a good soul in the old mammy. Soon, Ruby began to trust the old woman. By the time January had ended, Ruby found herself doing the light chores in the manse as quickly as possible so she could join Stella and Camellia in the cookhouse. Although she didn't say it out to anybody, Ruby found it almost pleasant there. Camellia treated her kindly, and even though she didn't really trust any white girl anymore, she put a lot of stock in that. Camellia made her think of Miss Donetta, and that reminded her that some white folks cared about their servants, no matter the appearances to the contrary. Listening to Stella and Camellia chatter as they fried chicken, rolled biscuits, and stirred gravy made Ruby warm up inside, at least for a while.

The days got wetter and colder as February rolled in. Everybody snuggled deeper into their shawls and hats as they went about their work. Mrs. Tessier came back from Charleston to check on a few things with Mr. York, and Ruby and Stella took care of her hand and foot. Since she stayed in her bedroom most of the time, Mr. York took the stairs to her bedroom every morning to go over The Oak's business.

From her place in the corner of the room, Ruby saw that Mrs. Tessier paid good attention to what Mr. York said. That surprised her some, since she'd heard Stella and Camellia say how little care Mrs. Tessier normally had for the plantation. Not only that, but Mrs. Tessier hardly ever took laudanum anymore, except for a couple of times a week, late in the afternoon. More often than not she skipped her opiate mix and spent her time either reading or writing letters to her children in Charleston.

Mrs. Tessier always wrote her letters in a cloth, high-backed chair by the window, her body draped in silk robes and leather slippers. When finished, she usually took a seat at a large roll-top mahogany desk, folded the letters into an envelope, then licked the seal and handed them to Ruby to give to Uncle Bob to mail in Beaufort. Other than her meetings with Mr. York and those letters, Ruby couldn't see that Mrs. Tessier had much heart for anything else.

It rained almost every day in early February. One day as the skies poured, Ruby joined Stella and Camellia in the cookhouse a few hours before dark.

"Put your hands to the gravy," said Stella, pointing Ruby to a skillet as she walked in. "Got rice to finish up."

Ruby moved to the table, skillet in hand. The kitchen was warm, but she still pulled her shawl tight. Although much colder in the north, the wetness of the ocean air chilled her worse than any deep frost. She put flour in the skillet, then added water and milk. "Got some leavin's from breakfast sausage?"

Stella pointed to a plate by the wall. Ruby took the plate and poured the morning's leftover sausage into it and cut it up. A few seconds later she carried the skillet to the fireplace and set it on a big rock in the corner.

As she waited for the skillet to heat, Ruby studied the white girl. Although Camellia tried hard to seem normal, Ruby sensed she had something heavy on her mind. She'd lost a lot of weight in the last few months and hardly ever looked her straight in the eye. Fact is, from what Ruby could tell, Camellia didn't look much of anybody in the eye. It was one thing for a poor white woman to look away from her betters in the white world, but something different when she wouldn't keep a steady gaze with a darky. Everybody knew that didn't make sense. Why should a white woman look away from a colored unless they had something real wrong eating at them from the inside?

Ruby washed her hands in the basin by the fireplace, then looked to Stella for another chore. "Cut up these apples," said Stella, pointing to a bunch of yellow apples on the table. "Put a little cinnamon on 'em."

Ruby took a knife to the apples and studied some more on Camellia. Maybe she felt out of place laboring side by side with the darkies. After all, she was the only white girl on the manse doing such a thing. Another notion came to Ruby. Maybe Camellia felt guilty because white folks held blacks as property. Ruby had heard of that. Miss Donetta had even talked about it once; told her how sad it made her that one person could buy and sell another.

Her hands busy with the apples, Ruby weighed one other idea. Perhaps Camellia carried around some burden. Was she fooling with some man? A good Christian girl passing out her favors before she stood before the preacher? Was that it? But no, it couldn't be that. Ruby knew Camellia went to church whenever she could. And she acted like a real Christian too, stopping by Josh Cain's house almost every day to do what she could for him and his children since his Anna had taken to the bed. A woman with that good a heart surely lived a chaste life.

Ruby finished the apples and put them in a pot.

Stella pointed her to the cinnamon. "You seed Obadiah lately?"

"Seen Obadiah," said Ruby, correcting Stella's grammar without thinking. "Have you seen Obadiah?"

"What?"

Ruby dropped her eyes at the slip-up. "Nothin'," she said, deliberately slurring her word. "Got nothin' to say."

Stella stepped closer. "I been watchin' you. Listenin' too. You got a strange way, somethin' in your speech. You talk real good one second, then sound like a field hand the next. I can't figure exactly what it is, but you're up to somethin' you don't want nobody to know."

Ruby glanced around, trying to figure what to do. She wanted to tell Stella and Miss Camellia the truth, to let them know she wasn't a common field hand, that she had learned her letters real fine from Miss Donetta. But doing that meant she was taking them on as friends, as people to trust. Could she do that? She'd decided the day she left Virginia she wouldn't ever do such a thing again. Making a friend meant you could lose that friend, and a woman with no last name had no power to do anything about that if it happened. No ma'am, it didn't pay to get too close to somebody, didn't pay at all.

She hung her head at the thought of living the rest of her life with nobody to call friend. What if she ended up on The Oak for a long time? What if she never found the chance to go back to Markus and Theo? She couldn't live forever without somebody who cared about her, somebody she cared about.

"I can read," she said softly, her hands still.

Stella stepped to her. "Your missy taught you?"

"Yes, back in Virginia."

"I heard of that happenin'."

"How does it feel?" asked Camellia, her eyes wide.

Ruby glanced at her. "You don't know your letters?"

"No, no chance to learn." Camellia dropped her eyes.

"I can't rightly say how it feels. Never thought of it that way."

"I think it would feel strong," said Camellia, looking back up. "Like you got some power, you know. Since you can read the words you got power to go into them, into the places they take you, the things the words describe."

"You did no schooling?"

"I know a few words. But I've been here since I was a small girl."

"Where's the nearest school?"

"Nearly thirty miles away. No way to get there."

"Your mama, your pa didn't teach you anything?"

"My mama died when I was young. My pa knows a little, his figures, reads some. But he never took time to teach me even that much."

"Most white girls can read some," said Ruby.

"But not many darkies," said Stella. "You know it's agin the law, don't you?"

"Sure I know. Why do you think I keep it quiet? Talk like a common Negro in front of everybody?"

Stella eyed her with a new respect. "You smarter than you let on."

"I don't plan to stay here all my life," Ruby said, admitting her hope straight out. "My smarts are all I have to get me out." She spread cinnamon on the apples and tried to focus again on her work.

Camellia wiped her hands on her apron and began to open her mouth, as if she wanted to speak, but Stella beat her to it.

"You able to read the letters Mrs. Tessier's children send her?"

Ruby shrugged. "I could if I wanted."

Stella picked up an apple, started peeling it. "Maybe it's a notion for you to do that." She kept her voice as calm as if telling Ruby to have a drink of water.

"Why should I?"

"Never hurts a darky to know what's goin' on in the manse," Stella said. "Never know when a touch of news might come in handy."

Ruby weighed the idea and saw it made sense, even though she couldn't see at the moment how reading the letters could aid her. "I seal the letters for her most times. Easy enough to read them if I want."

"Somethin' to study over," said Stella.

"Wouldn't that be wrong?" asked Camellia. "Snooping in somebody's letters?"

Stella laughed. "Lots of wrong things in this old world. One more added to it ain't gone break nothin'. Besides, what harm can it do? It ain't like we gone hurt nobody. Just gettin' a little news, that's all."

Camellia sighed. "It don't matter to me."

Stella turned back to Ruby and changed the subject. "I asked you if you had *seen* Obadiah. You never did answer."

Ruby shook her head. "He keeps coming around. But I have a man. You know that."

"That man be long gone," said Stella. "You best put him out of your head."

"Don't put a man like Markus out of your head too easy," said Ruby with a smile, suddenly more comfortable with the other two women. "He makes a woman forget other men; makes her forget everything, to tell it completely true."

"Still, a woman your age needs a man," Stella insisted. "Everybody expects it, counts on you havin' some babies."

"We have no master right now," said Ruby. "With Master Trenton off to school and Mr. York busy running things, nobody pays attention to me. I think I can go without a man awhile yet. Besides, like I said, I don't figure to stay here forever."

Stella shook her head as she set the apples in the fireplace. "You talkin' crazy when you say things like that. Hard for a darky to do any runnin', even a fella. You know what happens. A fella runs off, stays gone a few days, then shows right back up. He gets out there on his own and sees he's got nowhere to go. And what's he get for his troubles? A couple days hungry in the woods and a whippin' when he shows back up. So what good does runnin' do? A darky don't have a clue what to do when he gets off his rightful place. Where you figure you gone go?"

"Maybe I won't have to run," said Ruby. "Folks up North say men won't always own other men. Say the day is coming when we get our freedom."

"That's silly talk," said Stella. "Nobody down here gone let that happen."

"Folks up North say otherwise," said Ruby. "Say things got to change someday. Maybe a war will do something about it."

"I hear the Southern states will stand on their own if the Yankees get too uppity," said Camellia. "Pull right out of the Union."

"They might," agreed Ruby. "Some say a war will come for sure if they try it, though. I hope it does; anything for us to get our freedom."

"What we have then?" argued Stella. "Who gone do all the work on a place like this? And how we gone live if the master don't take care of us, give us clothes and food and such?"

"Don't know all the answers," said Ruby. "All I know is I don't plan on staying on The Oak all my days. Have to get back to Markus and Theo one way or another."

Stella grunted and started cleaning up the table. "Maybe. But until then Obadiah would make you a good man. He's free and all, got his own place, money too."

Ruby stared at Stella. "What do you care if I take up with Obadiah or not? He pay you to say a good word for him?"

Stella grinned. "Maybe I want you out of my house. Old woman like me needs to live alone."

Ruby smiled then, deciding to go along with Stella's talk about Obadiah. "He's a mite creaky for me, don't you think?"

"Age don't make that much difference. I be close to seventy, but I still got my eye on a buck or two."

The three women laughed, and Ruby's sense of friendship with Stella and Camellia warmed her even more. Although she didn't have Markus and Theo, she'd at least found a couple of friends. Not what she wanted forever, but for now it'd have to do.

"Will you teach me?"

Ruby faced Camellia. "What do you mean?"

"I want to read. Will you teach me?"

Ruby glanced at Stella, who shrugged. "Seems all backward," Ruby told Camellia. "A colored teaching a white girl. Not right, the way I figure it."

"That don't matter to me," said Camellia. "You know how to do something I've wanted to do all my life."

"What difference does it make if you can do your letters?"

Camellia squared her shoulders. "I love Trenton Tessier," she said firmly. "Stella knows it, others too. I think he loves me. But what kind of wife will I make if I'm so ignorant I don't even know my letters? Trenton's got enough reason to be ashamed of me. No reason to give him another."

"A man who truly loves a woman won't feel 'shamed of her no matter what," said Stella. "I told you that."

"That's true," Ruby agreed.

Camellia nodded. "He tells me it's okay. But I want to do all I can to make him a good wife. I got no dowry. Least I can do is learn my letters if I get the chance. Will you teach me?"

"Somebody else ought to do it," Ruby said. "Mr. Cain maybe. I see him with a book time to time. Maybe you can ask him one day when you go by to help him with his kids."

Camellia shook her head. "He's got too much else on his mind. I can't put another task on him. Besides, he's a grown man. It's not proper for him to spend time with somebody like me."

Ruby tried to figure how this could help her. Although she liked Camellia, she also wanted to take advantage of the situation if she could. Who knew what she'd need when the day came to take her leave? What help Camellia could offer?

A smile flickered on Ruby's lips. "I have a question. You answer it, and I'll teach you how to read."

"What's the question?"

Ruby glanced at Stella. "How does a body make his way up toward Columbia?"

"That be a dangerous question," said Stella. "Best you not go askin' it."

"I ask what I want," said Ruby. "She wants something from me, I want something back."

"I don't rightly know," Camellia replied.

"But you can find out."

"I could. Pa travels that way sometimes."

"That's what I want to know," said Ruby. "The way to Robertson's place, between here and Columbia; what road to take there."

"You gone get us all in trouble," argued Stella. "You run, and they gone come straight to me to see if I helped you."

"Just shake your frizzy head." Ruby grinned. "Tell them you had nothing to do with my running."

Stella looked at Camellia. "You best not aid her. It will cause us nothin' but aggravation."

Camellia's jaw tightened, and Ruby could see the torment in the white woman's eyes. Camellia wanted to help her, but Stella wouldn't let her. Ruby moved to the wash basin and dipped her hands in. Maybe she needed to do some stronger trading if she wanted to find out how to get to Markus. She looked at the thought from all angles but didn't see any harm that could come to her if she told what she knew.

"I got a secret," she said, facing the women again. "I'll give it to you if you get me directions. Plus I'll teach Miss Camellia how to read."

Camellia caught Stella's eye. Again Stella shook her head. "She'll run," the old woman warned. "And when she gets caught, she'll tell them we helped her. Then we'll all be throwed right off the place."

"But I want to read!" pleaded Camellia. "What will she do if we tell her? What can she do?"

Stella pulled at the edge of her bandanna. "All right," she finally agreed. "We can say we don't know nothin' if she runs. It be her word against ours. And she's new; nobody will take her side agin us."

"Okay," said Camellia.

"Okay," said Stella, facing Ruby. "You tell us what you got. Then we see how it weighs. If it be heavy enough, we find out the path to Robertson's."

Ruby smiled until her teeth showed. The three women sat down at the table as the apples cooked. "On the way here," Ruby began, "the day after Mr. York bought me in Charleston, we came to the creek. Mr. Cain and Mr. York found this man . . . "

Stella and Camellia held to every word as Ruby poured out her story. She told them everything except the part about them finding the money. When she finished, Stella pulled the apples from the fireplace, then clucked at Camellia. "Your pa say anything to you about this?"

"No, but I don't know why he should."

"You reckon he told Mrs. Tessier?"

"No way to tell."

Stella turned to Ruby. "You ain't told nobody else about this, have you?"

"I know my place. What good would it do me to get the overseer all mad?"

"No good at all."

"That's right."

Stella glanced at Camellia, then back to Ruby. "I reckon we got to get you some directions now, ain't that it?"

"That's the bargain."

"Okay," said Stella, "we'll do what we can. Give us a few weeks."

Ruby nodded. With what they would tell her, maybe she could take her leave of this place by the summer. She stood and took out some bowls for the apples. All of a sudden the world looked like a much happier place, much happier for sure.

Chapter Ten

A wet March rain fell, bringing a chill to the stately room where Trenton Tessier stood before his family. His back to a white marble fireplace, Trenton felt all eyes watching him. The last few minutes had been most unpleasant, and he needed a few seconds to compose his thoughts. He held his hands behind him, palms open toward the fire, and weighed what to say. His mother sat across from him in a tall rocking chair, her hands wrapped around a cup of hot tea. His two sisters, Martha and Miranda, sat on a leather sofa beside her, their eyes—an identical gray—almost pleading with him to listen to reason. Oil lanterns flickered on each wall, giving a soft glow to the room against the light fading outside. Calvin stood by the window to Trenton's right, his hands in his pockets, his eyes down. Trenton wanted to jerk him up and make him take his side, but he knew Calvin didn't have the strength yet to stand up to his mother and sisters.

Trenton tried to stay calm and find a reasonable way out of the corner he felt backed into. Although his desires stood at odds with everybody else's in the family, he didn't want to make matters worse. He quickly recalled the events that had brought him to this moment.

After spending most of February tending to matters on The Oak, his mother had insisted she return to Charleston as soon as March began.

"Mr. York runs the plantation quite well," she had written to Trenton. "No reason for me to stay here even one more day. The spring parties will soon begin in Charleston, and I simply refuse to miss them. Besides, I want to see Martha and Miranda, you and Calvin. I'll be there in a few days."

She had arrived by carriage, her feet warmed by wool blankets, her mind numbed by an extra dose of laudanum to get her through the trip. Four

*servants hurried out to carry in her baggage, and Trenton followed them to
greet his mother. Martha, Miranda, and Calvin trailed him. Driven by the
rain, they had all rushed back inside, Mrs. Tessier leading the way.*

*As she always did after a trip, his mother headed straight to her bedroom
to rest for a spell before attempting any further social endeavors. Once there
she removed her shawl and settled into the mammoth walnut poster bed with
a quilted cover at least three inches thick. A servant brought hot tea, took off
Mrs. Tessier's shoes, and placed the covers over her feet. Trenton put another
log in the fireplace. Mrs. Tessier drank from her tea, then waved everyone off.*

"Leave me to rest awhile," she said. "Then we shall visit."

And visit they had—close to thirty minutes already. The conversation
had quickly moved in the direction his mother wanted. She'd made her
desires plain and seemed bent on fighting anybody who stood against her.
Trenton now hung his head, wishing he could avoid the conflict, but
knowing he couldn't back down. What self-respecting man allowed his
mother to forge his future the way his mother wanted to direct his? The
fire behind him crackled, but Trenton felt no warmth from it.

"I'm not sure I can abide by your counsel," he said, staring hard at his
mother.

"We've dealt with this already," she replied, her eyes clear of the laudanum since her rest. "You must not rebel in this."

"But I'm a man now," he argued, his temper beginning to flare. "I cannot take orders from a woman, even my mother."

"You are a man," said his mother. "And I'm proud of that. But you're
a Southern gentleman. One who knows it's right to do best by his family."

Trenton looked at his sisters. Both of them were dainty women in colorful dresses with hoop skirts and tightly wound corsets. They wore their
brown hair in ringlets much of the time and kept multiple servants nearby
to wait on them hand and foot. They loved the Charleston social life and
attended all the best balls and knew just the right people. Both their husbands came from Charleston banking families with established names.
They had plenty of money, but that didn't seem to matter; they wanted
more and expected Trenton to make sure they got it. As a result, both of
them had taken their mother's side in this latest round of discussion with

him over the matter of a proper wife.

Trenton glanced at Calvin and started to leave him out of it but didn't have the grace to do it. "You're with me, aren't you?" he asked.

Calvin faced him, his freckled young face in anguish. "I'm not with anyone. I don't want to take a side."

Trenton studied his brother. Almost a copy of his father—blocky legs, wide hands and feet, thick jowls, thin of hair. A powerful, if not especially handsome, man. He wondered if Calvin would take after his father in other ways too, the hard edge of his manner, the rough talk and almost fierce pride.

"But you have to take a side," his mother said to Calvin. "This is family business, important to all of us."

"It's *my* business," Trenton fired back. "And I'm not pleased that all of you have taken such harsh positions against me."

His mother stood and walked over to him. "We're not against you," she said, more gently. "I really believe this is best. That York girl isn't right for you. We all know that. So do you, deep down." She reached for his hand, but he jerked it away.

"You can't take up with that white-trash girl," said Miranda. "Not fitting for you . . . or for her either, for that matter."

"Yes," agreed Martha. "Consider her in this. How's she going to feel if you marry her? She won't fit in any circle anymore. Not her own because she'll be too rich married to you, but still not yours because she's got no education, no quality. You're doing her a bad turn if you go ahead with this silly notion."

"Have you even asked her?" asked Miranda. "Maybe she won't have you."

Trenton remembered his last visit with Camellia. She'd seemed distant, especially when he said they needed to talk when he returned home in the spring. What did her silence mean? Did she still have feelings for him? A lot of time had passed since they were children. Perhaps what she'd said when they were young had changed. Maybe she didn't love him anymore.

He considered Martha's words. Was it wrong to marry Camellia? Would he be putting her in a situation where she could never find a friend? But who cared? He'd be her friend; she wouldn't need any others. He liked that notion; why should she need anybody else but him? Having a husband gave a woman all the companionship she required.

"It was a bad year on The Oak," said his mother. "You already know that. Yield down by close to ten percent."

"Are those figures from Mr. York?" asked Trenton.

"Yes," she said. "I met with him every morning while on The Oak."

Trenton's eye widened with genuine appreciation. When it came down to it, his mother could become very practical and firm-minded. Although she still took her laudanum on a regular basis, she didn't take it when she needed a clear head. She seemed to know exactly when those times arrived. *Best not underestimate her,* he decided. She tended to do whatever was necessary to accomplish what she wanted.

"You need a woman of means," said Martha, interrupting his thoughts. "We need you to find such a wife—for all of our sakes."

Trenton scrutinized Calvin again, hoping his brother would find some courage and offer his aid. But Calvin merely focused his gaze out the window.

"Why am *I* responsible for all of you?" Trenton asked in an aggravated tone. Then, pointing to Martha and Miranda, he continued, "You two are married; your husbands ought to provide for you."

"They do," said Martha. "But we also have an interest in our family's affairs. You can't cut us out just because we've got our own men. A quarter of what Father left belongs to us."

Trenton's skin crawled. His sisters were bloodsucking leeches. "What if I just handed it all to you?" he spouted. "Just said I didn't want any of it and married Camellia and left you all behind?"

His mother arched an eyebrow. "A noble notion. But what would you do? Where would you go? I'd feel compelled to relieve Camellia's father of his job as overseer, and also Camellia of hers, in the cookhouse."

"I'd bring her to Charleston," Trenton threw in. "I can get work. I'm an educated man."

"You're not serious?" gasped Miranda. "What a scandal! What—"

Her mother raised a hand to shush her. "I'm certain you could survive. But you have to admit that's rather rash talk."

"Maybe," pouted Trenton. "But it's something I've considered lately. I'm not like all of you. I can live without all this." He waved a hand over his family, over all the furniture in the well-appointed room, all the rugs and mirrors, chandeliers and paintings.

"Then why don't you try it?" his mother suggested.

"What?" asked Trenton.

"You have the choice," she said. "Leave school now, unless you can pay for it, of course. Find work. See how you do on your own, without any of the advantages your name brings, with none of the privileges our money provides. See how you like it for a while."

"But why should I?" he asked, suddenly scared and mad at the same time. "I can marry Camellia if I choose without giving up anything."

His mother shook her head. "No," she said firmly, "you cannot. If you marry her, I'll let go of any claim of you."

Martha and Miranda gasped in unison; Trenton straightened his back; Calvin held his breath.

"It won't matter," Trenton finally said. "A fourth of The Oak belongs to me."

His mother raised an eyebrow again. "Not yet. So long as I'm alive it's *my* property. Check the will if you'd like. That's the way your father left it."

Trenton's fists balled. He was trapped and didn't like it. "Are you telling me you absolutely *forbid* me to marry Camellia?" he growled, not sure he could believe what his mother had just said. "That if I do you'll disown me?"

"That's exactly what I'm saying," his mother said as simply as if announcing that dinner was served.

For a few seconds Trenton tried to imagine how poverty would feel, how he would adjust to it. Not having a house, not even a small one. No fine clothes or good food either. No servants at his beck and call. No carriage to carry him to high-spirited parties; no well-groomed horse and livery.

He lowered his head. Not only would he no longer have family, but his friends would desert him too. He'd end up with no one but Camellia. Would her companionship provide all he needed? Could he live without all the others? And what about her? She'd end up with nothing also. He pondered that. Would Camellia want him if he went to her empty-handed? She would if she truly loved him. But was it fair to ask her to marry him if he had nothing in his pockets?

Confused by his own questions, Trenton took a long breath and faced his mother again. "It's a risky game you're playing."

"I can assure you it's no game," she said sternly. "The Oak is in distress. We need you to marry well for that reason. But that's not all of it. Marriages of the sort you're considering never turn out happy. Can't hook a mule to a thoroughbred. Everyone knows it doesn't work."

"And what do *you* know about a happy marriage?" Trenton spoke without thinking.

His mother smiled patiently. "I've told you before. Your father and I understood each other. We made it work."

"Yes, I saw the way it worked . . . and I want something better," he fired back.

"You can have that," said Martha. "You can have it all. No reason somebody else can't make you happy. A marriage is what two people make it."

Trenton suddenly felt tired, worn out by the constant pressure his mother had put on him since his father's death; worn out by his sisters; worn out by the awareness that his family really did need him. Overwhelmed by all the responsibility, he wanted to sit down and rest his head on his knees.

"I don't know," he finally said. "I don't know what to do."

"Give it hard thought," said his mother. "No reason to decide today. The parties won't start for a few weeks. That's when we need to get busy, set you up with some proper girls; make the connections we need to make."

"You can at least consider other possibilities," said Calvin, stepping in for the first time.

"A good notion," added his mother. "I've done some discreet inquiring. A number of families with proper daughters in Charleston, a couple in Columbia, even a few in Philadelphia are open to your attentions. You do have other prospects . . . some women you haven't met."

"I know every eligible woman in Charleston," said Trenton.

"Then let's go beyond Charleston," said Martha. "Stay open to the possibilities."

"Will you do that?" asked Calvin.

"It can't hurt," said Martha.

Trenton sighed. "Remaining open will do no harm, I suppose. But even if I do call on other ladies, that doesn't mean I've made up my mind to forsake Camellia."

"Oh no," said his mother. "We quite understand your position on that."

Yes, he'd call on some other ladies, Trenton finally agreed. But he loved Camellia, and nothing would change that, no matter how intense the pressure his family put on him.

Chapter Eleven

A hard chill stayed around as March unfolded, frigid air that put frost on the ground several mornings in a row. The wind whistled through the little house where Ruby lived with Stella and caused her to shiver, no matter how much cover she laid over herself at night. Ruby and everybody else stayed inside as much as they could, their bodies close by the fireplaces, with coats and shawls, bonnets and hats on.

"I'll sure be glad when spring turns here for good," Ruby said to Stella about halfway through the month as they sat by the fireplace one night after finishing their labor for the day. "This wet cold makes me shiver like nothin' in the North, not even the snow. Makes everybody all glum too. Not much happiness around here it seems."

"Too many rough things happened 'round here for folks to feel much in the way of happiness," said Stella as she picked a blanket off the floor and laid it on her lap. "Mrs. Cain be still down in her head, rice prices don't rise any last year, and Mr. Tessier be gettin' colder by the minute in his grave."

Ruby picked up a piece of wood and dropped it on the fire. The glow from it warmed her some but not enough. "What you hear about Mrs. Cain? I teach Miss Camellia some readin' most every day and know she goes by to help Mr. Cain and his children, but she don't tell me nothin'."

"You don't have to talk sloppy around me," Stella said.

"I know," answered Ruby. "But I've been doin' it all the time lately so I don't forget—slip up in front of white folks."

"Nobody here will hurt you for knowin' how to read," said Stella. "We got good people running The Oak."

"I know," agreed Ruby. "Mr. Cain's one of them. That's why I asked about his missus."

"Camellia says Mrs. Cain just stays in bed all day and stares at the ceiling. Can't hardly talk."

"Something go wrong in her head?"

"Reckon so. Mr. York brought in a doctor from Beaufort, then one from Charleston. They took blood from the back of her neck a couple of times, but none of that did no good."

"I hear she won't take food."

Stella nodded. "She likely be not long for this world."

"That's too bad for Mr. Cain. I expect he loves her strong."

"I know that for a fact."

Ruby worked her cloth. Stella took a snuff dip from a can in her apron pocket. The fire crackled.

"I wonder about my boy back home," said Ruby.

Stella rocked but didn't speak.

"Theo's turned six now, living with his mammy."

"Good she there for him," said Stella, spitting in a cup on the floor by her rocker.

"He's a special boy," Ruby whispered. "Gets the visions. Said he saw me and him together again. I plan on seeing to it that his vision comes true."

"That's a high goal, yep it is. Hard to live out, though."

"Yes, that's true." Ruby picked up a needle and thread and folded her cloth in half. "I'll have to run someday to do it."

"I told you that be dangerous work for man or woman. White men have ways to find their runaways—dogs, rewards, fast horses. Even other Negroes help, sometimes for the promise of a few days off their labors, sometimes out of fear of getting caught helpin'."

"I wouldn't ever turn in one of my people. Would you?"

Stella stopped rocking. "Hard to say until it happens," she admitted. "If the price be high enough and I don't know the runner, I might. No reason to lie about that."

Ruby bit into her thread and tore it. "I guess you lived all your life right here. Never sold."

"Nope, never sold. Grew up with Mr. Tessier's mammy. She was a sweet woman . . . took good care of me all the time. I was sorry to see her go when she passed, yep I was."

Ruby's hands stilled. "I've just been sold the one time. But that's enough for me to know I'm against the white folks. Until then I had thought everything was all right, the way of the world, you know. Didn't make trouble, did my labor, and kept my quiet. But then, when they made me leave my baby, I saw for the first time how bad it was, how wrong for one person to have the right to sell another, push a body here or there, split up families. Can't be right, can it? The way this world is run?"

"It ain't for me to say. I hear the preacher sometimes when he comes through here; he says the good Lord set it up this way and reads from the Book that we's supposed to obey our masters."

"Yes, the Book says that, but it also says that Jesus came to set a man free."

"It's too complicatious for me."

Silence fell for a while. Then Ruby spoke again. "My Markus is a sweet man, like an apple pie. Sturdy too. Arms like fence posts."

"Sorry they took you two apart."

"They sold him in Charleston the same day as me," she said softly.

"I know. You told me the story."

"A sad day, for sure. But when I find him, we'll go for Theo."

Stella measured her words. Ruby still pined for her man, no two ways about it. But she needed to move on past him, find her another fella before some white man took out after her. Although marrying up with a darky didn't make it for sure that a white man wouldn't still push for her, it did make it a touch more trouble; added at least a little anxiousness to it.

"Obadiah still got an eye out for you," she said. "Even though you ain't givin' him much encouragement. He's a good man too, got money and everythin'."

Ruby shook her head. "No purpose in that. I got no hankering for any other man."

"I know that. But a man . . . well, you need somebody layin' beside you at night, if you know what I mean. Somebody to protect you from other men's notions. Girl, if that Mr. Tessier hadn't already met his Maker, you'd be in trouble right now from him."

Ruby cut off the cloth. Her hands trembled. "That kind of thing not much heard of on Mr. Rushton's place up in Virginia. It really happen down here?"

Stella clucked. "You still got lots of child in you, don't you? 'Course it happen; all the time."

"I'll kill the white man who comes for me," said Ruby.

Stella's face clouded. "Don't go talkin' that way. Get you in lots of trouble."

"I said it, and I'm leaving it said."

Stella watched the younger woman for a long minute, then moved to her mattress on the floor. "You keep that kind of talk to yourself. That my advice to you."

Ruby put up her sewing, dropped another log on the fire, and stretched out on the other floor mattress.

"I still say Obadiah is a man worthy of your thinkin'," Stella put in.

Ruby rolled to her side and stared at Stella. "He's least twice my age."

"That don't matter. Yep, lots of young bucks here will take up with you if you want. But what they got to offer? Obadiah's a free man, one with some dollars, a regular trade. And he's handsome too, big as an ox."

Ruby thought awhile before she spoke again. The fire burned lower. "I know a darky once who married up with a free man of color, and he came to live with her on the plantation. Gave up his good house because she couldn't leave hers. Wonder if it could work the other way around?"

Stella raised up. "What you mean?"

"Can a free man take a darky off the plantation?"

"Not if she don't have her papers, he can't. You know that. You got to have your pass, or they haul you right back to where you come from."

"But if a master gives the go-ahead, the darky could keep papers on her, show anybody that came asking that it's okay, legal and all."

"I reckon that's so, but what difference will it make? What you got on your mind?"

Ruby chewed a finger. Even though she'd given him no signs of favor, Obadiah had come to see her seven Sundays in a row. He brought her something pretty every time—a red ribbon one week, a piece of mint candy another, a small hand mirror on a third. "How much money you think Obadiah got?"

"No way to tell."

"Not enough to buy a woman her freedom papers, I expect."

Stella chuckled. "You fetched a pretty penny, I'm guessin'."

"Eighteen hundred dollars."

"Whoo-eee! That be as high as I ever heard of! You best be glad Mr. Tessier be dead. He'd come to you for sure with you costin' him that kind of money."

Ruby pulled her blanket tighter. "Men sure got the power in this old world."

"Nothin' much to be done about it, I don't spose. Seems like the Lord set it up that way."

"Think it's the Lord?" asked Ruby. "Or just the menfolk?"

Ruby chuckled. "You got some strange thinkin' goin' on in your head. Ain't you listened to the Bible?"

"Oh, I listened. Went to church right on the plantation back in Virginia. Preacher came all the winter, right up to the time we start planting."

"Then you know what the Book says. The man be the head of the woman, just like the boss be the head of the darky."

"The Book also says," Ruby insisted, "that Jesus makes no distinction between slave and free. The preacher didn't say that. I read it myself in a Bible in Mrs. Rushton's room."

Stella raised up and checked around, as if afraid somebody might be listening. "Keep that talk quiet," she advised. "Does no good to raise such things as that."

"Does me some good," said Ruby.

"Just stay shut up about it, that's all I got to say."

Seeing that she'd scared Stella, Ruby turned the topic back to Obadiah. "Obadiah never take a wife?"

"None I know of."

"How'd he get his freedom?"

"Same way as most. His pa—a white man—gave him his papers in his will."

"His pa must have been a good man."

"Some white men are."

"Why they keep us down, then? Why not give us all our freedom? They know it's not right to hold one people in slavery to another."

"You be askin' bigger questions than this old head can hold. You know how it is. They got to have us. What gone happen if we're not here? The whole place'll just fall apart. Every farm, every plantation in the South. Then how we gone eat? Who gone put a roof over our heads?"

Ruby sat up. "We do for ourselves," she offered. "White folks could pay us wages; we'd keep up their places. I hear tell of it up north of Virginia. People works for other people, same as now, but they get to choose where they work, where they live, when they come and go."

"Sounds mighty scary," said Stella, frowning. "Lots of things to work out before that can happen."

"People in the North, the 'abolutionists,' are calling for it now."

"Yes, I heard of them."

"Folks say they'll help a darky," Ruby dreamed aloud. "Runaways and everything. Say that if a runner can get to them, they'll fix him up right fast. Get him a job in the North, give him a new name."

"Sounds like a dream to me," said Stella.

"A good dream, though."

"Maybe. If you don't get killed tryin' to make it come true."

Ruby lay back down. "Maybe Obadiah got enough money to make a payment on me. Little bit at a time to Mr. York. After a while he could have paid for me, take me home with him."

Stella laughed. "I ain't heard of nothin' like that."

"Something to ponder," the younger woman replied. "I'd go with him if he could do something like that."

Stella shook her head. "You be conjurin' somethin'. Gone get you in trouble."

Ruby smiled and closed her eyes. "Might be."

"Take your care," warned Stella. "What's conjured in the night can get mighty dangerous in the light of day."

"People got choices they have to take," Ruby said firmly. "Just got to."

Stella finally lay back down. "Just make sure if you take your chance and fail, you don't get a whole lot of people hurt."

Cold fell on the room. Ruby put the covers over her head. "I'll use what I got on Mr. York if I have to. I been thinking about it. What can he do if I run? Whip me? Then I go to the law on him, tell them about the dead man."

Stella jerked upright, crawled to Ruby's mattress, and yanked the cover off Ruby's head. The old woman's eyes showed white in the shadowy room. "Men die all the time," she said. "Mr. York and Mr. Cain did what they could for that man at Mossy Creek Bank. The law ain't gone do nothin' to them."

"But they kept his money. What about that?"

"What money? You didn't tell us about no money."

"I heard Mr. Cain speak of it. Five thousand dollars. The law could take it from him."

"Maybe that be true. But you playin' a dangerous game. White men don't take to a darky gettin' too uppity."

"I wonder what he did with that money—"

"No tellin'."

"I heard Mr. York say he planned to keep it, least for a time until he could figure out what to do."

"Mr. Cain agree to that?"

"He argued some, but Mr. York seemed set on it, so he let it go."

"This be special news," Stella said, her face turned toward the low-burning fire. "But we got to take care what we do with it."

"What do you mean?"

Stella turned back to Ruby and took her hands. "I don't exactly know yet. But a body that knows somethin' about somebody else holds some power on them, that's the truth of it. If Mr. York kept this money, he ain't gone want nobody else to know about it. You already do, and he figures you won't talk. He's right about that. I won't talk neither. A darky with a blabbermouth don't do too well for too long. But still, somewhere down the road, you never know what might happen, how you could use this, how it might bring some favor to you."

Ruby watched the fireplace flicker and thought of Markus and Theo, then of Obadiah. "If I marry a free man of color, I surely get a pass to his place for Sunday, even if they don't let me move in with him. Am I right about that?"

"I expect so. They want you to birth some babies. Probably right eager to give you a pass to marry a free man."

"My babies born free or other?"

"Babies born to a darky belong to the plantation," said Stella. "No matter the parent."

Ruby twisted her hair. A plot formed in her head. She started to say it to Stella but changed her mind. Like Stella said, a darky with a blabber-mouth didn't do too well for too long. Best to keep her quiet for now.

Chapter Twelve

As soon as he could after the spring planting ended, Hampton York packed up enough clothes for about four days, brought out his favorite horse, and hauled into his saddle right after sunup. Then he set out for a spot right out of Beaufort for some gambling. A number of men always gathered there soon after the crop was in to play cards, watch some cock-fighting, race a few horses, and generally wash off some of the chill of winter with a few nights of hard drinking. York had joined this crew every spring for the last ten years, a group of men of high and low station, some arriving in carriages as wide as a small barn, others walking in with a sack-ful of clothes slung over their shoulders. Nobody cared much about station so long as a man carried enough money in his pockets to buy his way into a card game or to pay off a wager if he lost on a race.

His spirits high, York rode steady most of the day, stopping only a few times to eat, rest his horse, and stretch. He arrived in Beaufort late, put up his horse in a stable near the edge of town, and headed to an inn not far away. A chill ran through the air as the sun dropped, but York bought a bottle of scotch at the inn's bar and took it up to the room he rented. He closed the door, then poured himself a glass and slugged it down. After washing up, he slipped into a fresh shirt and pants and a tan frock coat, tucked the pistol he always carried into the coat's inner pocket, and headed back downstairs. After quickly eating at the diner next door, he returned to the inn's bar for another drink. His face warming from the alcohol, he leaned against the bar and surveyed the noisy crowd, noticing a decent poker game going on in the corner.

York grabbed the bottle of Scotch, made his way to the table, and asked if the game could use another hand. The men, four of them in various states of dress and drunkenness, shrugged and said "sure," and York took his spot in the game. With his first hand in play, he settled back with a big breath of relief. There was lots of strain in handling a place like The Oak, and York was glad he had Josh around to handle things when he left. He could count on Josh for that; always had, always would.

Playing confidently, he spent the next few hours at the card table. Coins clinked as men made and collected wagers. Men cursed or shouted as they won or lost. Liquor flowed fast and loose. A woman with red rouge on her cheeks and black hair stacked high on her head sauntered up to York every hour or so and offered to bring him a drink, but he shook her off.

"I never mix women with card playin', dear lady," he said, his words slurred by the liquor. "No way a normal man can give proper attention to both at the same time. See me when I'm finished." The last word slushed out of his mouth, and the woman grinned. York gave her money for a drink for herself, then studied the cards he held.

He lost that hand but won the next, lost the next two, then won three in a row. As the hours passed the stack of money by his elbow gradually grew larger and larger. Some players dropped out of the game, and new gamblers joined them. York recognized a man every now and again. A young gent named Tarleton sat directly across from him now, a fella with a thick nose and hands and shoulders to match. He seemed a pleasant enough man—from Savannah, he said.

Although his mind felt clouded by liquor, York still paid good attention to his cards, busily watching and evaluating the men around him. Young Tarleton did okay with his cards. York found him unusually quiet for a gambler, almost unnaturally so. Every now and again York caught Tarleton staring at him, as if he wanted to peek inside his head. Although it made him feel a little uncomfortable, York passed it off as Tarleton's effort to read his opponent's face for gambling purposes.

As midnight approached, York spat into his liquor glass, nodded to his playing partners, and announced he needed to give it up for the night. "I rode a long ways today," he said to explain. "Not so young as I used to be."

The men laughed, complained some that he was taking too much of their money, but then took a break from the game so he could collect his winnings and leave. A minute later, York left the table, slipped a chew into his cheek, and headed upstairs toward his room. About halfway up the steps, he heard someone behind him and was surprised to find Tarleton in his wake.

"Hang on there," said Tarleton.

York stopped and studied the young man closer. Not more than twenty-five or so. Dressed in black pants, a white shirt without a ruffle, and a dark green coat that tapered at the waist before flaring out and down to the back of his knees. A scarf the color of the coat hung around his neck. *Not a rich man, but not a poor one either*, York decided.

"What's on your mind?" he asked.

Tarleton looked around, then back at York. "Got a question for you."

"Okay." York's eyes clouded a little, and he realized just how tired he truly was.

"I'd rather not talk here," said Tarleton.

York's suspicions rose; he sobered up fast. "Why not?"

Tarleton nodded toward the door. "You'll see. Let's go outside."

York lightly touched the pistol in his pocket. "I won fair and square back there," he said, tilting his head toward the poker table. "Everybody in the room'll say that's so."

"I'm not talkin' about cards," said Tarleton, his eyes on York's hand where he had touched the hidden pistol. "I'm talkin' about Mossy Bank Creek."

York tensed tighter than a bowstring. Now he was the one who glanced around to make sure nobody had heard. When he saw no one, he faced Tarleton again. What did the man know? Was Tarleton the man he'd shot at?

Tarleton waved his hand toward the inn's front door. "Let's take a walk."

"I don't know anythin' about Mossy Bank Creek," York claimed.

"You bluff well," the younger man replied, "but I know otherwise. And unless you want everybody else in this inn to hear what I've got to say, you'll come with me and you'll do it right now."

York grunted but stayed calm. Tarleton hadn't brought the sheriff with him. That meant any claim he presented on the money must have some stain on it. Otherwise, why not get the sheriff before he talked to him? He wondered if Tarleton planned to kill him. But if he did he'd never find the money or ever know if York had it.

He tried to figure how tough Tarleton was. Although not a large man, Tarleton appeared real solid in the chest and shoulders. The two of them might come out pretty even in a fight. He had experience on his side to match Tarleton's youth. Could he depend on his experience to get him through?

Not seeing any option, York finally nodded. "Lead on."

Tarleton quickly led him outside. On the street he turned left and walked toward the stable. York wondered if Tarleton had a friend waiting for him there . . . somebody to ambush him, put a knife to his throat, and demand that he tell where to find the five thousand dollars. Tarleton shoved his hands into his pockets and moved into the stable with York at his heels. Then Tarleton stopped, lit a lantern, and held it up as they continued to the back of the barn. A couple of horses nickered as they passed.

"Quieter in here," said Tarleton, taking a spot by a hay bale. "Warmer than outside too."

York searched the dark past the glow of the lantern but saw no one.

"It's just me and you," said Tarleton, evidently anticipating his suspicion. "No need to get any more fingers in this pie if we don't have to. Know what I mean?"

York grinned but not pleasantly. So . . . Tarleton figured he had the money and didn't want to share it with anybody.

Tarleton hung the lantern on a post by his head and propped his booted foot on the hay bale. "No reason to hide nothin'," he started. "I'm the man you shot at down at Mossy Bank. You winged me in the thigh, but that got better. I been lookin' for you since."

York spat into the hay bale. "Didn't mean nothin' personal by it. Just protectin' myself."

"No grudge held."

"What were you doin' on Mossy Bank that day?" asked York.

"No value in tellin' that," said Tarleton. "It's got nothin' to do with us right now."

"Did you shoot that man who died?"

Tarleton shrugged. "What'd you do with the money?"

"Did you know the man?"

"Not important."

"What about Wallace Swanson? You know him?"

Tarleton shook his head. "None of this matters," he said, his tone firmer. "What does matter is what you did with the money!"

"What money?"

Tarleton's hand moved toward his side, and York tensed. "I had another man with me," York said. "If somebody found money, I guess maybe he's got it."

Tarleton shook his head. "You shot me but not enough to kill me. I doubled back toward the creek; lay down close enough to hear you talkin' with your friend, to watch you two diggin' the grave. I saw you with the box."

"What do you know about the box? What makes you think it contained money?"

A knife suddenly appeared in Tarleton's hand. York wondered how he'd pulled it so fast. "You don't need that. I'm not lookin' for trouble."

"Me neither," said Tarleton. "Just tell me where you hid the money, and I'll take it and go my way."

York tried to steady his hands. Although he'd scrapped with a lot of men, fought in a war, and killed one man face to face in a duel a long time ago, he had no hankering to get into anything deadly. "It ain't here," he finally said, realizing that since Tarleton knew the truth he might as well stop lying about it.

"Is it at The Oak?"

"You're a smart man. Knowin' where I'm from."

"I've done some checking," Tarleton said. "You're fairly easy to describe."

York smiled thinly. "Reckon that's true. So what you plan to do now?"

"I plan on you takin' me to the money."

"You expectin' me to just hand it over, let you go off with it?"

"That's what I expect."

"But you got no more claim to it than I do."

"Yes, don't that beat all."

York eyed the knife. If he took Tarleton to The Oak, who knew what might happen? No way would he just hand over the money. Why should he? Tarleton didn't deserve it; he'd killed the man at Mossy Bank. But why? He didn't know, and Tarleton surely didn't plan on telling him.

York thought of the sheriff but knew he couldn't go there. A sheriff wouldn't know who to believe. York spat again.

Tarleton waved the knife at him. "You might as well tell me. That's the only way you can leave here alive."

"You really plannin' on using that knife if I don't take you to the money?"

"No choice."

York shook his head but knew he had no choice either. Sometimes a man had to deal with matters, no matter how much he wanted to escape from them. He tensed, then spat tobacco juice into Tarleton's eyes.

Tarleton growled and grabbed his eyes. York charged him. Tarleton jabbed the knife at him, but York grabbed his wrist and bent it backward. Tarleton kicked his knee, and York almost fell as the blow caught him hard. He staggered but pulled back up, pressing harder on Tarleton's wrist. The knife fell from Tarleton's hand.

York let Tarleton go and scrambled for the knife, but Tarleton grabbed his shoulders from behind and pulled him back.

York twisted toward Tarleton just in time to catch a fist in the side of the head. His eyes glazed from the blow, and he tumbled backward. As he fell, he spotted the knife by the hay bale and leaned toward it. Tarleton jumped him as his hand closed on the knife. He jerked the knife up and Tarleton fell on it, the blade slipping through his flesh just below his ribs.

His heart pounding, York quickly pulled out the knife, threw it down, and shoved a hand over the wound in Tarleton's chest. Blood covered York's hand within seconds. He grabbed the scarf from Tarleton's throat and pressed it to the wound. Tarleton groaned.

"I'm . . . sorry," York stammered. "Sorry this . . . happened this way."

Tarleton lay on his back, his eyes already glassy in the glare of the lantern. As York stared at the man, he knew instantly that the knife had punctured his heart. Tarleton—no matter who he was—wouldn't make it. A wave of guilt hit York, but he fought it off. He hadn't gone looking for this, hadn't wanted it to happen. Why couldn't Tarleton have just left him alone? Why did he insist on making this so deadly?

"You got any last words?" York whispered. "Anythin' I can do?"

Tarleton stared at the ceiling, already unaware of his surroundings.

"Do you know Wallace Swanson?" whispered York. "Anybody named Ruth?"

Tarleton's eyes widened. "Lyn . . . nette."

York grabbed him by the lapels and lifted him up. "Lynette?" he whispered. "What is she to you?"

Tarleton didn't respond.

York started to ask again but knew Tarleton was too far gone. He thought of praying but didn't know how. At such moments he really needed Josh Cain.

Tarleton closed his eyes and took his last breath.

York watched the man for another few seconds to make sure he'd died. When he was certain, he spat and took a deep breath. What now? Not the sheriff. Too many questions he couldn't answer. Should he leave Tarleton here? No, the clerk at the inn had seen them leave together. What, then?

He spat again and made a quick decision. Moving fast now, he rushed to his horse, threw on his saddle, and readied the horse to ride. After taking off Tarleton's coat and wrapping his head and shoulders in it, he lifted the body and laid him across the horse. Wiping his hands, he looked around and found a shovel in a near corner. He wedged the shovel through a stirrup and grabbed the horse's bridle.

"Come on, boy," he whispered, leading the animal to the front of the stable. "Nice and easy."

At the stable door he eased it open and checked up and down the street. To his relief, he didn't see anybody. He led the horse out and turned right down the first alley he reached. The alley stretched about sixty feet to the end of the building, then opened up into a grove of pine trees. York led the horse deep into the trees, tied him securely, then rushed back to the alley and out onto the main street.

It didn't take him long to reach the hotel. There he nodded at the clerk, walked as normally as possible up to his room, gathered his belongings, and went out the back way. A couple of men passed him as he headed back down the street. He tipped his hat and nodded but didn't speak. Back at his horse, he adjusted Tarleton's body and the shovel, untied the animal, climbed into the saddle, and headed out of town. To his relief, nobody noticed.

He rode for at least an hour, his trail taking him through the woods as close to parallel to the main road as he could manage in the dark, but far enough away not to run into anybody on the road. When he knew he'd left Beaufort far behind, he dismounted, unloaded Tarleton and the shovel, and eased the body off the horse.

He found a nice spot about forty steps away and laid the body down. Within minutes he had dug a hole adequate for a man's body. The sweat pouring off his face, he hauled Tarleton into the hole, his coat still over his face, and stretched him out flat.

York lifted the shovel and threw in the dirt. When finished with the dirt, he picked up handfuls of sticks, pine straw, and leaves and spread them all over the grave. Then he stepped back and wiped his hands. He wished he could wipe the guilt off as easily. He'd messed up, but what could he have done? Tarleton had come at him with a knife. He had killed him in self-defense.

The moon gazed down with a sad face. York took off his hat and stared at Tarleton's grave. He wondered if the young man had any family, anybody at home waiting on him to show up in the morning.

Lifting his eyes to the moon, York offered the only words he could: "I ain't no man of the Lord. Not like my brother, Josh. But I'm sorry I had to kill this fella. It wasn't my plan to do it. I hope you can forgive what happened tonight. If I did any sin in this, I truly regret it."

Not knowing what else to say, he put his hat back on, climbed on his horse, and headed back to The Oak.

Chapter Thirteen

Trenton Tessier returned home in the midafternoon of an early day in May, his roan stallion followed by a two-horse carriage and a mule-led wagon loaded down with his belongings. Camellia watched him from the window of the cookhouse as he rode up hurriedly, dismounted, and handed the reins of his horse to Leather Joe. The sun burned down on Trenton's brown hair, and he seemed lit from heaven, like a returning king from a mighty victory in battle. Nodding to Leather Joe, he turned and headed up the steps to the manse.

"Young master be home," said Stella from behind Camellia. "Things likely to change around here now."

Camellia tried to stay steady. "You think he'll want to stay here and manage the place?"

"I hear that be his notion. 'Course, you know his mind better than me, I expect."

Camellia blushed but kept on making biscuits. "He and I were friends a long time ago."

"More than friends."

Camellia dropped a biscuit in a skillet, then started shaping another. "You think people of such different stripes as us can ever be man and wife?"

Stella laid down the chicken she'd been cleaning and wiped her hands on her apron. Ruby entered through the open door, a bucket of water in each hand.

"It ain't a matter of *can*," said Stella. "Most anythin' *can* happen. It's more *should*. And you *know* what I think about that. Trenton Tessier ain't got the niceness to marry such as you. He's got a hard streak in him. I know you ain't seen it, but it be there just the same."

Camellia's jaw tightened. "I know he gets haughty sometimes. But that's just his upbringing. He don't mean anythin' by it."

Stella gummed her lips. "I just sayin' my mind. You and me tell each other the straight, don't we?"

"I don't feel worthy of him," said Camellia, changing the conversation. "He's so refined and I'm so coarse. 'Course, I didn't worry about that when we were children; didn't notice it."

"Babies see the good in others better than grownups," claimed Ruby, emptying the buckets into a large clay jar by the wash pots. "Don't let so many things get between them."

"Sometimes I wish I could go back to being a child," Camellia sighed. "Don't we all?"

The afternoon passed, and after getting food to the servants and the people in the manse, Camellia hurried home to lay out supper for her pa and brothers. After everyone had eaten, Chester and Johnny moved out to the porch while Camellia cleaned up the table. Dishes in hand, she moved to the wash pot in the kitchen. Her pa followed her, a chew of tobacco in his jaw.

"You see Master Trenton yet?" he asked, a touch of anxiousness in his voice.

"No," she said, her hands deep in dishwater. "I reckon he's getting settled in."

York sat down at the table and took off his hat. "I want to ask you somethin', but I don't know if I should. I know this year has gone hard on you. You've not eaten well, lost weight. I've wanted to talk to you about it but wasn't sure how to start."

Camellia tried to figure how to answer. Her pa hardly ever sought her out like this. So why now? She studied his face. The last few weeks he'd seemed softer somehow, as if something had shifted, at least a little, in his insides.

"You know what it is," she began. "Mr. Tessier's death . . . Anna Cain's sickness . . . it all weighs on me, that's all. I worry about things too much. The burdens push me down, make me grieve."

"You can't fix the past," York offered. "Believe me, I know. Sometimes things happen that you don't want—matters get out of hand and then *slam*, before you look up, it's all past you. But nothin' you did caused the troubles, and there's nothin' you can do to fix them when it's over."

"But you got to try, don't you?"

York rubbed his beard. "Tryin' to change the past don't do much good. All we can do is keep movin' ahead."

Camellia dropped a cup into the water and faced him. He seemed almost sad, as if a burden weighted his heart. "What is it?" she asked, her curiosity high. "I can tell you got something on your mind."

York sighed. "I'm not sure how to say what I got in my head."

"Just say it," she advised. "No reason to hide anything."

"Okay. I'm worried about Master Trenton, what he might do . . . with the plantation, with me, and all of us."

"But you run this place," she said, confused. "He knows that; everybody does."

"He may want his own man."

Camellia brushed her hair from her eyes. "Who's better than you?"

When York dropped his eyes, Camellia noted the fright that had showed up a couple of times in her pa's face in the last few weeks. It looked strange on him; didn't fit somehow. She wondered if his rough ways covered up more of this fright than he liked to let on; wondered if his insides sometimes hurt in ways he could never admit.

"Tessier can bring in a man from most anywhere," he said. "Lots of people can do what I do."

Camellia sat by her pa, put a hand on his, and tried to assure him. "Trenton is my friend. He won't put us off The Oak. I know he won't."

York licked his lips. "You think he might ask you to marry him?"

Camellia pulled back. "You ought not to ask that. No reason to air a question that hasn't been asked."

"But you think he might?"

Outside, through the window, Camellia could see that the last of the day's shadows played on the ground. She didn't know how to answer her pa, didn't know what she'd say even if Trenton did propose marriage. How could she marry a man whose pa she'd killed? How could she do that without speaking out the truth about it?

"He won't put us off The Oak either way. Marry or not. He's not a mean man."

"We don't know that for certain."

Camellia stared at her pa, and an unpleasant notion rose in her head. She tried to put it away, but it stayed steady; she knew she couldn't deny it. Her pa wanted her to marry Trenton so he wouldn't lose his place on The Oak. Yes, perhaps he wanted it for her too, wanted her to marry a rich man so she could live a fine life. But he wanted the marriage for his own selfish reasons even more. Mad at her pa, she hung her head. Any softness she'd seen in him came from this—his fear of losing his job. What a mean, selfish man. He ought to . . .

Camellia dropped her eyes even farther as she realized she had some fault too. Would she want Trenton as a husband if he owned nothing? Would she marry him if he came to her with empty pockets, if he had no education and fine manners?

"You're hoping hard that I'll marry him, ain't you?" she asked.

"What man wouldn't be? I get no blame for that, do I?" He stepped to her and put a hand on her back. "You'll never again want for anything," he said. "The boys neither. What pa wouldn't want that for his offspring? That somebody could give them what he could never provide?"

"You've done just fine by us," said Camellia, hoping to lift his spirits. "Best you could."

"I've done okay. But it ain't much."

"You didn't get the advantages some men got. Look at Master Trenton. Born into everything, all of it handed to him, never had to work. Then a man like you, or Josh Cain for that matter, men as good as any, smart and busy, but you got nothing. Had to start from scratch, lower than scratch. Don't seem right that we live in that kind of world, that the Lord set it up that way."

"You think the Lord should've started us out all equal, is that it? Give us all the same amount of dollars when we come to the world? Somethin' like that?"

She smiled at the thought. "It ain't practical," she admitted. "But maybe that would make it more fair."

"What about the darkies?" asked York, playing out the notion.

138

"They get the same start as a white man?"

Camellia rubbed her forehead. "We're a ways afield from talking about me and Master Trenton."

"Seems so, but it's still a question to ponder, don't you think?"

"I reckon so."

"So you think the Lord played wrong with the darkies too?"

Camellia thought back to the day Marshall Tessier died, the day she noted the flour on her hands and Stella's. Other than skin color, she and Stella were pretty much the same. They ate the same food, bathed in the same river, wore the same clothes, wanted the same things—a good home, somebody to love and be loved by, a little happiness along the way.

"I suppose I do," she answered, voicing aloud what she'd thought for a long time. "The darkies are people too; they ought to have the same as we got."

"You blamin' a lot on the Lord, then."

"Oh, I don't blame it on the Lord so much as I do on menfolk. We're the ones who put others under the yoke, set up the divisions that keep folks apart."

"You got it all figured, don't you?"

She shook her head. "Nope, that's not it. But there's so much sin in this world that it's got to get the blame, not the Lord."

York moved to the window, and Camellia followed him. "We don't do as much talkin' like this as we ought."

He faced her, his eyes serious. "I'm not usually real free with my con-versation. Stay too busy for it."

"I hope we can change that some."

York stuck his hands in his pockets. "What will you do if Trenton asks you?"

She brushed back her hair and sighed. Should she let what had hap-pened between her and Marshall Tessier keep her from marrying Trenton? Like her pa said, the past was gone and she couldn't fix it. Should she let the past tear apart her future?

"I suppose I'll say yes," she replied, her mind suddenly settling on an answer to her questions.

"That'll solve a handful of worries; yours and mine."

Camellia smoothed her skirt.

"You're a beautiful young woman," York said. "So much like . . . " He stopped and looked down.

"Like who . . . like my mama?"

He toed the floor.

"Why don't you ever speak of her?" asked Camellia. "I've asked you over and over, but you won't ever talk about Mama."

"She's gone," said York. "No reason to talk about what's past."

"But you loved her like Trenton loves me."

"I hope he loves you as much as I did your mama."

Camellia folded her arms. "You look sad when you speak of her."

"I don't have her anymore. Never had her for long. I ought to feel sad, don't you reckon?"

Camellia studied him. His shoulders seemed so heavy. It wasn't just grief either, but a shadow that hung over him . . . something her pa knew but didn't want to say. "I have her red dress," she said. "The navy blue cape too, and some earrings and a Bible; least I guess it's all hers."

"What?"

"I found the things a few years ago, cleaning your room, under your gear. All in a box. I figured it was from Mama."

He frowned. "You ought not to go lookin' in a man's belongin's. Not proper."

"Are they Mama's things?" She had to know the answer.

"She married me in that dress."

"Was she beautiful?"

"Leave it be," he said sternly. "Whether she was or wasn't, don't make a difference. Your mama's dead. All that's past. We got now, and that's all. No good can come from lookin' over your shoulder."

"It hurt you when she died," whispered Camellia. "I can see it in your eyes."

"Lots of things hurt me," said York. "But I didn't let it whip me. Didn't then, won't now."

"Why didn't you marry again?" she asked. "You were still young . . . still are, for that matter. Lots of women be proud to marry you."

York kicked the floor. "Your mama was enough for me. Losin' her makes me unwillin' to put myself in a spot to lose another."

Camellia took his hand. So big and strong, yet so frail and weak too. Were all men like this? So easily hurt by a woman? "I hope Trenton loves me as much as you did Mama. If he does, we can get through anything."

"You are a naive girl," he said. "Sometimes even love ain't enough."

"Ours will be. You just wait and see."

Trenton came to her two days later, a couple of hours after midday, as she took a rest under the ancient oak that fronted the manse. He wore tan riding pants and black boots with a long-collared dark green shirt. Everything he wore looked new and fresh and every bit the right clothing for a wealthy plantation gentleman. Camellia stood as he stepped her way, brushed off the back of her plain brown skirt, examined her worn yellow blouse, and wished she had better clothes. At least she wore shoes today; he hadn't caught her barefooted.

She studied his face as he reached her. He seemed older than she remembered, as if he'd aged at least one year for every month since his father's death. His eyes wore the look of a man with a lot of shadows on his heart.

"Stay seated." He pointed her back to the ground. "I'll join you."

She dropped back to the soft earth, and he took a spot beside her. The sun drifted through the tree branches.

"Sorry I haven't seen you sooner," he said. "But I needed to handle a few things with Mother first. She's here for only a few days, then back to Charleston before the fever season starts."

"You don't owe me any explanations. Just wish you'd let me know when you plan to come see me. I'd like to have fixed up some for you."

He covered her hands with his. "No need for that. You look just fine all the time."

She smiled.

Trenton stared into the tree. "Remember when we were children? We used to climb this tree."

She glanced up. "It's been here a long time. Will be here a long time still, I expect. We thought it was the tallest tree in the world back then.

Thought we were doing what nobody else could do."

"Things were simple then, weren't they?"

Camellia sensed a bitterness in his words, as though he'd come to some discovery he'd never known before. "Life gets harder, that's for sure. Nobody can deny that."

He picked up a rock at his side and threw it sideways into the woods a few feet away. "The Oak had a hard year. Rice yield down, the land playing out some, not giving what it once did."

"I hear Pa talk. Know times are tougher than usual. He seems to have a handle on it, though."

"Your pa and I aren't always in agreement," said Trenton.

"Working men sometimes have troubles between them."

"He forgets his place sometimes."

Camellia's face bleached whiter. "His place?"

"Don't take offense," Trenton added quickly, obviously realizing what he'd said. "You know what I mean. He thinks he knows more about The Oak than I do, that's all."

"You saying he don't? He's run it for years while you've been off at school. He's not so educated as you, but he knows how to run a plantation. You got to admit that."

Trenton threw another rock. "I suppose that's true. But The Oak still belongs to me, right?"

"Nobody questions that. But my pa is a quality overseer. You need to know that if you don't already. The fact he don't own anything don't mean he don't know what he's doing."

Trenton touched Camellia's chin. "I've been all over the country— Charleston, New York, Philadelphia, even out to California once. But you're the prettiest girl I ever saw."

"You're lying, I'm sure," Camellia said, smiling lightly. "But I like it."

He smiled briefly back. Then his face darkened, and he took away his hand. "I want to make you happy."

"You will," she said, her breath short as she waited on him to say what he'd come to say. "We'll make each other happy."

Trenton turned away. She put a hand on his back, felt him trembling. Fear rose in her throat. She knew something terrible had happened. She thought of Stella and wondered if she'd told Trenton the truth about his father's death; if he knew now and wouldn't marry her because of it. "What's wrong?" she asked, not wanting to hear but knowing she must.

He faced her again, pain in his eyes. "I can't do it," he said softly.

"Can't do what?"

He shook his head.

"Tell me," she said. "What is it you can't do?"

"I can't . . . can't please them."

"Can't please who?" She feared she knew the answer before she asked.

"Mother, Miranda, Martha, and Calvin. They say I can't marry you, and tell me The Oak needs help . . . the kind of help only some rich girl can bring."

"But you said you wouldn't let anyone interfere with us!" argued Camellia, her anger rising at his words. "You said my birth—my low place in the world—don't matter to you."

"It *doesn't* matter to me!" he offered. "But it matters to Mother, to The Oak, to everything my father owned, all he stood for."

"You said yourself he was a scoundrel."

Trenton wiped his eyes. "He was, but I'm the elder son. I get the place when Mother passes, at least the responsibility for it. How's it going to look if I can't keep what my father left me? If I let the bankers take it because I can't pay off a loan or two?"

Made bolder by fear, Camellia put her hands on his hips. "Look at me!" Trenton obeyed.

"What difference should it make what others think?" she asked. "What it looks like? Sell the place, sell it today, take the money and live wherever you want. Buy a smaller plantation, a place not so grand. It don't matter to me so long as we're together."

He put his hands on her shoulders. "You're such a romantic. Too bad the world doesn't run that way."

"Why not?"

"I don't know why not. If I did, I'd fix it."

"So what are you saying?"

"I'm saying I'm trapped in my world as much as you're trapped in yours, and I don't know what to do next. I'm confused, that's what I'm saying—confused and angry and . . . afraid."

Camellia dropped her head on his chest. For the first time, it all started to sink in. She and Trenton wouldn't marry. With his mother's aid, he'd find someone else, someone who could bring a large dowry to the marriage, some status and connection. In spite of all she and Trenton had said to each other about their station not making any difference, everything had now come together to show them it did. She wiped her eyes and took a deep breath. *Maybe this was best,* she thought, trying to make herself feel better. Maybe the Lord wanted it this way. After all, she'd killed Trenton's father. How could she marry him?

Her heart breaking, she stepped back from Trenton. He studied his boots, his shoulders slumped. She touched his chin and tried to lift his face, but he pulled away. She sensed some words yet unsaid and then realized . . . "You've already found somebody else," she whispered suddenly. "Somebody more suitable."

He didn't respond, so she knew she'd hit the truth. "A rich girl in Charleston, is that it?"

"Mother," he explained it, his head still down, "knew this family from Columbia. I'd met the girl a couple of times, years ago. I'd never paid her any attention. But she's grown up now."

"So this time you did pay attention."

"I had no choice. Can I let The Oak fail, let down all the people who depend on me? Can I ignore all of them, do what I want, and forget what's best for everybody else?"

"Is it best for you if you marry somebody your mama forces on you?"

"I don't know." He sighed. "I don't know what's best for me—or for you, either. I mean, who knows if you'd be happy in a place like Charleston, dealing with all that comes with the city. You don't like society's ways, don't want to deal with it, aren't ready for it."

Camellia lowered her eyes and thought of the hours she'd spent with Ruby over the last few months, the way she'd started to read, the world opening up to her as a result. Had all that been for naught, nothing more than the fanciful dream of a poor girl wanting to become a princess? She nodded; yes, surely, that's what it had been. How prideful of her to think she could become good enough for Trenton.

"You're right," she finally admitted. "I'm not ready. I could be some-day, but I'm not now."

Trenton smiled and touched her hair. "I know you could. But is that really you? All the worrying about this and that; little things that don't matter to anybody."

"You're telling me I don't fit in your world?"

"I'm not sure I do either," he said wryly. "But I have to try. You don't. Marrying me might be the worst thing for you . . . the worst thing possible."

"I should never have let you go back to Charleston after your father passed away." A small sob escaped her throat.

"And I should never have gone. I wish I hadn't, but since I did I don't know what to do now, don't know . . ."

"This is it, then."

"I don't know!" he moaned. "But no matter what, I'll always love you. Even if I marry somebody else, I'll still love you. We could . . . well, you know . . . men do it all the time. Marry one woman but love another. We could—"

"I'm not a trollop!" she exclaimed, shocked that he would even sug-gest such a thing. "I won't share you with somebody else! How dare you think that of me!"

"I'm sorry," he said, shoulders slumped in obvious shame. "But it's such a terrible situation. Mother pressing me on one side, you on the other."

"I'm not pressing you," said Camellia, hurt at the notion she was forc-ing him to do something he didn't want. "You make your choice, do what you think best for the most people."

He stared deeply into her eyes. "I love you. That I know."

"Don't say that," she said. "Unless you plan to marry me. If you loved me enough, you'd tell your mother where she could go, and you'd do what you always said you wanted to do."

"She'll disown me if I do," he added bluntly.

"What?"

Trenton picked up a rock and threw it toward the woods. "Mother said she'd cast me away," he admitted. "I can't let her do that."

"So you're letting me go to keep your place."

"It's not like that and you know it," he argued. "It's far more complicated."

"Sounds simple to me." She leaned on the oak tree.

"You want me to give away everything?" he asked.

"Isn't that what you're doing?"

He threw another rock. "This is the biggest choice I've ever had to make," he said. "Mother says I have to decide now. The girl in Columbia has other suitors eager to take her hand in marriage."

"So she has you caged in."

"Looks that way." He spat out the words.

Camellia saw anger in his eyes. There was one thing she knew for sure about Trenton: He didn't like it when he felt trapped, forced to do what he didn't want. Although that trait scared her sometimes, maybe it was good this time, a shove for him to push away his mama's control.

Trenton waved his hand over the landscape. "I'll be giving all this up. Marrying you will change my life, your life, all our lives. If Mother disowns me, I'll come to you without a dollar to my name."

Camellia's heart soared. He sounded unsure again, as if he hadn't made a decision. "That makes no difference!" she encouraged him. "We can do without money, can show them how wrong they are."

"Mother might be trying to bluff me," said Trenton. "Might not disown me at all when it comes down to it."

"I don't care either way," Camellia insisted. "Just so we're together. But you ought to know this. If you bow to your mother here, she'll control you as long as she's alive."

"I can't let her do that," he said firmly. "Nobody can press me into doing something I don't want. Got that much of my father in me, I guess."

Camellia decided she'd said enough. Time to let him decide his own heart.

Trenton turned back to her. She saw a steely glare in his eyes, a fire that showed up every now and again. He put his hands on her shoulders, his face fierce. "You're right. If I marry Mother's choice, I'll never be a free man." Camellia held her breath as Trenton continued. "You and I will marry in May, next spring. That'll give me time to settle in here at The Oak, get to know the place, see what I can do to make it prosperous again."

Camellia tensed under his hands. A fear suddenly hit her. She knew how headstrong Trenton could be. What if he'd decided to marry her only to show his mother that she couldn't control him? Young men often acted out of pride and rebellion against a parent. Was this what he was doing now? Was that what she'd always been to him—a way to show his mother and father that he had a mind of his own? That he could and would stand up to them?

Trenton spoke again, his tone hurried now that he'd made a decision. "Mother will just have to live with it," he said. "Whether she likes it or not. She can't disown me; who'll run this place if she does? Calvin's not ready, and she certainly won't do it. She needs me, and she'll realize that soon enough."

When he threw his arms around Camellia, she relaxed and tried to let go of her fears. So what if he wanted to stand up to his mother? What real man wouldn't? He loved her . . . even if he hadn't remembered to *ask* her if she'd marry him. But so what? As long as he married her, what difference did it make that he hadn't proposed in a traditional way? So what if he hadn't asked her pa for her hand in matrimony? So what if he hadn't fallen to a knee, kissed her hand, and placed a ring on her finger as a token of his love? So what if he'd just assumed she'd marry him once he made his decision? He'd made the hardest choice a man in his situation could make, and she felt blessed that he'd made it in her favor. No reason to quarrel with him over the small details, no reason at all. Yet, as much as she tried to feel otherwise, her heart still fell a little, and Stella's hard words about Trenton rattled about in her head as he held her.

Chapter Fourteen

Later that day, as the sun began to drop, Hampton York closed a ledger book and leaned backward in the brown leather chair once occupied by Mr. Marshall Tessier. As he sat behind a walnut desk with brass drawer pulls, dust particles danced in the air. York rubbed his eyes and sighed contentedly. The guilt he'd felt over killing Tarelton had largely passed, and he felt like his old self again. Unless he missed his guess, young Trenton would soon ask his daughter for her hand, and all his worries would end. He rolled that notion around in his head, realizing that after they married he could come to this library anytime he liked.

He stared around the fancy furnishings. Although he did most of his work either out in the fields or in a small building not far from the largest of the barns, he came in here near the end of every week to write down a few crude notes about happenings on The Oak. Finely cut wood floors lay under his boots, and handsewn rugs of mostly gold colors lay over the wood. Shelves of books—he'd counted close to five hundred volumes—ran all the way to the top of the twelve-foot ceilings on two walls. A panther head hung on the wall behind the desk, a moose head on the opposite side. Yes sir, he deserved a place like this. When Camellia married Master Trenton, they'd probably live in Charleston most of the time, and he might just set up his office here.

Pleased with his dream, York took a key from a ring in his pocket, unlocked the bottom right-hand drawer of the desk, and slid it open. A stack of money lay in the drawer. After listening for a moment to make sure nobody was coming, he pulled two hundred dollars from the money stack, stuffed it into his pocket, and closed and locked the drawer. Standing, he patted the money in his pocket and headed to the door.

It's not really thievery, he thought as he did every time he took out a few extra dollars. *I run the place now; ought to earn more than the eleven hundred dollars a year they pay me. Besides, when Camellia and Master Trenton marry, I'll be part owner. How can a man thieve if part of a property is already just about his?*

His conscience almost quieted, York opened the door and stepped outside. He saw Ruby headed toward him, a wide smile on her face. He started to step past her, but she spoke before he could. "I come lookin' for you. You best go see Camellia."

Noting the lilt in Ruby's voice, York knew something good had happened. Could it be that young Trenton had . . . ? He started to ask but then decided he wanted to hear it from Camellia, whatever it was. "Where is she?"

"She be over to Mr. Cain's place," said Ruby. "Where she go every day about this time."

York nodded. Although it put a heavy burden on her, Camellia went to Josh Cain's almost every day to help Beth prepare supper. Josh had told her not to do it, but Camellia paid him no attention. She even refused to take the money he offered when he saw she planned on continuing.

"I'll go see her," York told Ruby.

"That be a good idea."

A few minutes later York found Camellia in Anna Cain's kitchen, making corn bread, with Beth and Lucy at her side. Josh entered through the back door, carrying a bucket of water in each hand. York nodded to Josh as he set the buckets on the floor.

"What brings you over?" asked Josh.

"I'm here to see Camellia."

"She's here, that's for sure," said Josh, washing his hands in the bucket. "Just about every day. She's a big help, though I fear she does too much for her own good."

"Don't talk about me like I'm not here," said Camellia, smiling. "I'm not a child anymore."

"I reckon you're not," said York proudly. "Young men from Beaufort keep droppin' by all the time. Interestin', though—she pays them no attention."

Camellia blushed as she placed the corn bread in the fireplace.

"How's Anna?" York asked Josh.

"About the same," said Josh. "Maybe a touch weaker. Seems to slide away a little more every day." His shoulders slumped as he spoke.

"The doc over in Beaufort don't know what to do?"

"Nothing to be done, he says."

York shook his head. He didn't understand why a man as good as Josh ended up with such sorrow while such good fortune had just fallen his way. "I'm sorry she's no better," he said sincerely. "I know these months been hard on you."

Josh swiped at his eyes and took Beth's and Lucy's hands. "Mr. York and Miss Camellia got things to talk about," he said to them. "We need to give them some quiet. Let's go check on your mama."

"I want to stay with Camellia," argued Lucy.

"She'll be here when she's finished. You know I can't seem to get rid of her." Josh winked at Camellia, then led the children from the room.

When they'd gone, York faced Camellia. "Am I the last one to hear your big news, whatever it is?"

She fell into his arms, her face joyful. He brushed her hair with his coarse hand. "You ought to just go on and get me out of my suspense."

"Trenton's planning to marry me," she said. "In spite of his mother."

"She's set against it, I'm sure."

"His whole family is. They want him to marry some rich girl from Columbia! Say The Oak depends on it."

York led Camellia to a chair and sat her down. "But you say Trenton's disobeyin' his mama."

"Yes, he says we'll marry next May."

York started to point out that the boy should've come to him first, but he felt so glad that he let it go. Another thought hit him as he sat down. "You say Mrs. Tessier told him The Oak is in some trouble?"

"Yes. Said that bad yields had put The Oak in some debt to a bank in Charleston."

"It's been down, but I don't see it as too bad," said York.

"The Oak's not in danger?" she asked.

"Well, we had a low yield the last couple of years, but things like that happen time to time. Nothin' to get all excited over unless there's somethin' happenin' I don't know about."

Camellia sat up straighter. "Then why is Mrs. Tessier saying otherwise?"

York put in a new chew of tobacco. "Got several possibles. One, The Oak's in trouble, and Mrs. Tessier is keepin' it hidden from me."

"Why would she do that? And how?"

"Don't know either answer, but it's a possibility. Maybe she borrowed some money on it for somethin' other than runnin' the place."

"What else?"

"The most obvious thing: Mrs. Tessier is lyin' to Master Trenton. She wants him to marry somebody else, so she makes up this poverty story to get him to go along."

"That's mean," Camellia said indignantly. "Why won't she welcome me like anybody else?"

York touched Camellia's elbow. "We don't live in that kind of world. People lie, cheat, do bad things. You need to know that for your own good."

"Seems sad to think that about folks."

"But it's true—you got to admit it."

"I need to tell Trenton she's lying to him."

"Even if that's what's happenin', it's not your place to do that."

"But if she's lying, he'd want to know that, don't you think?"

"What if she's not? You can't go tattlin' on his mama. He'll find out soon enough on his own, I expect. Leave it alone. We got more important worries right now."

"Like what?"

His mouth turned up slightly at the corners. "Like where will we get you a weddin' dress pretty enough to suit such a beautiful bride?"

"You're right, Pa." Camellia grinned. "Let Mrs. Tessier think what she wants. Me and Trenton will wed in a year, and there's nothing she can do to ruin that—nothing at all."

"I reckon you won't do this anymore." York waved his hand around the kitchen.

"What do you mean?"

"You know—come here to help out."

"Why not?" Camellia looked surprised.

"Won't have time, for one thing. The missus of The Oak can't be goin' around actin' like a common cook. Besides, you'll probably live somewhere else half the time or more. You know how that is . . . most rich folks get out of the hot, swampy land from May to October, out of danger from all the sicknesses."

"I hadn't figured on that," said Camellia slowly. "I suppose I got a lot of changes coming my way."

"Reckon we both do," York agreed.

When he stood to leave, she stood too. As he hugged her, a warm feeling ran through his heart. Even though Camellia wasn't his real daughter and he'd wanted this marriage for his own selfish reasons, he also wanted Camellia to find happiness. The truth that he hadn't wanted this marriage only for himself made him feel better about the rough things he'd done since last November, like the money he'd kept from Mossy Bank Creek, Tarleton's death in early April, and the slow, day-to-day taking of the funds from The Oak's profits since Mr. Marshall Tessier's death. Sure, Hampton York had his faults, but he wasn't a bad man, least not as he saw it.

He patted Camellia's back. He wanted happiness for her just as he wished it for himself. Of course, now that she had snagged her man—and a rich one at that—he saw no reason why both of his wishes couldn't come true.

Footsteps behind him interrupted his pleasant thoughts as Beth rushed into the kitchen. "I need some water!" she said, her eyes scared. "Mama is . . . Mama is . . . "

Camellia pulled away and ran toward Anna's room, and York followed. As he entered the bedroom, he saw Josh holding Anna and rubbing her arms and back. Anna's eyes were closed, and she lay limp in his arms. Beth ran in, a dipper of water in hand. Josh took the water and tried to pour some down Anna's throat, but it spilled on her chin and gown. When Josh gently opened Anna's eyelids, York saw that her eyes were rolled back. Just by looking at her, York realized that her time to cross from life into death had finally come.

His voice pleading, Josh talked to Anna as he held her. But she didn't respond. The last of the day's sun flooded Anna's sweet face, but the time when she could enjoy its golden glow had passed. Her breath slowed, and then stopped altogether as life ebbed away.

Tears rushed down Josh's face and Beth's and Lucy's too as they stood beside the bed. York wanted to comfort his brother but didn't know how.

To his relief, Camellia put a gentle hand on Josh's back and rubbed his shoulders. "She's gone," Camellia said. "You've done all you could."

Josh shook his head against her words, almost as if he could bring Anna back to life if he denied them, if he refused to accept the truth they spoke.

As Camellia continued to rub Josh's back, her hands as light as a butterfly, York saw the kindness in the young woman he'd raised and suddenly felt guilty again about his misdeeds—all the things he'd rationalized just a few minutes ago. Camellia's purity made him want to live better, worthy of her. But how could he go back and make amends for all his sins? And how did a man really know a bad thing from a good one? Nothing he'd done seemed that evil to him; it was more a taking of an opportunity than a crime. Tarleton had come at him, given him no choice. The money at Mossy Bank had showed up out of the air, and he'd never figured what to do with it. Yes, taking the extra dollars from The Oak bordered on wrongdoing, but he deserved the money, didn't he?

Shaking his head, York focused on the room again. Several minutes passed, the people as still as a grave in the middle of the night. Only the sounds of low crying broke the stillness. Finally Camellia broke the silence.

"You go on now, Josh," Camellia soothed. "Take Lucy and Beth. Let me provide what Miss Anna needs now."

Josh looked up at her, his eyes questioning.

York took Josh's arm. "Come on. Let me get you some coffee."

Josh stared back at his wife. "I can't believe it," he whispered. "Just like that; here one minute, not here the next."

"Mama's in a better place," sobbed Beth. "Mama always said when we die we go to the Lord in heaven."

Josh nodded. Camellia took Beth and Lucy into her arms and hugged them for several seconds, then faced York. "I'll make Miss Anna ready. Call Obadiah. We need a box built."

Josh turned to Anna once more, bent down, and kissed her cheek. "She's not hurting anymore," he said, sobbing. "The headaches are past. Least we can feel grateful for that."

"No man could do more for a woman than you did," Camellia said.

"I loved her," he replied.

He reached for Beth and Anna, picked them up. "I need to find Butler."

"He's in the yard," said Lucy tearfully. "Him and Copper."

York led them out while Camellia stayed in the room, shutting the door as they left.

"Camellia is a fine girl," Josh said gratefully. "Mighty mature for one her age."

"She helped us every day," agreed Beth, her eyes teary. "Don't know that we could've done without her."

"She cares for people," said York. "More than most anybody I know."

Josh nodded. York got his grieving brother a cup of coffee, and the two men sat down. "Go get your brother," Josh said to Beth. "Don't tell him yet. Bring him to me."

She rushed from the room, and York took a sip of coffee and pondered the way that life could bring great happiness in one minute and deep sorrow in another. A few seconds later Beth led Butler inside.

"I was playin'," he said, his young face innocent.

Josh moved to Butler and hugged him. Beth and Lucy held to Josh's legs.

"It's your mama," Josh told Butler. "She's gone to be with the Lord."

"Reckon we won't feel like playin' again for a while," said Beth.

"Your mama would want you to play," Josh said. "So we won't stop that."

The children then started to cry. As York watched them, he felt sad too, because he knew what it felt like to lose somebody you loved. It felt like somebody reached into your chest and pulled out your heart with his bare hands and then held it up and showed it to you.

Uncomfortable watching Josh and his children grieve, York moved to the back door, spat into the yard, straightened his spine, and reminded himself that he'd never again let anything like that happen to him. It might happen to others, even somebody as good as Josh. But it wouldn't happen to him. No sir, it would not.

Chapter Fifteen

Camellia saw a lot of things on The Oak change the summer after Anna Cain died. As he'd promised, Trenton started taking more and more interest in the plantation, splitting time between there and Charleston, talking a lot with her pa about ways to make sure The Oak produced as much rice as possible for sale at the highest price they could find. About the same time that Trenton got involved, his mother loaded up her belongings and headed out. Although she didn't follow through on her pledge to disown Trenton after he told her his plans to marry Camellia, she did let everybody know she didn't approve of his choice and wouldn't stay around to make arrangements for it. Trenton hung his head as her carriage headed out, but he didn't go chasing after her. Camellia and everybody else on The Oak had to give him credit for that.

Ruby married Obadiah in August that year, their marriage a simple matter under a canopy of thick oaks behind the servants' houses. Trenton gave permission for it after Ruby asked Camellia to convince him of its merit.

"Ruby will have babies if she marries," Camellia reminded Trenton. "Good strong hands to help you build up this place."

"Marrying a free man might give her notions," he argued. "Take her mind off her duties. And where will she live?"

"She knows she has to live here—we talked of that. Obadiah will split time from his place to hers. She can go to his house from Saturday night to Sunday."

"She's still with Stella while she's here, though. I have no other house to give her."

"She figures that. She and Obadiah will take one room, Stella the other."

Trenton finally relented, and the parson came to perform the nuptials. Ruby didn't much like having a white preacher marry them, but since Obadiah wanted it and Trenton said no heathen marriage would take place on his property, she gave in. Camellia stood on one side of her and Stella the other. The parson said the words, Obadiah and Ruby repeated them after him, and it was done. They walked away from The Oak as husband and wife.

Trenton gave Ruby three days off to get her marriage started. She spent it with Obadiah—either in his house or sitting on a quiet section of ocean front, not far from Beaufort.

After her three days ended, Ruby returned to The Oak, and she and Obadiah quickly settled into the rhythm of trying to make a life together.

For a little while Camellia was at odds with Ruby over her reading lessons. Camellia offered to give them up so Ruby could spend more time with Obadiah; Ruby suggested that since Camellia would soon become the master's wife, she ought to hire a real teacher to aid her with her letters. But the women said no to each other: Ruby because she said a "pledge made is a promise kept," and Camellia for two reasons—because she wanted to surprise Trenton with her ability to read and because she refused to ask him for money.

"I don't have dollars to pay a teacher," she told Ruby the first time the subject arose.

"Master Trenton would give it to you," Ruby suggested.

"I'm not asking him for money." Camellia frowned. "Maybe *after* we're married, but not until."

"You're a crazy woman," mumbled Ruby. "Get it while you can."

"Just be quiet and give me my lesson," said Camellia. So Ruby did. The two of them met at least three times a week, using some of the simpler books from the Tessiers' library as their guides for reading.

The hottest days of August set in.

Even though Trenton and her pa suggested she ought to stop,

Camellia continued to go by Josh Cain's every afternoon to do what she could to help. Sometimes she cooked, sometimes she cleaned, and sometimes she did some washing. Beth stayed close by her all the while, her big blue eyes so much like her kind mama's that it made Camellia want to cry. Josh stayed quiet most of the time, his eyes red from tears and lack of sleep. Lots of days he didn't come into the house until after dark, and every couple of weeks or so Camellia had to go get him to make him come in at all. She'd never seen a man so broken up, and her heart hurt for him.

One night, near the middle of August, as Camellia and the children ate supper, a storm blew up right about sunset, the heavy wind stirring up dust and bending trees in all directions. Soon after, rain started falling, sheets of water lit up by lightning every few seconds. Butler started crying for his pa, and Beth tried to soothe him, her tiny arms barely able to wrap around her brother's shoulders.

"I know where he is," said Camellia, drying her hands on her apron. "Same place he always is this time of day. He'll come home soon." She stared out the window. Butler wailed again, and Lucy soon joined him, their voices blaring out even louder than the storm.

"You think Pa's okay?" asked Beth, her voice shaky.

"You want me to go get him?" asked Camellia, noting Beth's fear.

Beth nodded.

Camellia grabbed a bonnet from a peg by the back door. "Stay here with Butler and Lucy," Camellia directed the girl. "I'll be right back." Camellia opened the door and ran outside, her feet splashing as she rushed toward a grove of trees about three hundred yards away. She saw Josh Cain before she reached him as a streak of silver cut the sky. He sat on the ground by Anna's grave, his back to Camellia, his clothes soaked.

"Mr. Cain!" she shouted as she ran. "Mr. Cain!" He stayed seated, as still as death.

She reached him and threw an arm around his shoulders. "You got to come in!" she yelled. "You catch your death out here, then what are your children going to do?"

He looked up, but without sign of recognition. She tried to pull him up. Water poured off his hat into his lap. She grabbed him by the shirt, but he still didn't move and she couldn't budge him. The rain pelted them, big drops that hurt as they fell. Camellia squinted back at the house; she could barely see the light from the lamps inside. She started to rush back but wondered what she'd tell the children. They'd wail for their pa and want to know why she hadn't brought him back.

"Come on!" she shouted. "Your kids are fearful for you!"

Josh stayed rigid, almost as if he didn't hear her. She squatted and took his face in her hands. He stared blankly at her. Then, without thinking, she slapped him! Just like that, an open hand to his cheek! He blinked and his eyes widened.

"I reckon losing your Anna hurts real deep!" she shouted. "Worse than just about anything! And I know you got to grieve her! But you got three children who need you! Three children who get scared when you don't come in at night and sit at the table with them, when you don't . . . don't take care of them like a pa should!"

She stopped to take a breath. But since Josh turned his head slightly, as if hearing her for the first time, she kept going. "I know it's not my place!" she yelled over the rain and wind. "But somebody's got to say it! You can't stay here by this grave forever; you got to get up and move on with your living! For your children, if nobody else! That's what your Anna would want! I know that's the truth!"

She stopped again as the rain drove hard across her face. Josh kept staring at the grave, and Camellia knew of nothing more to say. So she simply sat beside him, until the wind died some and the rain let up. Then she patted him on the back.

"It's done," she soothed, her voice softer, quieter now that she didn't have to shout over the storm. "But life's got to go on, you know that. You can't sit here every night for the rest of your days."

Josh Cain moved his glance from the grave to the sky, as if questioning the heavens. The rain had splattered on his cheeks, mixing with his tears. He suddenly looked young to Camellia—too young to have experienced the depth of hurt that Anna's dying had caused.

He's barely ten years older than me, she realized. *But life has already cut him deeply. Did life always do that? Like with her pa losing his wife, now Josh losing his? Did death stalk around all the time, taking a wife here and* a husband there, a child in one minute, a sister or brother in the next? It seemed that way to Camellia; as if nobody could ever count on tomorrow because death might grab them any second. Of course the Good Book said it just that way; that a body could never know when death might strike, that life was just a vapor that appeared for a little while and then vanished. She knew that people did one of two things in the face of such quick dying: They either figured they'd be dead soon, so they better grab everything they could right now, or they looked at life's shortness and eternity's length and decided they best do all they could to get ready for the time after the grave caught them.

Camellia patted Josh's back once more. He'd have to decide how long he'd grieve, she decided. There was nothing else she could do to aid him. She stood as the wind dropped some more, and the rain finally stopped. Smoothing some of her rain-soaked hair away from her face, she turned to go back to the children.

"Camellia?"

She twisted back to Josh. "Yes?"

"You think the Lord punishes us for our sin?"

"Not sure what you mean," she said, puzzled.

"You know, when we do wrong, does the Lord take his blessing from us? Worse still, does the Lord strike his hand against us if we stray?"

"The Book says the Lord disciplines us . . . least the parson said that once."

He sighed. "You think my losing Anna was the Lord's hand against me, trying to teach me a lesson?"

"I can't think of a sin bad enough for the Lord to strike down a wife just to teach a husband something," she offered. "You figure a parent would kill one child to punish a second one?"

"Don't guess I would."

"I can't imagine you did anything bad enough for this kind of heartache," she said gently. "You're a kind man."

He smiled, but only briefly. "You don't know me. I'm like all men, prone to weakness and sin."

"What kind of sin?"

He shook his head. "All kinds. Things I did—back in the war and all. Then things I haven't done, haven't said, haven't told."

"You want to talk about those things?"

He eyed her for several seconds, then put a hand on the muddy ground and pushed up. "You're a blessing to me," he said softly.

"I'm your friend. I care for you, the children."

"You're wise for your years. A woman of Christian virtue."

"You flatter me."

"It's the truth."

Glad to see him acting normal again, she took his elbow, and together they made their way back to the house. The children met them at the door: Beth with a cup of hot coffee in each hand, Butler with a couple of rags to dry them off. A few minutes later, after they'd both changed, Camellia into some of Anna's old clothes, they took seats at the kitchen table and sipped the coffee. Beth and the children sat with them for a few minutes but then, seeing their pa was fine, drifted away. Josh took a sip of his coffee, then set the mug on the table.

"Thank you for your kindness. You've done far more than you should have."

"The children need me," Camellia said, noticing his gentle eyes.

"You don't need to keep coming here every day," he said. "I know it's a burden, and you've got other things on your mind, with the marriage and all coming up."

"It's no burden," she insisted. "I love your children."

"But what about your own family?"

"Chester and Johnny work all day; I hardly see them except at night. They're old enough to get by without me. Your kids need me more."

"Still, you do too much."

"Are you telling me not to come anymore? That you don't want me?"

Josh sipped from his coffee. "No, not that. You're such a friend to Beth. But what you said there"—he nodded toward the grave—"you're right. I've got to move on. You helped me see it. It'll be hard, and I expect I'll have some lapses. But I have to look ahead. I can't let down my duties to my children. Anna wouldn't want that, and neither do I. I don't know how I'm going to do it, but I have to say good-bye to Anna. I have to leave my sadness and start over."

"You'll find your way," offered Camellia. "You have a good heart. You'll provide your children everything they need." She took another sip of her coffee.

Josh looked curiously at her. "I just noticed . . . you sound different lately. I can't rightly get it in my sights, but something . . . your voice, your . . . you seem more . . . mature maybe . . . your words?"

Camellia blushed. "You're the only one to catch it."

"What is it?" He sat on the edge of his chair.

"I'm learning to read," she said, feeling a thrill unlike any she'd ever experienced. "Trying to talk correctly, like the books do. Not sound so much like an ignorant girl. I don't always get it right, but I'm striving. Ruby is teaching me my letters."

"Ruby?"

Camellia clamped her mouth shut, hoping she hadn't gotten Ruby in trouble.

Josh quickly ended her fears. "Don't fret. I know some folks teach their servants to read. Ruby learned before she got here; what am I going to do about it now?"

Camellia relaxed. "I've learned with her close to six months. Ruby says I'm doing well. Faster than she learned, and she's real smart. I spend as much time as I can with it. "

"I'm proud for you," Josh said, leaning back. "Wanting to improve yourself, and not acting too good to let a servant teach you."

Camellia shrugged. "A servant can know as much as me. I grew up with the coloreds; don't see a lot of difference between me and them but the shade of my skin."

"Better keep such talk to yourself," Josh cautioned. "Not many around these parts agree with that view."

Camellia stared into her coffee. Beth ran in and got some water, then hurried out again. Camellia figured she should just drop the subject, but Josh surprised her by keeping it going.

"I wonder about it sometimes," he admitted in a whisper. "Especially when I read the Bible. You know, like Luke 4 and all. Where Jesus said he came to preach the gospel to the poor, deliverance to the captives, to set at liberty them that are oppressed. Seems to me those kinds of words give us all reason to pause, ponder some about what we're doing owning other folks."

Camellia glanced around, as if expecting somebody to jump on them for some bad crime. "I've heard preachers use the Bible to prove the case for slavery."

Josh nodded. "I've heard it too. But somehow it still seems wrong to me."

Camellia's hands loosened on her cup. "Funny," she said, changing the subject. "I've knowed you—uh, known you—for years but never knew you as a man of Scripture."

Josh sipped coffee. "We've not talked much until these last few months. No reason before then for us to truly know each other."

She nodded. Although they lived and worked on the same plantation, their lives had not touched much, except on the surface.

"I'm a believer," Josh said plainly. "Spend time with the Bible most every day, and some extra time with it on the beach most every Sunday afternoon. You like the parson at the Episcopal church?"

Camellia shrugged. "He's maybe a mite too fancy for me, but otherwise, I guess he's okay. Don't like to say much bad about a man of the cloth."

"You go to services some, don't you?"

"When I can. But we're over a day's ride away. Hard to get there."

"I hear some about the Baptists in Beaufort. Little more fire in their belly than the Episcopals."

"You ever go to church?" asked Camellia.

Josh dropped his eyes, as if suddenly ashamed. "Not as much as I ought," he admitted. "Don't feel worthy of it."

"Why not?"

"It's a long story, not for telling now. I've thought about going to the Baptist church sometime. Maybe I'll go soon."

"Pa says the Baptists do too much shouting for him." Camellia grinned. "And their preacher goes on too long—an hour or more."

"A little bit of religion seems to do York just fine," agreed Josh.

Camellia laughed, and peace flowed over her. For the first time since she'd known him, Josh Cain felt more like a friend than an uncle.

Without thinking, she spoke what had bothered her for a long time. "I don't see Trenton as too religious either. That scares me when I think on it too long."

"I'm certain it would."

"You think he'll change when we marry?"

When Josh focused on the floor and was silent, Camellia knew he had his doubts.

"I know the Bible says we ought not to unequally yoke ourselves. But Trenton was baptized in the church, so I know he's of the faith."

Josh faced her, concern in his eyes. "I don't know if that's enough. Seems to me that the Bible says we have to believe in Jesus when we get old enough to understand. I don't see anywhere that baptism as a baby does anything for our souls; how can it? We're not old enough to know about Jesus. The Book says we have to personally trust Jesus as our Lord."

Camellia had heard that too but didn't exactly know what it meant. She had been baptized as a baby but came to know the Lord better as she grew up. Was her faith not real if she'd never been splashed all the way under the water as a grown-up woman? But that didn't make sense. The water didn't save anybody; she knew enough to realize that. A person had to trust the Lord, and she'd done that . . . even though she couldn't put her finger on an actual day and time that it had happened.

"I guess I'll have to pray harder for Trenton," she said, more concerned for him than herself. "I know the Lord can change him, even if I can't."

"The Lord can change anybody; least the Book says it that way."

"I'm trying to read the Bible some now, but it's hard. I found an old one at the house. Ruby won't teach me from it, though. She's not of a religious nature."

"The Bible will help you, I'm sure."

"I still have so much to learn. Maybe you can teach me some." Suddenly, she was eager to learn from somebody as smart as Josh.

Confusion wrinkled his brow.

"To read," she emphasized. "You read so well."

"I'd be proud to do what I can. Although it won't take much for you to catch up with me."

As Camellia gazed into Josh's kindly eyes, a strange feeling ran through her . . . a feeling she'd never experienced with Trenton. She felt confused by it. What was this skipping of the heart? This heat in her face and shoulders?

"What kind of books you like so far?" Josh asked, interrupting her thoughts.

"All of them," she said, glad for the chance to think about something else.

"I like Dickens."

She smiled. She knew so little of this man whose children she'd come to love. "Will you teach me to read his books?"

"It's a small way to repay you for all you've done. Yes, I'll do it gladly."

Camellia brushed back her hair and relaxed. Josh Cain knew so much. And he trusted the Lord as she did.

"It's good to have somebody to talk to," he said wistfully. "I miss that."

"You listened to me," she replied. "When Stella brought me to you last winter."

He stared at her. "You doing better about all that?"

"I still get fearful sometimes. Worry that the law will find out and come for me. Have dreams about it from time to time. Feel guilty about marrying Trenton without telling him. Other than that, I never think of it." She chuckled.

"Bad things happen. Not much we can do about it. All of us have a few things we'd like to do differently if we got the chance, things we'd like to tell if we could. Can't always do it, though. Some things we have to keep buried, no matter how much we want to dig them up."

She eyed him closely. "You got things buried?"

He shrugged. "Might surprise you."

"You sound mysterious."

"Not so much, but I've neglected a thing or two I need to take care of."

"Your Anna has been sick."

"True, but that's not much of an excuse. I expect it's time to make some amends about a few things."

"You want to tell me about it?"

He paused, then shook his head. "Not tonight."

Camellia saw from his eyes that he'd say no more, so she let it drop. As the fire crackled, she simply sat by Josh Cain and drank coffee, appreciating the fact that for the first time she could remember, she had a fellow believer other than Stella as a friend. It surprised her that it had come this way, in a man she'd known a long time but not closely, a man who liked to read and thought a whole lot like she did. But that didn't take away any of the comfort it brought. As the rain started to fall again, she relaxed and talked and even forgot for a while that she would marry Trenton Tessier in the spring.

Chapter Sixteen

The next few weeks saw a visible difference in Josh Cain's stride. Although he still didn't laugh as much as in the past, the worst of his hurt over Anna's death seemed to slip off his shoulders. He talked a little easier with his children again, spent less time at Anna's graveside, set his hat on his head every morning with a hard shove, and turned his eyes toward the labor set out before him. Of course he had a lot of work to do, what with harvest days having arrived. That kept him so busy he didn't have too much time to grieve anyway.

By the time the next to last week of September rolled around and they'd been gathering the rice for several weeks, he seemed almost normal again, his steady direction to the field hands taking some of the harshness out of the frantic pace that Master Trenton and Hampton York set for them.

On Monday of that week he left his house early, eager to get started. At least three more weeks of harvest lay ahead. Mature rice stalks swayed in the breeze as far as he could see. He met York and they headed to the fields. The morning passed quickly. Josh and York stopped for only a few minutes for a bite to eat at midday. The afternoon pushed ahead. About halfway through it, Josh paused, took a breath, and looked up at the sky. Sweat soaked his shirt. On days like this, his body felt baked by the end of the day, as if somebody had laid it on the beach beside a bonfire to dry in the sun. He pulled a handkerchief out and wiped his brow. Clouds had begun to bank from the southeast, and he was glad. A little afternoon rain, if not too heavy, would cool the air some but not hurt the rice. He felt good about the progress of the work. They should get a good full crop this year, and from what he'd heard, prices were good.

He put his handkerchief away and thought of his plans after the harvest ended. He'd go first to the law in Beaufort, then over to Charleston. Although close to a year had passed since Mossy Bank, he'd do all he could to make up for his tardy ways. The wind shifted, and he checked the sky again. All of a sudden he noticed that the air felt cooler. He wrinkled his brow and glanced around the field. Everything seemed normal, but still he felt strange, suddenly tense. The breeze worried him. It felt too steady for this time of day all of a sudden, as if a huge silent hand was pushing it from behind, shoving it onto shore.

Josh shielded his eyes and squinted in the direction of the ocean. The clouds moved faster overhead and became darker too, like black cloth banking up from the south and spreading north. He checked the fields again, drained of all water for the last ten days. Close to three hundred darkies slaved away, their rice hooks busy hacking down the sheaves of rice. Another crew of workers walked behind them, laying the cut stalks in neat rows where they'd stay for a couple of days to dry. Later a third group would pick up the dried sheaves and tie them together, making ricks about seven feet wide and twenty feet long that they'd stack in the barn in piles as high as a man could stack them.

Josh adjusted his wide-brimmed hat. The field hands had labored since sunup and wouldn't stop until well past dark. Nobody got off in harvesttime—not even a pregnant woman, as much as Josh hated that. If a darky could move, he or she took their place in the fields. When the sun went down, they lit torches in the yard and barn so they could keep laboring.

When a couple of the older hands glanced up at the sky, Josh knew they felt it too. Although still baking hot, the temperature had dropped four or five degrees since mealtime, and the air seemed heavy, as if someone had squeezed it into a space smaller than it should fit. His pulse rising, Josh turned around and headed for the river. Several of the workers nodded at him as he passed, but he paid them no attention. His chin set, he reached the river in less than five minutes and stepped down to the bank. Mud sucked at his boots as he neared the edge of the stream. Bending, he studied the water flow, expecting to see it running north to south toward the ocean. He picked up a stick about the width of his finger and tossed it into the water. The stick drifted away in the slow current, slower than usual it seemed, but still moving south. Josh stood and walked with the stick as it eased toward a bend in the riverbed.

Keeping his eyes on the stick, Josh walked close to five hundred yards, to the place where the river turned and widened. The stick made the curve, and Josh followed it. Just past the bend the stick slowed, slowed, and then stopped. Josh squatted to the water and saw that the current had just about stopped.

Scared now, he stood and rushed back toward the manse to find York. He located him near a barn, directing a group of workers who were stacking cut rice.

"I need a horse!" Josh yelled to Leather Joe as he rushed to York. "Bring two!"

York looked up, and Josh pointed at the sky. "Come with me. I think we got trouble on the way."

York opened his mouth as if to argue, but Josh stepped close and stopped him before he could. "It's been building all afternoon. There's a blower headed our way."

"Ease yourself," said York. "We get somethin' every five or six years around here. Just had a big one a few years ago, in '54. Not time for another to hit us just yet. Even if it does, it won't be much this time—a hard wind for a few hours, some rain maybe. But the worst storms mostly ride on past us."

"You're probably right," Josh replied. "But you can't predict these things, you know that."

Leather Joe walked up with two horses.

York raised his eyebrows. "You goin' down to the beach?"

"Yes. Thought you might want to come too."

"I got plenty to do here," York argued.

"I know. But I want you to check with me."

York sighed and shook his head but mounted his horse. Josh climbed on his, and they galloped toward the beach, their horses' manes straight as the wind blew through them.

"The wind's coming from the southeast!" called Josh over the horses' thumping hooves. "Running in from the ocean at us!"

"It's not that bad!" York hollered back.

"I went to the river! Current is almost stopped."

For the first time, York's face clouded. "You thinkin' the river will back up?"

"I hope not! But that's my fear!"

They reached the trail to the beach within minutes. Josh led his horse through the trail and out on the sand. They darted onto the beach, the horses huffing, their hooves kicking up sand. Josh immediately saw the tide had pushed up much farther than usual for that time of day. Clouds loomed as far as he could see, the darkest of them to his right, from the south. The wind blew heavier here, and he had to hold his hat to keep it on. Sand whistled in the air and cut his face. The ocean looked gray, and the waves dashed to the shore with swells at least four feet high and white-caps that rushed toward them like soapy foam.

"Temperature is droppin'!" yelled York.

"I think we got one blowing toward us!" yelled Josh.

York cursed his agreement, spun his horse around, and rushed back toward The Oak. "We got to build up the dikes!" he called. "Get in as much rice as we can. Hope the tide surge don't push the river up too far, that the wind don't get too heavy!"

Josh spurred his horse up the trail. Although every planter on the coast knew that a hurricane could destroy a rice crop in any year, they all lived in hopes no bad one ever landed. Outside of an outbreak of malaria or typhus, folks in the lowlands feared a hurricane more than anything.

They reached The Oak and thundered to the barn, where Josh jumped off his horse. The wind here, although brisker than normal, wasn't as strong as at the beach.

"I got to warn Master Trenton," said York. "He'll need to get things in place at the manse."

Josh waved him off and started giving orders to the servants. Within minutes the place pounded with movement, people rushing in all directions, yelling and hollering. Josh barked directions, sending this servant that way and another off for something else. The wind gradually picked up, and every now and again dirt flew.

York rushed back up and jumped off his horse, his hand over his eyes to protect them from the gritty air. "You seen Camellia?!" he yelled to Josh.

"No. She not at the manse?"

"Not that I saw."

"I need to check on my kids," Josh yelled back.

"Go on. Get them safe, then get back here as fast as you can!"

Josh ran off, trying to figure how much damage might happen if a rough storm landed. He knew about the one in '54. It had beached ships in Charleston, knocked down houses, and killed hundreds of people. The tide surge had pushed salt water close to three miles up the freshwater rivers and flooded a lot of rice fields with the killing ocean water.

He reached his house and rushed toward the door. Beth, with Lucy and Butler right behind her, met him on the porch as he ran up. To his surprise, Camellia joined them, her hair blowing in the wind as it got a little stronger.

"I figured I better check on them," she said loudly. "Knew you'd have plenty on your hands to do."

He hugged his children. "Thank you."

"I got planks for the windows," Camellia added. "About to board them up."

"I'll help."

"No. You go on back. We're okay here. Pa needs you."

"You sure?"

"Yes."

"Won't Master Trenton miss you?"

"I haven't seen him. These kids need me more than he does anyway."

Josh pushed his hat down as the wind tugged at it. "Okay," he finally agreed. "But I'll get back here as soon as I can."

"I'll stay with them. Don't fret."

Josh hugged his kids once more, then stepped to Camellia and opened his arms. She moved to him and he wrapped his arms around her shoulders. A funny feeling ran through him as he felt her warmth, and his breath caught in his throat. Without warning, the way he viewed her shifted slightly, and the feeling scared him. Embarrassed, he hurriedly stepped away.

"You're a blessing!" he called over the wind, trying to cover his mistake. "A true friend."

Camellia waved him off, and he pivoted and ran out without saying anything else. Rushing back to the manse, he fussed at himself for being such a fool. Not only was Camellia promised to Master Trenton, but she was far too young for him. Besides, his dear Anna had passed only months ago; it was much too soon for him to get feelings for anybody else. Even worse, he knew Camellia had no care for him, at least not in that way. For all she knew, he was her uncle. How could she feel anything but a sisterly affection for him?

He reached the largest of The Oak's barns and almost felt glad for the approaching storm . . . anything to take his mind off his confusion about Camellia. "Get those animals into the barn!" he yelled to Leather Joe, pointing to a field where a group of cows were huddled against a fence.

All around him, chaos ruled. As the day progressed, the storm edged closer, the wind notching up in force. Josh, York, and everyone else rushed about, trying to do what they could to prepare for what lay ahead.

Dark fell at least an hour sooner that night, the early black caused by the clouds that now covered the sky as far as anybody could see. With Josh's children never going more than three or four feet away from her, Camellia did all she could to prepare for the storm. She put boards over the open windows, hauled in buckets of fresh water, piled all the candles in the house in one spot so they would stay dry, and hauled in food from the cookhouse.

Finished with that, she and the children dragged the kitchen table, the heaviest piece of furniture into the house, into the front room by the fireplace.

"Get your blankets," she told the children. "Put them under the table."

"We gone sleep there?" asked Butler.

"Yes," said Beth. "If the roof blows away or a big tree crashes on it, the table will provide some shelter."

"The chimney too," Camellia added. "That's why we put the table close to the fireplace."

Lucy and Butler, their eyes big, got their blankets without another word and slid under the table.

The wind howled as the night deepened. The house quivered every now and again, as if some giant had it in the palm of his hands and was shaking it. Something rattled against the ceiling from time to time as well, so Camellia knew that tree limbs and pieces of wood had torn loose from all kinds of places. After a few hours of pounding rain, water started leaking through the roof in numerous places. Before too long they had run out of buckets to catch the dripping wet.

"How bad will the wind blow?" asked Beth, her eyes wide in the glow of the candlelight as she sat by Camellia under the table.

"Don't know," said Camellia. "But not hard enough to blow down the chimney. If it gets too bad, we'll put out the fire and climb right up into it."

Butler balled his little hands into fists and lightly punched the legs of the table. "It feels stout."

Camellia drew him into her arms. "It is. That's why we'll stay here all night if the wind stays up."

"You bring a book?" asked Beth.

Camellia smiled. Lately, she'd started bringing books when she came to Mr. Cain's house. She practiced her reading on the kids. They seemed to like it and fussed at her when she didn't remember to bring one. "I brought a Bible."

"You bring that a lot," said Butler.

Camellia smiled again. Half the back cover of the Bible was missing, and the pages curled up some on the edges as if somebody had squashed it somewhere along the way. She felt good about being able to read from it, even slowly.

"I like the Bible, don't you?" she asked.

Butler nodded, and Camellia brushed back his curly blond hair. He looked a lot like his pa. A *handsome boy*, she thought. *Also like his pa*.

"Read somethin'," said Beth, jarring her thoughts away from Josh. "From the Bible."

Camellia crawled to the edge of the table so the fire could help her see and placed the Bible in her lap. "Here's a good one for tonight." She opened the pages to Matthew 7. "See if you like this as much as I do." She read slowly, hesitating over many of the words. "Whosoever heareth these . . . these sayings of mine, and doeth them, I will . . . liken him unto a wise man, which built his house upon a rock. And the rain . . . de . . . descended, and the floods came, and the winds blew, and beat upon that house; and it fell not; for it was founded upon a rock."

She paused, licked her lips, then continued, this time with more confidence, her voice louder to be heard over the wind. "And every one that heareth these sayings of mine, and doeth them not, shall be likened unto a foolish man, which built his house upon the sand: and the rain descended, and the floods came, and the winds blew, and beat upon that house; and it fell: and great was the fall of it."

She closed the book and looked at Butler, whose eyes had widened with every word. "Your pa's a man of the Lord," she soothed. "He's built his house on the Rock of Ages."

"So our house ain't gone fall?" asked Beth.

"No," Camellia promised.

"You read good," said Butler.

"She studies hard," Beth told him.

"Will you teach me?" asked Butler.

Camellia patted his head. "I'll teach you all I know."

Footsteps sounded on the front porch. Everybody watched as the door swung open and slammed against the wall. Josh staggered as the wind pushed him into the house. The rain fell in buckets past the door, and thunder rolled. Rain streamed down Josh's face. Camellia crawled from under the table and ran to the kitchen. A second later she returned, her hands full of dry rags. Josh had managed to shut the door and now stood by the fireplace, his clothes soaked.

"Dry yourself," she said, handing him the towels. He obeyed silently, swiping at his head with the rags as he pulled off his hat.

Beth moved from under the table and ran to him, her arms wrapping around his legs. "How hard is the wind goin' to blow, Pa?"

"Not hard enough to knock our house off the rock," said Butler, coming up behind her.

Josh quirked an eyebrow at Camellia. "Matthew seven," she said in explanation. "I read them Matthew seven."

Josh nodded and unbuttoned the top of his shirt. Camellia's mouth fell open and she dropped her eyes, embarrassed at seeing a man starting to disrobe.

Josh stopped as he saw her discomfort. "I'm sorry," he started. "I just . . ."

She glanced up, a warm sensation running through her face. "No, it's your house. *I* should go home."

He shook his head. "You can't. Nobody's there. Your pa, Chester, and Johnny are at the manse, orders of Master Trenton. He told me to bring you too, if I thought it safe enough."

Camellia looked toward the door. "How bad is it?"

"Not good. I almost didn't make it here. Too much blowing around out there—limbs, sticks, who knows what else? The manse is a long way to go in this."

"But my house isn't far," she insisted. "I'm sure I can get there."

"I won't let you. I'll try to get you to the manse if you want, but I won't let you stay alone at your house all night."

Camellia considered the manse. What would it feel like to sleep there? How strange! In spite of the fact that she and Trenton planned to marry in less than a year, she'd never even thought of that. She'd feel so out of place there, like a dog sleeping in a mansion, a stranger putting her head down where it didn't belong.

"I don't reckon it will look proper for me to spend the night in the house of my betrothed before the marriage," she said. "Even if a storm is blowing."

"I think most folks would understand."

"You think we can make it, then?"

"I'll do whatever you ask."

Beth stepped to Camellia. "Don't go. I'm scared. Stay here and read to us some more."

"Yes, stay here," added Butler and Lucy.

"Who's gone stay with us if Pa takes you?" said Beth, taking a new approach. "We're too scared to stay here alone."

Camellia looked at each of the children, then back at Josh. Water still dripped off his face, but not as heavily as earlier. His top shirt button remained loose, and his wet shirt stuck to his strongly muscled shoulders and chest. When a quivery sensation ran through her arms and face again, she realized she wasn't looking at Josh like an uncle. She dropped her eyes and told herself to stop thinking such evil thoughts. She and Trenton would marry in May, and Mr. Cain was her pa's brother—at least half—so she ought to stop acting like a schoolgirl just because he had unbuttoned a shirt button.

Lucy grabbed Camellia's hands and tugged her back toward the table. "You *got* to stay," she insisted. "You can't leave us here by our lonesome."

Not knowing what else to do, Camellia followed Lucy back toward the haven under the table. Josh picked up a rag and wiped his face again. "I best get a dry shirt. I'll change, then come back."

Camellia sat on the floor, still confused by her reaction to Josh. Butler climbed into her lap and handed her the Bible again. Hurriedly, she opened it and looked for a new passage to read . . . anything to take her mind off the fact that Josh Cain, a most handsome man, was changing his clothes in a room just a few feet away. Her eyes landed on Matthew 5, and she started reading. When Josh returned a couple of minutes later, she didn't even glance up. He took a spot on the floor nearby, and they all sat that way for a long time. Eventually, Camellia's voice got quieter as the children yawned, stretched out on their blankets, and fell asleep. Then Camellia stopped reading and put the Bible aside. Holding her breath, she looked up, almost hoping that by some miracle Josh had disappeared. But there he sat, dry shirt and all, hair slicked back, eyes gentle as he watched her. Outside the wind seemed to have softened.

"You read wonderfully well for somebody so new to it," he said. "You should feel proud."

"I read some every day. Trying to do my best."

He smiled and she relaxed some. He was her friend, and she could talk to him. As the hurricane raged outside, she and Josh talked more and more easily. They talked of the Bible and what it meant, of their faith and how they had come by it, their likes and dislikes in matters of all kinds. For some reason she couldn't explain, Camellia felt safe in spite of the storm, as if Josh Cain could take care of anything that might seek to harm her. She wondered why she didn't sense the same thing with Trenton but decided it was because Trenton was so much younger. A man his age hadn't experienced all that Josh Cain had, didn't have the same wealth of wisdom to draw on. After Trenton had matured, he'd probably carry the same strength in him that she now saw in Josh Cain.

The storm passed in the wee hours of the morning. Waking with a start, Josh quickly sat up, found his boots by the fireplace, and slipped them on. Camellia lay asleep under the table by Beth, her hair framing her face. Josh watched her for several minutes, listened to the sound of her breathing. An ache welled up in his stomach at her beauty, but then he thought of Anna and guilt pushed at his throat. What kind of man was he to feel this way about Camellia so soon after Anna's death? A sorry man, that's what kind. Of course, he already knew that about himself, had known it for a long time, ever since the war . . . ever since . . .

Not wanting to think of the past, Josh rubbed sleep from his eyes and decided to get going. No telling how much damage the storm had caused. He gently touched Camellia on the shoulder, and she awoke.

"I need to go," he said softly.

She sat up sleepily.

"I'll tell your pa and Master Trenton that you're safe."

"I'll see to the children, then come to the manse."

Josh smiled. "I don't know what I'll do without you once you marry. You've done more than anybody to get us through these last months. The Lord surely sent you to us."

Camellia waved off the compliment. "I'm doing what anybody would. I love your kids. They make me feel . . . needed."

Josh nodded, slipped on his hat, and stood to leave.

"You need some food," she said.

"I'll eat later." He headed to the door, then stopped for one more look at Camellia. "You're an angel."

"Go on," said Camellia shyly. "I'll get the children up. See you later."

He left then, stepped off the porch, and headed to The Oak. He found almost everybody else outside, their eyes wide with wonder as they examined the damage left behind. Josh saw Trenton almost immediately and told him that Camellia was safe at his house. His hair unkempt and eyes frantic, Trenton nodded but then hurried away toward the manse. Josh wondered why he didn't run immediately to see Camellia. A man with a good heart would do just that. It made Josh a little angry, but it was none of his business.

"I've done a quick check already," said York, now by his side. "Looks like some major roof damage to one of the barns. And three of the darkies' barracks are smashed."

"Any deaths?"

"None I know of; thank the Lord for that."

"You getting religious on me all of a sudden?"

"Hey, I'm coverin' my bets, that's all. I'm not a complete heathen."

Josh laughed. "You been to the fields yet?"

"Nope, that was my next stop."

Josh led York down the gravel path toward the first section of the rice fields. Neither man spoke; they knew what they might find, and it scared them. Their pace picked up as they neared the fields. Mud sucked at their boots, and water dripped everywhere. York reached the field first, Josh right behind him. York bent to one knee, took off his hat, and dropped his head in his hands. Josh caught his breath. As far as he could see, the fields were flooded. The ocean surge and rain from the storm had pushed the river over its banks and into the fields of mature rice. The wind had blown the rice down too . . . broken much of it, then left the rest bent sideways in the flooded mud.

Josh stepped into the field. Although much of the water had drained away after the peak of the river's surge, it still reached about halfway up his boots. He bent, cupped a hand in the water, and took a drink. The water gagged him and he spit it out.

York looked at him hopefully.

Josh shook his head. "Got some salt in it. Not as bad as the ocean water, but still some."

York dropped his eyes.

Josh sighed and stood. The storm had pushed and blown salt water into the rice fields, a death sentence for rice if the level was high enough. "These are the fields closest to the river. Some of the others are probably okay if we can get some sun real fast and dry it out before it rots."

York stood too and gazed in all directions. "It's a mess. At most, we might salvage half the crop. That's not even countin' the money it'll take to repair the dikes and canals, the barns and houses."

"We got our work cut out for us, that's for sure. But it could have been a lot worse. Not a full hurricane, I don't think, and we got all winter to worry about fixing things. Let's get in as much as we can, then do the repairs to get ready for next year's crop."

"You don't understand," York said slowly, as if in a daze. "The last couple of years have gone hard on The Oak."

"I know the yield's some lower, but all folks go through that. Some years you get more, some less."

"The Tessiers don't have much to see them through the lean years, that's what I'm tryin' to tell you."

Josh focused on his muddy boots. "What are you saying? What else can we do but repair the damage, get in as much crop as we can? After that, it's out of our hands. The Tessiers will do what they have to do. We have no control over any of that."

York rubbed his beard and addressed Josh as if talking to a child. "They could end up losin' the place. What do you think that means for me and you?"

"We find work with whoever buys it," replied Josh.

York snorted. "You're such a simple man. "What if they don't keep growin' rice here? Lots of folks are changin' over, going to island cotton. You know that."

"I could learn to grow cotton. So could you."

"But what about Camellia?" York asked. "She and Trenton are to marry in May. You think this won't change that? If he marries Camellia, Mrs. Tessier's already threatened him with losin' this place. She's pushin' him to make a marriage with somebody with money, family name. This storm"—he waved his arms over the damaged fields—"might have wrecked all Camellia's hopes. Trenton's too."

Josh stared at the rice, trying to decide whether he ought to say what he felt. As York hung his head, Josh stepped to him. "Look. We can speak openly to each other, right? We got that much between us."

York nodded.

"Okay," said Josh. "Here's what I got to say. First, it's not my place to speak about what Camellia and Trenton ought to do. That's surely up to them. But I have to tell you, if Trenton lets his mother push him one way or the other on it, then you best be mighty grateful if he ends up backing out of the marriage. Any man who can't see what a treasure Camellia is, any man who wouldn't marry her no matter whether he had a dime to his name or not, why that man ought to just go on and die because he's got nary a brain in his head. So, yes, all this is a hard thing—this storm coming and The Oak heading for tough times. But that shouldn't matter one bit to Trenton, not if he loves Camellia, and not if it's the right thing, the Lord's will for them to marry." Josh stopped to take a breath.

York tilted his head toward Josh. "That's a long speech, but a plain one."

"I believe it," Josh stated firmly.

York took off his hat and gazed into it, as if he could find the secret to life there. "I don't know . . . I been tryin' all my life to make somethin' of myself, somethin' for Camellia, my boys. But it seems that somethin' always messes things up. Here we got Camellia and Master Trenton all promised to each other. But this storm and the need for money could ruin everythin'."

Josh winced. Although he didn't like to think it, the notion came to him that York wanted Camellia to marry Master Trenton as much for him as for her. When he spoke, though, he didn't mention that. "If any of this ruins their marriage plans, maybe it's not the Lord's desire for them to become husband and wife."

York put his hat back on. "I don't know too much about the Lord's desire."

"I don't claim to know it either. But I do believe if a man looks to find it, he will. Yes, he'll stumble some along the way, get off the path here and there, but the Lord will keep giving him just enough light to take the next step."

"Wish I could trust that. But I'd rather trust myself, do things my own way."

"Like with the man at Mossy Bank?" Josh threw in.

"Yes, like that," York said sternly.

"You need to know I've made up my mind to find the rightful owner. I've waited too long already. Don't plan to wait any longer."

"Do what you want; the trail is cold for sure."

"I don't understand you sometimes."

York grunted and started walking back toward the manse. "Got no time to talk of this. Master Trenton will wonder where we are. Best get back."

Josh hurried after him, mad at himself for not standing stronger against his brother. As they reached the yard he saw Camellia headed toward them, her blue eyes bright. His legs weakened for just a second, and an unworthy thought ran through his head. He didn't *want* her to marry Master Trenton! If she did, that meant . . . He turned away and pushed the thought out of his mind. She *would* marry Master Trenton. She was promised to him, and Josh had no right to want anything else. Yet, he couldn't help but see a match with Trenton Tessier as a disaster. The man had no kindness in him, no good heart. Trenton would hurt Camellia; Josh knew it.

Facing Camellia and York again, Josh sighed. He had no right to think ill of Trenton Tessier. As bad as he himself was, Josh Cain had no right to throw the first stone.

Chapter Seventeen

The next four weeks passed like a buggy pulled by runaway horses for Trenton Tessier. He woke up every morning with but one desire in his head—a drive to get as much rice as possible out of the fields and to market. He pushed everybody harder than any master had ever pushed, and the field hands went into their houses way past dark every night. He spent almost no time with Camellia in those weeks. And when he did see her, he offered little by way of cheer.

"Seems like the whole world is against me," he moaned more than once. "No matter what I do, something awful still happens."

Camellia held his hand and offered encouragement, but nothing she said made any difference in his mood. Grinding his teeth, he barked and yelled all day; rushed here and cracked his whip there. When servants saw him they got out of his way, lest his roan stallion run them down with nary a notice from the angry man on his back. Trenton barely slept at night, and except for his attention to the harvest, the rest of his mind went blank, as if somebody had taken a painting and wiped all the color from it. His face took on a worn look with a lot of added lines and cuts way past its years.

When October ended, and the workers had harvested all they could, Trenton sat down at his desk in the study, added everything up, and discovered that he'd salvaged just over 70 percent of the crop—a result not quite as bad as he'd first feared, but not nearly good enough to keep the plantation from registering huge losses for the year. For a couple of days he walked around dazed by the depth of his misfortune. Again Camellia tried to talk to him, but he paid her no attention. What did a woman know or understand about a man's troubles? What could she do about them even if she did know?

About the only thing that cheered Trenton in those days was the fact that Calvin had come home at the first of the month. His mother had sent him, he said. Wanted him to aid Trenton any way he could. She knew from Trenton's letters that the storm had done major damage, and since she couldn't come herself, due to some pressing business with her sons-in-law, Luther and Gerald, she wanted Calvin there in her place.

Trenton met Calvin early every morning, and the two of them rode over The Oak in quiet inspection, discussing their next steps. Although Trenton didn't tell Calvin all the problems, he did offer enough for his younger brother to understand that things weren't promising.

"You have to go to Charleston and tell Mother the extent of the matter," Calvin said after his first few days home.

"I know," agreed Trenton. "She'll need to know everything so she can make the proper arrangements at the bank to tide us over until next year. I hate to face her, though. She will surely press me again about my plans with Camellia."

"She'll do what she has to do," Calvin assured him. "She's got your best interest at heart, even when she disagrees with you."

"She has *her own* best interests at heart," said Trenton bitterly. "You're still young, but you need to learn that now. Mother protects herself first and then looks to others next."

"You're a callous son."

"Perhaps. But give yourself time; you'll find out what I mean."

Finished with all he could accomplish at The Oak, Trenton squared his shoulders and got ready to go to Charleston. Although wishing with all his heart to avoid it, he knew he couldn't any longer. He told Camellia just before he left, "I'll come home as quickly as possible. Your father and I need to sell the crop; and I'm required to visit with my mother and family."

"I understand," she said gently. "I'm not going anywhere."

He took her hands. "I know I've not seen you much lately. But I've had so much responsibility."

She put a finger on his lips. "Don't worry," she soothed. "I know what happened. You don't have to explain."

He squeezed her hands. "We'll make plans for our marriage when I get back."

"Go," she said. "Write me letters."

His head snapped up with curiosity. She dropped her eyes. "I've . . . learned some . . . how to read," she explained.

"But how?"

"I study," she finally said. "Pick up things."

From her evasive answer, he got the sense she wanted to keep something hidden. He eyed her for another second, then let it drop. "Letters then. I'll try to remember."

He left the next day, a servant-driven carriage full of baggage following as he, Calvin, and York galloped out on their horses.

Camellia ate supper that night with Josh and his children. Although her pa had gone with Trenton, Josh had stayed behind to begin repairs on the fields, particularly the damaged dikes and canals that controlled the water flow. After she had prepared the food, Josh came in and helped her carry it to the table—biscuits, a cut of ham, and peas from the garden he kept behind his house. The children talked loudly as they ate, but Josh and Camellia were quiet. When everyone had finished eating, Beth asked Camellia to read to them. She brought out a copy of A Tale of Two Cities, by Charles Dickens, that her pa had gotten for her from the Tessiers' library, opened it, and struggled through a few pages. Butler became restless quickly, and after a few more minutes, Beth led him and Lucy out to the yard for some last-minute play before bedtime.

Camellia and Josh remained at the table. He drizzled some honey on one of the biscuits.

"Your reading is coming along fine," he said. "Wonderful for somebody who's as new to it as you are."

"Ruby says I'm almost to the point that she can't teach me much more."

"That doesn't surprise me. You're about to catch me too."

"I've got a long way to catch you. I want to go further, though," she said eagerly. "You know, to school and all. I feel like there's so much more I don't know."

"A body can never know it all. My mama used to tell me that."

"I never knew my mama." Camellia sighed.

"That is sad for a child," he agreed. "Especially a daughter."

"Pa won't speak much of her. I reckon it hurts him too much."

When Josh stared intently at his hands, she wondered what he found so interesting on them. "You never knew her, did you?" she asked.

"Nope. She married your pa before the war and was gone before I came to York and The Oak."

"You and Pa were separated for a long time."

"He headed out on his own the year he turned seventeen. Lived in and around Charleston, Savannah, made a living working horses for some stable owners, doing some gambling."

"You got back together about the time the war started."

"Yes, my mama died in '46. I didn't know where else to go. York had taken work at The Oak, asked me to come with him. I came here, then the war started. We both went off to fight it."

"You were mighty young for that."

He looked at his shoes, and she saw he felt bad about something. She changed the subject. "What's Pa told you about my mama?"

"Not a lot. Just that she was a beautiful woman and he loved her. You want to know more, uh . . . you need to ask him. I know she loved you, though. What mama wouldn't love a daughter like you?"

Through his hesitation, Camellia sensed Josh Cain knew more, but he wasn't willing to tell. So she said simply, "I want to know what colors to wear in what season. What a lady should say or not say in certain social situations, how to properly set a table, where to put the forks and spoons."

"All fine things to know," Josh replied. "Things a mama would teach a daughter. But my Anna never knew any of that, so I guess none of it is essential to be a good person, to live a fine life."

Camellia dropped her eyes as she recognized the truth of his words. A lot of her motive for wanting to learn came from her vanity—a desire to become a proper lady. In addition, she wanted to please Trenton's mother and the people she'd deal with after she married him. She pondered that for a second, her need to please people she didn't even know. She wondered if her hopes pleased the Lord; it bothered her to think that maybe they didn't, but she didn't see any way to do anything about it.

"I want Trenton to feel proud of me. His family too."

Josh's jaw firmed. Camellia got the impression he wanted to say something sharp, but he kept his voice even as he spoke. "Master Trenton did a fine job these last few weeks," he offered.

"He pushed hard. Stella said lots of the servants are upset with him."

"Sometimes a man has to push hard," Josh said. "Lots of people depend on him."

Camellia drank some coffee while she weighed whether to bring up what she'd had on her mind since the storm. Even though she knew times were tough, none of the men had told her any of the details because it wasn't proper to talk about such matters in front of a woman. Figuring Josh would tell her more than her pa ever would, she decided to go on and ask what she wanted. "How bad is it?"

Josh finished his biscuit and wiped his mouth. "Fairly bad. We lost a lot of crop. And we have to pay for all the repairs. Don't know yet what that figure will come to."

"Pa has seemed real upset lately. Trenton too."

"They both have a lot at stake here."

Camellia stood and started to clean off the table. "I know Trenton's mama is against our nuptials. I don't bring anything to the family."

"The woman is mighty selfish," said Josh, standing to help her with the dishes. "Trenton is much blessed that you would consent to become his bride."

Camellia laughed as she carried the metal plates to the wash bucket. "You're a touch loose in the head. Trenton is paying a high price to wed me."

Josh grabbed a rag and wiped off the table. Camellia eyed him curiously. "Not many men put their hand to cleaning."

"My Anna died, remember? Stayed in bed a long time before that. I know how to fix and clear off a table."

"I got a feeling you did it even before she got ill—that you aided her a lot whenever you could."

Josh shrugged, but she knew it was true. Josh Cain was different from other men, no two ways around it. He brought the towel to her bucket to wet it. She smelled the soap on his face where he'd cleaned up after his day in the fields. When he dipped the rag in the bucket and his hand touched hers, she jumped, as if something had jolted her skin. He apparently felt it too, for he paused and gazed at her as if she were a piece of gold. Her face flushed and she stepped away.

Wiping her hands on her apron, she tried to pretend that nothing had happened. Josh looked down and she eased away, glad he hadn't said anything. But then he stepped toward her, and her heart raced. She tried to figure what this meant; why she'd responded this way to a man she loved like a brother; why Josh Cain stirred something in her that she'd never experienced, not even with Trenton. She dropped her head in shame at her unfaithfulness to her betrothed. What kind of woman was she?

"I'm . . . sorry," Josh said, his face turning red. "I've tried to keep my quiet . . . but I just have to say this."

Josh took her by the shoulders and held her still. As he opened his mouth to speak, she held her breath, afraid he might say something crazy, like he loved her, that she made his skin tingle and his heart pound . . . just as he made hers do.

"You should not marry Trenton!" he blurted, his words pouring like rushing water. "I've been with him, know him well. He's got some fine qualities, that's true. But he's not right for you; you're too good for him, too fine. He's got no Christian heart in him, nothing of the Lord. If you marry him I fear for you, for your future, your—"

"No!" shouted Camellia, pulling away for good this time, her heart both relieved and somehow disappointed at his words. "I won't hear this, not even from you! I know he's not perfect—no man is. But he loves me. Otherwise, why would he stand up to his mother like he did? He's still young; he'll settle some after we're married. I'm sure of it! He'll change. I'm praying he will. I will trust the Lord to change him. He loves me; he'll do it for me!"

She stopped and stared at Josh, who looked stricken, obviously guilty that he'd upset her. "I'm sorry," he whispered. "I spoke out of turn. I have no standing in this, no right to speak. You and Master Trenton have to decide this, not me, not his mother, or anyone else. I hope you'll forgive me my brashness."

She put a hand on Josh's forearm. He stared at her, his eyes glazed. "You'll never know how much I respect you," she said. "You're so gentle . . . kinder than any man I've ever met. I know you're just trying to protect me. But I can't listen to you on this, no matter that you are my friend, my uncle."

Josh opened his mouth, and she waited for him to speak. Instead, he simply stepped back. "You should go. It's late, and you've had a long day. I'll take care of the rest of this." He waved over the kitchen.

Camellia nodded. "I'll come by about midday tomorrow. Check on the children."

To her surprise, Josh shook his head. "Maybe you shouldn't do that. You have plenty to do without taking care of us anymore. Beth's getting big enough to handle things around here anyway; probably time she started doing it."

Camellia's eyes widened. "I *like* coming by. It's not a chore."

When Josh shook his head again, she realized he really meant what he said, that he wasn't just being polite. Something had suddenly changed between them—a change she didn't like but didn't know how to fix. "But you're family," she argued. "I can't just stop checking on you."

Josh held up his hand. "I'm more grateful than I can say for all your aid these last months since Anna died. But you'll marry Trenton in the spring and won't have time for us anymore. It's time for us to adjust to that; might as well start now."

Camellia wanted to argue some more, to tell him she could see he was holding something back, some other reason for banishing her from his house. Yet his tone told her it wouldn't help, that he wouldn't tell her what was on his heart. Her spirit cracked as she realized she had to stop coming by every day; that she wouldn't see Beth, Lucy, and Butler much anymore; that she and Josh wouldn't talk about books and the Lord as they had.

"I'm . . . not sure I understand," she said. "Why can't I come by anymore?"

He smiled, but his eyes seemed sad. "I expect you don't. But it's best this way; I'm sure of it."

"What about . . . the children?"

"You'll still see them. Just not here. Not proper for you to come here, doing our chores for us."

"They can come to my house. I'll read to them there," she offered.

"They'll like that."

Tears sprang to her eyes, unbidden. "I'll miss our talks."

He nodded but didn't relent. "Go on now."

She walked slowly toward the door. As she reached it, she heard him move behind her and pivoted back to face him.

He smiled warmly. "If you ever need anything, you come to me. No matter what."

She smiled back weakly, then left the house. As she headed down the stairs, she took a deep breath. Marrying Trenton carried a mighty high price for her too, she realized sadly. Already she felt lonelier, cut off from people she cared about and who cared about her. Was it worth all this to marry Trenton? But how could it not be? She'd dreamed of this all her life. It had to be the Lord's will . . . and if it was, then surely the Lord would make up for any price she had to pay.

With York taking care of the rice sale, Trenton spent his first couple of days in Charleston sleeping late, eating big breakfasts, taking long walks along the sea wall, sitting at ease with a couple of his former school cronies, drinking brandy and smoking cigars. To his relief, his mother stayed away from him most of the time, coming down from her chambers to take her breakfast before he awakened and retiring before he returned for the evening. He met with York at the end of each day and gratefully heard that the sale of their rice had gone somewhat better than expected. With talk of war between the states more and more in the air, prices had risen some in the past year, and although nothing could make up for the 30 percent loss of the crop, they at least had not suffered from low prices with what they'd sold.

By his third day in the city, Trenton felt like he'd rested enough to finally face his mother. He arose earlier that morning and found her taking breakfast in the sunroom on the east side of the house. Eggs, muffins, grapefruit, coffee, and milk sat before her on the table. Fresh flowers added color. Three servants busied themselves in and out of the room, fetching and carrying this and that. Trenton kissed his mother on the forehead and eased down to a chair. The sun warmed his back.

His mother smiled thinly and applied butter to a muffin. "You sleep well?"

He warily took a cup of coffee, added sugar, and sipped from it. "Quite well."

He wondered when she would ask about the crop and what they were getting for it.

"I'm glad you've taken some rest," she said. "I know that harvesttime wears a man out. Always did your father."

"I'm recovered now, I believe."

"Mr. York is handling the business matters?" she asked.

"Yes. He's the expert in such things."

"He's a valuable man, no doubt about it."

Trenton took a muffin and bit from it as he studied his mother. Her hair had turned grayer since he last saw her. But her face looked calmer, as if she held a secret that gave her some power she'd always craved. He wondered what she had in mind. Her eyes were clear. Obviously, she hadn't taken any opiate yet.

"Your plans for marriage remain the same?" she asked.

He sat straighter as he anticipated her attack. "Yes, and I hope you've come to terms with those plans."

She smiled again. "You're a grown man. And a most stubborn one. Like your father that way. He hated it when I tried to make him do anything. Sometimes I think he deliberately took the opposite side in anything I suggested, just to show me I couldn't force my will on him. So I'll not try to push my desires on you anymore."

"I'm glad you've come to that conclusion," he said. "You'll come to love Camellia. I'm certain of it."

She took a delicate bite of muffin. "I believe that Luther and Gerald have plans for you this evening. They want to take you to dinner, talk over some business prospects."

Trenton eyed her curiously. "They've said nothing to me of this."

"They didn't want to bother you while you rested and asked me to invite you when I thought you were ready for it. They said they might have some interesting opportunities for you to explore."

Trenton lifted an eyebrow. "What kind of opportunities?"

"You men don't talk such matters before simple women like me. You'll have to go to dinner with them, see what they have in mind."

Trenton considered the matter as he ate his grapefruit. His mother's attitude made him suspicious. What kind of opportunities could Gerald and Luther know about that had escaped his notice? Yet, they were bankers. No harm in keeping up good relations with men who controlled vast sums of money, sums he would no doubt need if he wanted to see The Oak through to its next crop. "Will they come here for me?" he asked.

"Yes, I believe that's the idea. About eight or so."

Trenton buttered his muffin. He waited for his mother to ask more about the rice, but soon the breakfast ended and his mother retired to her room to get dressed for a visit she planned to make later that afternoon. Still unsure of his mother's intentions, Trenton became even more cautious about his meeting with Luther and Gerald. However, since he didn't have any basis for his distrust, he decided to just relax and go along with things. If they tried anything, he could handle it. Just had to keep his eyes open and his mind steady.

Luther and Gerald came for him in their four-horse carriage at precisely eight o'clock, looking almost like twins in their matching burgundy frock coats, black pants, boots, and white ruffled shirts. The mutton-chops on Luther's jowly face made him appear slightly silly, but Trenton knew Miranda liked them, so he didn't dare kid him about them. Gerald wore a stovepipe black hat that stretched his height almost to the roof of the carriage as they bounced down the cobblestone streets toward their destination.

"Where are you taking me?" asked Trenton, still suspicious of his brothers-in-law.

"To a quality establishment," replied Gerald, always the more talkative of the two. "A place for a gentleman to take his ease, share some quiet conversation."

Trenton glanced through the carriage window and thought of a number of clubs he'd visited in his school days. Places with fine burnished wood, tasteful thick draperies, food cooked from European recipes, wines and ports of classic vintage. The carriage didn't appear headed for any of them. "Is it a new place?"

"Stay patient," urged Gerald. "Good things come to him who waits." He smiled and pulled a cigar from a silver holder and offered it to Trenton. Not wanting to appear rude, Trenton accepted it. Luther produced a whiskey flask, took a sip, and handed it to Trenton.

"I'm not given to much whiskey," Trenton said, holding the flask without drinking.

"You're not a schoolboy anymore," encouraged Gerald. "You're the master of one of the largest plantations in the South. A man carrying that kind of weight needs to relax from time to time, get his mind off his responsibilities. Your father knew that, knew it better than most."

Trenton held the flask and tried to decide what to do. Camellia wouldn't want him to drink, and he didn't want to disappoint her. Yet what did she know about the heavy matters that plagued a man's mind, the toil of keeping up such a place as The Oak? He closed his eyes. Weariness settled on him despite the ease of the last couple of days. Loneliness hit him too, a sense that he had nobody but himself to depend upon. He took a long slow breath. Gerald was right; sometimes a man needed to lay down the duties he carried, enjoy a drink or two to ease his nerves. No harm in it, none at all.

He lifted the flask to his lips, and the liquid warmed him as it slid down his throat. He handed it back toward Luther, but his brother-in-law waved him off and produced a second one. "That one's for you," said Luther, winking.

Trenton hesitated again, but not as long this time. What Camellia didn't know wouldn't hurt her. Besides, she had no right to put shackles on his actions. For that matter, what right did any woman have to tell a man what to do? Even more, he and Camellia weren't even married yet. He smiled and took another sip.

The carriage turned left, passed under a streetlamp, and then headed west, out of the main part of the city. Gerald and Luther grinned at each other, Gerald's face pink even in the dim light.

"I hear the storm caused some significant damage to many of the plantations," said Gerald. "Rice crop in many places came in a lot scarcer than usual."

"Thankfully the price stayed up," added Luther. "Less rice to sell, a higher price to pay."

The mention of the storm made Trenton even more anxious. He felt like somebody had tied a leather band around his head and stretched it. Nobody but he and Hampton York knew the full depth of The Oak's losses from the storm. He took another drink to soften the tension.

"Hope it didn't hit you too hard," said Gerald, eying Trenton.

"It wasn't as bad as it could have been," Trenton said, deciding to play it close to the vest. "Lost some crop, though not as much as many."

Gerald nodded wisely. "Lots of men coming to the bank for loans. Figuring on a healthy crop next year to pay them back. Think you'll need anything of that nature?"

Trenton squirmed, took another drink, and hoped they'd reach their destination soon. He didn't like men like Gerald and Luther knowing too much about his business. "It's too early to tell."

Gerald glanced at Luther. His long chin, pointy in the passing shadows cast by the streetlamps, resembled a knife blade jabbed toward his chest.

"Mother says you have some business opportunities you think might interest me," Trenton said. "You talking shipping, property, what?"

Gerald cleared his throat. "Perhaps we should wait until we reach our club before we discuss those."

Trenton drank again from his flask. Gerald and Luther fell quiet. The carriage clicked along. The street turned from cobblestone to finely packed gravel. Trenton studied the houses as they passed. Although they weren't in the best section of Charleston anymore, they were still going by quality places: homes of old families with old money, money not tied up in land and field hands, money the house owners could get to if they wanted, cash they could use to pay off their debts and buy what they desired for their families. Well, Trenton had no cash money to speak of, almost none at all. Everything he owned came in the form of chattel or land and buildings. If he didn't come up with some cash to pay on his debts, he might need to sell some things, and if he did, then men like Gerald and Luther would swoop in on his property like snakes on mice and swallow it up at a bargain price.

Trenton wondered if that was the opportunity Gerald and Luther wanted to offer him: the chance to hand over some land or a few Negroes at a cheap price in exchange for dollars to keep The Oak running. He jutted his jaw. He wouldn't do that. No, he wouldn't. He hadn't taken over The Oak just to start selling it off. Such an act would destroy every ounce of pride he had left. No, he wouldn't let his father down that way, wouldn't give up what his father had labored so hard to build.

He drank again from his flask and felt the whiskey beginning to take effect. His eyes swam slightly, and his shoulders relaxed. He eased down in his seat and closed his eyes. The street moved along, the carriage turned here and there. Trenton's face warmed as the minutes clicked along; he felt slightly lightheaded. He took swallow after swallow of liquor, telling himself again and again that he needed this night, deserved it. Finally, the carriage slowed, made a right turn, then another left, and pulled to a stop.

"We're here!" exclaimed Luther, jumping eagerly to the street. "A most commodious place, I think you'll quickly agree."

Trenton, his legs unsteady on the gravel street, joined Luther and Gerald. He shook his head to clear it. A solid brick house, behind an iron gate at least seven feet high, stood before him. Four white columns ran along the front porch, and ivy climbed the bottom of the columns. The shades to the house windows were pulled. Huge oaks with moss hanging almost to the ground grew around the sides of the place. Somebody laughed from inside.

Gerald took Trenton by the elbow and steered him up the cobbled walk. "This is a discreet place. For men of means and quality. I think you'll enjoy it."

Trenton's eyes widened as he realized where they'd brought him. He tried to pull away, but Gerald held him tightly.

"A man of your years needs to visit an establishment like this," Gerald coaxed. "Prepare you for your marriage to come."

Trenton's face reddened, and he tried once more to escape. "Camellia will . . . will not like—"

"Are you going to let a woman keep you from exercising your manly rights?" asked Gerald, leading him up the steps.

"No, but . . ."

"No arguments," said Gerald. "Every man takes this step, most far younger than you. You've labored hard this season; you deserve to relax this way."

Trenton's head spun. He knew he ought to pull away and run, but he couldn't find the strength to do it. The liquor had made him weak. And, after all, he did need some relaxation from his troubles, so why not go along with Luther and Gerald this one time? They knew about things like this, knew what a man needed and didn't need. With Gerald on one side and Luther on the other, Trenton entered the house. A black man approached them, took Luther's hat, and led them into a parlor. Trenton took another drink. He heard somebody laugh in another room. The black man pointed them to a sofa and chairs. Trenton fell into the sofa. The room danced before his eyes. A fire burned in a marble-encased fireplace. The flames blurred. A woman with red hair stood before Trenton, then sat at his side. She smelled like musk.

Trenton tried to stand, but the red-haired woman giggled and grabbed him by the hand, pulling him back down. He squinted around for Gerald and Luther, but they had disappeared. The woman moved still closer. Trenton tried to move away, but the soft sofa had no more room. So he took another sip of whiskey and told himself he'd leave soon. As the fire danced, the red-haired woman touched his hair. He closed his eyes and blacked out.

The next thing Trenton knew he woke up shivering in a bed with silk sheets and thick covers. A bright sun washed over his face, and his mouth tasted like sour mash mixed with fireplace ashes. Pulling the bedcovers more closely around him, he rubbed his eyes and peered around. His pants and shirt lay neatly folded on a chair by the bed. He tried to remember what had happened the night before but couldn't. His head throbbing, he eased to the bedside and reached for his clothes. Suddenly, the room's door swung open, and a smiling woman rushed through it. Trenton's mouth fell open as his mother stood over him, her eyes bright with obvious glee.

Silence reigned in the carriage for the first part of the ride back to his mother's house. Trenton sat in a corner and pouted while his mother watched him with a pleased set to her lips, a confident glow in her eyes. Trenton tried to ignore her as best he could but found it impossible. Obviously, she'd set up the previous night with Gerald and Luther. A deep rage burned in him. She had no business scheming this way against him.

About ten minutes from the house, his mother smiled sweetly. Then he knew the time had come for her gambit to play itself out.

"What a shame if your precious Camellia should find out about this," she started. "Surely such a thing will upset her Christian sensibilities."

Trenton ground his teeth. "You devised all this, didn't you?"

His mother sniffed. "Does it matter?"

"To me it does."

Mrs. Tessier stared out as they passed the market section. Scores of people moved here and there in pursuit of their daily activities. "You've refused to listen to reason," she explained. "You gave me no choice but to take another course."

"You think I'll break my betrothal with Camellia to keep you from telling her of my indiscretion?"

"It is at least a thought, don't you agree?"

Trenton put his hands on his knees. "You're a mean woman."

"Not mean," she argued. "You may not realize it, but I've got your best interests at heart—the future of your children, this family. We've talked of this before; no use saying it again. I have nothing against Camellia. She is lovely. And from all I've seen, she carries herself well. But let me ask you straight out. If I approved of this marriage, would you feel as committed to it? If I loved Camellia, if I embraced her with open arms, would you want her as much as you do? Isn't it possible that at least part of your attachment to her comes from your desire to show me you're a man? Your efforts to prove you can stand up to your mother?"

Trenton stared out the window. Although he hated to admit it, his mother had touched a nerve. "I give you the point," he confessed. "But that doesn't change my love for her."

Mrs. Tessier chuckled. "If you loved her so much, why did you end up where you did last night?"

Trenton's heart fell as guilt touched him. "I took too much drink. Gerald and Luther, they . . . " His voice trailed off as he recognized he shouldn't blame them for his mistakes. A man of any character knew he needed to accept responsibility for his actions. And yet, if they hadn't taken him to that house, he wouldn't have gone there on his own. They did bear some of the blame—his mother too. His anger returned.

"I forbid you to tell Camellia of this," he said firmly.

"You're in no position to forbid me to do anything."

"So that's your plan?"

"I hope you won't force me to do so."

"What if I tell her?"

"That's your choice. She is a woman of Christian faith. Perhaps she will practice the grace of forgiveness."

Trenton's stomach rolled. "You're telling me I have to break the engagement, aren't you?"

"I'm asking you to do what's right for everyone, her included."

The carriage turned left and passed by the Battery. Trenton wiped his eyes. "I don't know. I'm tired and confused."

"You don't have to decide today; give yourself some time. You have other matters to occupy your thoughts for a while anyway. We both know the sale of the crop won't keep The Oak running this year."

"How do you know that?"

"I've talked to Mr. York. He's informed me what the crop brought. It's not enough."

Trenton squeezed his temples, not sure whether to believe her. Yet what difference did it make? Everyone knew he'd not made a full crop. "I figured on taking some loans," he offered. "Next year's crop will surely come in heavy, make up for what the storm destroyed."

"Any idea how much you'll need to borrow?"

"I planned on asking Gerald and Luther to do some estimates."

"Their bank will not loan you any more money if you insist on this ill-conceived marriage."

He glared at his mother. "You know that for certain?"

"I've arranged it as certain."

"You're a vicious woman."

"I'm a practical one. A right marriage will take care of everything. You'll see."

His head pounding, Trenton stared at the floor and tried to figure a way out of the trap his mother had set, but no escape appeared. "I cannot make that choice right now. I need some time."

Mrs. Tessier leaned over and patted him on the hands. "It's hard being a man," she said, smirking. "All the responsibility you carry."

Trenton wanted to grab her by the throat and choke the smirk off her face but knew he couldn't. Then he wanted to hang his head and cry at the injustice of it all. But he couldn't do that either. Tessier men didn't show weakness, especially when they knew how weak they truly were.

Chapter Eighteen

A few days after telling Camellia she shouldn't come by his place any-more, Josh left his children under Stella's care and headed out on horse-back. Although relieved that he was finally going to investigate the identity of the man from Mossy Bank, he also feared the trouble this would cause with York. Even if Josh never learned anything, York would take this as an act of betrayal. But what else could he do? The events at Mossy Bank haunted him, and he still worried that maybe the Lord had punished him for his silence about it.

Riding easy through the November morning, Josh tried to steady his heart as his horse clomped over the miles. A warm sun beat down on his back. He studied the blue sky, soaking in the color, wondering what it would look like on a piece of paper or canvas. He wondered if he could capture the pure blue of the morning, the soft touch of the puffy clouds that drifted by?

Anna's face rose up in his mind. She loved days like this; loved to go to the beach and ease her toes into the water as the waves foamed. She loved the sky and sea joining up at the tip of the horizon, the way the sun splashed color all over the place at sunup and sundown. She loved it when he tried to paint those images; when he put brush and paint to paper. Josh's eyes teared up. He hadn't drawn since Anna's death. How could he? Without her, he didn't see that much beauty anymore.

He forded a creek and headed a little more south. He and Anna had lived a good life together. She had birthed his babies, sat by him on Sundays at the beach as he read from the Bible and the children played in the water. What would he do without her? How could he go on living?

Then Camellia came to his thoughts. Like Anna, Camellia was a kind and gentle woman, but she was also stronger, at least of body. Nobody labored any harder than Camellia, not even a darky.

Josh considered Camellia's upcoming marriage and wondered how she'd fit into Trenton's world. A woman of her purity would struggle with it, he figured—the use of so much liquor, the women's gossip, the way so many of the men kept mistresses on the side. How could Camellia endure such things? He feared that Trenton wouldn't stay true to her; that he'd follow his father's poor example and take up with any number of women. Such actions would crush Camellia's heart!

Knowing he couldn't do a thing to aid her, Josh kicked his horse a touch and galloped on toward Beaufort. He entered the city late in the day, tired but anxious to talk to the sheriff. Although not nearly as large a town as Charleston, Beaufort held a charm all its own. Countless fine houses shaded by oaks and palms bordered the streets. Four good churches—Baptist, Methodist, Episcopal, and Catholic—gave people places to worship each Sunday. A library with over three thousand volumes housed great books. The Beaufort College provided education for the richest of the area's young men.

Josh eyed the hamlet with a mix of pride and shame as he headed to the sheriff's office on Bay Street. If you had a lot of money, Beaufort provided a fine place for a person to live. If not, well, Beaufort didn't look quite so inviting.

He turned a corner and headed down Bay Street, passing a bank, a large general store, the post office, and a score of other businesses and establishments. People headed this way and that. With the crops all in, lots of folks were in town, freed from their duties at their plantations and farms.

At the sheriff's office—a square wood building not far from the bank—Josh climbed off, tied up his horse, and went inside. He found the sheriff at a desk, his jail empty, his door and window open to catch the ocean breeze. The sheriff stood as Josh tromped in.

"Good to see you, Walt," he said, sticking out his hand.

"Been a while. Since Master Tessier's death, I think."

"Yes, I believe that's so. You have a minute?"

Walt pointed him to a seat, and Josh inspected him as he sat down.

Walt wore a brown shirt with a badge on it, gray pants, scuffed but clean boots, and a pistol in a holster on his hip. His black hair fell into his face, and his mustache curled all the way down to his chin.

"How's things on The Oak?" Walt asked.

"Busy. Hard work, you know. Good prices for the crop this year, but the storm hit us pretty hard. Cost us some crop."

"We got a lot of rain—wind too—but not too much damage."

"You got lucky."

"Reckon so."

"Things here in town going well?"

"All right, except for all the secession talk. This place is a hotbed for all that; lot of fire-eaters here, ready to go to war right now."

"You think South Carolina will really secede?"

"The Yankees keep pushing us on the slavery, I don't see how we can keep from it."

Josh sighed. "War hurts everybody. Hard things come from war."

Walt licked his mustache, and Josh shifted in his seat. "Look," Josh began, "I need to ask you a couple of questions."

"What kind of questions?" Walt leaned back.

Although he'd planned this out in his head over and over, Josh still didn't know exactly what to say now that the time had come to speak. He didn't want to say too much, at least not yet. No reason to set Walt to sniffing around if there wasn't a good reason.

"Close to a year ago," Josh finally said, "I was headed from Charleston to The Oak. I met a man about halfway between the two, at a crossing near Mossy Bank Creek."

"I know the place."

"Yes. Well, the man I met had a bullet in his back."

Walt raised an eyebrow.

Josh continued. "He wore real fine clothes and appeared to be about fifty years old or so. Mostly bald, but with a sandy-colored beard. I checked him but found no papers, no way to identify him."

"He still alive when you found him?"

"Yes, for a couple of minutes."

"A horse around? Any wagon or buggy?"

"None I saw."

"Curious."

Josh nodded. "He mentioned a name before he died. Ruth."

"Ruth?"

"Yes. I figured maybe it was his wife. No way to tell for sure."

"That's all he said?"

"He died real fast. No time for anything else."

A bee buzzed into the room. Josh watched the sheriff's face carefully, but it gave nothing away.

"You're looking for this Ruth, I reckon."

"Yes. Thought I'd check if you knew one in Beaufort."

Walt licked his mustache again. "Why didn't you come to me sooner? A shot man is a matter for the law."

Josh lifted his hat, stared into it. "I should have. But it happened the same week as Tessier's death. You had all that on your mind. I figured I'd see you soon after that. But I didn't. My wife took sick. Maybe you heard; she passed on."

"I hadn't heard. But you have my sympathies."

"Much obliged. Anyway, by the time all that had happened, months had already passed. With one thing and another, time just got away."

Walt shrugged as if it didn't really matter. "You might try Charleston. Sounds like you found this man as much in their part of the world as mine."

"I'll do that next. Just thought I'd start as close to home as I could. No way to tell if the man was headed north or south, coming this way, that way, or the other way. This Ruth might live just about anywhere."

Walt leaned back. "I don't know a Ruth right offhand. And I know just about everybody in town."

"I'm sure you do. That's why I stopped here first." Josh fingered his hat. "That's what I wanted to tell you."

"You bury the man?"

"Yes. Said a few words over him."

Walt nodded and Josh stood to leave. "Let me know what you find," said Walt. "A shot man gets a lawman's blood pumping, you know. A good mystery makes for an interesting day. Don't get much of that around here."

"You'll let me know if you come across somebody named Ruth?"

"Sure will."

Josh turned to go.

"One more thing," said Walt.

Josh stopped.

"I don't know that this connects," said Walt. "But a man rode through here back in February. Looking for a man he described a lot like Mr. York. He didn't know his name though, just his description."

"He say what he wanted with this man?" When Walt narrowed his eyes, Josh got the distinct impression the sheriff was enjoying the moment.

"He said he and the man had exchanged some remarks."

Josh laughed lightly, hoping it threw Walt off a little. "He wouldn't be the first man to exchange remarks with York, if it was him."

"He said he took a shot at the man."

"Pretty honest of him to confess that."

"He said the man he was looking for had taken something that belonged to him."

"That's a serious charge."

"He said it happened in November, last year. I figured that at about the same time Tessier died. Seems like I remember noticing a cut on Mr. York's arm when I visited The Oak for Mr. Tessier's funeral; the time I talked to the darky and Miss Camellia. You think any of this goes together?"

"Sounds like a mystery to me."

Walt studied him with a straight stare, and Josh kept his eyes steady too. Any false move here, and Walt might end up stirring up far more than Josh wanted stirred. "This man say anything about a shot man or a woman named Ruth?"

"Nothing."

"Perhaps it's not connected, then."

"Perhaps."

"I'm sure York would gladly talk with you about it if you want. Should I say something to him?"

Walt lifted his eyebrows. "No, suppose not. The man didn't ask me to do that, and I don't know for sure it was Mr. York."

"You give him York's name?"

"No, but if he asked around town much, he'd surely get it."

Josh nodded. "Thanks for your time," he said, putting on his hat.

"Always glad to assist," Walt answered. "Any way I can."

Josh took a couple of steps, then turned back to Walt. "The man give his name?"

"Yes, now that you mention it. Tarleton, he said. Ike Tarleton."

Josh shook his head. "Never heard of him."

"Have a good day."

Josh left and headed back to the street. For several seconds he stood there and tried to figure what to do next. Although not sure what he'd expected from Walt, he was unsatisfied with the visit, disappointed that he'd not done more to make up for his slackness in handling the matter from Mossy Bank. He felt dirty, as if he'd stepped awfully close to something that didn't smell too good and the aroma had stuck. Mounting his horse, he headed toward the Baptist church. He might just stop and go in. Maybe a few minutes of quiet in their fine white building would calm his spirit some. He hoped so. Otherwise, he didn't know what he'd do to make that happen.

Chapter Nineteen

By the time November came, Ruby had settled into marriage with Obadiah without much of a hitch. When his work allowed it, he stayed with her in the back room of her house on The Oak, and when he couldn't, he picked her up in his buggy every Saturday right as the sun went down and drove her to his place, a four-room white house with two glass windows on the front, a small spot for a garden out back, and two red rugs that he'd bought from a dead man's widow in the main room.

Ruby always cooked for him when she got to his house; fixed him fine meals from the goods he kept stored in the cabinets he'd built in his kitchen. The cabinets stretched from the floor almost to the ceiling and covered one whole wall. The first time she saw them her mouth fell open, and she stepped back to take a better look. Smooth arches ran across the cabinet tops, and finely cut figures of men and women in all manner of dress and doing all sorts of labor decorated the sides and fronts.

Her eyes awed, Ruby touched the dark wood and ran her fingers over the carvings. "Where you get such fine wood?"

Obadiah smiled so widely that all of his big teeth and gums showed. "When you makin' a box for white folks, they don't much ask how much wood it take. I get a bit extra most of the time. Use it for my house, my cuttin's."

Ruby studied the carvings up close. "You got white folk and black folk cut in here."

"Look real hard," he said. "Maybe you see somethin'."

Ruby's eyes widened. "They be doing different things. Some chopping wood, some cooking, some riding horses, some dressed all up like they going to church. Coloreds and white."

"Study the faces," he insisted again. "See what you can see."

She obeyed, but nothing came to her. So he touched one of the figures, ran his fingers around the man's tiny face.

"I see it now!" Ruby suddenly said. "That be Mr. Tessier! His missus got his picture hanging on the wall in the manse. You've carved the master."

Obadiah beamed and waved his hands over the shelves. "I done a carvin' of everybody I cut a box for. All the folks that have passed in my years around here."

"Black and white," said Ruby. "In the same wood. Best hope no white folks ever see this. They might not like it that you put them in the wood with the coloreds."

Obadiah stepped back. "Reckon not. But I tell you the truth. When I cut a box for them, it don't matter what shade they got on their skin. After they get laid in the ground and stay there for a while, the bodies all end up lookin' 'bout the same."

Ruby smiled and studied Obadiah with a new appreciation. The man did have a wise way and a gentle hand. Add that to the fact that nobody told him what to do when he got up every day, and you had a worthy mate. True, like all free people of color, he still couldn't leave the county without a pass from a white sheriff, and he couldn't buy other folks' property without special permission. But all in all, he still lived a life a whole lot better than hers, and his situation made hers a whole lot easier than it would have been without him.

The months since her marriage had passed quickly, with her labor at The Oak and her time with Obadiah more than filling up her days. Stella and Camellia proved steady friends. Ruby came to see them both as people of worth: Stella, a true companion, and Camellia, as close to one as any white girl could ever be with a darky.

Given her comfortable life, Ruby found it tempting to settle in and give up her hopes of running off to find Markus. After all, people treated her nice here, as well as back in Virginia. Obadiah loved her, gave her sweet gifts, watched after her as if she had gold dust on her skin. Sometimes, when she lay down beside him at night to sleep, she felt a peace running through her bones, a peace that made it hard to consider anything that might shake it loose. Yet, she didn't want to give in to the feeling. To do so meant the loss of something she'd only learned about herself since the sale from the Rushtons': the loss of her fiery desire to live as a free woman, to find her man and boy again and run off with them to a place where nobody could put chains on anybody, where nobody could tell anybody when to start work and when to stop, when to eat and when to sleep. She feared that if she lost that part of her heart, then she might as well go on and die, because that's what had kept her alive ever since she got sold off from Virginia. But how do you keep such a thing burning in your soul, she wondered, when a man treats you as well as Obadiah treated her? When you had friends to talk to and a safe place to live and plenty enough to eat?

Ruby talked to Stella one day about it all near the middle of November, the way she didn't want to go back to her old sense of comfort and ease. Buying and selling people, splitting them up from those they loved was wrong—no way around it—and she wanted to stay mad about it, no matter how settled she became.

"You know how I've been," she said one day as they made apple pies. "Always asking Miss Camellia about roads and such. I did the same with Obadiah for a while. Found out all the ways in and out of Beaufort, which ones lead to Charleston, which to Columbia. Figured I'd need to know all that for when I run off to go to Markus."

"I told you that runnin' talk is foolish," said Stella, laying out a crust. "They just catch you, haul you back, and give you a beatin'. Mark up that pretty skin you got. Hurt you bad."

"I figured how much food I'd need too," continued Ruby, ignoring Stella's warning. "Figured it'd take about three, maybe four days, if it all goes good, to get to Markus. Then we will run off and go for Theo. I even saw a map once, in the telegraph office in Beaufort. Obadiah took me there while he sent a telegraph to a man up in Philadelphia whose wife had died down here. Obadiah was doing the box. That map showed the whole country of these United States, the oceans and everything, pretty map hanging on the wall. I saw our spot on it, down toward the bottom.

I studied it while Obadiah did his business, saw where Virginia was, got it all in my head, how I have to go through North Carolina to get to my boy, Theo."

"Hand me that bowl," said Stella.

"I believe I can do it," Ruby continued as she handed her the bowl and grabbed one for herself. "But now I don't know that I want to do it. Oh, I still want Markus and my boy. But I don't know—I got it fine here; Obadiah treats me nice. And it gets hard to keep Markus and Theo in my head. Sometimes I can hardly remember how they looked. That breaks my heart—the way the face of somebody you love with all your heart can just fade right away."

Stella halted and stared at her. "Now you're talkin' good. You got to let the past go its way. You livin' here now. Nothin' to be done about Markus. Theo either, for that matter. They got their own lives to lead, and the Lord will take care of them just like the Lord took care of you."

Ruby folded the edges of the piecrust. "I feel like I'm letting them down, though," she said sadly. "I believe they're expecting me to come— Theo especially. You know, he saw me in the vision . . . saw me and Markus coming for him."

"You got no way to do that," said Stella. "You got no money; you are a colored and a woman on top of that. How you expect you can get away from here when nobody else can do it? You too weak for all that, too frail."

"Maybe Markus will come for me," Ruby announced hopefully.

"It been over a year," said Stella. "Maybe long enough you need to put that hope in the grave where it belongs."

As they finished up the pies, Ruby let the talk of running drop. But the temptation to give up her dreams to go after Markus and Theo only got stronger. When the end of November drew close, the weather turned nasty, rainy, and cold, with clouds low in the sky. One day Ruby found herself in the parlor of the manse in midafternoon. The fire was burning, but not really enough to make her warm, so she pulled her shawl close to her shoulders. For once nobody else was around. Ruby moved slowly, a feather duster in hand, but not too busy. The sound of a horse thumping in the muddy yard brought her to attention. Who was riding on such a day as this?

She stepped to the window and saw a man in a gray rain slicker on a soggy brown horse. The man rode right up to the steps, his slim body straight in the saddle, his black derby hat low to keep the rain off his face.

Leather Joe appeared out of the slashing rain as the man dismounted and took his horse away toward the barn. The man tipped his hat to Leather Joe, then stepped onto the porch.

Glad for company to break up the dreary day, Ruby moved quickly to the door and opened it. The man tipped his hat once again.

"Greetings," he said. "My name is Sharpton Hillard, and I'm here to talk with Mrs. Marshall Tessier."

"She not here," said Ruby. "She's in Charleston, where she stays most of the time. Master Trenton is with her."

Hillard nodded. "It's my understanding that the overseer is a Mr. York?"

Ruby eyed him suspiciously. "You talk funny."

Hillard's lips twitched slightly. "I'm not from these parts. Hail from Richmond now, and Washington, D.C., the great capital of our nation, before that."

Ruby's eyes lit up. "I started up in Virginia. Richmond."

"A fine city in spite of its Southern leanings."

Ruby looked around, as if expecting someone to slap her. "You best not say that kind of word out loud. Somebody here might take some offense."

Hillard nodded gravely. "Forgive my tongue. Sometimes I let it outrun my judgment. Now, I asked about Mr. York."

"He's down at the house by the biggest of the barns this time of the day, I expect. Keep a desk down there, do his business."

Hillard tipped his hat again. "Thank you for your help," he said, easing down the steps. "When I go through Virginia again, I will think of you."

Ruby watched him go, her curiosity high. Why did a man from so far away want to see Mrs. Tessier? Mr. York? Especially a man who plainly didn't take to all the ways of the South?

Although she knew she shouldn't do it, Ruby couldn't stop herself. As Hillard disappeared around into the rain, she pulled her shawl tighter, slipped off the porch, and hurried after him. Maybe she'd learn something if she listened, she figured . . . something that would make a good story when she talked to Stella that night.

Sitting in a hard chair behind a boxy desk in a two-room building about twenty feet from the barn, Hampton York lifted his face from a ledger as he heard a knock on the door. Rain drummed on the roof, and a fire crackled in a hearth a few feet to the right of the desk. "Yep," yelled York.

The door opened and Hillard entered. "I'm Sharpton Hillard," he said quickly. "May I have five minutes of your time?"

"What's the nature of your business?" asked York, suspicious of any man out in such ill weather.

"May I sit down?" Hillard took off his hat and pointed to a chair on his side of the desk.

York examined Hillard head to toe. Not a lot taller than a hoe handle and just about as thin. His nose looked a little off-center from his brown eyes, as if somebody had stuck it on without reference to the rest of his face. A rain slicker covered him to his waist. Black wool pants ran down to his muddy boots.

York took out a fresh pack of tobacco, pulled off a chew, and offered it to Hillard, but the man refused.

"Look," York said, putting the tobacco in his cheek and laying the pack on his desk, "I'm a busy man. Lots on my mind."

Hillard sat down without permission, put his hat on his knee, and ran his hands through his thick brown hair. York fiddled with his papers, his nerves tight. Hillard seemed a little too sure of himself.

Hillard cleared his throat. "This is a delicate subject. But I've come here concerning the disappearance of a man back in November, a year ago."

York's hands stopped, and his eyes narrowed. His face turned blank, as it did when he played poker and he didn't want anyone to read his emotions. "You think we'll fight a war anytime soon?" he asked, hoping to change the subject. "I hear the fire-eaters in Charleston talkin' about it pretty good, seceding and all."

Hillard shrugged. "If the Southern states try to leave the Union, I expect some bloodshed. A lot counts on who gets elected president next time around. But that's still a long way off."

York spat tobacco juice into his cup. "You come a long way for somethin' that happened a year ago."

Hillard tapped his hat. "I've spent the time going from town to town, asking questions."

"You say your man disappeared? You figurin' he's dead maybe?"

"I'm surprised you'd guess that, but yes, that is my fear."

"But you're not sure about it?"

"No, not at all."

"Where's the last place anybody saw him?"

"We last heard from him in Charleston. He was supposed to go to Savannah, traveling by horseback. He disappeared somewhere between the two towns."

"You sure he got started to Savannah? That he didn't go off somewhere else?"

"Not completely, but why would he go anywhere else?"

"You tell me. What was his business? Any motive for him to head off somewhere you didn't expect?"

Hillard tapped his hat again. "He had a motive, I'll say that."

York chuckled slightly. "They always do."

"We have reasons to think he didn't run off."

York put in a new chew of tobacco. "You keep sayin' 'we.' I take it you work for somebody?"

"That is correct."

"Who?"

"I'd rather keep the name of my employer to myself, least for now."

"Suit yourself." York rolled the tobacco in his jaw until it settled. "I got another question. Why you so bent on findin' this gent? He kin or somethin'?"

Hillard raised an eyebrow, and York watched him with steady eyes, his mouth still.

"He carried five thousand dollars," Hillard finally said. "My employer would like to find that money."

"I reckon he would," said York, leaning back. "That's a sizable sum. That's his motive for runnin' too, I expect. Take that money and go. How you think I can help you?"

Hillard tapped his hat. "I'm not saying you can. But I'm going all over this area. Have already checked in Savannah, Charleston, Beaufort. Now I'm visiting plantation to plantation, farm to farm, anybody and everybody who might have some information about this."

"Makes sense," said York.

"But you can't help me."

"Reckon not."

Hillard pushed back his chair, put on his hat, and stood to leave. "I met the sheriff down in Beaufort," he said suddenly. "Walt is his name, I think. He said I probably should come by here."

"He say why?"

"No, nothing direct. Just that since yours was the biggest in the area, I should make sure to see you. I got the feeling he knew something, maybe, but didn't want to say it to a stranger."

York chewed hard but tried to look calm. "Walt's a good man. Not much of a lawman, though. A little too lazy for it."

"You mind if I ask around your place?" he asked.

York paused. He didn't like the idea of Hillard nosing around The Oak. Not that he worried about Ruby; a darky knew to keep quiet about white folks' affairs. But what if he talked to Josh? For all he knew, Josh had already talked to Walt. "Why don't I do it for you?" he suggested, hoping to get Hillard off the property before Josh met him. "Save you a little time."

Hillard tapped a thigh as he considered the offer. "That's real gracious of you, what with you being such a busy man and all."

"Glad to do it. I'll nose around a mite, see if I hear anythin'. Where should I find you if somethin' turns up?"

"Why don't I come back through here in a few weeks?" said Hillard. "If I don't find any answers by then."

"That'll do good." York stood up. "Come see us again if you need."

Hillard moved toward the door, and York followed him. As Hillard reached the door, he turned quickly back to York. "You ever hear of a man named Wallace Swanson?"

York froze, his face shocked. Hillard waited—a hint of a smirk on his lips. York grunted, then found his voice. "Why you askin'?"

Hillard reached in his pocket, pulled out a tintype, and showed it to York. "You by any chance know this woman?"

York found it hard to control his breathing. His hands tightened into fists before he could stop them. "You askin' a lot of questions for a stranger."

Hillard smiled lightly. "Simple questions, though. You know Swanson or this woman?" He held up the picture again.

York pondered whether to answer. If Hillard asked around, he'd find out from most anybody that he'd once known both Swanson and the woman in the picture. Perhaps Hillard had already done that. Either way, he might as well tell the truth; better to do that than have Hillard catch him in a lie. "I've been in their acquaintance—sure, both of them. But that was a long while back. What they got to do with your missin' man?"

When Hillard smirked again, York decided he didn't like the man. Too high and mighty, as if he knew something nobody else had yet figured out.

"I'll be in touch," said Hillard, opening the door.

"You do that."

Hillard left, and York stepped to the porch. He spat into the mud as he watched the other man splash toward the barn. For a few seconds he thought of following Hillard, of going quietly after him, catching him off guard, and shutting him up for good. A truly bad man would do just that: shoot Hillard in the back and bury his carcass in the muddy ground where nobody would find it. A dead man could do him no harm.

York spat into the rain again. Hillard walked into the barn, then reappeared on his horse a few seconds later and pounded away into the murky day. York pivoted and stalked back to his desk. The notion of killing Hillard rose again. He'd already killed Tarleton. What difference would one more make? But he'd killed Tarleton in a fair fight—no sin in that. Was it different to ambush a man?

York took a big breath, knowing he couldn't do it. Killing a man without warning didn't sit right with him, no matter how much he wanted to keep the money. York spat toward the fireplace. No, he was a lot of things, but he wouldn't sink to bushwhacking. He'd just have to cover his tracks, that's all. Make sure that Hillard never talked to Josh or Ruby. York spat one more time. The tobacco juice sizzled as it hit the fire. Hillard complicated things a lot, he sure did.

Crouched by the door, Ruby had darted away the instant she heard Hillard move his chair. Now, squatting by the side of the house, her heart pounding as hard as horses' hooves, she held her breath and watched Hillard ride off. Although she'd not heard every word, she'd caught enough of the talk between Hillard and Mr. York to know why Hillard had come to The Oak.

After York left the porch, she rushed back to the manse and entered through the back door. Quickly, she checked the room to make sure it was empty. Seeing no one, she eased to a corner and sagged against the wall. The day at the creek came back to her, the day Mr. York and Mr. Cain found the dead man and his money. She'd wondered every now and again what Mr. York had done with all those dollars. Had he given it to Mrs. Tessier or the sheriff in Beaufort? If so, why hadn't he told that to Hillard? Since he didn't, that meant he'd kept it.

Ruby wondered if Mr. York would come remind her to keep her mouth shut. But what if she didn't? What if she threatened to tell Hillard what she knew? That wouldn't sit well with Mr. York, she knew that. But what could he do? Wouldn't the law haul him away for keeping the money? And, if they hauled him away, he couldn't do a thing to harm her.

A small smile crawled to her face. Knowledge brought some power—maybe not a lot, but some. Was it enough to bargain with Mr. York? If he came to her, she might just try to find out.

After Sharpton Hillard left, York sat for a long time, pondering what it all meant. Was Wallace Swanson alive? Had he sent Hillard down here to look for the man at Mossy Bank? If so, he best take real good care how he handled Hillard. But what did Swanson have to do with Mossy Bank?

York considered another question. What did Sheriff Walt know? Had Josh followed through on his threat to go see him? What had Josh told him? Apparently Walt hadn't told Hillard that much. Thank goodness for that. But what should he do about Josh? Have it straight out with him? Or stay quiet and see what turned up?

York closed his eyes. Josh had told him plain out he planned to do some asking around. But why did he have to do that? It caused all kinds of troubles. York's jaw set. His brother seemed weak sometimes, too soft in the conscience. That trait put them at odds from time to time. But how could he get mad at him for that? A man didn't control his conscience, did he?

Pulling out another chew of tobacco, York opened the bottom drawer of his desk, took out the money box, dug out Swanson's picture, and held it up close. After a few seconds he put it back, closed his eyes, and remembered the woman's picture Hillard had shown him. Although he'd only briefly seen the picture, the image had cut fast into his memory. He saw her again, a tall, stately looking woman he knew as Lynette Wheeler—never heard any other name. Was Lynette the same as Ruth? Had she somehow survived the typhus after she sent her last letter? Had she changed her name? Although more mature of face and form in the tintype, she appeared as fetching as ever, her hair parted in the middle and flowing down to her shoulders, her eyebrows full and arching, her lips prim and perfectly shaped.

York's heart pounded as he thought of Lynette. Although he hated her now, he'd once loved her stronger than any man had ever loved a woman. Camellia looked so much like her it hurt.

Slowly, almost reverently, York opened his eyes and let Lynette's face fade from his mind. Then he slid the money box back into the bottom drawer, locked it, and decided he needed to forget Lynette Wheeler. And, no matter what it took, he had to make sure of one thing—that Camellia never saw Hillard's picture of her mother.

Chapter Twenty

December 1859 rolled in even wetter and colder on The Oak. Camellia waited every day for Trenton to come home, but he didn't. She asked her pa over and over what had happened in Charleston that would make Trenton stay away so long, but he just shook his head and said he didn't know.

"I expect it's his mama," he offered. "Or he's workin' with Mr. Gerald and Mr. Luther for financin' to keep The Oak on her feet for another year. Bank business can get complicatious."

Not knowing what else to think, Camellia accepted the explanation and kept waiting. Toward the end of the first week of the month she received a short letter from Trenton, but it offered little to settle her questions.

> *Greetings from Charleston,*
>
> *How wonderful to be able to write you a letter. Glad you can read it.*
>
> *Please forgive my long-delayed return. As you would expect, these are difficult times and much is at stake. I will divulge all when I see you next.*
>
> *With deepest affection,*
>
> *Your loving Trenton*

She took the letter to Stella and asked her what she thought it meant. The aged servant sucked her gums and shook her head. "Ain't for me to say," she offered. "But that boy got somethin' goin' on, that's for sure."

Christmas came, and the plantation shut down so the Negroes could celebrate. But neither Trenton nor Mrs. Tessier returned home, and Camellia truly started to worry. Folks in the South almost always traded the city for their plantations during Christmastime. For Mrs. Tessier and her whole family to stay away meant something strange was surely happening.

She yearned to ask Josh Cain his opinion about it all, but since she knew how he felt about Trenton and she didn't want to hear anything mean about her betrothed, she kept away from Josh. He'd stayed distant from her ever since the big storm anyway, his cold shoulder a barrier she didn't know how to get past.

With nowhere else to turn, she spilled out her concerns to Ruby one day during their reading time. But Ruby didn't offer any good word either. "Stella says you should get shed of him."

"I don't need you repeating Stella's sorry talk," Camellia stated, quite offended that the two would take such a stance. "Neither of you know Trenton. He's a gentleman with me. Never treated me anything but nice."

December ended, then January as well.

February arrived, with still no word from Trenton. With May only three months away, and a wedding promised for that month, Camellia found it hard to sleep at night. Her appetite dropped off almost as much as in the winter after Mr. Tessier's death. Even her books failed to comfort her; she lost the desire to read. Without Trenton, why should she bother? Wanting to please him had motivated her desire to better herself. Without that, what was the use?

She studied some over the fact that she'd set so much of her future toward her plans with Trenton and thought maybe she shouldn't do that quite so much. But what girl wouldn't? A girl lived her whole life preparing for the man she'd marry. Any charms she enjoyed, any gifts or talents she possessed went into the effort to find and enrapture her man. Well, she had enraptured Trenton, or at least she thought she had. Had something happened to upset that? If so, if he'd changed his mind about their marriage, why care about anything anymore?

Toward the end of February a second letter arrived from Trenton, this one even more confusing than the first.

Dearest Camellia,

I know these last months have been as difficult for you as they have for me. Please know of my caring thoughts for you and my desire to see you in the near future and explain all. Things are almost prepared here, and I'm most anxious to return to The Oak. I know you are a woman of great faith and I'm glad for that. Please pray for me. The future is at stake.

With kindest regards,
Trenton Tessier

Although not certain about the exact meaning of the words, Camellia knew she disliked their lack of sentiment, the failure to show any statement of love or affection. How could he act so callously toward her?

Her frustration growing deeper every day, Camellia went to her pa. But, once again, he failed to offer much comfort. "Master Trenton is like most every man I know. Not given to a lot of sweet talk in a letter. He's comin' home soon, like he says. Stay easy. He'll get it all straight when he arrives."

In spite of her pa's advice, Camellia's mood soured even more. For the first time, she began to feel angry at Trenton. How could he leave her so uninformed? Was he planning a wedding without even talking to her? Shouldn't they be making preparations together? True, she didn't know anything about the kind of wedding that Trenton would want. But did that give him the right to set it all up without her? But what if he wasn't making preparations? Wasn't it already too late if he hadn't started getting ready? She didn't know what was worse—the notion that he was preparing a wedding without her or that he might not be planning a wedding at all.

March entered as it often did in the low country—a season of winds and rain that left everything soggy and swirling. In the second week of the month, on a Monday, when the rain actually stopped and the sun broke out shiny and glaring, Camellia slumped out of the cookhouse after finishing breakfast. When she heard horses approaching, she faced the cedar-lined road that led to the manse and saw Trenton's roan stallion pounding homeward, black mane flying freely. For a second, her anger flared. Once again Trenton had acted without telling her! How dare he treat her so poorly? She glanced down at her stained apron and plain dress. Every time he came home he caught her in work clothes, never gave her warning so she could prepare. What kind of man did that to a woman?

Trenton pulled up his horse as he reached the manse and slipped from the saddle with a flourish, his gray cape flaring over his shoulders, his clean black boots hitting the gravel and pivoting like the arriving general of a triumphant army. Leather Joe appeared from the barn and took the horse reins. Trenton patted the old servant on the arm.

Seeing the gentle gesture, Camellia's anger disappeared. Trenton was a kind man, in spite of his faults. If he wanted to arrive unannounced, he had every right to do so. Besides, he thought her beautiful no matter what she wore; he'd told her that time and time again. She started moving toward him, a wide smile on her face.

"Master Trenton be home!" Leather Joe shouted. Several other servants appeared beside Leather Joe, each of them ready to step lively at the command of the master. Ruby and Stella came down the steps of the manse. Camellia tried to appear unhurried. "An anxious woman can scare off a man," Stella often told her, "so don't rush up like a starry-eyed little girl." After all, Camellia was a woman now and possessed of some comeliness—lots of people said it. That ought to give her confidence.

Then why did her heart race so? Why did her face feel like it had a burning brick under the skin? She slowed as much as she could make herself and noted how much older Trenton seemed. He'd sprouted mutton-chops, giving his face a more mature look, more like his father than she'd ever seen him. He pulled off his gloves and tossed them to Ruby, the act of a dashing young master in charge of his surroundings.

Camellia heard hoofbeats again, about thirty yards away, and managed to pull her eyes off Trenton long enough to turn and see two coaches coming up the lane. She recognized the first one—a black carriage pulled by twin chestnut stallions—as Mrs. Tessier's. The other, a dark brown coach with red curtains pulled over its windows, was unknown to her. She wondered who Mrs. Tessier had brought to visit.

Concerned more about Trenton than the two carriages, she pivoted back to him, her smile wide. To her surprise, he stood at attention facing the carriages, his shoulders straight, his eyes focused, every bit the attendant waiting on someone important. The two carriages rushed past Camellia, the horses' hooves clopping across the wet earth. Gravel clattered as the coaches reached the manse and ground to a stop. Camellia glanced again at Trenton and tried to catch his eye but failed. More servants poured out of the house and barns, all eyes on their master and his guests. The carriage drivers jumped down, stepped swiftly to the coach doors, and opened them.

Camellia stopped and waited respectfully. As Mrs. Tessier climbed down from the first carriage, Trenton took her hand and led her to the top of the manse steps. She paused there and faced the second carriage. Trenton dropped his mother's hand and moved to the brown carriage, taking off his hat as he reached the door. The gesture disturbed Camellia; her throat squeezed shut, and she found it hard to breathe. A hat appeared through the door of the carriage—a plumed, forest green hat covering a woman's head. Auburn hair styled in ringlets spilled from beneath the hat and reached the woman's shoulders. She wore a tan coat with a long cape and a dress the color of the hat. The woman reached for Trenton's hand; he gently took it and helped her down. Her boots crunched lightly on the gravel. Trenton tucked her hand under his elbow and turned to his mother.

Stella stepped to Camellia's side as Trenton led the woman up the steps of the manse. Mrs. Tessier took the woman's hand and led her to the edge of the porch. Trenton trailed them, then moved to the woman's side. Mrs. Tessier faced the gathered crowd—at least fifteen people now, house servants included. Everybody held their breath.

"We are home," Mrs. Tessier pronounced grandly. "My son and I."

Trenton touched his mother's elbow, and she paused. He waved his hand over the crowd. "I'm pleased to return," he proclaimed, his voice deeper than Camellia remembered, "to the home of my birth; to the home where I plan to sire my own children."

Stella put a hand on Camellia's back to steady her. Trenton extended a hand toward the woman with auburn hair. Camellia studied her face—the porcelain skin, the high cheekbones, the full red lips. Tears stung Camellia's eyes.

"Steady child," whispered Stella.

"This is Miss Eva Rouchard," Trenton announced. "Of the Columbia, South Carolina, Rouchard family. She is to become my wife in April of next year. She is a woman of great quality, and I know you will come to love her as she will come to love all of you. I ask you to make her welcome at The Oak."

Camellia's knees buckled. If not for Stella's strong grip holding her up, she would surely have fallen to the ground.

Hampton York got the news within the hour as he rode up to the barn from the rice fields. Leather Joe filled him in as he dismounted.

"Master Trenton come home," said Leather Joe, taking the horse's reins. "Him and Mrs. Tessier."

Just then Josh rode up and climbed from his horse. "The Tessiers are home," York told Josh. "Wish they'd give us a little warnin'."

"They brung another woman too," continued Leather Joe. "She be a red-headed lady from Columbia."

York waved him off and adjusted his hat. He didn't care to hear the servant's gossip about some Charleston socialite who had come home to keep company with Mrs. Tessier for a few days before she took off again.

"Master Trenton say he gone marry this woman. Eva Rouchard is her name."

"What's that?" York faced Leather Joe.

Leather Joe dropped his eyes. York took him by the shoulder. "Speak it again," he demanded.

"It be troublesome news, that's for sho," said Leather Joe. "But Master Trenton tell us all plain as day that he gone marry this Miss Rouchard come next April."

York dropped Leather Joe's arm and stalked toward the manse. Josh caught up with him in five steps, grabbed his elbow, and twisted him around. "There's nothing you can do! He's made the announcement!"

York faced Josh, his face set with rage. "He made an announcement to Camellia too! You know that! I'll not abide this! He thinks he can treat Camellia this way, come traipsin' in here all high and mighty and throw her aside like she's nothin' more than some tart he's dallied with from a brothel. Tellin' her nothin' in advance, givin' none of us any warnin'. He's got no right!"

"Rights have nothing to do with it, and you know it. It's the way of our world. A man like Trenton can do just about anything he wants."

"But he loves Camellia; I know that, she knows that. It's his mother. She's forcin' this marriage."

Josh let go of York's arm. "Maybe he does love her, who can say? But if he loved her the right way, he'd never let his mother force him to this. If he can't or won't stand up to her, then maybe it's best for Camellia; you ever think of that? A man who's so weak he can't follow his heart and do what he knows is right is not much of a man, not one I'd want any daughter of mine taking up with."

"It don't matter!" growled York. "He broke his vow to Camellia. I can't let him get off scot-free doin' that. I got to go to him, talk some sense into him!" He stepped toward the manse again, but Josh grabbed him once more and held him back. York jerked his arm away, his face a dark scowl. But this time he didn't move.

"What are you going to say?" asked Josh. "What demand can you make? Trenton's got the power here; you know that! All you'll do is make him mad, more set in his decision. You'll set Mrs. Tessier off too, and she's not a woman you can trifle with."

"So what advice you givin'?" York asked. "You tellin' me to just sit by and let this go?"

Josh toed the ground with his boot. "I don't claim to have any answers to this. But I have to tell you the truth as I see it. I don't see Trenton Tessier as worthy of Camellia. She's too fine and pure for him. He's got some good qualities, sure. He's smart and determined and willing to labor for what he wants. I admire all that. But he's mean in his bones too, looking out for what's best for him, not anybody else. He's not sensitive to the ways of a woman; like the way he didn't warn Camellia about this marriage announcement, didn't break off their engagement first. What kind of man would do that? Not a good one, that's for sure. Not honorable either." He gazed straight into York's eyes. "You're blessed that Trenton has done this. So is Camellia."

York shook his head. "You don't know what you're talkin' about."

"I think I do."

"Try tellin' that to Camellia."

"You need to go to her," Josh urged. "Help her through this."

"Somebody else can go to Camellia. I'm not good at talkin' with her, never have been. I plan to go to Trenton," said York.

"You know you can't do that. You'll be stepping out of your place."

York took off his hat and stared into it, as if looking for the answer to the world's deepest mystery. Although still angry, he knew Josh was right. He held no power here, no real choices. "This ruins it all. Every hope we ever had."

"Go to Camellia," said Josh gently. "She needs your care."

"You go to her. She sets a high store by you, and you're better with words than me."

Josh toed the ground again with his boot. "I . . . can't go to her. Wouldn't be fair."

York grunted. "What do you mean?"

Josh looked up then, displaying a sadness deeper than any York had ever seen in him, even when Anna died, even when . . . "I . . . I got feelings for her."

York froze.

"I know it's wrong," Josh continued. "It's not been long enough since Anna's passing, and Camellia's got no such inclinations toward me. Even if she did, I know you would never allow it. I'm not good enough for her either—no man is. But I've come to think highly of her, and if I went to her, I couldn't do it with a clear conscience. I don't want her and Master Trenton to marry, plain as that. Anything I said would be stained by my feelings."

York almost chuckled but, seeing the lost look on Josh's face, held it in. "She thinks you're her uncle."

"I've not told her anything different."

"You think I should?"

"I told you that some time ago, before Anna died, before I . . ."

York set his hat back on. "I can't do it. Can't tell her about her mama. Don't want to hurt her, especially now."

Josh nodded. "I know. And I agree completely. With the pain that Trenton has now inflicted, I don't want her to find out her mama wasn't exactly the chaste woman she believes her to have been."

York put a hand on Josh's shoulder. "I don't know what to say about your thoughts toward Camellia. You know you are my brother, my only true friend. But I got to tell you honestly: I want more for Camellia . . . no offense or anythin'."

Josh smiled, but only briefly. "None taken."

York started walking slowly toward the manse, and Josh followed him.

"I need to tell you something else," Josh said, "while we're talking plainly. I traveled to Beaufort back in the fall. Talked to Sheriff Walt."

York tried to stay calm. "That's no surprise. What did you tell him?"

"I didn't tell him about the money, or even that you were there. Just that I had come on a dying man and he'd spoken the name 'Ruth.'"

"You didn't mention me at all?"

"No."

York stopped and faced him, confusion in his stare.

"I didn't see the need," explained Josh. "If the money belongs to Ruth, I want to get it to her. No reason to get the law mixed up with that. No reason to tell about you either. You didn't shoot anybody."

York pulled out a chew of tobacco and stuck it in his jaw. "You beat all."

Josh grunted. "I should have told Walt a long time ago."

"Maybe." York tried to figure how this connected to Hillard. "You ask Walt to keep this to heart?"

"Yes, thought that wise."

"He seem okay with that?"

"You know Walt. He's a quiet man most of the time."

York chewed his tobacco.

"One more thing," said Josh. "Walt mentioned some man asking for somebody that matched your description. Said a man named Tarleton had come to see him."

"Tarleton?" York could feel his face going white.

"Yes, said he was looking for somebody he'd had a fracas with."

York cleared his throat. "You figure he's the man who shot me at Mossy Bank?"

"That's my guess. Best you keep your eyes open, in case he shows back up around here."

"Reckon I should." York started walking again. "Seems things get more mixed up every day. More reason than ever for me and you to stick together. You're still the best friend I ever had."

"I'm the *only* friend you ever had," said Josh quickly, grinning. "Nobody else can put up with your meanness."

York smiled slightly. "Maybe so. But I got to say again I agree with you that you're not good enough for Camellia. She's made for better than either of us."

"I know," replied Josh. "That's why I'll not tell her of my leanings for her."

"You're a wise man. No reason to confuse her or cause hurt to yourself."

"You still want to talk to Master Trenton?"

York spat. "I don't reckon so, least not yet. Next April is a long time away. A lot can happen in that time."

"You're not giving up your hopes for him and Camellia, are you?"

"A man ought never give up his hopes."

"Guess not."

York patted Josh on the back as they reached the manse. Right now he needed to hold his peace with Trenton Tessier. As he'd said himself, April was a long way off. Who knew what kinds of things could happen between now and then?

Part Three

The camellia is a wondrous flower that seems
always to bloom when winter is bleakest and
the joys of spring lie yet so far away.

Chapter Twenty-One

In the first couple of months that passed after Trenton brought Eva Rouchard to The Oak, it seemed to Camellia that somebody had shoved a pitchfork right through her heart. She ached so much with grief that her whole body felt like one large stab wound. Although she knew the sun still rose in the morning, the spring still brought a greening to the earth, and the dogwoods and azaleas still bloomed as the spring passed and summer entered, she paid no mind to any of it. Trenton's betrayal shut off her sight for anything beautiful, anything pleasurable. So far as she could see, God had pulled a heavy cloud over her head and closed out everything bright the instant Eva Rouchard stepped down from her carriage.

A faithful friend as always, Stella tried to talk her out of her sadness. But Camellia refused to hear anything.

"I'm ruined," Camellia said when Stella told her she was better off without Trenton Tessier, since he obviously was the kind of man who married for money. "Shamed and humiliated. Everybody knew about his promise to marry me."

"That be right," Stella claimed, frowning. "He made the promise, then broke it. Everybody see that as shame on *him*, not you."

"I'm not good enough for him," argued Camellia. "Everybody sees that too. Just look at Eva Rouchard. She's got all the qualities I'm lacking—all the polish and station."

"I don't rightly know her," Stella said. "Maybe she be a good woman, maybe not. But she ain't no better than you, and everybody who knows you knows that. You as fine a young lady as anybody in these parts has seen for a long spell. Now that Master Trenton is out of the way, menfolks from all over the county will soon come to your door, askin' for you to sit with them. They been doin' that already, but your pa kept them away."

Camellia refused to listen. She had no interest in other men. And, no matter what Stella or Ruby or anybody else said, she knew the truth when she saw it. Trenton had chosen Eva Rouchard because of her refinement, her education, her beauty—all the things that Camellia York didn't possess. Who could blame him for that? Any man in his right mind would make the same decision. Who knew what she would've done if the situation had come up the opposite way? What if the Lord had birthed her into a family like Trenton's? What if Trenton spoke poorly, dressed roughly, carried no good breeding in his blood? Would she have married him?

Of course, it did surprise her that Trenton never sought her out to explain his decision. At first that made her angry. Even though she didn't deserve him and understood that, he might at least have told her that to her face or sent her a letter explaining his change of heart. A gentleman would've given her that courtesy, wouldn't he? Trenton owed her that; didn't he?

The days stretched out longer and longer as spring ended and summer arrived. Trenton, his mother, and Eva Rouchard left The Oak in late May, their carriages and his horse heading out for cooler climes like an army on parade.

Camellia watched them go, her anger stoked even higher at his callous manners. The anger didn't last that long, though. Why should it? So what if Trenton hadn't told her in advance? So what if he didn't talk to her a single time in his weeks on The Oak? Why should a man of his station explain anything to one of the hired help? No one had ever made any public announcement of their marriage, so no formal breach of it had occurred. If she wanted to get mad, she ought to direct it at herself, at her stupidity for thinking that somebody of her origins could ever, should ever aim so high as to take a man like Trenton as a husband. To even imagine such a thing showed her ignorance, her complete silliness. Fairy tales didn't come true, no matter what the books said. Her self-confidence ebbed as her anger slowed.

The long days of summer bore down. The breezes from the ocean felt heated, as if somebody had run them through a big fireplace before spewing them out. Camellia labored side by side with Ruby and Stella but didn't talk much. Stella kept trying to make her feel better, kept trying to get her to talk like normal again, but she always refused. Why should she waste energy on useless words?

Every now and again Camellia saw Josh Cain coming or going from the fields, and she considered walking over to his house and sitting on his porch and pouring out her troubles. He'd listen in a way nobody else would, she knew that. Yet she hesitated for a couple of reasons. First, he stayed gone more than usual these days, sometimes for several days at a time to locations he never mentioned. He always asked Stella to look after his children when he took off, and this made Camellia sad. It gave her a second reason for not going to him. He'd made it plain she shouldn't come to his place anymore. Although she never knew exactly why, she suspected it came from his dislike for Trenton. If she went to Josh, he'd tell her she was better off without Trenton; that he obviously didn't love her or he wouldn't have dropped her.

That, more than anything, kept Camellia from going to Josh. She couldn't stand to hear him say that Trenton didn't love her. She couldn't face that, at least not now. Trenton did love her, no matter what had happened. No, he wouldn't marry her, but she understood that. He deserved better, and The Oak needed more. But that didn't mean he didn't love her. A man could love one and marry another; he'd told her that a long time ago. Yes, she'd lost him as a husband, but to give up the notion that he still loved her hurt too much, made her humiliation more than she could bear. So she stayed away from Josh Cain.

Camellia stayed alone as much as possible that summer; gave up her reading too. Before she knew it, her language had slipped back into the way she had talked before Ruby had taught her a single word. But she didn't care. Why should she? Without Trenton, she had no cause to make herself fancier, more sophisticated. Truth was, the notion of doing so had obviously been silly from the beginning. A woman of her station shouldn't try to fix up and put on airs that didn't really belong to her. Easier to put a lacy bonnet on a pig than for somebody with no fineness in her blood to act as if she had quality.

With every other pleasure gone, Camellia found her only solace at the ocean. When she finished her labors in the afternoons, she often slipped away from The Oak and made her way to the beach. Her head uncovered, she usually took a spot on the ocean side of a favorite sand dune, her small body perched there like a nesting bird. From the dune she liked to watch the waves as the sun dropped, her eyes searching the horizon, as if hoping to see a ship arrive, a ship that she could board and sail away on forever.

Sea gulls darted overhead as she sat, and the wind played with her hair. Often she dug her bare toes into the soft sand and imagined what it would be like to wear shoes every day, to have more than one pair of shoes. She tried to pray as she sat there, her hands clasped in her lap, her heart yearning for some word, some sign, some reason to leave her grief and start over with her life. At times she wondered if she should leave The Oak; if she should take a wagon down to Beaufort and catch a ship to some distant city like Charleston or even farther, perhaps to the North—that strange exotic land where no plantations existed and people wore heavy coats from October until May. Is that what the Lord wanted for her? Should she leave this place and seek her happiness somewhere else? But what would she do there? How would she live? What about Chester and Johnny and her pa? Who'd care for them? They still needed her, depended on her.

She shook her head as she thought of her pa. She longed to talk to him, but he'd seemed angry with her since Trenton broke off their engagement, as if he blamed her for Trenton's decision. In one way she agreed with him. Her lack of quality caused Trenton to leave her for Miss Rouchard. But couldn't her pa at least have offered her a touch of sympathy? She needed that, hoped for it. But it never came. He stayed gone even more than usual these days, always in the fields until Saturday night, then in Beaufort until late Sunday. He took trips too, as often as he could get away, sometimes to Charleston, sometimes to Savannah or Columbia, wherever he could find a horse race, cockfight, or card game, some excitement to put blood in his face, some chance to wager the few dollars he earned.

Camellia's eyes watered. In spite of his failings, she loved her pa and worried about him. Since Trenton's announcement about Eva Rouchard, he'd become even more distant, like a man bent on nothing but the present, a man with no use for the future, no desire to see it come. He drank as much as he could when the workday ended and took wagers on anything he could find.

She knew he'd put all his hopes in her marriage to Trenton. But should it ruin his life when it failed to happen? He made eleven hundred dollars a year as overseer. Not enough to make a man wealthy, but enough to give him a comfortable life. Most men didn't make that much. Why couldn't he settle down and take care of his family the way he should? Why couldn't he give Chester and Johnny the kind of example they needed to see in a father?

Camellia knew the answer as soon as she asked the questions. Her pa wanted more, had always wanted more, had always seen himself as capable of improving the station God had given him at his birth. He tried to make it seem that he wanted more for his children, but Camellia saw through that, understood that he wanted it even more desperately for himself. It was as if he believed that money and status could give him happiness. But could it? She didn't know. What would happen to her pa now that she'd crushed his hopes?

The days slipped away. August rolled in. Finding herself more and more drawn to the waves, Camellia went to the ocean almost every day. One day, about midmonth, she found herself once more sitting on her favorite dune, with the sea gulls darting in and out. She picked up sand and let it drift through her fingers. The tide ebbed and flowed. Tears ran down her face.

Lifting her eyes, Camellia stared into the ocean. Whitecaps topped the green water. The waves pushed in and sucked out, pushed in and sucked out. The roar of the waves seemed to speak to her, to whisper to her soul. The whisper told her to come to the water, to let it soothe her aching heart, her battered spirit. Where would the waves take her if she walked into them? If she stepped into the foam and headed out to sea and never turned back? Where would her body go? Where would they find her?

More tears dropped onto the sand. She knew such notions didn't please the Lord, but she couldn't help it. How could she go on living, now that Trenton had chosen to marry another?

She picked up another handful of sand and let it slide through her fingers. Life slid away just as easily, she decided. Like sand running out one day at a time until nothing was left . . . nothing, nothing. She wondered about life after dying: Did a person go to live forever with Jesus or not? What if that person didn't deserve Jesus? What if the person had tried to live right but failed at the end? What if the person walked into the ocean and never turned back? If the ocean pulled them away and down, down to the dark under the waves?

The ocean rolled in and rolled out. Again she heard it calling her name. "Camellia, Camellia . . ." The sound seemed so real, closer and closer.

"Camellia! Camellia!"

She glanced up at the sound.

"Camellia!" The ocean beckoned to her, tugged at her.

"Camellia!"

She stood and turned toward the sound and saw Johnny running toward her, his wavy hair mussed by the wind. She held her hand over her brow to block the sun's glare and hurried toward him. He looked small and frightened. He reached her, out of breath, and pointed toward home.

"Chester is bad sick," he panted. "Pa sent me for you."

"I knew he was ill earlier today. Is he worse?"

Johnny nodded. "He's real sick. Pa says it might be the malaria."

York was right: Malaria did take hold on The Oak. Camellia threw herself into nursing Chester, her mind numb to any personal danger. So what if she took sick? So what if the disease hooked into her flesh and killed her? She had no reason to go on living; she might as well die of malaria as take her own life in the ocean.

Having seen a less severe outbreak of the disease the year she turned twelve, Camellia knew what to expect. Fever that would come and go; chills that would make the teeth chatter and the body shake; headaches so bad the sick screamed out in pain; heavy sweats that soaked the sheets and blankets; nausea and vomiting until only dry heaves were left.

Given time and good doses of quinine, most of the sick would recover. Yes, they'd get the fever again from time to time, but never again quite as intense as the first attack. But those who didn't recover progressed to even worse symptoms and a bloody dry cough; pain all over the body, but most severe in the back, head, and eyes. Seizures afflicted them too—convulsions that caused them to bite their tongues and fall out of the bed. Dark water poured from their body fluids. Only a miracle could save them if they got the dark water, and most were not saved.

Camellia spent most of her waking hours inside, sponging off Chester with wet rags; carrying out and washing the bedclothes that his sweaty body made filthy by the middle of every day; pouring thin soup down his throat when she could get him to swallow. Three days after Chester took ill, Johnny went to bed too. One day after that her pa fell over from fever and, in spite of all his efforts, couldn't get back up. Only Camellia remained healthy. Her back ached from a lack of sleep, and her frail frame dropped every ounce of excess weight because she found no time to eat. But she never took the fever. *God's irony*, she thought.

Stella dropped in on her every now and again, her arms heavy with cooked food and clean rags. She asked Camellia if she could stay and aid her, but Camellia always shook her head.

"You got enough to handle," she said in a quiet moment near the end of the second week of the outbreak on one of Stella's visits. "The sickness is all over The Oak."

Stella put the food on the table. "This come hard on us this time. Reckon Master Trenton's choice of Miss Rouchard mispleased the Lord. This be his anger spilt out."

Camellia pushed her hair back. "Trenton is not here to speak a defense. And I know it's no time for me to arm-wrestle with you either. But I don't see your reasoning. If this sickness be the Lord's vengeance on Trenton, why did the Lord hit everybody else with it? He's not even here.

For all we know, Trenton's folks are as well as they can be."

"The rich folks don't stay in the lowlands in fever season," agreed Stella. "The swampy air be bad. Gives the sickness."

"Exactly. So how is all this the Lord's punishment?"

Stella grunted and spit snuff into a cup. "The Lord be makin' it hard on The Oak, the thing Master Trenton loves the most, even more than he loved you."

"Then why is the Lord making it hard on me?" asked Camellia, waving toward the bedroom where her family lay sick. "I had nothing to do with Trenton's choice, but I got three near to death back there. What have I done to cause the Lord to strike down the ones closest to me?"

"You be askin' mighty deep questions. I got no answers for them."

Seeing no conclusion, Camellia sighed. She took a loaf of bread out of Stella's basket. "Who else is sick? Anybody getting better?"

Stella arranged the rest of the food on the table. "About one in ten or so on our place, it seems. "Darkies, the white folks. Strange, you know? When the sickness comes, it don't worry none whether it take out after white or black. They be all the same. Color don't keep you well nor make you sick. Seems the Lord made us equal that way."

Camellia nodded. "I hear they got it down in Beaufort too, all over the county. The doctor took ill the first couple of days, so nobody's able to do much about it."

"Ruby shows no signs of the illness. Obadiah neither. That be a good thing—lots of work for him right now. Reckon no matter what happens, somebody can make a livin' off buildin' boxes for the dead."

"I wonder if the malaria hit Charleston?" Camellia whispered. "Columbia?"

"Columbia be inland so far it's not likely. Charleston, who knows? That be where Master Trenton is?"

Camellia shrugged. "I can't say where he is. He and I don't talk anymore. He could be somewhere in the middle of the ocean as far as I know."

Stella dropped the clean rags by the food. "Time you put that man out your head. He's long gone from you. You the best for it, though I know you got no eyes to see that today."

A low moan sounded from the bedroom where the three men lay.

Camellia tilted her head at the sound. "I best go to them, and you best get back to the manse."

"I come again when I can," said Stella.

"Thank you."

Stella headed to the door.

"How's Josh Cain?" Camellia asked, suddenly realizing she'd not seen him since her pa fell sick.

"I ain't seen him for a couple of days," Stella said. "I know his girl Lucy took ill; don't know about the other two."

"But he's well?"

Stella stared at the floor. "I ain't sure. Last time I knocked on his door, he hollered for me to keep on goin'. Said he didn't want me to come in. Feared I'd take the sickness from his house."

Camellia's heart pounded as she thought of Lucy, ill only a short distance away. How strange that in spite of their closeness she hadn't talked to her much in the last few months. She hung her head, ashamed that she'd stayed away from the children because Josh didn't want her around anymore. No matter that he didn't like her, she shouldn't have let him keep her from the children. Now Lucy lay on a bed dripping with sweat and aching with pain, and Camellia hadn't even gone to offer her aid. What kind of friend was she? Not much of one, that's what kind. She wondered about Beth and Butler. If anything happened to one of those children, she'd never forgive herself.

"You going by Mr. Cain's place from here?" she asked Stella.

"I'll go knock at least; offer my care."

"Tell him . . . tell him . . . " She hesitated, not sure what to say. "Tell him I'll come as soon as I can. Tell him of my prayers for him and his children."

"He'll appreciate those prayers. Mr. Cain puts much stock in the Lord."

"I know."

Stella left the room, and Camellia trudged back to her pa and brothers. As she opened the door to their bedroom, she wiped her brow and made a vow that if she lived through this, she would go to see Josh Cain's children as soon as possible to make sure they all knew of her love for them.

Chester died six days later, just as the sun came up. Weary beyond words, Camellia left him and stepped outside for the first time in days, her heart as low as the bottom of the ocean. She hadn't eaten—best she could remember—in at least three days, and the blue calico dress she'd worn for over a week hung on her as loose as a sack. Her hair lay weary on her head, and her eyes held no color she could recognize as she looked into the tin dipper that she used to draw water.

Standing on the front porch, she glanced up at the clear sky and wondered how the sun could shine so brightly in the face of all that had happened. It just didn't seem right. She stretched and wiped her eyes, her feelings crushed. Although her pa and Johnny lay on their pallets in the back room, their fevers finally broken, their bodies weak but taking food again, she'd lost Chester, his thin body finally yielding to the illness. To her relief, she saw Ruby and Obadiah headed her way in Obadiah's wagon.

"I need you," she called to them.

"We feared you might," shouted Ruby.

A few minutes later Obadiah picked Chester up and carried him out, his big black hands gently cradling Chester to his chest.

"You nursed him all you could," Ruby said as she stood with Camellia, watching Obadiah carry Chester away.

"I know," said Camellia, "but I don't feel like it. I feel . . . feel like I should've saved him somehow. Found a way to make him better."

"You take on too much," soothed Ruby. "You are not a miracle worker, no matter how much you try."

Camellia followed Obadiah to his wagon, kissed Chester one last time on the cheek. Although a head taller than her, Chester looked so small. Death did that, she realized. Shrunk a person down in size. Obadiah loaded him into the back of the wagon as Ruby took Camellia's hands.

"I'm not one to give advice," said Ruby, "but I feel like I got to say something."

Camellia squeezed her hands.

"You have moped about a long time," Ruby began. "All the spring and summer. But now you got to get back to living. All this"—she waved over

Camellia's house—"and all this"—she waved over The Oak. "You can't let any of it wreck what's inside you. You know what I'm saying."

Camellia stared at her, confusion on her face.

"Look," said Ruby, "I have learned my lesson. Life will bring lots of hurt our way, like storms that come in the summer. You can't tell when they come nor how much damage they'll do before they go. But they come, and there's nothing we can do to stop them. All we can do is figure out how we'll act when they hit us. Will we let them knock us over for good? Ruin everything so we can't ever fix it again? Or will we rise up again after the storm passes? Put ourselves back to the toil to make something of life? Will we let the storm blow away what's inside us—the steady stuff, the stuff of the heart, the soul? That's the matter you got to settle with yourself. You say you're a Christian girl, but where's your trust in the Lord now? Where's your faith gone? Is the Lord truly with you or not? Or has the Lord gone off and left you all by your lonesome? Is the Lord as undependable as Master Trenton? Is that what you think? What you got in your head? Well, if you got no more trust in the Lord than to give up and go on moping forever, then it seems to me that's not much trust."

Camellia stayed quiet, listening, so Ruby continued. "Yes, it's true that you had a hard year. Master Trenton showed his true stripes and left you standing with your hands empty. That's a hard knock. Now this sickness killed your brother. That's surely a rough grief, and you will need some time to get past it. But you're not dead yet. You're still a beautiful woman, got friends who love you strong, and you're smarter than most. What do you plan to do with all that? What will you let the Lord do with it? That's the questions you've got to face."

She patted Camellia's hands, then dropped them as Obadiah stepped back and climbed on his wagon seat.

"Think on it," Ruby said. "See what you come up with."

Camellia nodded as Ruby joined Obadiah and they rode off. She stepped back inside her house, and, for a long time, just stood and looked out the window, her mind swirling. What right did Ruby have to give her such a speech? A darky—especially with no trust in the Lord—should not take such liberties as to offer advice to a white girl, even one as low in station as she. And yet . . . Ruby's words hit her straight in the heart.

Perhaps she had let Trenton's choice shape her more than it should. Maybe she had forgotten the Lord too quickly. Was her faith so weak as to let a couple of hard knocks push her right off it? If so, it wasn't much faith to begin with.

Tears began to fall. Although she was not yet twenty, it seemed like the weight of at least a hundred years lay on her shoulders. She stared out over the field toward Josh Cain's house and saw him walk onto his porch. He held his hat in his hand, his head down. Quickly, she ran to the porch and called out to him, "You okay?"

He glanced toward her, sadness in his posture. Her own shoulders sagged. "What is it?" she yelled. "Who?"

Josh stumbled down the steps, and she ran into the field to meet him. They met halfway between their houses, then stopped.

"Lucy," he sobbed. "She's gone to be with her mama."

"No!" cried Camellia. "Not Lucy!"

Josh stared at the sky. "She passed last night. Obadiah came for her this morning before the sun rose."

"I lost Chester this morning," she sobbed.

"I'm so sorry," he said.

"I should have come to Lucy, tried to help," said Camellia.

"Nothing anybody could have done," sobbed Josh. "Nothing to do." He opened his arms, and Camellia fell into them, the weight of the last few months pushing her into his strong embrace. For a long time the two of them stood under the heat of the early fall sun, tears running down their faces. Camellia grieved over the loss of Trenton, over the deaths of Chester and Lucy. But mostly she grieved that she hadn't really talked to Josh's children in months, that she'd let her disagreements with him over Trenton keep her away from loving friends.

"I've been such a fool," she sobbed. "In so many ways, over so many things."

"Shush," Josh soothed. "You've had your hands full."

"That's not it. I stopped seeing the children, talking to them, reading to them."

"Blame me for that," he said. "I told you we didn't need you anymore. Put you off from coming."

She gazed up into his tear-filled eyes. "We've both been fools. But you were right about Trenton; I have to admit that now."

"That's past," he claimed. "No use saying who was right or wrong. What's important now is trying to move ahead. Doing what we can to go on living. You told me that after Anna's passing, and it's true. You need to remember it now."

Camellia brushed back her hair. "We have a lot of grieving to do before that."

"Life is hard," he agreed. "But the Lord's grace is sufficient."

"You really believe that?" she asked seriously.

"I've found it true in the past. I suppose I'll test it again now."

She nodded. "I guess I will too."

Chapter Twenty-Two

After the malaria sated its appetite and left the county, Hampton York slowly regained his strength and returned to his labors. By harvesttime he seemed at full speed again, almost as if he thought he could replace all the work of the Negroes who had died with his own two hands. He cursed and ranted at the servants from the first threat of day to way past sundown, his voice growing hoarse from barking orders; his lips cracked from spitting tobacco; his face, hands, and neck baked by the sun.

In spite of the fact that Trenton planned to marry the wealthy Eva Rouchard and therefore solve their need for cash, York still believed that the survival of The Oak rested on his shoulders. The account ledger told him the hard truth every time he looked at it—The Oak had fallen deeper into debt. If the upcoming crop didn't gather in full and healthy, the Bank of Charleston might foreclose on the place before any nuptials could take place. Who knew what would happen then? The Rouchard family might call off the wedding, and somebody else might purchase The Oak and push him right off the place.

Driven by his fears, York became angrier and more desperate. Although Trenton showed up in late September to labor beside him, he didn't want anything to do with him. The young master's betrayal reminded him again of something he'd always known—you couldn't depend on anybody. If a man planned on making anything from life, he had to take matters into his own hands, wrestle fate to fit his dreams.

For reasons he couldn't explain—even to himself—York found it most unbearable to be around Camellia. No matter how much he tried to think otherwise, he saw her as a failure. He'd depended on her, but she, like everybody else, had let him down. If she'd only treated Trenton nicer, given him more of what he wanted, if she'd only . . . York sought to push away the hard feelings, but the notion hung on him like the smell of a wet dog. York had worked hard all his life, looking for his one big chance to get what he'd always wanted out of life. Now it seemed that Camellia had ruined his only remaining chance. And he just couldn't help but blame her. So he stayed away from home more and more, not going home most nights until she and Johnny had finished supper.

He missed Chester, of course. What pa wouldn't miss his son, especially such a fine boy as Chester? But what could he do? While he lay on his bed, too sick to do anything, the boy's life had been in Camellia's hands. And she'd not managed to nurse the boy back to health. York knew the malaria had taken many folks—forty-four Negroes and two whites to be exact—but, once again, he couldn't help but feel that Camellia had failed there too.

With each day that passed, York grew more sullen, his anger spilling over even to Josh. He didn't like it that after they finished the harvest, Josh started disappearing some again, often for days at a time. Of course he knew what Josh was doing. But why should he bother about Mossy Bank? It was so long ago. True, Josh wasn't telling anybody about the money, but who knew when his questions would stir something up? What would happen then? Somebody would come for the money, and that would cause a lot of trouble. It would also ruin his one last hope for a better life—even if it was purchased with someone else's money. *Maybe*, York thought, *he needed to talk with Josh and settle this once and for all.*

That year the harvest turned out better, and York got a good price for it when he took it to Charleston for sale. Yet, it still wasn't as good as he'd hoped, and his mood didn't brighten much. The Oak had fallen too far behind for one good crop to make up the difference. Plus the malaria had killed a lot of darkies, and it would cost a lot to replace them.

Unsure what else to do, York toiled in the fields until sundown every day, and although exhausted, he stopped by the small house near the barn to make his notes. At the end of every month, he pocketed as much money as he thought he deserved. Whereas before he had excused his thievery by pointing to Camellia's upcoming marriage to Trenton, now he passed it off by figuring that since Trenton had betrayed him, he owed him

the dollars. Either way, he kept taking the money, in spite of the fact that
The Oak couldn't really afford it anymore.

Mrs. Tessier and her family came home at Christmas. The place shut down
for three days of celebration, but York didn't do much by way of enjoy-
ment. In four months Master Trenton would wed Eva Rouchard, and all
York's dreams would end. The only thing that gave York any comfort was
the fact that by the time Christmas had ended and Mrs. Tessier had taken
everybody except Trenton back to Charleston, his cash total—the Mossy
Bank money, his gambling winnings in the last couple of years, and his
skimming from the plantation—totaled almost nine thousand dollars.

If circumstances had allowed him to spend the money, York might
have felt rich. Next to the Tessiers, he figured he had as much cash as anybody in the county, and if it came down to paper dollars, he might actually have more. Yet his fear wouldn't let him enjoy it. Trenton could
discover his thievery; Hillard could show back up; Josh could stir up a hor-
net's nest; or Ruby could spill his secret. How could a man feel any comfort with so many things out of his control? How could a man make use of
his wealth if somebody could take it from him at any minute? York's fears
grew stronger.

As the year 1861 dawned, York slowly reached a point where he knew he
either had to *do* something, or just give up and stop trying. Sooner or later
somebody would find out about his money. When they did, he'd have no
explanation for it, and they'd take it away. The time had come to do
something bold, something that would either make him or break him.
Chester's death had pushed him to that conclusion. Life didn't last long;
you might be shoved out of it and into the dark of death at any minute.
Best act when you got the chance. But what should he do—and how?

He thought some about all of the war talk that had become more serious since Abe Lincoln's election in the fall and South Carolina's vote just
before Christmas to pull out of the Union. Would Lincoln truly go to war
to keep the states in place if others followed South Carolina? How would

a war affect York and The Oak if it happened? Not given to politics, he figured a war didn't matter much to him either way. If one started, it'd surely end real fast. If anything, it'd push up rice prices in a hurry. Men fighting a war had to eat, and rice kept and shipped just fine. Maybe a war would be a good thing. Yet he also knew the Yankees would try to stop rice shipments if a war came. They'd try to bottle up the ports like Charleston and Savannah, maybe Beaufort too. Of course, they might not manage that. But if they did . . .

Unable to do anything either way, York put his worries about a war aside and went back to thinking about his situation and how to make the most of it. Near the middle of January, an idea came to him as he sat by the fire after Camellia and Johnny had gone to bed. It made so much sense once he thought of it that he wondered why it hadn't occurred to him earlier. It gave him the one chance he'd always wanted, the moment to truly test his notion that a man had to depend on his own strength, his own abilities to make what he wanted of life. One way or the other, if he had the guts, this possibility provided him that opportunity: the horse races in Charleston, the first week of February.

The fire crackled as he weighed the idea. The wealthiest men from all over the South—Savannah, Raleigh, Macon, Columbia, and Charleston—gathered every February for four days of festivities. Money drenched the air. Women in colorful dresses under wide parasols with darkies beside them to meet their every need dazzled one another and their menfolk with their high-pitched laughter and genteel ways. Horses neighed and stomped in their stables. The smell of mint juleps and straight scotch whiskey rode whatever breeze the weather brought in the height of the day. Short, skinny jockeys, mostly black, wore silk blouses, shiny pants, black boots, and hats that matched the blouses. Races took place every day at the Washington Course near Charleston on the Saturday, Sunday, and Monday before the first Wednesday of February. Three races of four miles each on the first day; three races of three-mile heats on the second day; and three races of two-mile heats on the third.

York had attended the races many times, often with Mr. Tessier, and he loved them even more than a game of cards. He loved the smell of the stables, the lather on a horse's neck after a run, the thud of hooves rounding a corner as a finish line beckoned. Maybe most of all, York loved the wagering that always accompanied the races. From poorest to richest, every man with a nickel in his pocket laid down a bet or two. The wagering brought the blood to the sport, raised the heat of the excitement, and guaranteed that before the day ended, somebody would end up in a fight over disputed odds or an unpaid wager.

Like all other men, York lost more wagers than he won. Yet, also like all other men, York felt certain that the next race he wagered on would surely come home a winner. After all, he knew horses better than most. He could tell by the lift or drop of a head how a horse felt that day; could see in a horse's eyes whether or not he liked to run; could rub his hands over a horse's flank and measure the power of his haunches. A man with as much horse knowledge could surely pick out a few winners if he really set his mind to it, he figured. Well, this year, he decided, he wanted to set his mind to it. He really did.

Four days before the races were to begin York packed up his finest clothes, told Camellia he'd return in about a week, and called Josh into his office near the barn. His beard trimmed, York pointed Josh to the chair across from the desk.

"You're headed to the races, I guess," said Josh.

"Yep, thought I would. Take some rest for a few days."

"You deserve it. Worked hard all year."

"Both of us did."

Josh opened his mouth to speak further, but York stopped him. "No use sayin' it. We both had some rough months, heavy grief. Talkin' about it won't make it any better."

Josh rubbed his brow. "I'm not sure I agree with you. I feel like we need a long talk about a lot of things."

"What kind of things?"

"I've been thinking," Josh said slowly. "I feel like I need to make some changes. I'm not sure I'm as happy here as I once was."

"Who is?" York threw in.

"We got things between us," said Josh plainly. "Things that give me hard feelings sometimes."

"We're men. That kind of thing happens."

Josh nodded.

York considered telling Josh to stop talking with folks about Mossy Bank, but he knew it wasn't the right time. Maybe when he returned from the races. "I'll come back by the end of the week. We'll get things straight then."

He stood and put out his hand to shake Josh's. When Josh looked confused at the gesture, York quickly pulled his hand away. Suddenly, York knew something really *had* changed between them, and it was all his doing. Against Josh's wishes York had kept money belonging to a dead man. Then he'd stolen from The Oak. Finally, he'd killed a man to keep his secret. A little at a time he'd become a bad man, a man so bent on self-ish ends that he did whatever it took to accomplish what he wanted, including blaming Camellia for what couldn't be her fault—his son's death and Trenton being a snake of a man.

York studied the matter for a second. Was this the way a man turned evil? Not in one big step, like going over a cliff, but a choice at a time—a little matter here, another minor choice there, each decision going further and further from the right way, each one leading him more and more down a path away from goodness?

"See you in a few days," he said, hoping his voice sounded normal, not as mean as he felt.

Josh nodded and York walked out, climbed on his horse, and headed north. The sun rose to his right, and he settled his hat tightly on his head. Every dollar he owned lay in the saddlebags under his legs. With some luck and guts, who knew what he could win with it?

Her arms folded, Ruby stood quietly on the front porch of the manse and watched Hampton York ride out. She shivered in the light breeze of the clear day. Although months had passed since the fever hit The Oak and it had missed her entirely, she still suffered from a newfound fear in her bones. Her skin felt thin, as if somebody had brushed all the heaviness from it, and her eyes lay low in their sockets, wary and unsteady. Worst of all, she'd had bad dreams almost every night since the malaria had come—dreams that brought a vision of the Death Man with them, the Death Man with yellow teeth, fingers like pointy sticks, and a voice that cackled worse than any crow. The Death Man wanted her, she knew it for sure. He didn't care that she was still a young woman; he had set his red eyes on her head and planned on getting her soon.

As York disappeared in the cedars, Ruby felt tears falling on her skin. Guilt stuck like a wad of dirty cloth in her throat. She'd gotten settled on The Oak; had let her care for Obadiah cause her to forget her pledge to Markus and Theo. She'd curled up in her comfort like a turtle on a rock and taken her ease. What kind of mama would do such a thing?

She tried to calm her mind. The Death Man had showed her what she thought she'd put aside, maybe forever. If she ever wanted to see Theo and Markus again, she had to go *now*, because nobody ever knew when the Death Man might come and snatch them right out of life, right out of any chance to wait, right out of any chance to do something in some day yet to come. Truth was, nobody ever knew if tomorrow would ever get here. Lots of times tomorrow got stabbed in the heart and died before the sun ever rose on it. The country fever that had killed so many darkies had reminded her: If you want to do something, you best do it today.

Ruby remembered her dreams: Theo crying and calling for her, his little hands reaching out as if he saw her a few steps off but couldn't reach her. He seemed pale and sickly in the dreams: His hair was gone, and it looked like he was losing his black, like somebody had rubbed the stain from his skin. She would reach for him in the dreams, begin to feel the warmth in his pale fingers . . . and then the Death Man would step between them, his yellow teeth bare and sharp, his cackling laugh a reminder that he saw and knew and wouldn't let her touch her boy. She always woke up then, her breath gasping, her body wet with sweat, her heart pounding like a drum. She knew the meaning of the dreams. The Death Man wanted somebody—maybe her, maybe Theo, maybe the both of them.

The breeze whipped her skirt at the ankles, and she shivered again. The time had come. The dreams told her so. She had to leave now or forever give up her notions of doing it. Yes, she had come to care for Obadiah in ways she never expected, but he wasn't Markus. Even if he was, she still had Theo; he still called her; he still had his vision. How could she, so long as she drew breath, give up her boy?

Her hands jumpy, Ruby left the porch and hustled to her bedroom. All around her the plantation seemed still, as if the weight of the dead still lay on it, causing everything to move in slow motion. What better time to take to the woods than now, while everybody remained cold from winter? With Master Trenton off with his fancy woman, making ready for his marriage, Mr. York gone away for some gambling, and Obadiah at his place for a few days, it gave her the perfect chance. If she did this just right, it might take a day or so before anybody but Stella would even know she'd gone.

In her room Ruby stopped and thought about what she'd need. Her old plans—buried in her head for longer than she wanted to admit—rose again. Although she had no idea exactly how long it'd take her to walk the seventy or so miles to Robertson's place, she figured she could do it in four or five days—even with a lot of stops to hide and wait—so she'd need enough food for at least that long. She'd take a heavy shawl for the cold and rain and a hatchet in case she had to go through the woods and cut through heavy brush. She'd need her shoes too. Couldn't go barefooted that far in February. She remembered the map she'd scratched out after seeing the one at the telegraph office and pulled it out from under her mattress. After brushing away the dust, she studied the rough markings and found them just as she remembered: pretty simple for anybody with a good head on her shoulders.

She'd leave after dark, go west on the main road that led from the ocean up toward Columbia. She'd keep her ears open for horses, wagons, anybody else on the road. If somebody approached, she'd run into the woods, hide until they passed, then go forward. She'd hide in the woods during the day.

According to what Camellia had told her, the road would fork about a day's walk inland, and she'd need to take the north path. Another day's walk and she'd have to head due east. Robertson's place stood south and east of Columbia, not far after she crossed a small river called the Richland. Once across the river, she'd have to look for a road that curved off to the left. An old chimney stood right at the curve; she knew that because Camellia had asked her pa one day how to get to Robertson's plantation, and not knowing why she'd asked, he'd told her. If all went well, Ruby would find it.

Ruby slipped the map into her pocket, pulled the blanket off her bed, and gathered up her two dresses, her three bandannas, her shawl, and the brush she used for her hair. She started to grab the stack of ribbons that Obadiah had given her, then hesitated. How would she explain them to Markus? She grabbed one of the ribbons, the brightest red one, and tied it to the handle of her brush—one to remember Obadiah, but no more.

After tying the bundle in the blanket, she hid it under her mattress, left the room, and hurried to the small building where Mr. York kept his office. A couple of minutes later she reached the back door and stepped inside as if going in to clean the room. After closing the door, she waited for her eyes to adjust to the dim light, then walked straight to Mr. York's desk, opened a drawer, and took out a piece of paper and a writing pen. Her fingers scratched out a simple note.

Mr. York,

I am gone. I expect you know where. You ought to look in the wrong direction. You know why. You give me what I want; I do the same for you. Secrets ought to stay secrets. I expect you agree.

Ruby

She folded the note, put it in her pocket, and hurriedly left the room. The cookhouse was her next destination. To her relief, nobody was there. She quickly pulled several cuts of bread, a large piece of cured ham, and a sack of pecans from the cabinet, and wrapped it all up in a burlap sack. Next she took two canteens from a shelf by the window, filled them with water, and hid them in the sack with the food.

Her excitement rising, she headed to the door. Stella almost ran into her as she darted out. Her eyes bugged wide. Stella glanced at the sack of food, then up at her.

"You mighty hungry it looks like."

Ruby nodded, her eyes down.

Stella grabbed her elbow. "You up to somethin', I can see it."

Ruby glared at her. "You got it right!" she growled. "I am doing what I said all along I was going to do. I'm leaving this place. Figured now was the time."

"I thought you had settled with Obadiah. Ain't he treatin' you right?"

"He treats me fine, but I got a baby in Virginia, a husband at Robertson's. I made them a vow, and I aim to keep it."

Stella squeezed her elbow. "You gone get yourself whipped is what you gone do. Runners don't never get away, you know that. They set the dogs on you."

"I'll be long gone by the time they get the dogs out. Unless you tell, nobody will miss me for a long time."

"They'll know where you goin'. Mr. York knows where they took Markus."

"Maybe, but it will take him a while to get home and head there. If I go fast, I can get Markus and be gone before anybody ever reaches us."

Stella let go of her elbow. "You don't even know if Markus is still there," she warned. "Maybe they sold him off."

"If I don't find him, I'll keep on going. North next."

"You crazy, that's for sure. A woman right in the head would stay with Obadiah. He's a good man."

"I know, but I *got* to do this. The malaria killed a lot of folks. So what if I stayed alive this time? You get that close to the Death Man, it teaches you a lot about living. How you got to grab hold of it for all its worth while you got it."

"I lived a long time, so I reckon I know that's for true. I seed lots of folks alive and kickin' one day, deader than a hammer the next. Never know what day the Lord's gone call a body home."

"I got to go," said Ruby. "Got to see my man again, my baby."

"I ain't gone stop you," Stella said. "You do what you got to do."

Ruby hugged Stella, then stepped back. "Take this," she said, pulling the note from her pocket. "Give it to Mr. York when he comes back. Give it to him when he's alone."

Stella took the note. "What's it say?"

"It's a reminder, you know, what I told you about Mossy Bank Creek. With me gone, he got nobody who can tell what happened back there."

"Nobody but Mr. Cain, his brother." Stella put the note in her pocket.

Ruby nodded, then thought of Sharpton Hillard. "One more thing. This man came by here. Name of Hillard. He asked about Mossy Bank."

Stella's eyes widened. "What'd he want?"

"Asking Mr. York what he knew, didn't know. Mentioned a name, a Wallace Swanson. Wanted to see if Mr. York knew him."

Stella's mouth stopped gumming. "What'd he say about him?" she whispered.

"Not much. Just wanted to know if Mr. York knew him or not."

"How'd he answer?"

"Said he knew him, so what?"

"That all?"

"Yes, who is Swanson?"

A tiny grin appeared on Stella's face. "He be a ghost. Done raise up from his grave."

"Now you're the one talking crazy."

"I reckon I am."

"Well, I'm leaving at dark," Ruby insisted. "Tell Camellia she's a good woman and to stay patient. The right man will surely show up someday."

"I'll say that to her."

"And tell Obadiah . . . " Ruby choked as she thought of him, how well he had treated her. "Tell him he is a good-hearted man and that I'm not running 'cause he's not. Tell him if I didn't already have a baby, a man I loved, I couldn't find no better man than him."

"I'll tell him your words."

Ruby hugged Stella once more, her body shaking with grief at all she was leaving.

"Go on now, child," said Stella, stepping back. "You got things to make ready."

Wiping her eyes, Ruby walked away. Although it cut her heart, she had to do it. Theo and Markus were waiting on her.

Chapter Twenty-Three

Hampton York spent Thursday and Friday in Charleston at the stables near the racetrack just a short way out of town. He had a simple mission those days. Study every horse that would run in the two-mile heats on Monday over the loamy track that sat at the center of the racing arena. Size the animals up and down, see which ones seemed frisky, which ones tired, which ones hurt, which ones healthy.

The stables housed over sixty horses, but only eleven planned to run in the two-mile races. The others would take their places in either the four- or three-milers. All the races would end in front of a grandstand that seated close to a thousand people.

York walked and chewed tobacco as he made his way in and around the stables. The horses stomped and kicked and neighed all around him. The smell of manure, feed, straw, and liniment filled his nostrils. Although focused on the eleven who would run the race he knew the most about, he inspected all the horses, admiring their long legs, deep chests, muscled haunches. At times he wondered how they could do it— run three heats of races, the longest the four-milers, the shortest the twos. Only thirty minutes separated the heats, and only the strongest and most conditioned horses survived as champions.

Although a man with a sharp eye for a good horse, York didn't put himself up as an expert on any of the races but the two-milers. The others were too long, too unpredictable for his taste. Even in the two-milers, the things that could go wrong were too many to list. But in the longer races, that list just lengthened.

York passed scores of other men as he went about his business. Some of them worked with the horses, their hands filled with buckets and brushes, their boots covered with mud and hay and manure. Others wore fine clothes, tall stovepipe hats, and cravats on their necks and studied the horses as closely as he. These were the wagering men, the wealthy who lived for the sport of the race, a time when they would test their sense of a good horse against every other man with enough courage to drop down some dollars.

Although careful, York chatted with some of the men as the days passed, flattered them in the effort to get them to talk about the various horses, their strengths and weaknesses, how many races they had won, how many they'd lost. Nobody looked at him as if his questions were out of place because a lot of other men were doing the same thing. Men that planned on making big bets always did this. What smart man wouldn't?

When he could, York found out who owned a horse and carefully watched the owner. Did he look clean or smell of the drink? Did he talk a lot with a lot of bragging, or did he keep his quiet, act almost humble? He'd learned a long time ago that the appearance and habits of a horse owner often gave some clues to the condition of the horse.

As the sun dropped on Friday, York left the stables and headed back to the inn he'd taken just outside of Charleston. He arrived back at his hotel room just after dark, took off his coat and the money belt where he kept his cash, and lay down for a long nap. When he awoke he washed up, slipped on his coat and the money belt, and headed back downstairs. On the street, he checked the moon and figured it close to ten o'clock. Hungry, he headed to an inn near the water where he knew he could get a good bite of tasty food.

He ate quickly and quietly, his appetite fueled by nervousness. All around him he heard bits and pieces of the talking, half of it about the races, the other half about politics. Now that six other states had joined South Carolina in pulling out of the Union, would war start soon? Most of the men figured it would.

Although he listened to the talk, York didn't care much either way, so long as folks left him alone. If the Yankees tried to take on the South, the war wouldn't last long—everybody knew that. So without adding to the conversation he finished his food, left the inn, and headed to a saloon just up the street. Twenty men crowded the saloon, and a thick cloud of smoke rose in the air as he walked in and headed to the bar. York searched each face in the crowd but saw nobody he knew. Out of nowhere a sense of loneliness hit him, a realization that, other than Josh Cain, he had nobody he really thought of as a friend. York ordered a scotch, put in a new chew of tobacco, and turned his back to the crowd.

Camellia and Johnny loved him, he figured, but not because he much deserved it. He knew he'd not done well as a father; that he'd spent far too little time with them. But what could a man do without a good woman? Didn't he have to do his labor first; manage his family second? Most men had wives to look after their family, to take care of hearth and home.

He ordered another shot of whiskey.

Lynette.

He saw her in his mind, her hair the same rich brown as Camellia's, her eyes as blue, her skin the same color. Lynette had grown up in a Columbia church orphanage, her parents the victims of a fire that had burned down their house when she was only eight. He'd met her in June of 1842, in a place a lot like this, except it had been in Savannah, where he lived at the time, making his living for the most part at a poker table. She'd come to the bar with a card player named Wallace Swanson, a man who'd seen her obvious beauty and taken up with her soon after she left the orphanage the year she turned sixteen.

Although Swanson had a good eye for women, his card playing didn't amount to much. When York won most of his money that night, Lynette had quickly shifted her affections to him and left Swanson broke of pocket and heart when the bar closed.

Now York swallowed the last of his drink and ordered another one. A poker game in the corner of the room broke up. Five men sat down and started another one. York rubbed his head and tried to put Lynette out of his mind but failed.

What a woman! It hadn't taken him long to fall in love with her. How could he resist? Although rough in manner and speech, Lynette carried her wondrous body like a goddess, and her face melted a man's knees. When she smiled, and she always smiled when she wanted something, the whole room lit up. Nobody could resist that smile.

He didn't find out she had a two-year-old daughter until two weeks after they met. "A woman friend takes care of her most of the time," Lynette had explained. "I give her money; she keeps my baby."

"Whose is it?" he'd asked bluntly.

Lynette didn't bat an eye. "Swanson's."

"You two married?"

"No."

"Why not?"

"He never asked."

York faced the bar crowd again. Lynette's straightforward manner had surprised but not shocked him. He wasn't a saint either.

"I'm with you now," she'd said as she smiled and snuggled her head onto his shoulder. "You won't throw me and my baby out because of my wanton ways, will you?"

York breathed deeply. Her smell made him drunk. She needed him! No woman had ever moved him so. "No. I won't throw you out."

Within the month they were married. A few weeks later he found out she had another child on the way—and it would be too soon for this baby to have been his. Anger boiled in him for a few days, but then Lynette favored him with a kiss that made him feel like a king, and his anger disappeared.

Later he asked her why she'd chosen him over Swanson, who was the father of her two children. Lynette had shrugged. "I'm almost twenty. Had another baby on the way and needed somebody to take care of us. Swanson loved me but didn't do well when it came to making a living. You seemed better at it."

The words had cut York as she spoke them. She'd not even pretended to love him. Of course that explained what happened later. But he'd not worried about that then. She'd love him someday, he figured. He'd treat her so well she'd come to that.

York took another drink and shook his head against the memory. Women were crazy. Men were crazier. He watched the poker game for a while, put in a fresh chew. A fight broke out in the corner of the bar but didn't last long. A man staggered past with a trickle of blood running down his chin. York remembered more of his early days with Lynette.

His gambling luck had turned pretty sour within months after he met her, and he had started losing at the card table. By the time she'd given birth to her second baby, a boy she named Chester, he'd pretty much run out of money and knew he had to do something different. With a wife and two children to tend, he needed steadier work than the luck of the draw, the fall of a card.

"I know a man I've gambled some with," he told her one night. "He owns one of the biggest rice plantations in the South; he told me once he needed a man like me to help him manage things. I know how to do that. There were rice plantations all over where I grew up near Georgetown. Man said if I wanted, he'd set me up to run his place."

"I don't see myself prospering too well in the middle of nowhere," Lynette argued. "Not my idea of a fine living."

"You think this is better?" He had waved his hands over the room he rented above a general store. "No spot of our own, no place for the children to grow up, no promise of a wage tomorrow."

She had tossed her head, and he knew he hadn't convinced her. But when she didn't argue, he kept talking. "The man's name is Marshall Tessier," he said, hoping she'd like it that he had a plan to care for her and the children. "He's got an old man as overseer, won't last much longer. If I do good, he'll give me the job when the old man passes. I can make over a thousand a year with Tessier. We'll do fine there, you'll see. You take care of the kids, I do the work. It's better than depending on a card game."

Although not happy, she'd finally relented, and they had moved to The Oak soon after and settled into their new life. Over a year passed. Lynette seemed to accept her situation; said little against it; did the things a man expected of a woman; bore him a son, Johnny.

York hit the bottle one more time. He didn't want to remember all this. But how could he forget? If Lynette had only stayed with him, he might have turned out a better man, a man of good character. But she hadn't. In April of 1844, when Camellia was almost four, York had awakened on a clear day and found Lynette gone without a word or a trace. Just like that. Vanished like a cloud off the ocean. He looked for her, of course, but knew in his bones what had happened. She'd run off, how or where he never knew.

Had she started scheming the day he told her of the job on The Oak?

Had she gone back to the woman who had kept Camellia for her? Had she sent that woman out to search for Swanson and tell him that Lynette wanted him back? That's all he could figure, especially since seeing the picture Hillard had shown him. She and Swanson had gotten together again. But how did either of them connect to Mossy Bank?

York grimaced. He wondered how long Lynette and Swanson had lived together before she'd written him the letter about her having typhus. Were they happy? Had she loved Swanson all along? Although he knew he shouldn't, he felt almost glad the typhus had killed her. Why shouldn't he? The woman had betrayed him, hurt him deeply. She deserved to die young. Why should she get any pleasure from life after what she did?

He remembered the picture, taken before she got sick. She sure looked pretty, he had to admit that. He chugged his scotch and remembered again how alone he was. How he had nobody to depend on but himself. Trenton Tessier had broken off marriage to his daughter. Chester lay under the dirt. And now it looked like his half brother, Josh Cain, was no longer on his side. From where York stood, life had handed him a sorry deal. True, he had some money. But what good did it do if he couldn't spend it? Should he just take it and ride out and never come back? But what about Camellia and Johnny? He couldn't just leave them. He'd sunk pretty low, but not that far yet. Then what? What could he do?

He finished his drink. He'd decided there was only one thing he could do: try to turn the money in his saddlebags into a whole lot more. Take one big gamble and see how much he could make. Either hit it big . . . or lose it all. Hit it big enough to truly make a difference, or let it go and stop torturing his head with visions of something grand.

He paid the bartender, then moved to the poker game and asked if he could sit in. The men nodded. He took a spot at the table and pulled out a few dollars. For the next couple of hours he stayed in the game, kept his winnings and losses about even, and drank some more. A couple of the men left the game, and after a few more hands, York followed them. He hadn't come to Charleston to play poker, not this time anyway. Not enough money in a poker game to make much difference to him one way or the other.

Stretching, he stepped outside. The cool night air sobered him some.

He checked the moon, figured it close to midnight. He spat and walked fast toward the stable where he'd put up his horse. A couple of men passed him, but he paid them no attention. At the stable, he saddled up, checked the equipment and supplies in his saddlebags, and led the horse outside. Once on the street he mounted and rode west. It didn't take long to reach the stables at the racetrack. About a hundred yards away he dismounted and tied his horse to a tree in the woods.

After getting his saddlebags, he left his horse and slipped through the woods toward the back of the stables. To his relief he heard nobody talking. As he had expected, everybody had taken to their beds. A dog barked in the distance but not close enough to raise any alarm.

Outside the back of a barn York peered around. He knew the horse he planned to back tomorrow, a tall black animal named Blacksmith with a white band around his left forelock. One of the three favorites, the animal looked fit and ready. Early odds said he would run at about three to one.

A touch of shame hit York as he sat down, but he quickly pushed it away. So what if he wanted a little edge in tomorrow's race? Who even knew if what he planned would make any difference? He couldn't take care of every horse in the race, just the one. If the horse he planned to bet on didn't run well or if another he hadn't seen as a real rival suddenly took off like nobody expected, it wouldn't even matter. The way he saw it, he wasn't fixing the race, just tilting it a little. And it wouldn't even hurt the horse he hoped to slow down, just maybe throw him off a little. He took a deep breath and held steady for close to an hour. The dog stopped barking. The moon dipped behind some high clouds.

York thought of Lynette again. After she'd left him, he found life dull and useless. He tried to do good by the children but had no heart for it. They belonged to Lynette, not him, why should he care for them? Stella had done most of their raising; he realized that now and felt a touch guilty for it. But what could he have done? The war with Mexico came not long after Lynette left, and he and Josh rode out to fight it. Mr. Tessier had let him go.

"A man who won't fight for his country ain't much of a man," Tessier had said. "You've done well for me since you came. Come back when the war's over. I'll keep your job for you." And that's just what the plantation owner had done. The two years away had given York time to bury Lynette far down in his mind. But now her memory had risen again.

— Checking the moon again, York figured it had to be around three in the morning. He decided he'd waited long enough. His heart smooth and slow, he stood and slipped through the shadows, around to the front of the barn, and opened the door. After easing inside and closing the door, he faced the horses. They stood motionless, their faces toward him, their backs to the rear of the stalls.

York rushed to the tallest horse among the eleven that would run the two-milers, a chestnut with wide haunches and clear eyes. Bob's Bullet, they called him—undefeated in his last five races. He'd go off as the favorite tomorrow.

"He's hands-down the best horse in the stable," one man had told him earlier. "If he's at the top of his form, he'll run them all into the ground."

Grabbing a tall bucket, York filled it with oats. He took ten apples and a bag of sugar from his saddlebags, cut up the apples with his pocketknife, and threw them on top of the oats. The sugar followed the apples. He produced two bottles of straight whiskey from his coat pocket and poured them into the bucket. Then he poured water from a nearby water trough over the mixture.

As the smell of the mash rose in the air, York stepped to the tall chestnut and hooked the bucket over his head so he could easily get at it. The horse sniffed it, then stuck his snout down and took a bite. York waited until the chestnut had eaten everything in the bucket, then filled it again with the same ingredients. Again the chestnut ate the mixture. York filled it one more time. This time the horse finished about half the bucket, snorted, lifted his head, and licked his lips. York again offered him the bucket, but the chestnut shook his head in refusal. York removed the bucket and stepped back; he'd done all he could.

Hurrying now, he quietly washed out the bucket, refilled it with water, and offered it to the horse. The chestnut drank from the water, then lifted his head.

Satisfied, York made sure the bucket was clean of any leftover evidence, then set it down and slipped out of the barn. Back at his own horse, York led the animal back into the woods, mounted, and headed back to

Charleston. Only one thing left to do—put the nine thousand dollars on the stout black and hope for the best. One way or the other, tomorrow would change his life. At three to one odds, he'd either go home a rich man . . . or never go home at all.

To Ruby's surprise, her escape to Robertson's plantation brought no more trouble than a long walk in the woods. As planned, she moved only at night and slept during the day. Her nights moved swiftly, and she made better time than she expected. Although she ran up on some farm dogs every now and again, they didn't bark for long, and she eased past them with little disturbance.

All through the first night she thought she heard horses pounding after her—heavy hooves racing to run her down and trample her into the earth. Her body shook with fear and chill, and she wondered why she'd ever thought she could get away with this. Then, however, when the first night ended and the sun came up, she knew that most of her fear had come from her own head. No horses rumbled after her, no dogs panted over her scent.

Her food lasted her the whole three days it took to reach Robertson's. When her canteens ran out, she filled them in creeks that she passed. The only trouble she faced came when she tore her skirt in some brambles the second morning as she looked for a resting place and when she twisted an ankle on a rock as she climbed down a creek bank to get water.

She reached the outskirts of Robertson's plantation near the morning of the fourth day. She knew so because she saw a sign with the plantation name painted in black hanging on a white fence as she walked down the road. The sign turned her to the left, and she followed the road until the sun came up. Then, her heart pounding, she crept off the road, lay up for the morning under a thicket of heavy brush, and studied what to do next. Now that she'd reached the plantation, how would she find Markus? How would she know what house he slept in?

Unable to come up with any other answer, she slipped out of the thicket about midday and headed through the woods in the direction the sign had pointed. To her relief, she found a creek about an hour after she started. Sneaking up the creek bed, she came to a bend and stopped. Crouching low, she rounded the bend and saw the plantation several hundred yards away. Tall pines and more heavy brush surrounded the cleared cotton fields.

Relieved, Ruby moved through the brush until she found a spot that gave her a good view of the fields and barns that lay about a hundred yards past the trees. From there, she kept her eyes steady. The darky houses—fifteen of them from what she counted—sat a good three hundred yards beyond the barn and behind the plantation manse. She spotted Markus about an hour later, his broad body strolling toward the barn. Her heart jumped as she saw him, and a wide smile creased her face. She'd done it! As simple as that! Markus looked as fine as ever, strong and healthy. He ducked into the barn and stayed there a long time. But then he came out, his arms full of tools—a shovel, a rake, and a hoe. He carried them to a shed nearby and stepped behind it, out of sight.

The day moved slowly, but Ruby stayed patient. She'd waited a year and a half for this; she could wait a few more hours. As dusk fell, she saw Markus again, this time by the well, his thick shoulders pulling water up in buckets and pouring it into a trough. A few minutes later field hands from all over the plantation started walking to the trough to wash up.

Ruby knew the routine. The servants would eat now. If the plantation was big enough—and this one certainly was—they'd get bread and stew or beans, or even some meat from a main cookhouse. They'd carry the food to their quarters and add anything they had there stored from the gardens the masters let them keep.

As the servants washed and the sun started to drop, Ruby decided she had to move closer or lose sight of Markus. Leaving her belongings, she eased from the forest and crawled across the field, keeping her eyes on the water trough. The Negroes started moving toward a larger building, no doubt the cookhouse, a little nearer the plantation manse. They carried tin plates and cups. Ruby reached the back of a small shed and squatted by the chimney. Markus stood less than thirty yards away, his back to her. She heard his low voice and wanted to jump out of the shadows and run to him but knew she didn't dare. A thing like that would start a ruckus, and she didn't want that. She smelled corn bread and potatoes, and her mouth watered. It didn't take the field hands long to get their food and scatter to their quarters.

Ruby tried to figure where Markus lived. Only on rare occasions did a darky family get their own house. Most shared quarters with a number of others: single folks sleeping on rows of pallets, couples getting small rooms off to the sides. Tattered blankets hanging on nails served as the only doors in the houses. Even married couples found privacy hard to come by. A fireplace in the largest room served as the only heat. A body took relief in the outdoors, usually from a common outhouse near some woods.

Markus waited until near the end of the line to get his supper. Ruby kept her eyes on him as he disappeared into the cookhouse. A couple of minutes later he walked back out, his plate waist high. Her heart rose as she realized Robertson's folks had treated him well. He headed toward a house about forty feet away, climbed the two-step stoop, and disappeared inside.

Ruby eased back to the ground and prepared to wait some more. Now that she knew where Markus lived, she'd stay there until the middle of the night and everybody had fallen asleep. Then she'd go in, shake Markus awake, lead him back outside, and off they'd go. Just like that. No more white folks telling them what to do. No more waiting to see her man or boy. No more "Master this and Master that."

She smiled at the notion of running free. They'd make it North; she knew it for certain. Hadn't her plan worked just fine so far? She and Markus would find somebody to give them a job. She'd work hard and so would Markus. With war talk all around, who knew? Maybe the Yankees would show the Southern folks a thing or two, and all people could go free. She knew not to wish too highly, but today why not? She'd made it to Markus; anything was possible. She and Markus would take a little house, put curtains on the windows. She'd keep it as neat as anything. When people asked her name, she'd add one . . . maybe Hudson. She'd always liked the sound of that: Ruby Hudson. A last name of her own and one she had decided upon herself.

With her nerves taut, the first part of the night passed slowly for

Ruby. But gradually it did pass. The birds stopped chirping, the frogs ceased croaking. Dew settled on the ground and bushes, and a chill fell on Ruby's head. She wished she'd brought her shawl from the woods. The moon climbed high, crossed the middle of the sky, and started to drop. Ruby stirred. The time had come.

She rose silently and stretched, her eyes on the door of Markus's house. A second later she slipped across the ground to his front stoop. There she paused and listened. Nobody stirred. She smiled, feeling blessed. Although she didn't put such store in God as Stella did, she sure felt something—or was it someone?—watching her tonight.

She eased to the door and opened it without a sound. In the glow of a small lantern sitting on the mantel over the fireplace, she counted six men on pallets in the front room. She studied their faces but didn't see Markus. She drew in her breath. Had she gotten the house mixed up? She peered at the men again, but Markus wasn't there. She figured he must be in a side room.

She held her breath and stepped to the wall by the lantern. A man rolled over and she froze, but then he snored and fell back asleep. Ruby lifted the lantern off the mantel and eased out and down the hallway. She came to a blanket hanging over a doorway and pulled it back and looked inside. Markus lay on a pallet on his side, facing her direction. She gasped and almost dropped the lantern. A woman lay beside him, her head sticking out of the blanket that covered them both.

Ruby steadied the lantern and tried to breathe. Who was this woman? She held the lantern higher and studied the woman's face. Not pretty, at least not to her. Was she . . . no, she couldn't even ask it. It didn't make sense. Markus had sworn to love her forever, to come to her when he could. But how could she deny what she saw? He had a woman resting by him in the dead of night. A man didn't do that unless he had taken up with the woman, chosen her as his.

Tears threatened Ruby's eyes, but she wiped them away and ground her teeth. What could she do now? Keep on running? Leave here and go North all alone? But wait! Just because Markus had a woman didn't mean he didn't still love her; that he wouldn't still leave with her. After all, she had taken Obadiah in marriage but left him. How could she leave now, without talking to Markus, offering him the choice? She had to do it, couldn't live with herself if she didn't.

Her mind set, Ruby put the lantern on the floor and squatted by Markus. Then, as gently as she could, she touched his shoulder and shook it. His eyes popped open, and he jumped slightly, but not so much as to disturb the woman beside him. Ruby pressed a hand over his mouth. His eyes widened as if haunted. She held up a hand, telling him to keep quiet. When he nodded and his eyes warmed, she knew he recognized her.

She pointed to the door. "Outside," she whispered. He nodded and got up. A minute later they exited the house and eased down the front steps. Ruby led Markus into the woods. Panting, she sat down by a tree and, taking his hand, pulled him down beside her. He embraced her there, the moon beaming overhead. Stars twinkled. Ruby felt like heaven had come down. She kissed Markus and he responded.

"We been apart a long time," she said softly when the kiss ended.

Markus held her close, rubbing her shoulders and back. "You scared the fool out of me. Thought you was a dream. But I reckon not."

"No, I'm real enough." She kissed him again, then leaned back into his arms once more. They stayed that way for several minutes, the quiet of the night making it seem like old times back before they were sold. Ruby relaxed, knowing that nothing could ever go wrong again. Markus would run with her. They'd make it North. Life would turn out wonderful. Maybe there was a God after all.

"I guess you done run," said Markus, finally breaking the silence.

"You mighty smart to figure that out," she teased. "Of course I ran."

"How did you find me?"

Ruby smiled. "I heard them call the name Robertson when they took you. I've been picking up information since then. Got some friends at The Oak—where I went—people who helped me. Even saw a map. Took me some time, but I got it done."

"You goin' North, I reckon."

"Suppose I am." She eyed the moon, figuring they had less than four hours before daylight. She raised up, her hands clutched around her knees. "Be sunup soon. If we're going, best we get started."

She felt him stiffen, saw him turn eyes toward the ground. She took his chin, pulled it up to look at her.

"I don't reckon I can go with you," he said.

Ruby's breath caught.

"I done run twice," he continued. "About six months after I come here, and again about four months after that. I took off toward The Oak both times. Had heard the name Hampton York when he bought you. Did some checkin', just like you did. Figured I could find you, if I got lucky. But they caught me."

He lifted his shirt, and she saw in the moonlight the scars cut deeply into his flesh. She ran her hands over them. They felt like knotty ropes, all raised on his back.

"I'm sorry they whipped you. No man has the right to do that to another just 'cause he wants to be free."

"Robertson got every right," said Markus. "Least the law says he does."

Ruby sighed. "You saying you're not coming with me?"

"Another whippin' will kill me," he replied sadly. "It'll come worse than the first two, always do. Robertson done said if he got a darky that runs three times, he just goes on and sets them plumb free to go be with Jesus."

"But they won't catch us," argued Ruby.

"I done told them about you and Theo," said Markus, his voice grieved. "They beat it out of me the second time, where I planned on goin', why I planned on goin' there. They'd come straight to The Oak if I run, then to Virginia when they learned that you had run too."

Tears came to Ruby's eyes again; this time she didn't push them away. She wanted to get mad at Markus, but she couldn't. Everything he said made sense. How could she fight him? She didn't want him dead, and she knew the unwritten law among white folks. A darky got two chances to settle down but no more. A third run meant sure death. Yet she still felt angry at Markus, disappointed that he wouldn't take the chance and flee with her.

"What about that woman?" she asked, tilting her head toward the shanty. "She keeping you here?"

Markus shrugged. "I ain't gone lie. She nursed me after the second whippin', kept me alive. I took up with her after that, figured I owed her that. Figured I wouldn't ever get back to you."

"You love her?"

Markus took Ruby back into his arms. "Not like I love you. But what am I gone do? Robertson wanted me with a woman; you know how that is. No way to stand up to him. I got to do what he says or get whipped again, and that'll kill me for sure."

Ruby's anger left her. She didn't want Markus dead, didn't want to have caused it. "What about Theo?"

"I don't know. I think of him every day. But what can I do? I got no way to go to him."

"You reckon he's still with Mammy?"

"Sho he is, why not? The Rushtons is good folks; they'll take care of him."

"I don't know that I can make it by myself," she said. "It's a long way for a woman to go alone."

"It's a mean old world," Markus told her. "But I got no way to fight it right now, none at all."

Ruby weighed her choices. Without Markus, she couldn't go North, least not yet, not without some time to scheme. But what did that leave her? Only one thing. She'd have to go back to The Oak. Retrace her steps. No doubt Mr. York would put some punishment on her. Probably not a whipping if she came back on her own. Lots of darkies disappeared for a few days, then showed back up. Sometimes little or nothing was ever done. With Stella's help, Camellia's too, plus what she knew about Mossy Bank, Mr. York might let her off pretty easy.

She faced Markus. "I supposed I need to go, then."

"Back to The Oak?"

"No choice that I can see."

"I am most sorrowful."

She took his head in her hands and held him close. "I don't blame you. Nothing for you to do."

He cried in her arms.

"I want Theo back," she said, determined. "And there'll be a time when it will happen. I feel it somehow, and Theo said he saw it."

"I hear maybe a war will come. Maybe the Yankees will whip the white folks down here; change things around for everybody."

"That's not likely."

"A man can hope."

Ruby kissed him then, knowing that she'd probably never see Markus, her man, again. The two of them sat together in the cold of the night, with the stars bright overhead. They held each other for another few minutes. Then she knew she had to go. After one last embrace, she stood and walked off without looking back. She'd still go to Theo; yes, she would. The time would come for that. She didn't know when or how, but it *would* come. But now she knew that when she did, she'd have to go alone.

Chapter Twenty-Four

With the heats set to start at one o'clock, York got up late the next day, dressed in his best clothes, and ate a slow meal. About eleven o'clock he started for the tracks, his nerves jumpy from coffee and excitement. Once there he took a spot near the main road where he could watch the rest of the spectators arrive. They came all through the noon hour—a combination of the wealthiest and the poorest the region had to offer—the wealthy to drink aged whiskey, show off their clothes and carriages, and talk about the latest rumors about an upcoming war; the poor to spend a day away from the constant drudgery that ate up their days like a hungry dog on a bone.

York paid no attention to the poor. Why should he? Their wagers would cover a dollar here, maybe five there. Nothing like the amount he had come to gamble. His eyes steady, he inspected the rich as they arrived: the women in their long hoop skirts and silk hats carrying parasols as they stepped down from their horse-drawn carriages; the men in shining black boots riding prancing horses. Negroes drove the carriages, helped the ladies down, led the gentlemen's horses away as they dismounted. As if drawn together by a special scent, the wealthy immediately began mixing together—their obvious refinement pulling them to a high spot of ground under a stand of tall oaks not far from the track. By the time the first race of the day went off, close to five hundred people had gathered, at least two-thirds of them from the best of the state's society.

Dressed in a ruffled blue shirt with white cravat, mustard-colored trousers, long-tailed black coat and clean black boots—all purchased at a quality shop in Charleston—York easily mixed with the wealthy. Although many of the crowd knew each other, enough strangers were there for his

269

presence to cause no alarm. The crowd continued to swell as the first of the heats approached. The wagering took place quietly among the crowd under the oaks; there were no loud shouts of bragging or argument here. Nothing as crude as that. No, the men here struck up gentle conversations about the merits of this horse or that one, the strengths and weaknesses of their dams and sires. Then, after a few minutes of such chatter, one or the other man would tip his hand, offer a gentleman's opinion that this or that horse would carry the day in the race about to start. The other man, if he chose, would take another opinion, champion a different horse. They'd talk quickly of odds, who got them and at what amount. If agreement could be reached, the wager would be laid.

Although careful not to lay too much with any one man, it didn't take York long to find takers for his low-key but firm support for the black. Not wanting to set off any unusual suspicions, he spread his money out among nine different men—wagering a thousand with one man, fifteen hundred with another, eight fifty with a third, and so on until he had placed eight thousand, eight hundred dollars on the heats. In most cases, he got his three to one odds with all of his opponents choosing either the chestnut or the dappled gray over his black. Fortunately for him, the Tessiers had gone to Columbia to continue making plans for the upcoming nuptials and so were missing the races this year. Otherwise, in spite of his care, someone might have heard about his wagers and wondered about his source of money. As it was, anybody who knew him and heard of it would probably figure he was putting the money out for Master Trenton.

Finished with the wagering, he eased away from the oaks and took a spot in the stands that fronted the track by the finish line. He had only a few more minutes before the first heat began. He noticed his hands shaking as he sat down. For the first time since his decision to take this action, his nerves hit him hard. What if he lost?

He squeezed his hands together, as if trying to press the blood from them. So what if he did? He'd go back to The Oak, do his job as long as Master Trenton would allow it. If the time came when Trenton got rid of him, he'd take the thousand or so that he had left and start out somewhere else. True, he'd never get his dream if he lost. But a lot of men never got their dream. Why should he expect any different? Why should fortune smile on him more than any other man?

He thought back to the day he and Josh found the man at Mossy Bank, the way they'd talked about their hopes. Josh's desires seemed so small; all he wanted was a simple life with a loving wife, a happy family, and a chance to serve the Lord. How could a man keep his view so low? Wasn't there more to living than what Josh wanted? It seemed so little, so . . . well, so pointless. Shouldn't a man want the kinds of things York sought? Shouldn't a man desire to make his mark in the world; shouldn't he want a fine house and lots of land and the admiration of his neighbors? Shouldn't he want his picture hung over the mantel of a mansion? Why else did a man exist but to scrape and fight and claw as hard as he could to reach the top of whatever world he found around him at his birth?

The hour of the first heat approached. York left the stands and made his way to the stables. Although staying out of the way, he eased in and out of the area that stabled the horses to run in the two-milers. He particularly watched the black, the chestnut, and the gray for any unusual signs. Although the chestnut seemed quiet, he didn't know enough of the horse's normal temper to figure if that should put him at ease or upset him. Not wanting to draw any attention, York soon left the area and made his way back to the stands.

He pulled his hat—a new broad-brimmed black one that matched his coat—tight over his eyes. The next hour and a half would seal his fate. If the black won, he could take his winnings and move to the second part of his scheme. If the black lost, all that would end forever. No portrait for him over any mantel. No fancy school for Camellia. No mark made on the world. Nothing but daily work at the whim of another man for the rest of his days.

The horses exited the stable, and York followed them out, a new chaw of tobacco in his cheek. People crowded in around him. The horses pranced onto the track toward the starting line. The jockeys—their colored silks bright in the spring sunshine—held the horses back. A light breeze whipped through the horses' manes. The crowd whistled and cheered as one horse, a tall roan, reared up, his front legs pawing the air with eagerness to run.

York stroked his beard, neatly trimmed for today. He felt as eager as the roan, ready for this to happen. Ever since he and Josh found the money at Mossy Bank, he'd sensed that something like today would occur. It just had to. That money had seemed destined for his hands, as if Fate had reached out and placed it in his lap. Since then he'd done all he could to make the most of it. True, taking money from The Oak bothered him some when he dwelt too long on it, but any sane man would see that he deserved those dollars. He'd responded just like any other normal man. He'd grabbed the chances that came his way and sought to make the most of them. Just as he'd told Josh he needed to do.

The horses reached the starting line. The crowd rose to cheer them off. A man in a tall stovepipe hat and a navy frock coat stood at the starting line, a pistol in hand. The horses tensed. York held his breath. His chest ached with fear. The man in gray fired his pistol, and the horses darted away. When the black stumbled briefly, York thought he might fall, but the horse regained his footing and thundered off after the horses in front of him. He passed two of them by the first turn, his long mane stiff in the breeze. The dappled gray lay three horses off the lead, the chestnut just in front of him. A smallish bay led the race, but York didn't worry much about him. Known for his early speed, he had failed at the end in every race he'd ever run.

The first mile passed slowly, each of the horses trying to keep a steady pace. At the halfway point, the black passed another horse. Now he ran fourth—the bay, the gray, and the chestnut all in front and in that order. For another quarter-mile the black gained no ground. Sweat broke out on York's face. His chest felt like someone had shoved a hot brick into it. He knew the black didn't have to win all the heats, just have the best combined time in them, but he also knew that the first heat often set the stage for the next two. The four leading horses turned the last corner and headed for home. York began to shout.

The chestnut moved easily, seemingly without effort. York wondered if his late-night mash had messed up his stomach at all. The black lay just behind him, equally as fast. York breathed once but then stopped again. The little bay hadn't faltered, neither had the gray. The two of them ran side by side, the bay near the rail saving ground on the turn. The black's neck stretched forward, and his speed hit another level. His hooves pounded the ground. The crowd roared as the chestnut seemed to hesitate. Just like that, his legs seemed to move slower, as if somebody had poured swamp mud under his feet, and the black sped around him as if passing a stump in a field. Now the black gained on the front two. York punched his fist into the air over and over, keeping time with the pounding hooves.

The three horses ran neck and neck as the black pushed his way between the bay and the gray. The bay veered out, and the three horses bumped. The gray hesitated, his hooves suddenly tangled, then he went down. The crowd gasped. The gray's jockey rolled off the horse. The gray's front legs collapsed and he rolled forward. York groaned. The last two horses shoved forward, less than five paces from the finish line. The black bounced into the bay once more. His neck reached for the finish. The bay arched his nose. The black pounded one last huge lunge and beat him by less than a neck.

The crowd roared, some in triumph, the others in outrage. York ran from the stands toward the judges' box at the edge of the track by the finish line. Three men with tall black hats talked quickly to one another. The crowd waited for the judges to decide if any foul had occurred.

York glanced back at the track. The gray was standing, his jockey beside him, reins in hand, checking the horse's legs. From what York could see, both horse and jockey appeared fine—shaken but not seriously hurt. He wondered if the gray would try the next heat or give it up for the day.

He eyed the judges again. They continued to talk. Three other men had joined them; York figured they were the owners of the horses involved in the bumping. Each of them made their case; each defended their horse and jockey.

Everybody else held their breath. Finally, after what seemed like forever, the tallest of the judges turned to the crowd. "The judges are all agreed," he shouted. "In the first of the two-milers, the winner is Blacksmith, owned by Jeremy Ruger of Augusta, Georgia! Time is 3:16."

York almost collapsed. His knees wobbled. For the first time he could remember, he wanted to cry. Although he had two more heats to go, fortune had fallen well so far. The chestnut had quit in the last stretch; the

dappled gray had taken a fall. Now only the bay seemed like a serious con-
tender, and everyone knew the small horse had fine early speed but no
staying power. If he ran true to form, the next two heats wouldn't go well
for him.

York tried to stay calm while the horses rested for the next heat. If it
all went as this first race had indicated . . . no he couldn't count on that
yet. He had to wait; had to stay patient.

Within thirty minutes, the horses were back at the starting line,
minus the dappled gray. The starter fired the pistol again. The horses galloped off. Again the bay took off first, but this time he didn't last as long
as in the first race. The chestnut ran well for the first mile but then started
laboring with every step. By the time they reached the last half-mile, he
had dropped to next to last. Blacksmith lay near the front until the final
turn, then passed a thick-shouldered roan in the last hundred yards to win
by three lengths.

York dared to breathe again. The impossible now seemed possible. He
sweated for the next thirty minutes, not looking at anybody, not wanting
to break the spell of the moment. The third and last heat began. This time
the chestnut ran like everyone had expected him to run from the beginning and won the race by a neck over the roan. The black finished third,
but it didn't matter. His time stood at 9:52, the best by seven seconds over
the next best finisher. The crowd roared—some with approval, some with
disgust.

As Blacksmith crossed the finish time, York didn't even rise to his
feet. His shock was so great he didn't think his knees could hold him. For
several minutes he stayed in place. Just like that, in three heats that lasted
barely ten minutes, he'd moved from a low-class white to a man of means.
Finally, that reality sank in, and he jumped to his feet. He spun around to
find somebody to tell but found no one—nobody he knew, no friend. For
a second his shoulders sagged. Here was the biggest moment of his life,
and he had nobody with him. But then he remembered how much money
he'd won, and all his sadness disappeared. How could he feel low? He had
close to twenty-seven thousand dollars. Not enough to buy a plantation,
but more than most men made in a lifetime.

York chuckled as he considered what he hoped to do. It might take him a while, and he'd have to take care to choose the right moment. But if he pulled it off, people would talk about him for a long time. If his scheme panned out, he'd make a mark all right, more of one than even he'd ever imagined.

He put in a new chaw of tobacco and headed out of the stands to collect his winnings. Maybe he'd take a couple of days and celebrate, he decided. With the kind of money he now had, he could celebrate real well.

Chapter Twenty-Five

His hands in dishwater scrubbing out the frying skillet, Josh looked out the window at the rising sun and mapped out his work for the day. When York took time off like this for the races, he took on a lot of extra duties. The only way he could get them done and still take care of his family was to start early and stay steady. He thought of Ruby and knew that today he'd have to make a decision about what to do. When Stella had told him three days ago that she'd not come home the night before, he'd decided to give the situation a few days before sending out anybody to search for her. A lot of servants ran off from time to time but then showed back up with no real fuss. He wanted to give Ruby time to change her mind and come back. So far, though, she'd not come home, and something had to be done. If York came back and found out Josh had let her go without a search, he'd raise a ruckus.

With Beth helping, he finished cleaning the dishes and got ready to leave. Slipping on his hat, he heard a knock on the door.

"I'll check it," called Beth.

Josh moved to the front room.

"There's a man here," Beth called.

Josh stepped to the front door. A man in a long black coat stood there, his hat off, his forehead wide, his eyes clear.

Josh stuck out a hand and introduced himself. "You're out mighty early this morning."

"I'm Sharpton Hillard," said the man, shaking Josh's hand heartily. "I checked at the manse. Master Trenton and Mr. York are both away. I was told you're next in charge. Can I speak with you a minute?"

Josh stepped back, let Hillard in, and pointed to a chair by the fireplace.

"Would you like a cup of coffee?" Beth asked him.

"That would be mighty nice, young lady."

Beth disappeared to the kitchen. Josh noted Hillard's accent but didn't comment on it as he settled in his chair. Josh stood by the fireplace.

"I'll not waste your time," said Hillard. "I rode through here back in November, talked to Mr. York. He tell you of my visit?"

Josh shrugged but didn't answer. Until he knew more, he wouldn't let on to Hillard what he and York discussed or didn't discuss.

"Okay," said Hillard, with a slight smirk. "I told Mr. York I'd come here looking for information about a man who disappeared somewhere between Charleston and Savannah a while back."

Josh fought to stay calm. He knew his face must have blanched white. "What's that got to do with The Oak?" he asked quietly.

"Nothing necessarily. Just that I've been looking for this man for quite a while. Trying to find out what happened to him. Asking from place to place, you know. Seeing if anybody knew anything."

"I suppose Mr. York said he didn't."

"Exactly."

"Then why have you come back?"

Beth entered with a cup of coffee. Hillard accepted it gratefully and took a sip. Josh tilted his head at Beth, his signal for her to leave the room.

Hillard lowered the coffee cup. "Two reasons. One, I was told that a man named Tarleton has been looking for Mr. York."

Josh remembered the name from Sheriff Walt in Beaufort. "So?" He wondered if Hillard had talked to Walt, and if so, what Walt had told him. He hoped Walt had kept his mouth shut.

"It seems Mr. Tarleton has gone missing."

"What's that got to do with York?"

"He was seen with Tarleton about the time he disappeared, in Beaufort."

"You accusing Mr. York of foul play?"

Hillard held up a hand. "I'm not accusing anybody of anything. Just curious, that's all."

"How does any of that connect to your missing man?" Josh sat down on the fireplace hearth. He felt like Hillard was weighing him, testing his mettle.

Hillard drank from his coffee. "My man and Tarleton were traveling together."

"Sounds like maybe you need to find Tarleton. He might know what happened to your missing man."

Hillard nodded. "Tell me about Mr. York."

"He's the overseer here," Josh answered. "Well known in these parts. He's some good, some bad . . . like most men, I expect."

"Anybody could tell me that," challenged Hillard. "I want to know what kind of man he is; what kind of character he has. Is he a liar, a cheat, could he kill a man?"

Josh raised an eyebrow. "We could all kill a man," he said gently. "Don't you think?"

Hillard let out a big breath. "I hear he's your brother. You wouldn't be protecting him now, would you?"

Josh chuckled lightly. "I don't think my brother needs a whole lot of protection. If you've asked enough to know we're kin, you know that too, I suppose."

Hillard shook his head but didn't challenge Josh further.

Josh waited, kept his breath calm. In his gut, though, he started to fume. Why hadn't York told him about Hillard? And did York know Tarleton? Had something happened between them?

Hillard set his coffee cup on the floor.

"You said you had two reasons for coming here," Josh challenged.

"Yes."

Josh sensed Hillard's pleasure, like a man who'd just caught a bass bigger than his skillet could hold. His muscles tensed.

"You ever hear of a woman named Ruth Swanson?"

Josh's hands clenched as he fought to stay easy. He figured Hillard had certainly talked to Sheriff Walt. "Don't know a woman of that name," he answered truthfully. "Why do you ask?"

Hillard crossed his knees. "I hear a man of your description has been asking about a woman named 'Ruth.'"

"So what?"

"Maybe Ruth Swanson is the woman you're asking about."

Josh felt his heart speed up. Who was Ruth Swanson, and how did she connect to Mossy Bank? Was she the dead man's wife? A daughter maybe? But what should he tell Hillard? Would Hillard accuse him of murder if he admitted to finding the man at Mossy Bank? Josh considered his choices. He could stay quiet, or he could come clean and see what happened.

"I found a man," he said calmly, careful to leave out anything about York. "At Mossy Bank Creek in early November, 1858. Somebody had shot him. He died within a couple of minutes. Before he passed, he spoke the name 'Ruth.' I tried to get more, but that's all he said. I buried him there; you can find the marker if you go look."

"No sign of who shot him?"

Josh thought a second, wanting to tell the truth but not put York in any danger. "A search of the woods found no one."

"No horse or anything?" asked Hillard.

Josh shook his head. "No horse and no papers."

Hillard put both boots on the floor. "You find any money on the man?" He asked the question almost lightly, as if he was talking about twenty dollars or so.

"No," Josh said quickly, glad Hillard had asked the question in a way that allowed him to answer correctly without lying. "Nothing on him at all."

Hillard's brow wrinkled, and Josh decided to take a gamble. "Why are you looking so hard for this man? He kin or something?"

"No," said Hillard. "I'm just doing a job."

Josh kept the initiative. "So who is Ruth Swanson?"

Hillard slapped his hands on his knees and stood. "Don't worry. She's nothing to you. You can stop looking for her."

Josh stood too. "I'd like to know. Feel kind of obligated. The man at Mossy Bank spoke his last words of her. I told him I'd tell her that."

"The man's name was Quincy," said Hillard. "He was delivering some money."

"To who?"

"I don't know. That part is not my business."

"You working for Ruth Swanson?"

"That part is not your business." Hillard headed to the front door.

"Where you going now?" asked Josh, following him onto the front porch.

"To Mossy Bank Creek."

"You looking for the money?"

"Don't you think I should?"

"That would make sense."

Hillard put on his hat. The sun baked down on his face.

"How much?" asked Josh.

"Excuse me?"

"How much money?"

"More than you and I will ever see," Hillard said. "That's for sure."

As Hillard walked off, Josh watched him go. Somehow, though, he figured he'd see Sharpton Hillard again. A man like Hillard had some bulldog in him. Once he got his teeth into something, he didn't let go too easily. What would happen then? So far Josh had protected York. But what would he do when Hillard returned? He couldn't lie for York if Hillard pinned him down. Josh wouldn't do that, not even for his brother.

Reentering the house to tell Beth he was leaving, Josh's anger at York boiled higher. York shouldn't have put him in this position! He'd wanted to tell the truth and hand over the money from the start. But York had insisted that he keep it. Now look what had happened! No matter their innocence, they'd both look guilty when all this came out. Even if people didn't see them as murderers, they'd at least conclude they were thieves. Josh didn't have much but his good name, and now he was afraid of losing that.

Grabbing his hat, Josh hugged Beth and Butler and left the house. On the way to the barn for his horse, he realized he couldn't blame it all on York. He'd failed too. A man of any solid virtue would've done the right thing from the beginning, no matter how much his brother told him otherwise. He was weak, Josh concluded, as spineless as one of the jellyfish that washed up dead from time to time on the beach.

At the barn he took his horse from Leather Joe, mounted, and headed to the fields, still trying to figure what to do. Should he go after Hillard and tell him everything and let matters fall out from there? No, not yet. Not until he'd talked to York first; made clear his plans. He owed York at least that; owed it to him for a lot of reasons, one more important than the others. He'd give him one more chance to come clean and hand over the money. After that, well after that, he needed to do something else. He needed a fresh start.

Josh's mind skipped back over the last few months. Nothing good had happened to him or his family in a long time. Maybe the Lord wanted him to hear something in all this. Maybe the Lord wanted him to pick up his last two children and move away from here, away from York and the constant temptation he seemed to bring. Until he could get stronger and stand up to his brother, he needed to stay away from him.

At the fields Josh dismounted. In front of him the land stretched as far as his eye could see. Scores of servants were already busy, their steady energy the fuel that made the plantation hum. For several seconds Josh studied the darkies. An uneasy feeling rolled through him as it often did when he stopped to think about the system that made his job possible. The servants were trapped. He could leave The Oak and escape his brother's heavy influence anytime he wanted. But these people couldn't do that. No matter how heavy the hand that ruled them, they were bound here, their lives not their own, the result of their labor belonging to somebody else. Even their wives and husbands, their children, were owned by another. Did God approve of this? Had God ordained it? If so, why? Why did Josh Cain deserve freedom, but the darkies didn't?

Josh remembered Ruby and recalled from talks with Camellia that Ruby had a husband and a son. Had she fled The Oak to try to find them? Could he blame her? What would he do in her place? What right did he have to run her down like a horse that had run off? Put dogs after her?

Josh's heart felt heavy. He'd heard some of the war talk, and part of him wanted it to happen. A war would change things forever; he knew that wars always did. What if the Yankees came? He'd have to fight again, would have to leave Beth and Butler. But he wanted no part of a war; he'd done that once and didn't want it again. War had changed him . . . hurt him . . . made him so guilty. No wonder he felt unworthy to go to church, that he spent every Sunday he could on the shore, reading his Bible, rather than sitting in a church pew.

As a sea gull fluttered overhead, Josh envied its freedom. The bird could come and go as it pleased . . . no duties, no worries. He took off his hat, wiped his brow from the hot sun, and reached a decision. He did need to leave here, not only to escape his brother but also to free his heart of the guilt caused by what he saw in the fields every day.

Another image crept into his head: Camellia. He didn't understand his feelings for her. She stirred something in him, but could he trust that? He knew he missed the company of a good woman. Was his attraction to Camellia the result of loneliness and nothing else? No, that wasn't all of it. Camellia wasn't just any woman. She had a glow about her, a goodness that attracted him like no one he'd known except Anna. Yet Camellia seemed to have no such feelings about him. How could she? He was an uncle to her, nothing more. If he didn't leave soon, he'd surely confess his feelings for her.

He put his hat back on. A fresh start would be good for him, and for Beth and Butler too. They could put the hard times behind them; go far away where not even a war could reach them, where he could put his feelings for Camellia out of reach. It would take several weeks to check on a few things. But then he'd go to York and spell out his situation. Yes, he'd loved his time with Anna on The Oak. But the time for a new start had come.

Josh scanned past the fields, toward the ocean. Although he couldn't see the water, he could sense its movement—in and out, ebb and flow, waves crashing on shore in one moment, waves receding in the next. Crash and foam, then a slow but steady and unstoppable retreat. He took a big breath. Life passed the same way. Full and advancing in one moment, then back and away in the next. Success one day, then failure to follow. Joy and sorrow, one after the other. A wave and a crash, a tide in and a tide out.

Feeling better now that he'd reached his decision, Josh made one final decision. He'd do nothing about Ruby. After all, if he'd been in her place, he probably would have done the same thing.

Chapter Twenty-Six

Her hands busy opening jars of preserves, Camellia paid no attention to the sound of approaching horses as the last Friday of March 1861 passed its midway point. What did she care who came and went on The Oak? She had plenty of jobs to do that gave her no time to look about or ask questions about anything beyond her small world.

In the months since the malaria had passed, her days had settled into a dull but steady routine. On every day but Sunday she got up just before daylight, fixed breakfast for her pa and Johnny, then headed off to the cookhouse. She labored there all morning, took a little time off at midday, then went right back to work from midafternoon until suppertime. After supper, she helped Stella and Ruby clean up, then went back home to get food on the table there. Nothing upset the pattern, and she liked it that way. In addition to all the sadness the last year had brought, it had also taught her a couple of hard lessons. One, don't expect too much because just when you do, some hard thing will snatch it right out of your hand. And two, don't try to get beyond your station, because no matter how virtuous you live, a person belongs at a certain level. If you try to climb above it, you always get smacked right down.

Camellia dipped the preserves into a dish, then stepped to the back door to dump out some dirty water left over from that morning. The sun hit her face as she reached the porch, and she tilted her eyes so her bonnet could block the light. She heard a horse clomp close by. It sounded like somebody had ridden right up to the front of the cookhouse. *Pa,* she thought. *Come for some food.*

She banged the bottom of the pan to get out the last of the water. Her pa had seemed strange the last few weeks, almost pleasant. He walked around with an odd smirk on his lips, almost like he knew something good but couldn't tell anybody. But she knew if she asked him about his mood, he wouldn't give her a straight answer. She figured he probably won a few dollars at the races. Gambling winnings always made him feel good, at least for a while.

Camellia scrubbed the pan with a rag. Her pa had felt so good when he came back from Charleston that he hadn't even punished Ruby for her disappearance from The Oak when she showed up a couple of days after he returned. That surprised everybody, but why should they argue if Mr. York wanted to go easy on the darkies?

Stella and Camellia had questioned Ruby hard about what had happened, and she told them all about Markus, how he'd settled in with another woman and given up his hopes of fleeing. Sad for her, but glad to have her back safely, they took good care of her over the next couple of weeks, giving her extra food, doing her chores so she could recover from her travels. A couple of days after she got back, Josh Cain had come to the cookhouse and pulled Ruby aside.

"He told me never to run again," Ruby told Stella and Camellia later. "Said since I came back on my own, Mr. York didn't plan to do anything this time. If it happens again, though, he said he had no doubt Mr. York would see to it that something rough came to me. Said I'd set a bad example, and Mr. York wouldn't let me get off free if I did it again."

"I hope you heed his words," Stella warned. "You got no reason for takin' off from here. It's a good spot. Best you gone get."

Ruby scowled. "I still aim to go to Theo. Markus or not. You know why."

"You heard Mr. Cain," Stella insisted. "And what about Obadiah? He took you back this time. Don't know about a next."

Ruby nodded. "He's a fine man, it's true. But like I told you, I give up my hope to see Theo, I might as well die."

Stella shook her head. "You gone learn sooner or later, child. Hard way or easy way, I don't rightly know. But you gone learn."

Footsteps behind Camellia brought her back to the present. Heading back inside the cookhouse, she almost dropped the wash pan. Trenton Tessier stood in the kitchen doorway, his brown hair framed in the sunlight, his eyes bright but also somehow sad.

Camellia straightened but kept her reserve. Trenton held his hat in his hands. She waited for him to speak, to tell her why he'd lowered himself to come to the cookhouse. Didn't he have a wedding fast approaching?

When he finally spoke, his tone sounded gentler than she could remember in a long time. "May I have a few minutes with you?"

Camellia hadn't heard from him except by letter since he'd left The Oak the fall after the storm; hadn't seen him except at a distance since he brought Miss Eva Rouchard home. "You're master of the place," she said as casually as she could muster. "You can speak with any of the hired hands."

"I know you're angry," he said wistfully. "I cannot blame you for that."

Again Camellia held her peace.

"May I sit down?" He indicated the table.

"You own the place. You can sit anywhere you like."

Trenton dropped his hat on the table, pulled out a chair, and sat, his body erect. "Please sit," he said, indicating a chair.

Camellia took a chair opposite him and studied her hands.

"I should have told you about me and Miss Rouchard. I should have written you a letter, let you know somehow. But I didn't have any words, didn't know what to say, how to explain what had happened."

"You owed me no explanation. White-trash folks like me aren't worthy of your kind. You can do as you like. We have to live with it; that's the way of the world. I know that now." There—she liked the way that sounded, and the firm set of her tone, her face, and jaw. She'd used her best grammar too. There was no reason to sound like an ignorant girl at a time like this.

Trenton put his hands on the table, palms down. "I'm not a good person," he offered, his voice weaker. "Not good enough for you."

Camellia's heart softened a little, but not completely. He could put on the charm when he wanted. She kept her eyes steely as she spoke. "You did what you had to do. For your family, I see that plainly. It hurt me, yes, I cannot deny it. But you had no choice."

Trenton's eyes searched hers. "I'm sorry that the malaria took your brother. I feared for you as well."

"I survived. Many didn't. You know that, of course. Many of the Negroes passed on."

"It has gone hard on The Oak," he continued. "Seems like every day brings some new cause for worry with it."

"I'm not much versed in the business of The Oak. My pa doesn't tell me of his work. Are things not better?"

Trenton stroked his forehead, as if in pain. "Worse, if anything. Yield was down again the past year, even though prices stayed steady. Over forty darkies dead from the fever last year, you know that. The bank loan mounts."

"Does my pa know this?"

"Most of it."

"He works night and day," she said, feeling protective of him. "Treats this place like he owns it. Nothing would hurt him more than to see The Oak fail."

"I know," Trenton agreed. "Nobody faults him for any of this."

Camellia pushed back a loose strand of hair. Trenton's sadness touched her. He seemed more humble than she'd ever seen him. She thought of Eva Rouchard, the money her family possessed. How could she blame Trenton for doing what he'd done? Perhaps she would have made the same choice.

"I wish I could do something," she said, honestly grieved for Trenton's worry. "But my limitations are many." She stood and faced him, her arms folded. She wanted to stay strong and put all this behind her. "Look," she started, "I don't know what brought you here today, but I want you to know I forgive you for any meanness you may have displayed toward me. I've accepted your decision, made my peace with it, taken it as the will of the Lord. We're different, you and I, we cannot deny that. I believe we could have made it, but not easily. So let's leave it in the past and set our hearts forward to the future. That's my desire, and I'm sure you join me in it."

She took a deep breath and hoped the speech sounded sincere. Although she didn't know for sure that she believed all of it, she certainly hoped she'd convinced Trenton she did.

Trenton stared at her, as if seeing her for the first time. "You've changed," he said, his tone almost reverential. "Much more mature. Not a girl anymore, but a . . . a woman of deep thought, steady mind."

Camellia brushed back her hair, wishing she'd had time to prepare for this meeting. Even though Trenton didn't love her anymore, she still wanted him to think her beautiful.

"I'm less innocent." She sighed. "Less naive."

"There's something else too . . . your voice, it's . . . your language is different, like you've been . . . "

"I've learned to read," she said, moving back to the table opposite him. "I told you that. I've continued to learn more in these months since . . . Mr. Cain loaned me a few books; I got others from the manse library. I didn't think anybody would mind."

Trenton smiled slightly. "Nobody stays here long enough to mind. Not that we would anyway. I'm proud of you."

"I did it for you, wanted to fit better with your friends and family, wanted to make sure my backward ways never shamed you. Figured if I could do my letters, I might learn more of your world, find out how to make my way in it."

He dropped his eyes. "You could make your way just fine. You have more charm and natural grace in your little finger than most women have in their whole bodies."

Camellia waved off his compliments. She knew better than to trust them. "No cause to say such things. That time is way past."

Silence fell on the room. Trenton picked up his hat and stared into it. Dust particles danced in the sun's rays as they baked through the open window.

"I'm sorry I hurt you," Trenton said. "That was never my intent."

Camellia's heart weakened some more. He sounded so sincere. She wondered again what had happened to him, why he'd come to her now, after all this time, when his wedding was just weeks away. Her heart suddenly pounded harder. Had he broken off his engagement; come to his senses and returned to her? Was that why he sat here now, his eyes troubled, his shoulders slumped? He appeared so frail, like a twig that a light wind could snap at any second.

Trenton stood and walked to the window, his back to her. She stayed still and watched him. Something about his posture made her tense;

something in it told her he had something important to say, something that didn't come out easily. She wondered again what had brought him home. Had he come to ask her forgiveness before his marriage? But she'd just offered it to him. Why was he staying? Was her first thought right? Had he broken off the engagement? But what would she do if he had? What if he again asked her to marry him? Would she say yes?

Camellia squeezed her hands into fists and chastised herself for thinking such silly notions. Trenton hadn't broken off any wedding plans. He'd simply come home to make his peace with her before he started his new life. She admired him for that, appreciated his good heart. Nobody had made him do this; he deserved her appreciation.

He pivoted and faced her again. His eyes looked empty, like a swamp drained of every drop of water. She tried to figure why he seemed so blank.

"She's dead," he said, as if announcing the color of his hat. "A carriage hit her a month ago."

Camellia immediately thought of Mrs. Tessier but knew she would have heard if such a thing had happened. So it had to be Eva Rouchard. A carriage had run over Eva Rouchard!

"Most bizarre thing you ever saw," continued Trenton, his voice a dull monotone. "She stepped out on the street after dinner. Had taken too much wine maybe; nobody knows for sure. The carriage crushed her spine. Doctors did all they could, but she died."

Camellia's heart raced with an odd mixture of grief and . . . hope? Yes, that was it! Hope. Although she knew it wasn't right, she couldn't help but think it. Eva Rouchard was dead! What did that mean for her and Trenton?

She shoved the questions away, fought again against the selfish pleasure that tempted her. How tragic for Eva Rouchard! How her parents surely grieved!

Trenton gazed at her, his eyes strangely dry. Against her best instincts, Camellia stood and moved to him, her arms open. He fell into them, his head on her shoulder. Camellia touched his hair and tried to clear her head.

"I need you," whispered Trenton. "More than ever. You're the only friend I have in the whole world, the only one who truly cares for me."

Camellia thought of pushing him away, of telling him he couldn't just run back to her when things turned sour, that he couldn't treat her that way, like a loyal dog he came home to every now and again when he felt lonely. What he deserved was her disdain, her unending anger, her strong rejection. Then why couldn't she do it? Why couldn't she push him away? Was it love? This sense of pity she now felt? The feeling that he needed her and she'd never turned him away before, not even in his worst moments? Was her kindheartedness a sign she loved him no matter what he did, no matter how poorly he treated her? Unable to answer, she held him close.

"I'm here," she soothed. "Right here."

"After all I've been through," he continued, "after all it's cost me, cost us, we may still have to sell The Oak."

Camellia's blood rose. Was the plantation all he cared about? Was that why he seemed so empty? The notion that he and his family would lose it? But surely not! What kind of heartless man would worry more about his finances than the fact that he'd just lost his wife-to-be? Not Trenton. His faults didn't include such coarse meanness.

"Nobody knows what will happen now," he said. "Mother is coming here soon; hard decisions have to be made."

Camellia's heart thumped heavily. Would Trenton look for another woman of means? Her face blushed with hurt again.

"I need you," Trenton whispered, his head still on her shoulder. "No matter what happens, I'll never forget that again."

Although she knew she was a fool, his words melted all her anger. In spite of everything he'd done to her, she still cared for Trenton Tessier. Whether she loved him or not, she didn't know right now. But, no matter what the future held, her concern for him would never change.

Chapter Twenty-Seven

The day after Trenton Tessier returned, Josh decided the time had come to face York—not only to tell him he was leaving but also to warn him about Hillard. He found York talking to Leather Joe by the barn, the sun bright on his shoulders.

"Got a minute?" asked Josh.

York looked up. "Sure."

Leather Joe walked away. York moved to a wagon by the barn, propped a boot on a wheel. He wore the same pleased expression he'd carried ever since he came home from Charleston. Although he figured he knew why, Josh had never asked him about it. Now he decided he would. "How much did you win?"

"A bunch," York stated.

"How much money you got now?" Josh asked.

"More than you would expect, I can tell you that."

"Got your stake with a dead man's money," Josh said plainly. "I ought to have made you take it back."

"Don't let your mouth overload your back," York chuckled. "Can't make a hound give back a rabbit once he put his teeth into it."

"I could've made you," argued Josh, "if I'd been stronger. But I wasn't. I was weak—I know that now."

"You got a busy conscience. That's your biggest failin' so far as I can see."

Josh kicked the side of the wagon wheel. "I've done a bit of thinking the last few weeks. That's why I came to talk to you."

York spit tobacco juice into the hay by the wagon.

Josh kept talking. "I've always let you take the lead. Even when I knew you were wrong. When you drank too much and got in fights. When you took the money on Mossy Bank. When you worked the servants too hard. When you . . . well, when you pressed Camellia to marry Master Trenton, even though you knew he wasn't good for her."

"Is that what this is about?" growled York, his face gradually turning red. "Your hankerin' for my daughter?"

Josh kicked the wagon wheel. "No. Not all of it at least. Yes, I want to tell her she's not my niece. But you say you don't want her to know what kind of woman her mama was, so I've kept my peace about it. I don't agree with that anymore, though. Camellia's a grown woman; she can take a hard truth. I know she can."

"You think you know her better than me?"

Josh studied York for a second. "Yes, better than you."

"If you were any kind of man, you wouldn't wait for me to tell her," he challenged. "You'd tell her yourself."

"I would, but I prefer you do it. It's your right."

"It's not time," York said, laughing. "Least not yet. Until I know what Trenton will do now that his woman got hit by that carriage."

Josh sighed. "Beats all, don't you think?"

"Life is sure fragile."

"You figure Trenton will come back to Camellia, don't you?"

"No way to know. But it's possible." York grinned. "Strange how things take turns, ain't it? Almost makes you believe there's a Lord and he's on my side."

Josh's temper took over. "I can't stand by anymore," he said heatedly. "Let you run over people, over me."

York squinted hard at him. "You sound angry. Not like you."

"Guess I am. Not all at you either. You've just acted like you've always done, and I should expect that. I'm blaming myself, my failures. If I'd put my foot down a few times, maybe I could have turned you around, kept you from falling into bad things."

"I could take offense at your meanin', little brother. Yes, I've stepped off the beam every now and again, I admit it. But I never claimed to be no example of virtue. Never saw no callin' to holiness or nothin'. Didn't get the Jesus streak that your mama put in you. I'm just a regular fella tryin' to make a livin'. To scrape a couple of dollars together as he goes along."

Josh waved him off. "I'm sorry. I know I sound high and mighty when I shouldn't. I have plenty of logs in my own eyes I need to clean out before I go after the splinter in yours. But I just can't do it any longer. So long as I'm with you I'm trapped. I can't turn you over to the law; no good brother would do that. But I can't just stand by anymore either and watch you take advantage of every situation, every person. It's too hard on me, and on my 'busy conscience,' as you call it."

York removed his hat and eyed Josh curiously. "What you plan on doin'?"

"I've spent the months since Lucy's death in deep sadness," Josh continued. "I got two loved ones in Oak soil now. That's changed me, caused something to shake loose." He gazed out over the plantation. "This doesn't mean much anymore. It's a way to make a living but not much else. I'm not happy these days. Find my mood low and sour."

"If you'd take a drink every now and again, it'd ease you out some." York grinned.

Josh didn't smile. "Without realizing it, I've come to blame myself for Lucy's death; Anna's too."

"That's a crazy notion."

"I don't know. Maybe I've done something wrong to cause her passing, displeased the Lord. I know better in my head, but my heart says otherwise, and it's hard to make your heart stop talking, even when what it says is untrue. I feel like I have to make some changes, some amends, or I'm going to lose somebody else."

"You really believe the Lord punishes one person because of the failin's of another?"

"I'm not a preacher," Josh said intently. "All I know is that sometimes it seems that way. It's a ripple, I think. Like throwing a rock in a pond. The rock one person throws sets off a splash he can't pull back. It washes out from there and touches people a long way off, people who don't deserve to get touched. The bigger the rock the worse the splash, the ripple that follows. It's not exactly the Lord hurting one *because* of the sins of another, but the effect turns out the same."

"If the Lord hurts your loved ones because of your sin, what does that mean for my loved ones?" asked York, sincere now.

Josh grinned this time. "You saying you've got a few sins on you?"

"A whole sackful," York admitted.

"I expect you're better than some men, not as good as others," said Josh. "All of us are sinners."

"So my loved ones might suffer for my failin's?"

"Maybe they already have."

York spat into the hay. "Don't like that notion."

"None of us do," said Josh. A bee buzzed near his head, and he brushed it off.

"You're the best man I've ever known. I don't think the Lord has taken your Anna or Lucy because of nothin' you've done."

"I've got plenty of sin staining my soul."

"You're as white as snow compared to most men," argued York.

"Not comparing myself to other men. Comparing myself to the Lord."

"You thinkin' of that matter back in the war?"

"That, plus not doing the right thing after Mossy Bank."

"You've tried. I know it; so do you."

"I didn't try hard enough. I never made you give back the money."

"That's my sin, not yours."

Josh kicked the wagon wheel again. "A man named Hillard came through while you were at the races."

York straightened. "He say what he wanted?"

"He wanted a lot."

York spat at the wagon wheel. "I figured he'd show back up someday. What did you tell him?"

"I told him about finding the man at Mossy Bank."

"I would have preferred you hadn't done that."

"Not yours to say," Josh said quietly.

York spat again. "He mention the money?"

"He asked about it, but I didn't tell him you had it."

York eyed him. "You surprise me."

"I wanted to warn you first. Thought that fair. Give you a chance to give it back of your own accord."

"I'm obliged you didn't tell him."

"You've kept secrets for me."

York nodded knowingly.

"It's the last time I do it, though," claimed Josh. "I figure we're square now."

"I reckon we are."

Josh stared out past the barn. "Hillard told me about a man named Tarleton. You know anything about him?"

York clenched his fists. "Not your worry."

"You kill him?"

York's jaw tensed, so Josh knew his brother wouldn't say anything else. "Hillard asked me if I knew a 'Ruth Swanson,'" Josh said.

York's eyes widened. "I reckon you told him no."

"That's right."

"You figure that's the 'Ruth' you been lookin' for, though?"

"Yes. Who do you think she is?"

"No way to tell."

"You don't know anyone by that name either?"

York fidgeted. Josh could see his brother struggling, almost as if he had one arm tied to two horses pulling in different directions. When York finally spoke, his face showed a seriousness Josh hadn't seen in his whole life.

"I don't know for certain," York began, "but the man my Lynette run off with back before the war . . . his name was Wallace Swanson."

Josh grunted. "You figure Ruth is connected to him?"

"Don't know. But there's a picture."

"A what?"

"A picture was in the bottom of the money box. It's Wallace Swanson. Older than I remember him but still him. I'd know that face anywhere. I'm sure he took Lynette and run off with her. I've hated him for a long time."

"So Ruth might be Swanson's wife? So what? What's that got to do with us?"

York shrugged.

Josh took off his hat and tried to slow his thoughts. "Let me get this straight. We find a dead man—his name is Quincy, by the way. He's carrying five thousand dollars and a picture of Wallace Swanson, the man who fathered Camellia and Chester. As Quincy dies, he speaks of a woman named Ruth. Then Hillard asks me if I know a Ruth Swanson? What's all this telling us?"

"Don't know."

"Wallace Swanson is Camellia's true father," Josh stated. "She needs to know about this."

York stared defiantly at him. "Why?"

"You know why."

"It'll do her no good," said York.

"But if he's alive, she needs to know."

"I see no good to come of it. He's shown he don't love her, running away with her mama, leaving her behind. If he cared about her, why don't he come back and get her years ago? I know I've got lots of faults, but I've stayed true to Camellia and Chester, treated them as my own all these years. I don't want to give her up to a man she's never known. No reason to do that."

Josh nodded with understanding. York made sense. But still this added another secret to keep. He hated to think of it and felt glad that he'd set his heart on leaving. Another thought came to him. Maybe York wanted to keep this secret because he hoped Trenton would come back to Camellia now that Eva Rouchard was dead. Maybe he wanted to keep her believing he was her father so he could claim his place on The Oak if Trenton and Camellia ended up marrying.

Could York be that callous—even with Camellia? Josh didn't know, and he had no right to ask. Besides, he was planning to leave soon. "She's your daughter," he finally told York. "Not my place to interfere and I won't." But Josh had also decided the time had come to tell York one last thing. He faced his brother straight on. "I want you to know I'm leaving."

"What?"

"It's simple enough. I'm leaving The Oak, soon as I can."

York didn't blink. "What will you do for work?"

"I don't know yet. But I can find something, I guess."

For the first time, York seemed confused. "Where are you goin'?"

"I don't know that either. West, I expect. With war almost certain, I want to get away from it if I can. Figure there's plenty of work there, Texas maybe."

"But you're an ocean man."

"They have an ocean, the Gulf; or perhaps I'll go all the way to California."

York scratched his beard. "What if I said I don't want you to go?"

"Don't know that it would matter. My mind is set."

"What if I said I'd tell Camellia about Wallace Swanson? She'd know you and she weren't kin. That'd give you a clear path to her."

Josh studied him. "You won't do that. I think you're counting on her and Trenton coming back together. Besides, I don't know if that's the right thing to do right now. She seems to set no store by me."

"You think Trenton will want her?"

"If he's got any head at all on his shoulders, he will."

"I expect he'll need to find another woman of means."

"That's no reason to marry," Josh said, fire in his eyes.

"A man does what he has to do," York shot back. "I can understand his choice real well."

"Then you don't know anything about love."

"I reckon I don't."

Josh straightened, stuffed his hands in his pockets. "I'll help you get the crop in the field. But you'll need to find another man after that. Keep this news to yourself for now, if you would."

"I prefer you stay."

"I can't do that."

"Suit yourself, then."

"After the crop is in."

"I'll miss you, Brother."

Josh nodded but didn't respond. Right now, with so many secrets pounding around in his head, he wasn't sure he'd miss anything about The Oak except Camellia and the sound of the ocean on Sunday afternoon.

Chapter Twenty-Eight

Mrs. Tessier's carriage rolled back up the drive to The Oak about mid-morning a week later, her horses muddy from the rainy day she had chosen for travel. Leather Joe and the house servants met and unpacked her bags as she arrived, their shoulders hunched against the chilly spring rain. Hampton York watched her from his workroom, his body tense. Since Josh had told him that Hillard had shown up again, he knew he needed to ask fast. No more time to wait on Trenton to make up his mind about Camellia.

After Mrs. Tessier disappeared inside the manse, York moved back to his desk, sat down, and tried to stay calm. But he found it hard; he had so much to consider. Would Master Trenton ask Camellia to marry him? If so, maybe he could hold back on his desperate plan. How could he know? How long should he wait to see? And what about Hillard? He'd return soon. York knew he had to act quickly or he'd lose his chance forever.

He put in a chaw of tobacco. No matter what happened, he'd keep the money. If Hillard turned up, he'd take Johnny and Camellia, go straight to Charleston, get the cash out of the bank where he'd left it, and leave the area to start all over somewhere else. It wasn't his first choice, but he could do it if necessary.

The morning passed, the afternoon began.

A couple of hours later he heard a knock on the door. "Come in," he called.

To his surprise Stella walked in, her bandanna wet from rain. "Mrs. Tessier wants to talk. Come as soon as you can."

York sat up straighter. Mrs. Tessier usually came and went without any contact between them. If she wanted him to know something, she sent the message through Master Trenton. Yet, based on what she wanted, this might actually make his decision easier.

"She say what she wanted?" he asked Stella.

"No, she not tell me nothin'."

"Do you know the last time Camellia and Trenton talked?"

"Reckon you ought to ask your own daughter about that. Not my bidness to go mixin' there."

York eyed the old woman sharply, sensing she knew more than she let on, but he'd learned a long time ago that what Stella didn't want to say always went unsaid. If he wanted to know why Mrs. Tessier had beckoned him, he'd just have to go and find out.

"Go on then," he said, waving her off. "Leave me be."

Stella left without another word, and he sat for a few minutes trying to figure this latest turn. Did Mrs. Tessier want information? Then why not ask Trenton? If not that, then what? He couldn't think of anything good. Most likely she planned to blame him for The Oak's troubles, then tell him she didn't need him any longer. So what if she did? That would just force him to act, one way or the other.

Ready to get on with it, York brushed off his pants, left the room, and slopped through the mud to the manse. There he wiped his feet on the porch mat, walked inside, and headed upstairs to Mrs. Tessier's bedroom. Once there, he took a deep breath, then knocked on the door.

"Enter." The voice sounded heavy.

York stepped inside. Mrs. Tessier stood by her window, her bustled dress a dark red. Her hair was pulled back in a severe bun, and her eyes seemed buggy, a little pushed out. Her skin, always white, now looked like winter frost.

"Sit," said Mrs. Tessier, indicating a chair beside her bed.

York took the seat. Mrs. Tessier folded her arms and faced him. She'd lost weight since he last saw her.

"Thank you for coming so quickly. I don't know an easy way to say this," she offered. "But I believe we're going to need to sell The Oak."

York rocked forward, his hands on his knees.

Mrs. Tessier raised a hand, and he stayed seated.

"You know how things are," she continued. "Nothing we've tried these last couple of years has turned out well. We got the storm, then the malaria swept through. Add that to low yields, and even good prices can't make up for it."

"It's been hard," he said. "Got to admit that."

She sighed. "Then this thing with Miss Rouchard. A strange happening. Heartrending for all of us."

"That must have come as a shock to everybody."

She smirked. "I expect you to feel pretty good about it. Figure you see it as another chance for your daughter to marry my Trenton."

York's face flushed. "You're a hard woman."

"I'm a practical one," she countered. "If I were you, I'd want the same thing for my child."

York felt an odd admiration for Mrs. Tessier. They had a lot in common, he decided. Both would do what they needed to get what they wanted. "You lookin' for another wife for Master Trenton?"

"Don't know if there's time. He's got to go through proper mourning. You know our customs."

"A wife of means could still save things," York said. "Get us over this bad spell. Give us another year and we'll do just fine, I tell you that for sure."

"You'd give up your hopes for your daughter to save The Oak?"

York wanted to spit but saw no cup. "If The Oak goes, so do her hopes."

"Not if she marries Trenton. Losing The Oak will hurt; I'll not lie about it. But we won't be completely broke. We have other houses—one in Charleston, another in Columbia."

"Why don't you sell one of those places?" asked York, not certain she wanted any advice but offering it anyway.

"I could," she said. "But neither of them would bring in enough money to pay off the bank. Besides, truthfully, I don't want to do it. I've never liked living here, you know that. I much prefer Charleston, even Columbia, to this place. A plantation is a man's world, not mine. I'm not good at it—never have been."

"What about Trenton? Don't he want this for his own? Somethin' to run, to make prosperous?"

"I'm certain he does," she replied sarcastically. "But what Trenton wants is not most vital at this moment. If I can find a buyer to give me a fair price, I can take the money and put it aside, assure my family of a steady income for a long time. No more worries about weather, about crop yields, about darkies getting sick and dying."

York tried to think. She'd said so much so fast he didn't know how to soak it all up. He wanted to tell her to lower her spending some, just for a while, not waste so much on imported clothes, on the finest wines, the best furniture. If she cut back, even for a couple of years, he could take the extra money and pay the bank until The Oak recovered. He'd work the hands from sunup till midnight . . . himself too. He'd work everybody until they couldn't move anymore, and they'd produce the best rice crop anybody had ever seen! And that one great crop would earn so much The Oak would never face this kind of problem again. He knew he could do it if Mrs. Tessier would just give him the time; if she'd find a way to keep the bank at bay for one more season.

"I want you to make The Oak ready," she said, taking a chair at her desk across from her bed. "Figure out how much things are worth. What we can expect to get for the hands, the livestock, the land and house. I want to sell it as one piece if I can; keep the servants here if possible. You'll need to get the house painted—all the buildings too. Repair the dikes, the canals. Put it all in its best order. Make The Oak shine."

York's heart was pounding. He wanted to shout but knew he couldn't. A man of his station didn't dare talk back to a lady like Mrs. Tessier. "I can't believe you'll really sell her," he said, almost in a whisper.

Mrs. Tessier sighed. "I know it's not what my husband would want, but I see no choice."

Driven by desperation, York knew the time had come. He had to say it now, or he never would. "What about you? What if you married again? I know you've surely had suitors . . . wealthy men who can provide what you need."

When she glared at him for a minute, he thought she would dismiss him for his forwardness. But then she grinned and seemed to relax.

"I've considered that. At one time—even as distasteful as it was—I figured that's what I'd do. But then Trenton came to his senses and agreed to marry Miss Rouchard, and I no longer saw the need."

York's fists balled in anger at the way she'd dismissed Trenton's engagement to Camellia.

"No offense meant," Mrs. Tessier said, noting his red face. "But you know a match between Camellia and Trenton wouldn't have worked. She's a fine girl, I'm certain of it, but too much separates them. It's that simple."

York unclenched his fists as he recognized the truth.

Mrs. Tessier continued. "Now it's too late for me to take a wealthy husband. The bank is quite insistent that I pay up immediately, and my cash situation simply won't allow me enough time to find a proper man. Even if I knew one with the money to make a difference, it's a bit too forward to rush a marriage, then immediately ask for cash. I'm bold but not that much so."

York bowed his head. He'd prefer to wait for Master Trenton's decision about Camellia but couldn't. Unless he did something, his worst fears would come true. A new owner would bring his own overseer. He thought of his money and knew he didn't have any choice anymore; he had to act.

"Can you get things ready?" Mrs. Tessier asked, breaking into his musings. "I'm depending on you."

He stared at her. She seemed smaller than normal, almost frail, more approachable than he'd ever seen her. It was now or never. She'd reject it out of hand, of course, but he had to try. What did he have to lose? So what if she said no? He'd hand the place over to Master Trenton and ride out within a week. But if she said yes, what possibilities that would bring!

The feeling he got when he made a large wager rushed through York's stomach—a fluttering of his insides, half fear, half joy at putting so much on one possible outcome.

"I got a proposition for you," he said, his voice more confident than he expected. "Somethin' that might save The Oak. You know what this place can do; it's kept your family livin' high for a long time. No reason to lose that if you don't have to, am I right?"

She shook her head. "I'm afraid there's no proposition that will make any difference. Just do what I've asked. Get me a fair price for the place, and I'll hand you a worthy bonus when it's done."

"How much money you figure you need to keep the bank off your back for a year?"

"I don't see where that's any of your business," she said stiffly. "Besides, nobody's got that kind of money."

"But what if they did?" he asked, not caring anymore if he made her mad. "How much would it take?"

She folded her arms. "Just do what I told you!"

"I know where I can get close to twenty-seven thousand," he said. "That much do you any good?"

She licked her lips. "Who's got that kind of cash?"

"Never mind about that. I know where to get it."

Mrs. Tessier tilted her head curiously. "That would go a long way toward paying off the bank. But it's senseless to talk of it; nobody's got that kind of money, least not anybody who'll give it to me."

York stood and walked to the window. If he told her about his money, she'd surely accuse him of stealing it from her. How would he answer her charge? Outside, the rain pattered to the ground. He surveyed the scene, the level ground, the line of oaks draped in wet moss, the marsh beyond. His choice sat right in front of him—his first and only chance to put his picture in the entryway of a fine house.

He turned back to Mrs. Tessier and tried to figure what she'd do. If she fought him, he might end up accused of embezzling money. Jail might follow. Even if he beat the charges, some folks would always see him as a crook.

"What are you up to, Mr. York?" Mrs. Tessier asked, her voice low. "Tell me now or leave. I haven't the time for such mysteries."

York made up his mind. He crossed the room and dropped to one knee in front of Mrs. Tessier.

"What are you doing?" she shrieked.

York grabbed for her hand and held it. "I'm askin' you to marry me."

She jerked her hand away. "You're insane! Get out of my room! Do what I told you, or I'll put you off the place!"

He stood and moved closer to her, stared down into her eyes. Fear crawled onto her face.

"I've got the money," he whispered. "I've got enough to give us another year. We can make it that long. Produce a full crop; put us right on top again."

She tried to move away, but he put a hand on each of her shoulders and held her in place. Her face flushed, but she stopped struggling and stood still, her eyes locked on his. "I don't believe you," she panted. "How would you come by such a sum?"

"I do some wagerin'. Been at it for years. I win a lot."

She seemed interested now but not convinced. "A man needs a high stake to wager enough to come up with that much. Where'd you get your stake?"

York started to tell her about the man at Mossy Bank, then thought of Sharpton Hillard. Who knew what Mrs. Tessier might have heard? Just as Hillard had come to The Oak asking questions, he might have done the same in Charleston or Beaufort, Columbia too—all the cities where Mrs. Tessier lived. If she'd heard of Hillard, she might add it all up and make him give back the first five thousand. If he didn't have that, he didn't have enough. In addition, if the law got mixed up in all this, it might ask questions about how he got the rest of it.

"Never mind where I got a stake. All that matters is what I have now, enough cash to save The Oak."

Mrs. Tessier gently lifted his hands from her shoulders. "You stole it from me," she said icily. "You've had free rein of the place, and there's lots of dollars coming in and out."

"Not as many as I've got," he said. "You know that. Besides, Master Trenton checks the books regular. I could never have taken this much from The Oak."

Mrs. Tessier rubbed her hands together, her anger apparently ebbing some. "You're a strong man, Mr. York. But I'm sure I can make a case against you. Enough dollars go through here for you to skim some off the top if you'd like."

"You're right," he said, seeing no reason to lie. "But somebody would have noticed the amount I've got. Besides, I can get witnesses to tell of my wagerin', how I've won over the last few years. Like at the races in Charleston; men will swear to it."

"I'm sure they will." She seemed calmer now, trying to figure him out.

She moved toward her dresser, picked up the pitcher, and poured herself a glass of water. "But I can still take you to the law, claim the money you've got . . . least most of it."

York shrugged. "I'll hide it."

"A few days in jail might change your mind on that."

"But it might not. I can be real stubborn when it comes to money; you ought to know that. I'm not a soft man. Besides, what good will a trial do you? Sure won't help you sell The Oak. Fact is, a trial will slow things down. Not what you want, I expect. Who wants to buy a property that's all tied up with some court matter? Not many, that's for certain."

She drank from her water. "You may be right," she admitted. "Scandal does no one any good. But what makes you think I'd marry you just to save this place? It's not my favorite spot, you know that."

York noted the change in her tone, realized she no longer dismissed the notion out of hand. He smoothed down his beard. "You know how much money this place can make. If you sell it, you've got the money from that but no more income. You'll have to go easy on your spendin', no matter how much the place fetches. Otherwise, who knows how long the cash will hold out? And you've got your children to consider. If you spend all the money on your own pleasures, what will you leave them when you pass on?"

He moved to a chair by her desk and perched on the end. "But if you keep the place, you've still got its value, plus the money a crop produces each year. A fine lady like you can do a whole lot of things with that kind of cash, don't you think? And we've had a rough spell of luck these last few years. Time for it to turn. I'll do rice this year, then gradually plant some cotton. With war comin' soon, prices for both will go sky-high. We'll make a fortune and never have to worry about the bank again."

Mrs. Tessier arched an eyebrow. "You have a good argument. But a marriage will cause all kinds of problems. If Trenton and Camellia were not well matched, what says we will be?"

York grinned. "That's easy. They would have married for love, least what they know of it. Their differences would have shown up fast. You've said that yourself. Those differences would have crushed that love, crushed it like a boot on a spider. But you and I know better than to fret over such love notions. We'd be marryin' to get somethin' we want. A business arrangement . . . nothin' more nor less."

"I take it you're not a romantic."

York hesitated but only for a second. "A long time ago I was. But who's that childish anymore? Life don't treat romance real good if you ask me. Finds a way to snuff it out at every turn."

Mrs. Tessier drank again from her water. "You give me reason for thought. I have to admit that."

"Strictly business," said York. "Nothin' else expected."

"What will people think?" she wondered. "My friends in Charleston?"

"They'll think you married a handsome man," York said. "Tell them I swept you off your feet."

"But you're no gentleman, and ladies of my quality don't marry a man who's not a gentleman."

"I'm a captain," he said. "Military rank carries good status."

"That may not suffice."

He smirked. "Then tell them it was for love. They know you didn't get that with Mr. Tessier. Tell them this time you did. You couldn't resist my charms. They'll find it movin', sentimental even."

"They'll never suspect it was for money, that's for sure."

"That's right. An overseer makes a livin' but not any money."

Mrs. Tessier walked hesitantly closer, until she was standing over him. "You're a surprising man."

He grinned again as he stood and looked into her face. So far his plan had gone better than he expected. "I reckon I am."

"You can prove to me you have the money?"

"I can."

"This will surprise our families," she said.

"Are you tellin' me yes?"

She held out her hand, and he gently took it and kissed it. She accepted the kiss, then stepped back. "When do you think we should do this?"

Thinking again of Hillard, York knew he needed to wed as soon as possible. "How soon will the bank demand its money?"

"Let's marry in a month," she said. "Near the end of the month. Here on The Oak. A simple affair. The parson from Beaufort can do the ceremony."

"That'll please me just fine. You'll inform your sons?".

"Yes."

"I'll tell the servants," he said. "They'll need to make the place ready."

She smiled and eased to him again, put her hands around his neck, and touched his long hair. "You might look real fine in some good clothes. Real fine indeed."

Chapter Twenty-Nine

Trenton got word in the study from Ruby about an hour later that his mother wanted to see him in her chambers as soon as possible. "Can't it wait until evening?" he asked, busy with some figures.

"I just deliver the message," said Ruby. "That's all."

Trenton dismissed Ruby and put down his pen. When his mother called, he had to respond or risk her cold anger. Although he detested being at her beck and call, he buttoned the sleeves on his shirt and headed to his mother's bedroom. *Probably more bad news,* he thought as he reached her door. Seemed lately that's the only kind they got.

He found her lying on her bed, but she sat up as he entered and pointed him to a seat. He rested on the edge, his hands on his knees.

"Thank you for coming so quickly," she said. "I have something to tell you before you hear it somewhere else."

He noted the gravity in her tone. "Should Calvin be here?" he asked, not wanting to leave his brother out.

She shook her head. "This is between us for now. Mother to elder son. Calvin will know soon enough."

"Is it about The Oak?"

"Yes and no."

He waited. She took a spot on the bed's edge. "I'm going to marry again."

He rocked back, confused. "Who? You've said nothing of this!"

"I know," she soothed. "It's happened suddenly. But I want this; believe it's best for us."

He sat blankly, trying to think of eligible men who might have wooed his mother without his knowing it. No one came to mind. "Who is it?" he asked again.

"This will surprise you," she started, "and you will not like it. But I've made up my mind, so there's no point in argument."

"Just say it."

"Hampton York."

Trenton froze. "Hampton York! It can't be true!"

Mrs. Tessier waved him off. "It's not your business. I can marry again if I choose."

"Not him!" fumed Trenton. "Yes, marry again if you like—I prefer that quite honestly—but not York! What possible reason could you have to wed him? He's far below you. Marry someone of means, or at least some title, not a man who can bring neither to your bedchamber."

Mrs. Tessier studied her son. "Let me get this straight. You think it permissible for you to marry Camellia but not for me to marry Mr. York? Your inconsistency surprises me."

"I know it's not logical," he said, standing now. "But I grew up with her, and she's beautiful and I . . . I've always wanted her. She brings out the best in me. When I'm not with her I get confused, make bad choices. It's like . . . like she's my conscience or something."

Mrs. Tessier laughed. "You know I'm against it. That's why she's so attractive to you. And yes, she's got virtue and you don't, but you *think* you want it. Ah, that's charming as well. Plus, she is a stunningly attractive woman. No wonder you have desires for her. But I can tell you from experience that men like you don't change, not even for one as pure as Miss Camellia. Yes, if you married her, you'd try to alter your stripes. You'd strive to live up to her high morality, but you'd fail. You're too much like your father not to fail."

Her voice became distant as she continued, and her eyes seemed to see something a long way off. "Somewhere—maybe it would take a few years—but somewhere down the line, you'd see another woman, some spectacular new thing in town or a darky in the servants' quarters. She'd catch your fancy. You'd fight it for a while, but to no avail. You'd get drunk one night and end up in the woman's bed, and then where would you and your sweet pure wife be?"

"I wouldn't do that," said Trenton. "Not to Camellia."

"You already have." Mrs. Tessier smirked. "Or have you so soon forgotten? You'd do it again too. Oh, she'd forgive you, at least the first few times. But you'd despise her for it, for the weakness it would show. You'd despise her because you'd despise yourself. Gradually, you'd grow cold and distant toward her, and the wonderful Miss Camellia would grow sad and hurt and miserable."

Trenton scowled. His mother's words stung him, but he didn't know how to argue with them. "Why would you marry York? I don't understand."

"He's got money," she said. "Simple as that. Enough to satisfy the bank until we can bring in a solid crop."

"Where'd he get that kind of money?"

"He says he won it gambling."

"That's a lot of luck."

"He says he's been doing it for years."

Trenton did some quick figuring. "It doesn't make sense."

Mrs. Tessier shrugged. "I'm not sure. All I know is he says he has it, and I need it. I'd prefer not to marry again, but since you didn't succeed in saving The Oak, I have to do it."

"Not exactly my fault that my intended got hit by a carriage," said Trenton, back in his chair.

"Still, it's a fact. We put our hopes in you, but they didn't come to fruition. Now I can't wait any longer. The bank will own the place in three months if we don't do something. Mr. York is our only chance."

"He stole it from us," snarled Trenton. "He's probably been robbing us blind for years. We ought to put the law on him, make him explain his sudden wealth."

"If we had time, I might agree. But we don't, so we'll do nothing of the kind. In fact, you need to get off your high horse and accept this. I'm going to marry Mr. York, and he's going to become lord of the manor around here. Not only will you not put the law on him, but you'll begin to show him some respect."

Trenton's jaw dropped as his stomach rebelled, and a vile taste rose in his throat. "I'll not allow this," he whispered, his voice cold. "No cheap, white-trash overseer will become master of The Oak. What a slap in the face! I'd rather lose the place to the bank; least it would sell it to someone worthy. If York takes over, we can never hold our heads up again . . . not here, not in Charleston, not anywhere."

His mother moved to his side. "You need to calm yourself. If Mr. York's money allows us to save this place and make it profitable again, then it won't matter what people say. You know how it works. If you have money, people keep their mouths shut, least to your face. If we give this place up, everyone will know why. Talk about shame. How will that feel? To go back to Charleston with our pride lost. Who'll accept us then?"

Trenton took his mother's hands and tried to stay calm. Maybe she'd respond to gentleness, if not to logic. "I can't let you do this," he said in the most loving tone he could muster. "I just can't. It's a matter of honor."

Mrs. Tessier chuckled. "What do you know of honor? You're a spoiled rich boy, who never had to practice any honor."

"You're right. But maybe it's time I started. Maybe it's time I stood up to you, to what you want, to the way you've taught me."

"You're talking nonsense," she said. "It's done, and you have no choice but to accept it."

"A man always has choices. Always."

"What are you going to do?"

"What I have to do," he replied. "Nothing more, nothing less."

She grabbed him by the shoulders. "Stay out of this! You had your chance. Now it's up to me!"

He shook her off and left the room, his hands clenched into fists. Nobody would tell him what to do, not even his mother. Maybe especially not her. No matter what happened, he could not let this come to pass, not so long as he had a heart beating in his chest.

Trenton burst into Calvin's room a few seconds later, his anger now hotter than when he'd left his mother's room. "Have you heard?" he shouted.

Calvin nodded. "Ruby told me. All the darkies know it. But nobody knows why."

"York stole from us!" Trenton complained. "She's marrying him for the money, to keep the bank at bay!"

Calvin jumped from his chair, his young face confused.

"We can't allow it!" continued Trenton. "Father surely wouldn't!"

"But what can we do?" asked Calvin, by the fireplace now, his back to the mantel.

Trenton paced the room, his eyes wild. "The only thing a gentleman can do. York has offended us; we cannot let it stand. We'll go to him, demand that he return the money and leave The Oak. We don't need him now. I'll run the place." He rubbed his hands together as he warmed to the possibilities. "If York takes our offer, we'll let matters end there; won't get the sheriff involved."

"Will we go to the law if he doesn't?"

Trenton stopped and faced his brother. "We'll not have time for that. An inquiry could take weeks, maybe months. And I'm sure York can get witnesses to his gambling winnings. I know his reputation. If we go through the law to reclaim the money, the bank will have us before we finish. No, if York won't cooperate, we'll have to take matters into our own hands."

"What do you mean?"

"You'll go to Josh Cain," Trenton said. "Make our challenge through him."

Calvin's face bleached. "A challenge?"

"Yes."

"Are you sure? It's illegal now."

Trenton stepped over and stared out the window. The road leading from The Oak stretched out before him. Clouds drifted through the sky as the rain blew out. He knew the route he'd just chosen brought many risks, maybe mortal ones. But what other path could he take and still claim any pride as a man?

"I'm sure," he said. "The law will do nothing, never has. I cannot let this stand if I ever hope to hold my head up again. York has aggrieved us. Not just with the stolen money—which is certainly offense enough—but with the proposal to Mother as well. A man of his station doesn't wed a woman so far above him. It's an offense to our name, you know that."

"But he's not a gentleman," said Calvin. "A challenge is not permitted to one who isn't."

"He's a captain," said Trenton, pivoting back to face his brother. "Officers are always considered gentlemen."

Calvin dropped his eyes. "He might kill you."

"True, but I have no choice. People of our station must defend their honor."

Calvin nodded, but without much conviction. "What about your hopes with Miss Camellia? If you kill her father, she'll surely not marry you."

Trenton bit his lip. "She loves me, and she and her father are not close. She has not told me this, but I know it's true. When I have the money again, I can keep The Oak and still marry her if I choose. She'll forgive me, even for this."

"You have great confidence in her love."

"Yes, I do. She's wanted to marry me since I was a boy." He tossed back his hair and moved to Calvin, put a hand on a shoulder. "Will you serve as my second?"

"If that's what you want."

Trenton patted Calvin's shoulder. "York will probably tuck tail and run. No duel will ever occur. And if it does, I can handle myself, you know that. Father taught me—you too, remember? He fought two duels, killed two men; he knew the craft and passed it to us."

"York is a dangerous man," said Calvin. "A former soldier as you said."

"But not a duelist," Trenton threw in quickly. "I'm not afraid of him. I have to do this."

"You'll write the letter of challenge?"

"Before the day is out."

"Then I'll take it to Cain," Calvin said, sounding confident now.

"You'll tell no one else. We don't need anyone trying to stop this."

"As you wish."

"I expect York will leave in peace."

"I pray that you're right."

Trenton grinned. "I didn't know you were a man of prayer, young brother."

"These are unusual circumstances," said Calvin. "Perhaps you will forgive me my sudden religiosity."

Although stunned by the news of York's proposal to Mrs. Tessier when he heard it from Stella as he washed up in the barn at the end of the day, Josh didn't let it bother him. With the money he'd put together, York might just pull this off and get his picture over the mantel after all. Josh wondered for a few seconds what such a marriage would mean for Camellia but couldn't see much harm from it. If Master Trenton didn't marry her, she'd find another young man soon enough. Either way, a match between York and Mrs. Tessier didn't look to harm her.

What an irony, thought Josh as he headed home. York's marrying Mrs. Tessier relieved Trenton of the need to marry a woman of means and opened the way for him to marry Camellia. Had the Lord set all this up this way? Made a path for Trenton and Camellia so odd as to be almost funny, if not so strange?

No matter, Josh decided. It wouldn't change his plans. He'd get the crop in the field, then take Beth and Butler and go west. With the fire-eaters in Charleston and Beaufort and a hundred other cities calling for war any day now, he wanted to leave before that happened. He'd seen war before and knew what a mess it could make of things. The sooner he could get shed of this part of his life and start the next, whatever that might be, the better.

The last of the sun beat down on his back as he reached his house and stepped onto the porch. After checking inside and not finding anybody around, he moved back to the porch and sat down on the steps. A light breeze blew in from the ocean. A rooster crowed in the distance. Josh took out a handkerchief and wiped his brow. He stared out over the land and thought what a pretty picture it would make to paint it. Since Anna's death he hadn't done any drawing. He dropped his head. Maybe when he got settled somewhere he could start again. Hearing footsteps, he glanced up to see Calvin Tessier headed his way.

"Afternoon, Calvin," said Josh, pocketing the rag and standing in surprise at his appearance. "Shouldn't you be preparing for supper?"

Calvin kept his chin up, his back straight. Josh knew from his posture that something important was up.

"I'm here because I have important affairs to attend," Calvin said.

Josh tilted his head. "I assume those affairs include me, otherwise you wouldn't have come to my house."

"You assume rightly."

Josh noted that Calvin's hand shook at his side.

"I'm here by the request of my brother, Trenton Tessier," said Calvin in a most formal manner. "To express a formal challenge to Hampton York for the offense he has given to every member of the Tessier family."

Josh put his handkerchief in his pocket. "A challenge is dangerous business."

"Master Trenton is aware of the dangers." Calvin's voice broke slightly.

"What is the nature of the offense?"

"The offense is twofold," stated Calvin, his heels together. "First, Master Tessier has cause to believe that Hampton York has practiced thievery against his family. Taken money that does not rightfully belong to him."

Josh bowed slightly. "If that is so, then I can understand your position. But what gives you cause to believe such a thing?"

Calvin cleared his throat. "Hampton York claims to possess money that he could in no way have managed to acquire on the salary he receives. How else could he accumulate such funds if not by thievery?"

"He is a gambler, you know."

"An extraordinary one, if he's got as much money as he says."

"You said you claim two offenses."

"Yes, and the second is as bad, if not more so, than the first. Hampton York has asked our mother to marry him."

Josh smiled slightly. "Who can control matters of the heart? I do not see the offense in this."

"It's not yours to see or not see," stated Calvin haughtily. "It is your task to take the letter of challenge to Mr. Hampton York."

Josh sat down on the porch steps and tried to ease the tension some. "I assume there are conditions that would appease Trenton's offended spirit."

"Yes, they are threefold." Calvin stared straight ahead, above Josh's hat. "First, Hampton York will return the money and offer an apology to the Tessier family. Second, he will retract his proposal to Mrs. Tessier. And third, he will pack his belongings and take his leave of The Oak within seven days from this day."

"Those are hard conditions."

"They are not negotiable."

"And what are the consequences if Mr. York refuses?"

Now Calvin seemed even more hesitant, a little unsteady in his knees. He glanced down for a second before he faced Josh again. "You know the tradition of the code duello. If Hampton York refuses the conditions of appeasement, then he—as challenged—will choose a second, pick a weapon, and designate a time and a place. Then he will meet Master Tessier at the stated time and place, and they will face off for the duel."

Josh took off his hat and stared into it. Things had suddenly become real serious, and he wanted no part of it. "Not many men resort to duels anymore. They're illegal, you know that. Perhaps the courts would suit Mr. Tessier better."

"A duel is still an honorable man's way of settling disputes," said Calvin. "No matter that they have fallen somewhat out of fashion."

"I suggest you ask Trenton to consider the courts. He is a young man. No reason to put his life at such risk as this."

"He knows the dangers," Calvin insisted. "I can assure you of that. Will you carry the letter of conditions and challenge to Hampton York, or should I communicate them through someone else?"

Josh stood and took a step toward Calvin. "Look, Calvin. I know you and Trenton. You don't need to do this. So what if your mother marries York? So what if he's got some money? Maybe he won it gambling, maybe he took some of it from you. Is it worth Trenton's life—and yours too, maybe? That can happen, you know. A second in a duel sometimes gets caught up in it; has to protect the honor of the one dueling. This whole notion isn't smart. I've seen York with a pistol. He knows what he's doing. He's not going to back down from this, if that's what Trenton is counting on. He won't do it, I can tell you that for sure."

Calvin blinked, and Josh saw sweat on his young face. "Tell Trenton to let this pass," Josh coaxed. "Tell him it's not enough to die over."

"Please take this letter to Hampton York," said Calvin, his voice cracking slightly as he lifted an envelope from the inside of his jacket pocket and handed it to Josh.

"I will. And you will take my message to Trenton."

"We'd like a response by the morning."

"I'll tell Mr. York."

After clicking his heels once more, Calvin pivoted smartly and hurried away. Josh watched him go, his heart heavy. Then, settling his hat back on, he left the porch and went to find York. Although he didn't think York would care what he had to say, he wanted to do all he could to get him to give back the money. Then he'd leave The Oak.

Josh found York by the barn, talking to Leather Joe. After asking Leather Joe to give them privacy, he immediately handed York the letter and told him what Calvin had said. York listened intently but without comment. When Josh had finished, York gave the letter back.

"Open the letter," York commanded.

Josh quickly obeyed.

"It say what you just told me?" asked York.

Josh read it. "Yes, the offenses, the conditions to satisfy the offended, and the challenge if the conditions aren't met. He also requests that we keep this between us. No public proclamation of the challenge."

"I'm some surprised. I didn't expect Trenton to like the idea of my marryin' his mother, but I didn't expect him to act so rashly."

"He's a boy," said Josh. "Hotheaded. Not clear in his thinking."

York's eyes narrowed, and Josh saw his meanness rise up in them.

"He thinks he's good enough to marry my daughter, but I'm not good enough to marry his mother."

"He's impudent," agreed Josh. "But is that any reason to kill him or be killed by him?"

"He's tryin' to take somethin' from me," York said coldly. "That's reason enough, I reckon."

Listening to his brother, Josh knew in a fresh way that he'd never understand him. Although the same father's blood coursed through their veins, they were so different. "How did you come by the rest of the money?" he asked. "Other than what I found at Mossy Bank?"

York waved him off. "Gamblin'. I did real good the last couple of years."

"That's a lot of winnings."

"Five thousand wagered right can go a long way close to twenty-seven thousand now."

"You don't plan to give it back, do you?"

"No."

"What if I told Mrs. Tessier what we did at Mossy Bank?"

"So what? It wouldn't change nothin'. She wouldn't care, and the trail is too cold for the law. Walt probably wouldn't even investigate."

Josh felt guilty. "I'm a fool. Look what this has brought. If I'd only taken the money to Walt from the start, none of this would be happening."

York chuckled. "You beat all. Any guilt here rests on my head, not yours. Yet you'll carry the load around like it's your fault. All that conscience of yours again."

"Maybe you got too little conscience."

"I ain't arguin' that."

"You have enough to save The Oak?" Josh asked.

York spat into the side of the barn. "It'll give us another year. We make a strong crop, we come out of debt. If we don't, all bets are off."

"So you're gambling again?"

"Yep, for sure."

"Hardly seems worth it."

"Maybe not to you, but I got no choice. Here's my chance to get that picture over the mantel."

Josh nodded. "Your dream. What you've always wanted. But is it worth dying over, killing another man?"

York shrugged. "To me it is. I don't expect that's a surprise to you."

"I won't stand as your second. Won't take any part in this."

"I'd like you by me. But I can understand if you choose otherwise."

"I choose otherwise," said Josh firmly. "I won't watch you die, and I won't help you kill Trenton. That's one guilt I don't want to carry."

"I'll ask Johnny then."

"He's real young for something so serious."

"You leave me no choice."

"Guess not," Josh said slowly.

York stuck out his hand. "Will you pray for me?"

"I don't know what I'd pray," Josh replied, taking his hand.

"Pray my aim will go straight." York laughed, obviously trying to break the tension.

"Maybe not that," countered Josh. "But I will pray that either you or Master Trenton will come to his senses before either of you takes a bullet."

"I'd prefer my prayer," said York, "but I'll take yours if you insist."

Josh squeezed his brother's hand, then dropped it and stepped back. "He's requested a response by morning. I'll write up the letter. I'll write that you will not return the money and depart; that you'll not apologize or retract your proposal; that you are accepting the challenge."

"What you figure he'll do after that?"

"Knowing him, I expect he'll write you a letter inviting you to choose a weapon, a place, and a time. He'll keep it formal, in accordance with the code, the rules of the duel."

York lowered his head. "What will you do?"

"I'll write him a letter outlining your response. Then I'll step aside and leave it to you and Johnny as your second."

York nodded. "I hate it comes to this. But I can't do what he wants."

"What about Camellia if something happens to you?"

"She's a grown woman now. She can care for herself, for Johnny."

"What if you kill Trenton? She'll hate you for it."

York didn't look up. "I reckon that's better than if Trenton kills me."

"It's a rough time," Josh claimed.

"It surely is."

Josh trudged off, both heart and feet heavy. Nothing good could come of this duel. No matter what happened, somebody would almost surely die.

Chapter Thirty

Camellia knocked at the door of Josh's house right after supper that night, her shawl gathered around her shoulders against the spring chill. Beth and Butler answered the door. She hugged them both as they welcomed her.

"Pa's finishin' in the kitchen," said Butler. "I'll go get him."

Beth held up a doll as Butler ran out. "I made it from an old dress of Mama's."

Camellia admired the doll. It had brown buttons for eyes. Beth led her to the front room, where wood burned in the fireplace.

"I know I'm gettin' too old for dolls, but I still like them," said Beth, her eyes bright.

Josh and Butler stepped into the room. "Good to see you," Josh said quietly, pointing Camellia to a rocking chair.

"I needed to talk to somebody," she began, "about Pa and Mrs. Tessier."

"I'm glad you came," Josh replied. "Wanted to talk to you too." He took a spot on the edge of the hearth.

"I guess you heard about the marriage," she said as she sat in the rocking chair.

"Yes, he sure surprises me sometimes. He tell you?"

"No, I heard it from Ruby."

"Everybody's tongue is loose."

Camellia glanced at Beth and Butler, and Josh noticed. "Why don't you two give us grownups a few minutes to talk?" he asked them. "Maybe Miss Camellia can visit with you for a while after that."

Beth started to argue, but Josh held up a hand and stopped her. She and Butler reluctantly tromped out.

"They're growing up fast," said Camellia. "Especially Beth."

"I fear I don't do well with her. Don't know how to handle a young woman. She's still hurting from Lucy's death, Anna's too."

"Perhaps you should marry again."

"Seems we already got a marriage to handle. Guess we don't need another one just yet."

"Can we let him do this?" she asked fearfully.

"Don't see what we can do about it."

"But he doesn't love her."

"Maybe not, but it's not ours to say one way or the other. Your pa's capable of it, you know."

Her eyes lowered to the floor. "I see little evidence of that. He's a hard man."

"He loved your mother, you should know that. Loved her as much as any man has ever loved any woman."

"Then why does he never speak of her?"

Josh stood and threw a piece of wood on the fire. "I don't know that I have the right to say. Your pa ought to answer that question for you."

"What's the big secret?" Camellia blurted. "Nobody will talk of her—not Pa, not you, not Stella. Nobody who knew her will ever say anything. I'm tired of that: the dropped eyes when I ask questions, the way people look away. Why won't they tell me about her? Did she murder somebody, do some terrible—?"

She covered her mouth as what she'd never considered hit her. People didn't talk of her mama because she *had* done something bad, something not worthy of remembering, something they thought a daughter shouldn't know.

"What did she do?" she asked quietly as she tried to grasp the truth of what she'd just figured out. "What is it nobody wants to tell me?"

Josh shook his head.

"Tell me!" she insisted. "Secrets like this do no one any good—not me, not Pa. It's time for it to end! I'm a grown woman. Whatever my mama was, I want to know, deserve to know."

Josh sat back down and focused on Camellia. "I guess you're right. You should know the truth. You're right about secrets too. They'll eat you up after a while. I've told York more than once he needed to get this out. But he never wanted you to know, and I didn't see it as my place."

"Stop protecting me," urged Camellia. "You're my friend, aren't you?"

"Okay." He took a deep breath and said it straight out. "Just remember all this is from what York's told me. I never knew her myself."

"Okay."

"Your mama wasn't a chaste woman." He said it quickly but firmly.

"What do you mean?"

He told her the story. How York met Lynette and fell in love. How he married her and took her baby girl into his heart. How she birthed Chester about seven months later. How York's luck turned bad and they moved to The Oak to make a steady living. How her mama ran off less than two years later, not long after giving birth to Johnny.

"Your pa kept you and Chester after she left," continued Josh. "You weren't his, but that didn't matter to him. He loved you because he loved her; raised you as his own because she was part of you; all he had left of her. You kept her alive for him; he's told me that over and over through the years."

Camellia listened intently as he talked, her heart rising and falling with the story. When he finished, she folded her arms and leaned back, rocking slowly to combat the confusion, the grief she was feeling.

"I have the red dress she wore the day they married," she whispered. "A navy blue cape, a pair of her earrings, and a Bible. That's all. Found them a long time ago in Pa's trunk. Don't know how he got them."

"She sent a box," explained Josh. "And told York she was dying of typhus."

"It's hard to believe. After all these years, hearing this."

"It's true. I've got no reason to lie."

Camellia stopped rocking. "He's not my father," she said quietly.

"He's as close to one as you're ever going to get. Don't shortchange what he's done for you."

She looked at her shoes. "I've not always thought well of him."

"He sometimes makes it hard to do that."

"Ruby said Mrs. Tessier is marrying him for money. I don't understand that. Didn't know he had any."

"Ruby ought to talk less. Why a man and woman marry is not my business, nor yours, nor hers."

"Does Pa have money?"

"You need to ask him that."

Camellia nodded. Then another idea hit her. She focused on Josh. "You're not my uncle."

"No. I'm your friend."

Camellia remembered the feelings she'd had for Josh, the way he made her breath come in short gasps the time she saw him without his shirt. Maybe she'd sensed this somehow, known it all along as only a woman can know things about a man. But now it didn't matter. Trenton loved her and surely would come back to her. Now that her pa planned to marry Mrs. Tessier, she and Trenton would face no more obstacles to their matrimony. Then why didn't she feel more joyful?

The fire shifted as Camellia tried to sort her emotions. The notion of Trenton proposing scared her more than anything else. He'd walked away from her once. Would he have done that if he truly loved her? And she'd never told him what had happened at his father's death. What would he do if he knew? Confusion ate at Camellia's stomach. A proposal from Trenton would cause a lot of upset, and that made her fearful.

"Who's my true pa?" she asked, hoping to settle her jumbled thoughts.

"That's one you need to ask York."

She stared into the fire, her mind stunned at how much she still had to find out.

"I need to tell you one more thing while we're getting secrets out of the way," said Josh.

"Yes?" She stared back at him.

He smiled, but his face wore a heavy sadness. His eyes were so kind, so gentle, unlike the eyes of any man she'd ever known. He wasn't her uncle, he believed in the Lord as she did, and he made her breath come in short gasps.

"I'm leaving The Oak," he said.

Her face turned white. "What?"

"I'm taking the children and going away from here in a few weeks."

"But why?" She felt lost, as if somebody had just dropped her in a forest in the middle of the night a thousand miles from home.

"How can I explain it? Lots of reasons." He turned and pointed toward the fireplace. "I used to draw."

"I remember the sailing ship. It was good."

"I don't draw anymore," he said sadly. "Not since Anna, then Lucy. Too many hurts here, too many memories that cling to me like big rocks. I need to shed myself of all of that. Plus, your pa and me, it's true we're brothers, but I'm not good when I'm with him. I let him take me on paths I don't want to go. I'm not blaming him, but I'm weak; don't follow my best instincts when I'm with your pa."

"You're the strongest man I've ever met."

"Then you need to meet more men." He grinned.

She smiled too, but only briefly. "I don't want you to go," she said, her voice pleading, sad. "I need you here."

"You'll be fine," he said softly. "You've got a strength few possess. You'll marry Trenton, move to Charleston, and raise some wonderful children."

"That's all I ever wanted. A loving husband and a good family; somebody to talk to me, to hold me when I'm cold; somebody to sit by the fire with and read good books when I get old."

"You'd think that wouldn't be too much to ask." Josh sighed. "But sometimes it's hard to find, even harder to keep."

"I still grieve your Anna."

"So do I. I pray Trenton will make you happy," he said. "You deserve it."

Camellia again rocked slowly. "You've never liked Trenton."

Josh waved her off. "It's not my place to speak ill of him."

Camellia stopped rocking. "But I want to know what you think. I trust your judgment. Why don't you like him?"

Josh hesitated, but she waited. The fire cracked as a piece of wood shifted. Finally, he spoke. "Please understand that whatever I say about Master Trenton is influenced by my care for you. I . . . I want only the best for you and don't believe he can provide that."

"Why not?"

"Many reasons. First, from what I can see, he's always taken you for granted. Treated you without respect, figured you were there for his taking when and if he asked. Next, how could he ask Miss Rouchard to marry him if he loved you? You can't tell me he did it to save The Oak. What kind of man would do that to a woman?"

Josh's voice rose as he talked. "Now you're going to just welcome him back with open arms? You need to respect yourself more than that! He's hotheaded too, just like his father; you know it's true. Yes, he can give you all the fine things you'd ever want, but those aren't the things that count in the long run." He paused to catch his breath.

"Maybe worst of all," Josh continued, "he's not a believer. I know I have no right to say anything; I'm not worthy of judging another. But a man's faith tells a lot about the kind of man he is. You're a believer in the Lord. How will you two mix that?"

He stared at her, as if waiting for an answer, but she was stunned to silence. Her eyes watered as she realized the truth of his words.

"Hey," he said, pulling out his handkerchief and wiping her eyes. "I didn't mean to hurt you."

"I asked for your opinion."

"Yes, you did."

"Is he worse than other men? Can he change?"

Josh put his handkerchief away but didn't respond. She pressed him. "Do you think he'll change if he marries me?" He shrugged, and she saw again he didn't want to hurt her.

"All men have their faults," he finally said. "And if anyone can lead Trenton to the Lord, that person is you."

"You have no faults. None I can see."

He dropped his eyes. "You have poor vision. I'm the most unworthy man of all."

Camellia studied him. "You've said that before. More than once. Why is that?"

"I'm like Paul, chief of sinners."

"I don't see it, nor why you would unless you're being falsely humble."

"You don't know me," he claimed. "What happened during my years at war."

"What did happen?"

He shook his head. "It's past. No need to burden you with it."

"You may never get the chance again," she coaxed. "What with your moving away and all."

He paused and was silent a long time.

"I'll not ask you again," she finally said.

He stood and shoved his hands in his pockets. "I'll miss you when I leave. You've been fresh air to me."

She stood and stepped toward him, her heart heavy as an anvil. "When will you go?"

"After the crop is in the field. Maybe second week this month."

"I can't believe you'll move from here; take Beth and Butler from me."

"They love you," he said.

"I love them. Will you draw again after you move?"

"That is my hope."

"Draw me something someday, send it to me?"

"I will look forward to that."

He opened his arms, and she fell into them. Her breath choked in her throat. She wanted to tell him she loved him too, but how could she mean that? Wouldn't Trenton soon ask her to marry him? Wasn't that what she'd counted on all her life? So how could she run away from it now?

As she leaned into Josh's chest, she listened to his heartbeat and wondered why hers felt like it wanted to stop.

Chapter Thirty-One

Camellia rushed home after leaving Josh, her mind spinning with questions, her heart pounding with confusion. She'd learned so much in the last hour, so much that it seemed she'd become a different person all at once, more mature, more aware of everything around her. She found her pa sitting on the front porch, a chaw in his cheek, his chair tilted back on its hind legs, a contented, pleased expression on his face. One part of her wanted to scold him for his proposal to Mrs. Tessier; another wanted to comfort him for all the troubles her mama had caused him.

He smiled as she reached the top of the steps. She took a chair by him and tucked her shawl closer to her chin.

"I reckon you heard," he started.

"Yes."

"I hoped to tell you face to face, but news like this don't keep long."

"Why, Pa? And don't tell me love."

He looked sharply at her, and she felt bad about her tone.

"I don't need to explain my doin's with Mrs. Tessier to you," he said. "Why we're marryin' is between us, like it is between any man and woman."

She stared out into the dark yard. Stars blinked down. She turned back to her pa, determined to talk to him, set on making amends for the harsh way she'd thought of him for a long time. "You loved my mama, didn't you?"

"Yes, I did. Powerful love I had for her."

"She loved you."

He spat into the yard. "I like to think she did."

"Tell me about her."

He rubbed his beard. "Not much to say. She died young; the typhus got her."

"I don't remember her."

"That's a grief to me. You look just like her."

"Not much like you, though. I always wondered some about that."

He eyed her suspiciously but didn't speak. She shivered as the night chill ate into her bones, but she didn't plan to leave the porch until she said what she wanted to say.

"Tell me about her."

He dropped the front legs of his chair to the porch floor. "She's dead and gone. No reason to drag those memories out right now. I got a new life ahead of me. You want to talk about that, I'll jabber all night. But what's over is over. Best to leave it buried."

"Josh told me about my mama," she said softly. "I made him."

York cursed and spat again. "Josh sometimes talks more than he ought."

"I gave him no choice."

"Man always got a choice to say no."

"Be mad at me, not him."

"What'd he tell you?"

"All of it. The way you met, she already with me, Chester on the way. How she stayed a couple of years, gave you Johnny, then took off. The way you loved her; the way you took care of us children all by yourself."

"I didn't do too good by you three, but it was the best I knew how," he said.

"You should've told me. It would have made me more understanding, more patient, more . . . " Camellia stopped, and her eyes trickled again. "I've not been a good daughter," she continued. "I've judged too fast, seen the worst real easy instead of looking for the best. I'm sorry for that."

"I tried to protect you," he mumbled. "Didn't want no more hurt to come your way. No reason for a child to think poorly of their mama, no matter how bad that mama might be."

Camellia reached over and patted him on the knee. "You are my pa. No matter about any of this."

He shook his head. "Your pa is a man named Wallace Swanson. Josh tell you that too?"

A light breeze caught her hair and blew it into her face. Wallace Swanson. The name meant nothing to her. How could Wallace Swanson be her father?

"He still alive?"

York leaned back again and stared into the yard. "Don't know for sure. Maybe so."

"He feels dead to me. Just a name, nothing else."

"If he's alive, he's up North somewhere, that's all I can say."

"Wonder what he looks like."

"Maybe you can find out someday."

She brushed her hair from her eyes. "Things are changing. *I'm* changing."

"Things are always changin'. People too. It's one thing you can hang your hat on."

"This is more than normal, though. You and Mrs. Tessier marrying, Josh leaving."

"He tell you about that too, did he?"

"Yes."

"Man keeps his mouth shut a long while, then runs off with words all of a sudden, like a stream after a heavy storm."

"Why's he leaving?"

"Not for me to say."

"He says he needs a fresh start somewhere. Too many memories here."

"I can see how he'd figure that."

Camellia paused and wondered again about Josh's past, why he spoke ill of himself so often. "Why's he so hard on himself?"

"What do you mean?"

"You know, how he says he's so unworthy."

York shrugged. "Some things men don't like to talk about."

"You two stick together, don't you?"

"Used to for sure. Not so much right now, though."

"What will happen to us, Pa?"

He spat into the yard. "Future's not always clear. One day one thing, the next day another. But the way I see it, me and Mrs. Tessier will marry, I'll make The Oak prosperous again, everybody will live happy ever after."

"You believe that's possible?"

"Don't see why not."

"What about me and Trenton?"

"If he loves you, he ought to wed you. Nothin' to keep him from it."

She thought of Josh. "How do I know if Trenton really loves me? He put me aside real fast when he found Eva Rouchard."

"His family forced him to that."

"He should have stood up to them."

He cocked his head at her. "You havin' second thoughts about him?"

"Not sure what I feel. Confusion more than anything else . . . fear too maybe. Scared he'll ask me, scared he won't."

"Don't marry him, then. Don't need to anymore with me marryin' Mrs. Tessier. I can give you what you want. Can send you to fine schools, dress you up real pretty, make you a lady like none other in the South."

She smiled. "Pa, that's your dream, not mine. I never really wanted any of those things. Sure, they'd be nice, and I've thought about them because I knew Trenton desired that for me. But I don't desire them, pine for them. I'm a simple girl, easy to please when it comes to matters of a house, clothes, food, and such. I just want a man I know for sure loves me, will take care of me."

"Trenton might not be that man, then," he said quietly.

Her eyes widened. "You've always encouraged me and Trenton. You feel different now?"

"Maybe I don't need to encourage it anymore."

"Now that you're marrying his mother."

"Right."

"You wanted me to marry him for his money, didn't you?"

He stood and moved to the porch rail, then sat on it and stared at Camellia. "I won't deny that's part true. But I figured you loved him too. That way everybody came out to the good. You married the man you loved, improved your lot in life—mine too in the bargain. Make both of us happy. Any sin in that?"

She had no answer to that question. "You think he loves me?"

"I think he wants to love you but isn't sure how."

"What does that mean?"

He sighed loudly. "Men like Trenton Tessier worry more about what they want than they do what the other person wants. They don't realize it, but they're born to privilege, born to rule and bark orders. They do it with the darkies, with their hired help, with their wives. In his eyes, he's above right and wrong because he's above the laws that govern other folks. He does what he desires and expects everybody else to accept it."

"You sound angry at him."

"Maybe I am."

Camellia sensed something deeper behind the words but didn't know how to get at it. "How's he taking your proposal to his mother?"

"Not good, I can tell you that."

"Have you talked to him?"

"You might say that. He says I'm not good enough for her."

"She didn't think me good enough for him."

"Yes, I think there's a fancy word for that."

"Irony."

Another question came to Camellia. "I hear you have some money."

"People sure do talk a lot."

"Do you?" she asked.

"Some."

"Enough to keep The Oak from the bankers?"

"At least for another year."

"Mrs. Tessier marrying you for the money?"

He smiled. "She's marryin' me 'cause I'm handsome and charmin', don't you think?"

"Where'd you get your money?"

"Everybody wants to know that. I'm a gambler, remember?"

"That's a heap of gambling."

"I'm good at it."

Camellia moved to the rail by her pa. "What do I do if Trenton proposes to me?"

He gazed into her face in the moonlight. "What do you want to do?"

331

"I don't know."

York spat off the rail. "Maybe you won't face the choice."

"You don't think he'll ask?"

"That ain't it. He may be dead."

She froze in place. "I don't understand."

York sighed again. "I ought not tell you this, but you'll find out soon enough anyway. Master Trenton has challenged me. Claims I stole money from The Oak. Also says I offended the family name by proposin' to his mother."

"You can't fight him!"

"It ain't my choice. He's offered the challenge."

"You can refuse it! You have to refuse it!"

"You know what happens if a man refuses a challenge. He's a laughing-stock. He'd post me all over—Beaufort, Charleston. I'd have to leave the state."

Camellia nodded. She knew what happened if a man turned down a challenge. The challenger put up posters all over the place, signs and letters that told what a coward the man was, how he'd refused an affair of honor.

"What are his conditions?" she asked, hoping to find a loophole.

"I give him every dollar I got, take back my proposal to his mother, and leave The Oak."

Camellia frowned. No way her pa would accept those conditions. "You can't duel," she argued. "It's illegal."

York chuckled. "It's illegal on the books, but men do it all the time. The law don't do a thing."

"But you might kill him!"

"And he might kill me."

She stood and paced the porch. "But you can't! He can't!"

"It ain't my doin'. He challenged me. I got to face it or leave."

"Then let's leave! Josh is doing it; we can too!"

"And go where?"

"I don't know, it doesn't matter. We'll go with Josh, wherever he goes," she insisted.

"He wants shed of me," her pa stated honestly. "Don't think he'd like my taggin' along."

Camellia's mind swirled, but she saw no way to fix this, no way to keep her pa from dueling Trenton. Yet she refused to give up. Somehow, someway, she'd keep this from happening.

"Mrs. Tessier know about this?"

"I don't know. Probably not, and you shouldn't go tellin' her."

"She won't marry you if you kill her son."

"Maybe not, but I got a feelin' about her. She's a surprisin' woman. But one thing is for sure: She won't marry me if I run or if Trenton kills me."

"You can't kill him," she repeated. "You just can't."

"Go tell him to take back his challenge, then. That's the only way to make sure nobody dies."

"I can do that," she agreed. "He'll listen to me. He has to."

When she left her pa, Camellia headed straight for the manse, her head set on getting Trenton to back off the challenge. Ruby led her to him in the study, and he stood quickly as she entered the room. He indicated a seat for her, but she refused to take it and remained standing instead, a heavy desk between them.

"You cannot challenge my pa!"

He waved her off. "I'll not talk with you of this. It's not a woman's place to interfere in such matters."

"You have to."

"No, I don't. Your pa shouldn't have told you."

"You think you can kill my pa, and I'll still marry you?"

When Trenton glared at her, the memory of Marshall Tessier, his father, suddenly came back to her . . . the way his eyes had changed when she fought his advances.

"I haven't yet asked you to marry me," he said coolly. "But if you love me, you'll marry me no matter what happens between your pa and me."

Camellia staggered back, her spirit crushed. For the first time she saw in Trenton a trace of what both Josh and her pa had described—his arrogance, his sense of privilege above other people. For several seconds she stood stunned, trying to figure what had happened. Had he just shown this side of himself to her for the first time, or had it been there all along and she'd refused to face it? Tears threatened, but she angrily wiped them away. "What's happening to us?"

Trenton's face softened again. He circled the desk and opened his arms. He seemed like his old self, but she refused to go to him. So he dropped his arms but stepped close. "It's okay," he soothed. "Please forgive me. As you can imagine, I'm under a lot of strain. This proposal from your father stunned me. I cannot let it stand."

"But you'll be killed!"

"Perhaps not."

"Then my pa will be killed!" She stepped back a pace. "How do you think this makes me feel? One of the two men most important to me will almost surely die!"

"It doesn't have to be that way," he argued. "He can accept the conditions, and I'll retract the challenge."

She backed up another step. "You have no idea what you're doing. My pa will not retract anything. He's a soldier at heart, always has been. A man as tough as any alive. You ought to know that. He's cunning and brave, prideful too—in his own way as prideful as you. One of you will die in this unless you retract."

"I cannot do it. It would ruin my life."

"Better a ruined life than none at all."

"Not to me."

"Then you refuse?"

"Yes."

"Does your mother know?"

"No, and you will not tell her."

"If you kill him, I . . . I don't know that I can marry you. He's a hard man, but he has done his best for me, Chester, and Johnny."

"We'll face that when the time comes," he answered stoically.

She shook her head, surprised at the words she'd just spoken. "I fear that Josh may be right about you," she said, again stronger than she knew she could be.

Trenton smiled, but not playfully. "Mr. Cain's opinion of me is not high?"

"I don't understand you."

"It's not your place to understand me," he said, moving close enough for her to feel his breath on her cheek. "It's your place to stand by me, to support my decisions. That's what a good woman does for her husband; she stands with him. No questions, no quarrels."

He put his hand on her shoulder and pulled her close. She closed her eyes and leaned into him, eager to rest in his strength, eager for somebody to hold her against all the forces pushing at her insides. She felt like she did when an ocean wave crashed over her head and she gave herself to it. The water just carried her away, carried her away, and all she had to do was relax and enjoy the power of the water, the might of its pull. Trenton's lips touched her forehead, and she raised her eyes to meet his. She saw a grin on his face, but this time the grin seemed all crooked—not a grin of joy at her love, but a grin of triumph at his power. He believed he could have her, she realized, have her whenever he wanted. He believed in his control over her, in his privilege, believed that all he had to do was ask and she'd come running. Could she give in to that, allow him that much authority over her? Only the Lord should have that much dominance over another person; only the Lord should receive that much obedience.

Camellia pulled away from him and ran from the room. Until she understood what she felt, she couldn't stay with Trenton, couldn't let him kiss her and put her under his dominance again.

On the stairs she almost stumbled but kept going. She'd done all she could for Trenton and her pa. No matter what happened now, it was beyond her control. The duel would surely happen. After that, who knew what to expect?

Chapter Thirty-Two

As Josh expected, neither York nor Master Trenton backed away from the prospect of a duel. Within the next seventy-two hours, Trenton had written a second letter, this one inviting York to name a weapon and a place and time for the settling of their dispute. York chose 7 A.M. on Saturday morning, five days hence, April 13. A spot on the beach about two miles from The Oak would serve as the staging ground. Pistols, York decided, a Colt .51 for each man. The traditional ten paces apart. Each man would bring one second, and each man would fire one shot per round. If both men were still standing after the second round, the seconds would step in and allow either man to back away from the contest, honor intact. The doctor from Beaufort would stand as aid to the wounded if necessary.

Although he carried the letters to and from York and Master Calvin, Josh tried hard to keep from getting caught up in the emotion of the matter. He'd seen enough death and didn't choose to experience any more. To the best of his ability he kept his focus on preparing to leave The Oak. He told Beth and Butler of his plans. Beth cried and told him she wanted to stay. He held her close and sought to soothe her by telling her he'd move them to a spot where she could go to school; that seemed to settle her some.

The days before the duel passed quickly. Josh talked to York almost every morning, trying to get him to offer Master Trenton a compromise, maybe give him the money at least, but York refused. He'd won the money, he kept repeating. No reason for him to give Trenton Tessier something that belonged to him.

Work on the plantation continued as if nothing had changed. The field hands moved to the rice fields every morning, slaved in the hot sun that had already started to bake down, then came home about dark each night. It seemed odd to Josh, the way things kept on moving, the way normal routines still happened in spite of the possibility of death hanging just around the corner. Of course nobody but he, York, Camellia, Johnny, and the Tessier brothers knew about the upcoming duel. But still it struck him as odd that life could just ease along while so much change stood so close on the horizon.

To the best of his ability, when he wasn't helping his kids pack for their move, Josh stayed alone a lot of the time, took long walks on the beach, tried to keep his thoughts away from the grief he felt about leaving Camellia. She deserved better than him, he knew that. But still he had feelings for her he couldn't deny. And it wasn't just loneliness anymore either, nor the desire to have a mother for Beth and Butler. No, it was more than that—deeper, he knew that. She possessed every trait he'd ever valued in a woman—honesty, goodness, intelligence, and natural grace. She loved the Lord and tried to live a holy life. In addition, she was prettier than the ocean at sunrise. Yet she belonged to another. So he might as well put her out of his head. In just a few days he'd leave The Oak, leave her and everything connected to her.

His preparations complete, Josh met with York near the end of the day, down at the beach where York would square off against Trenton the next morning. York paced off the distance that would stand between him and Trenton and checked the footing in the sand. Sea gulls squawked overhead; waves crashed on the shoreline. Josh looked out to sea, his heart heavy but resolute. York stepped to him and also scanned the horizon. A steady breeze blew in their faces.

"I wish it hadn't come to this," said Josh.

"Not my choosin'."

"I've suggested a compromise. Give back the money; offer him that satisfaction at least."

"We already spoke of this."

Josh nodded. "The crop's about planted. I'm ready to go. So I'm leaving early tomorrow. Before this happens. I don't want to see it, either way it turns out."

"I know."

Both men fell silent. Josh kicked at the sand with his boot. "I feel like I've failed you. By deciding not to stand with you in the morning."

"You ain't failed nobody. Been a good brother to me."

"Not like you've been to me."

"I ain't done much."

"You stood by me after Mexico."

York shook his head. "We're even on that. You owe me nothin'."

"I'm not a good man," Josh said, a tear coming to his eye.

York put a hand on his shoulder. "You're the best of men."

"If I could just go back." Josh sighed. "Do that one thing all over again, maybe then . . . "

"What happened there just happened. Nothin' you or anybody else could have done about it."

"Wish life gave us a chance for do-overs," said Josh sadly. "But once something is past, it's over."

York chuckled slightly. "I thought you believed in do-overs. Thought you believed the good Lord gave us all a chance to start again."

Josh nodded. "I believe that in my head, but it's hard to get it lodged in my heart."

"You got to have faith," said York.

Now Josh laughed. "You sound like a preacher."

"Yes, and the salt in the ocean is really flecks of gold."

Both men laughed.

"I'll miss you," said Josh.

"Likewise."

"Take care of Camellia."

"She is past the age she looks to me for much care."

"You know what I mean."

"I'll do my best."

"You've done well by her. Be proud of that."

York spat. "I did the best I knew how. You plan to tell Camellia bye?"

"No more than I already have."

York turned and put a hand on his shoulder. "I wish you'd stay until this matter with Master Trenton is finished. Camellia might need you if I don't come through it."

"She'll marry Trenton if that happens," Josh replied quickly. "She won't need me."

"And if I kill him?"

"Then she'll find another man to marry. She'll have plenty of offers."

York faced the ocean again. Josh put his arm around his brother's shoulders. The ocean rolled and swelled, pushed in and out.

"May the Lord bless you," Josh said.

"You too, Brother."

"Thought you didn't believe in the Lord."

"I cover my bets, either way."

Sleep came reluctantly to Josh that night, and about the time midnight came, he realized why. He had one more thing to do before he could leave, one more thing he wanted to finish. Climbing from his bed, he stepped to his closet, pulled out a couple of things he'd already packed, set them up, and started to work. It took close to three hours, and he wasn't that pleased with it when he'd finished.

After putting his things away, he crawled back into bed and fell asleep this time, as contented as any man could be in his circumstances. Only a couple of hours after dozing off, he awoke suddenly, the sound of knocking bouncing through his head. It took him a couple of seconds to realize somebody was at the door. Hurrying, he slipped on his pants and a shirt and rushed to answer before the knocking woke the children. To his surprise, Sharpton Hillard was standing on his porch, his hat in his hands. The first streaks of the morning sun had just started to mark the sky. Josh stepped back and asked Hillard in.

"Sorry to come so early," said Hillard, taking the seat Josh offered. "But the matter is urgent."

Josh threw a log on the fireplace and lit a candle on the mantel. "You want some coffee? Take a minute to heat some, but glad to get it."

339

"Not now. Just need to talk with you. I rode most of the night."

"What's the rush?"

"Guess you haven't heard about Fort Sumter. South Carolina forces fired on it yesterday. It's all the talk in Charleston. War is here for sure."

"War is foolishness," said Josh. "Lots of good men will die."

"You are not a secessionist?"

"I've seen war. Nobody ever wins, no matter their cause."

Hillard spun his hat on his fingers. "I didn't come to talk about the war. Though that did give me cause for hurry. Want to get back North soon as I can."

"This about Mossy Bank?"

"I found the grave," said Hillard.

"Quincy."

"Found the marker you left on it."

"You find any money?"

"Nope. Found this, though." He reached into his pocket and pulled out a piece of paper wrapper for a chaw of tobacco.

"So?"

"Mr. York chews store-bought. I've seen him with this brand."

"This is not proof of anything."

"Oh, come on, Mr. Cain. I admire you trying to protect your brother, but maybe you weren't the only man at Mossy Bank that day. Mr. York was there with you."

"So?"

Hillard sat his hat on his knee and stared hard at Josh. "Look. I've done a lot of talking to folks these last few months. From what I hear, you're a honest man, not given to bad things. But Mr. York, well, he's got a different kind of reputation. Folks say he does what suits him, not a mean man but a cunning one, out to take care of his own interests before anybody else's. He—"

Josh held up a hand. "He's my brother. I won't hear you bad-talking him."

Hillard nodded, took a big breath. "Okay, I understand. Here's all I'm asking. Was he there? Is it possible he took the money? Maybe you know about it and are covering for him, maybe not. Maybe he took it, and you don't even know. That's all I'm asking. Is it possible he has it?"

Josh stood and focused on the flickering fire in the fireplace. How could he tell Hillard what had happened? How could he turn in his brother? What would that do to York's plans, even if he lived through the next hour or so? If he told on him and Hillard took the five thousand away, would he still have enough to keep The Oak from the bankers? If not, would Mrs. Tessier still marry him? If not, York would never get his picture over the mantel in the manse, and he'd blame Josh forever for his failure. Telling on York might destroy his whole life. Could he do that after all York had done for him?

Yet, how could he tell a straight-out lie? Mr. Hillard had asked him directly about York and the money. Could he pretend he didn't know about it? He thought of York, even now already at the beach, about to face off against Master Trenton. He might be dead within the hour. He faced Hillard.

"Tell me who Ruth Swanson is," Josh insisted. "Who you work for and where this money was headed. You come clean with me, and I'll come clean with you."

"You're asking a lot," said Hillard.

"I know. But so are you."

Hillard twirled his hat. "Okay, here's the way it is."

Josh sat back down. Hillard told him his story. As Josh listened, his eyes widened. What Hillard said changed everything.

Five men gathered on the beach right after sunup, each of them dressed in their best frock coats and ruffled shirts. As they had agreed, neither had brought any of the three witnesses the dueling code allowed them. York wore a new black hat, stiff of brim and braided with gold. Trenton came hatless, his close-cropped hair catching the first rays of light. Calvin stood by Trenton, Johnny by York. According to the code, both seconds had already searched each other to make sure neither carried any weapons. On this day, only the combatants could hold firearms. The doctor stood close to thirty yards away and out of line of any potential fire, no matter how wildly aimed. The sun warmed the men from the east. A touch of a breeze ruffled York's beard as he stared at Trenton.

"As the challenger's second, I am duty bound to give you one more opportunity to meet my demands and retire from the field," said Calvin, his tone steady. "Will you apologize for your offenses, or shall we go forward?"

York simply spat tobacco juice for his answer.

"We'll go forward," Johnny called. "The claim to offense is without merit."

York smiled proudly at his son for the way he had risen to this situation. No matter what occurred today, his boy had shown courage, and his chest swelled to see it.

"Then you give us no choice but to go forward," Calvin proclaimed.

"The choice is yours," said York, speaking for the first time. "I have no desire to shoot anybody, but I will if I must."

"Do your worst," Trenton replied, eyes narrowed. "And I'll do likewise."

Calvin produced a coin from his pocket. "Choose heads or tails. Winner chooses firing position, loser chooses firing signal."

Johnny nodded. York had spent the last few days teaching his son the dueling code, so Johnny now knew his rights. "Tails!" he shouted bravely as Calvin flipped the coin. The coin hit the sand.

"Tails!" shouted Calvin, eying the coin. "Choose your position!"

Johnny glanced at his father. York tilted his head left. He wanted to fire with the sun to his left, away from his dominant eye. Johnny walked to the spot his father had chosen.

Calvin nodded. "Firing signal is 'Ready.' I will call it."

Everyone nodded. Trenton turned to Calvin, and Calvin lifted a rectangular box to chest level and opened it. A pistol lay in the box. Calvin lifted it out and handed it to Trenton.

"As we agreed," said Calvin as Trenton examined the weapon. "Colts, 1851. The combatants will take ten paces in opposite directions. At the signal 'Ready,' they will fire their first round at will. If both men miss, the offender has another chance to make his apologies and retire from the field. If he refuses, the two combatants will again meet in the middle, will reload and commence action again, this time taking nine paces before firing. Such action will continue at closer ranges each time until one or the other of the men either retires from the field or receives a mortal or disabling wound. If both men take wounds but without any mortal or disabling wound, the combatants will then decide whether to continue or retire. Are these instructions clear?"

York spat and nodded.

"Yes," said Trenton.

"Then we shall load weapons." Calvin looked at Johnny, who pulled a Colt from his waistband, slipped a bullet into the chamber, clicked it shut, and held it ready. Calvin likewise prepared Trenton's weapon. According to code, Johnny handed the pistol into York's left hand, his least dominant one and Calvin did the same with Trenton, thus protecting against either man firing early. Johnny's hand trembled as he pulled it away.

"Stay steady," whispered York, seeing his son's fear. "A man needs a clear head with matters like this."

Johnny dropped his eyes. York quickly hugged him. "I'll be fine," he whispered. "But just in case, if anythin' happens, go to Josh Cain. Tell him . . . tell him to provide for you . . . to . . . tell him he has my blessin' regardin' Camellia. He'll understand."

Johnny nodded.

"Move away now," urged York.

Johnny stepped off about twenty steps.

York and Trenton glared at each other, as if one could scare the other away.

"Prepare to take your positions," said Calvin.

York thought of Camellia. If Trenton ended up dead, she'd never forgive him. "Take places!" ordered Calvin.

York pointed his pistol toward the sky, his elbow at waist level, and moved to his spot. Trenton did likewise. The breeze played with York's beard. He hoped the wind wouldn't knock his aim off line. The ocean rolled in and he heard its rush. A bird chirped in the distance. York thought of Trenton. The boy had guts; he had to give him that. He wondered about Trenton's thoughts, whether the boy truly knew that he might die in the next few moments. If it didn't seem real to York and he'd killed a number of men, how could it seem real to a young man like Trenton?

York reached his spot and pivoted to face Trenton.

"Stand ready!" called Calvin.

York's legs tensed, and his eyes narrowed. His finger twitched on the pistol trigger.

"Prepare!" yelled Calvin.

York switched his pistol to his right hand and tried to say a silent prayer but couldn't. What did a man pray at such a time? That God would let him shoot down another man? He thought of Josh. Josh would pray for him; always had. Not that it did much good, but maybe it didn't do any harm.

"Seconds retire!" yelled Calvin.

Johnny and Calvin stalked off another twenty paces from the duelists, then came to a stop and faced the combatants again. A second of quiet fell. York spat. A bird chirped. Clouds shifted. A fly buzzed. York's mind raced. He thought of all he'd done, all he could have done. He hadn't lived a good life and knew he ought to ask God's forgiveness but didn't know how. Would he die? Would Trenton die? What happened to a man after he died?

"Ready!" Calvin's signal to fire cracked through the air.

York jerked his pistol to shoulder height, his eyes aiming the weapon even as he lifted it. He heard a shot fire and thought for an instant that his finger had squeezed off his weapon before he'd aimed. But then the dirt splashed at his right boot and he realized that Trenton was the one who had fired hastily, not him. His finger eased off the trigger, and he stared across the distance between him and Trenton, knowing that the boy's inexperience had just cost him dearly. Trenton had fired his round and missed and now stood straight ahead with no protection and no choice but to stand and let York take his shot.

York kept the pistol aimed as his chest heaved! He was alive! Not even wounded! He wondered what would happen after he killed Trenton. Would everything change for the good? With Trenton gone, would Mrs. Tessier still marry him? Probably, he figured. She was like York—did what she had to do. He'd marry her with no more troubles. His picture would hang over the mantel! Would that satisfy him? Make him content? He didn't know, but he'd sure like finding out.

"It seems you've missed your mark!" he shouted to Trenton.

"Take your shot!" responded Trenton. "That is what the rules require."

York grunted at the young man's foolish bravery. "The rules allow me to offer you the option of leavin' the field. I now grant you that choice."

"I am a man of honor," called Trenton. "And you are a thief! How can I retire and leave you to mock me? A man of your station making light of a man of mine? I could never show my face again. I will not leave the field without you taking your round."

"Let it go!" shouted York. "You're still alive. Nobody but us will ever know."

"I'll know!" argued Trenton. "That's what matters most!"

"I offer you the choice one more time," York called. "Leave me be and I'll not shoot."

"Let it end!" Calvin shouted to Trenton. "Your honor is not worth your life!"

"He'll fire or I'll kill him!" answered Trenton. "You know what the rules demand! As my second, you must enforce them!"

Calvin squared his shoulders. "You have heard his choice!" he shouted to York. "And I am a witness to it."

"You leave me no release," called York. "I'll do what is required."

Trenton stood to his full height.

York raised his pistol. Trenton stared straight at him. York imagined Trenton lying dead on the beach, his blood pouring into the sand. But would Mrs. Tessier marry him if he killed her son?

Confused, York spat and tried to clear his head. With Trenton gone, Mrs. Tessier would have no choice if she wanted to hang on to her fortune.

York aimed carefully. All of his anger suddenly poured into his fingers, anger at the way men like Marshall Tessier had treated him, anger at the way Mrs. Tessier had looked down at Camellia, anger at the fate that gave some folks a higher station in life than others. A man like Trenton Tessier deserved to die, he figured. He and others like him had laid hurts on the shoulders of others for a long time. He ought to suffer, to feel pain like others had felt it.

York's face dripped with sweat. He spat one last time and pulled the trigger.

Josh ran onto the beach just as York fired his pistol. His heart dropped as he saw Master Trenton crumple to the ground. Mrs. Tessier and Camellia trailed Josh, their skirts dirty with sand they'd kicked up in their rush, their faces wet with sweat. Josh ran to Trenton and knelt beside him.

"My knee!" shouted Trenton. Josh stretched Trenton out and saw blood soaking his pants in his right leg. He pulled at the hole the bullet had made and ripped it wider to examine the wound. Then the doctor appeared. Josh stood with everyone else and watched as the doctor wrapped cord around Trenton's thigh. Josh pulled out a handkerchief and pressed it against the wound. Trenton groaned and gripped his leg with both hands. His mother ran to his side, took his head in her lap.

"You have crippled me!" Trenton shouted at York.

"If you don't die of blood loss or get the gangrene, you'll live," York said softly. "Consider yourself a blessed man I didn't aim for your heart like I could have."

"You should have killed me!" moaned Trenton. "I don't want to live like this, half a man."

"I figured maybe dyin' would be too good for you," said York. "Too easy. Best to let you live a while longer. Maybe see if you can learn some things, turn out a better man."

"You'll pay for this!" Trenton screamed, his empty pistol still in his hand. "This is not the end of your dealings with me!"

"I'll kill you the next time," said York. "You be smart now and let matters go." He stood and faced Josh and Camellia, pointed at Mrs. Tessier. "What are you all doin' here?"

"I came to stop this," Josh explained. "Sorry I'm too late." He and York moved away a couple of steps, Camellia and Johnny trailing them. Mrs. Tessier stayed with Trenton.

"Why didn't you kill him?" Josh asked.

"Maybe I'm gettin' a conscience."

"You still plan to wed his mama?"

"If she'll have me."

"But you just crippled her son."

"I let him live. She'll thank me for that."

"Is that why you didn't kill him? So she'd still marry you?"

"You never know about me, do you? Just when you think I did somethin' for a right reason, you suspect I did it for a bad one?"

Josh lifted an eyebrow. No matter how long he lived, he'd never understand York.

"I thought you were gone," York said.

"I was going to be but . . . Hillard came this morning."

York paused, and Josh saw the questions in his eyes. "I told him. All about the money."

York's face hardened. "You beat all."

"It's okay," said Josh. "That's what I came to tell you." He motioned for Johnny and Camellia to join them, then led everybody a couple more steps away. "Hillard told me everything," he continued, his tone low so the Tessiers couldn't hear. "He works for Wallace Swanson. Swanson's a rich man now, living in Richmond. Made a lot of money running a general store, then bought and operates several hotels, some houses. You name it, he's got his fingers in it."

"He must have changed a heap since I last knew him," York said with resentment.

"Apparently so. Anyway, Swanson sent a man named Quincy down here to look for Camellia and Chester."

York glanced at Camellia. "What's he want with her? And Chester's dead!"

"He's their pa, remember. He sent the money to them!" Josh said. "Wanted them to know he was alive; wanted to make up for leaving them so long ago."

York frowned. "I don't get it. Why would he do that all of a sudden? After all these years?"

"You'd have to ask him. Hillard didn't know the answer to that."

York faced Camellia. "You know about the money?"

"Yes, Josh told me just a few minutes ago."

"I wouldn't have kept it had I known it was for you and Chester. I got my faults, but I wouldn't take from you or the boys. You got to believe that."

"I know," she said.

"I'll give you the money," he said. "All of it."

Josh dropped his eyes in gratitude for the good that remained in York.

Camellia raised her chin. "I don't want it. Got no need for it. I know how much you want this chance with The Oak. You do with it what you want."

"That don't feel right," York said.

"Doesn't matter," she insisted. "I have no desire for money from a man I never met."

"But he's your father."

She shrugged.

Wanting to give York and Camellia some privacy, Josh moved off and back to Trenton. He was standing on one leg now, holding on to Calvin. When Trenton stared toward Josh, a snarl on his lips, Josh saw how much he hated York and anybody connected to him. As Calvin leaned in close to Trenton and handed him something, Josh glanced away. Camellia, York, and Johnny stood in a small circle, their voices low. Josh took a deep breath and gazed toward the ocean. He'd miss this place, the beauty of the sea, the smell of the salt air. He looked one last time at Trenton and Calvin. Blood ran from Trenton's knee into the sand; he still held his pistol at his side.

Josh's blood suddenly ran cold. Trenton had propped his left hand on Calvin's shoulder and now lifted the pistol to an aiming position with his right!

Josh yelled, throwing his body between Trenton and York. The pistol fired as he moved. A crack sounded, and the bullet caught Josh in the left side of his chest. He fell to the sand, the right side of his face landing on the beach. The ocean rolled in at eye level. Strange, how different the waves looked from here, the way they slid in on the sand all white and foamy, Josh thought. He heard voices and felt pain in his chest. Then everything seemed a little darker, as if somebody had slid a cloud over the sun. He saw York's face and then Camellia's and wondered how they could be on the ground as he was.

Josh tasted blood in his throat. "I'm glad Trenton . . . didn't kill you," he whispered to York.

"Me too."

"Now you . . . your picture . . . the mantel."

"Don't talk," said Camellia.

Josh smiled lightly. "Stay . . . with me," he murmured.

"I'm here."

"I . . . I love you," he said.

"We'll fix you," she replied softly.

"Beth . . . Butler. Care for them."

"You'll take care of them," she answered.

The doctor moved to Josh, rolled him to his back, and examined his wound. "Need to get the bleeding stopped. If I can do that, he's got a chance."

Josh smiled again. "I got a chance."

"Let's get him out of here," said the doctor.

York and Johnny gently lifted and carried Josh toward the doctor's carriage. Camellia took his right hand and squeezed it as they walked.

"Mexico," Josh said. "I need . . . to confess it."

"I'm here," she said.

They reached the carriage and laid him in the backseat. Camellia climbed in beside him. The carriage headed toward The Oak.

"Middle . . . of the night," he whispered.

"Later," Camellia said. "Tell me later."

Josh closed his eyes. "Got to . . . say it now." He panted. "Before it's too . . . late."

"It can wait," she pleaded.

"I was asleep . . . in a camp, hundreds of men. I woke up, saw this man, short, hat over his head, covered in blankets, standing over . . . York." Josh paused to draw breath.

"Not now," pleaded Camellia again.

Josh opened his eyes. Camellia looked so lovely, but she didn't understand, didn't know that before a man died he needed to say things, needed to speak things he'd never said to anyone. He didn't want to carry the guilt in his heart when he stood before Jesus.

"I saw . . . a weapon. He had it . . . pointed at . . . York. I pulled my pistol . . . killed him."

Camellia glanced at York. "I don't understand," she cried. "It was war. Men die in war."

York nodded gravely. "Men, yes. But this was . . . he was a boy."

She looked back to Josh, her confusion evident. "A boy?"

"A boy," said York, speaking for Josh now. "Not more than ten or eleven. He was starving. Armies, ours and the Mexicans, had been in his area for a couple of weeks, taking what they needed. The boy slipped into our camp, Josh woke up, saw him standing over me, the pistol in hand. Josh shot him before he knew."

Camellia leaned closer to Josh. Tears streaked his face. She put her lips to his ear. "You didn't know," she whispered. "You were just a boy yourself."

"I'm sorry," he whispered back, his eyes wet.

"The Lord forgives you," she soothed. "The Lord forgives you."

Josh took a deep breath. "One more thing," he whispered. "Hillard . . . told me."

"What?"

"Your mother . . . is . . ."

"What about my mother?" she asked.

He smiled lightly. "She's . . . she's alive."

His mind switched off then. Even though he could vaguely hear Camellia calling his name, he could no longer answer. Then her voice disappeared completely, and he heard nothing more.

Chapter Thirty-Three

The next three weeks passed like a dark dream for Camellia.

Once they'd carried Josh back to his house, the doctor got the bleeding stopped and saw that the bullet hadn't hit his heart. After that, he told everybody he wanted to let Josh rest at least a day before he tried to get the bullet out. The next morning he drugged Josh with laudanum and went after the bullet, carefully digging into Josh's chest with sharp instruments and a pair of forceps. After what seemed like hours to Camellia, the doctor lifted out the bullet with bloody fingers and dropped it into a tin cup. Everybody breathed a sigh of relief.

"We're not out of the woods yet," the doctor cautioned after he'd finished. "He'll bleed some more. Then we wait to see if any infection sets in. If not, he might just make it. Only the Lord knows."

Although everybody took turns sitting with him, Camellia, Beth, and Butler did the most. Day and night, somebody stayed by him all the time. Fever came on him the fourth day, a raging heat on his face and hands that made his body almost scorching to touch. He talked out of his head for almost a week after that, his words making no sense, words about a boy in Mexico, words about Anna, Camellia. Sometimes he shouted the words, sometimes he whispered them, sometimes tears poured down his face as he talked. Every now and again, he even spoke some Scripture, his voice soft as he mouthed the phrases. He lost weight, his bones poking through his skin like tree limbs in the winter when the leaves have fallen off.

Camellia prayed more than she'd ever prayed. Not just for Josh, though she usually started and ended her prayers with her concerns for him. But she prayed also for Trenton, for her pa, for herself. Everything had become so confused in the last week. Things she'd felt certain about for years were now so mixed up she didn't know what to think or feel.

Sharpton Hillard visited her while she nursed Josh, his words assuring her that what Josh said was true. Wallace Swanson and her mother had sent the five thousand dollars as a way to make amends for the sorry way they had treated her and her brother so many years ago. Why they'd sent it now Hillard didn't know. But yes, they were alive, living in Richmond. Her mother went by Ruth now, her middle name. Not even York had known it.

Camellia tried to figure out her feelings about the Swansons but couldn't. What did it matter if they were alive? They meant nothing to her, were no more real and solid than a fog that rolled in off the ocean on a winter morning. So what if they'd sent her and Chester some money? Did they think that would make a difference? Could they soothe their consciences so easily? She wanted to talk to her pa about all of it but didn't know where or how to start. So she said nothing to anyone about what Hillard had told Josh.

The talk of war bothered her a lot too. Seemed that the whole country, led by South Carolina's example, had gone mad with the zeal for glory. Although news didn't get to The Oak real fast, it did eventually reach them. Within days after the duel everybody knew that Yankees and Confederates were now at war. Camellia prayed about that too, but since she didn't know if or when it would affect her and her loved ones, she tried to keep it out of her head.

Of all the feelings that confused her, none bothered her more than her thoughts about Trenton. She worried about his leg. Although the doctor had done everything he could to prevent it, gangrene had set in pretty fast, and the doctor had been forced to amputate just over the knee. She knew this not because anybody from Trenton's family talked to her, but because she went by the manse every day and talked to Stella and Ruby.

Her heart ached as she tried to figure out her feelings about him. How could he have taken a shot at her pa after the duel had ended? What kind of man shot at another when he wasn't looking? Was it possible to love a man who'd do something like that?

About a week after the amputation, Calvin showed up on her porch and told her Trenton wanted to see her. Although scared of the meeting, she also wanted it, needed to talk to him and give him a chance to explain. Surely he'd lost his head to do such a thing; no man in his right mind would take such dishonorable action against another. She followed Calvin back to the manse and found Trenton in his bed, a pair of crutches beside him on the covers. He motioned for her to take a chair, and she quietly obeyed. Calvin eased out of the room. Camellia folded her hands in her lap. A soft breeze from the window pushed her hair back. Trenton's eyes lay dark in their sockets. He seemed to have aged ten years.

"I am a cripple now," he said. "Your pa made me one."

She saw hatred in his eyes. He seemed completely different now, not at all the young man she'd cared about so much, the young man she'd . . . loved. Had he always been like this and she'd never seen it, or had life gradually done this to him, the hurts and hard times slowly carving fury from a good heart, bitterness out of a sweet spirit?

"I'm sorry about . . . about . . . " she tried to say.

"My leg," he snarled. "My leg, you can say it. Your pa cost me my leg!"

Camellia started to remind him that he'd issued the challenge but decided against it.

"I ought to be leading soldiers," he said. "Defending my home, my family from the Yankees. But with this—" He pointed to his knee.

"Be grateful you don't have to fight," she said, hoping to make him feel better.

"Grateful? What an idiotic thing to say. The Yankees want to destroy everything we own, what we stand for, what makes us who we are, and you want me to feel grateful?"

Camellia sighed. "I don't know what I'm saying. I'm so mixed up, confused."

"I meant to shoot your pa," he said. "Not Josh Cain. I want you to know that."

"That's supposed to make me feel better?" Her voice sounded angry, and it surprised her. She didn't want to feel mad at Trenton. How could you marry someone you didn't like?

"Your pa offended my mother. I had to defend her honor."

"So you tried to shoot my pa when he wasn't looking?"

"He crippled me. I was in shock. Surely you can understand that."

"He could have killed you in the duel."

"I would have preferred that."

Camellia leaned closer, took his hand. "Look," she started, "I cannot speak for what my pa did or didn't do with your mama, whether it was respectful or not. But was it worth dying for, worth his life or yours? I don't see it, don't understand it. Look what it's brought. Josh Cain near death, you with this . . . crippled. Was it worth that?"

Trenton pulled away and touched his thigh above his missing knee. "My mother is still going to marry him."

"What?"

"Haven't you heard? They talked yesterday. Seems she's appreciative your pa didn't kill me. Said she can understand what he did, why he did it. She figures I gave him no choice but to duel. He told her he didn't kill me for her sake, not mine. She found that . . . charming." He spat out the last words as if spitting out sour milk.

"She tell you this?" Camellia leaned back in amazement.

"Yes, last night."

"So there's going to be a wedding on The Oak after all." She wondered if her pa was still legally married to Ruth Swanson or if all their years of separation gave them a common law divorcement, but it was above her head, so she let it drop.

"Soon as we know whether Mr. Cain is going to live or die. Your pa didn't want to marry until then."

"He's hanging on," she said, dropping her eyes. "But we don't know if he'll make it."

Trenton shrugged as if it didn't matter one way or the other. Camellia thought of her pa and Mrs. Tessier. Since she'd not taken the five thousand from him, her pa still had enough to save The Oak, at least for now. Trenton picked up a crutch, reached out and tapped her chair on the arm with it. As she faced him, a heavy weariness hit her, a bone-tired feeling from the nights with Josh, the thinking about all that had happened in the last few days, the worry about Josh and Trenton.

"I need to go," she said quietly. "We'll talk again soon."

"Please not yet," he replied.

"I don't know what else to say right now."

"Don't you want to know?" he asked.

"Know what?"

He smiled slightly. Some of the years seemed to peel off his face, and she saw something of the old Trenton again. But could she trust it anymore? Or was it just a mask he put on when he wanted something?

"What will happen to us?"

"I don't understand."

He pushed back the covers, lifted both crutches, and eased to the side of the bed, his right pants leg pinned at the thigh. A few seconds later he stood unsteadily and faced her. "I'm getting better."

"I'm glad."

Moving slowly, he stepped to her and bent as low as his crutches would allow. "You will forgive me if I don't bow," he said, his eyes peering deeply into hers. "But my infirmity prevents it."

Camellia's heart thudded. This made no sense! What was he doing?

"I have a question for you," he said. "I don't think I've ever actually asked you this question before."

Camellia wanted to run. He couldn't do this now, not while so much remained unsettled, confused. Yet how could she run? She'd dreamed of this almost every day since she could remember.

Trenton reached for her hand and she, unable to run, extended it. He took it and kissed it gently on the palm, then the top. Then he said the four words she'd always wanted to hear him say: "Will you marry me?"

Camellia's heart seemed to stop. The breeze dropped to nothing. It felt like the whole world held its breath. She wanted to smile but couldn't. She wanted to shout yes but couldn't. She wanted to stand up and take Trenton in her arms and hold him close and protect him like a mother protected a child. But she couldn't do that either. She felt nailed to her seat, her mouth glued shut. A sudden realization hit her, something she now saw she'd known all along but couldn't admit. But now it all made sense for the first time, more sense than anything had ever made sense. No wonder she couldn't say yes to Trenton Tessier!

"I'm a little unsteady on my feet here," Trenton whispered. "An answer would be greatly appreciated."

She blinked and focused on him again. "I'm sorry. But I can't marry you."

He staggered back onto the bed. She knelt by his knees, looked up into his face. He seemed stunned, as if somebody had hit him with a boat oar. "It's not right," she soothed, confident in her feelings for the first time in a long time. "It wouldn't work."

"Why?" he asked, his eyes focusing again.

"It's more than one thing."

"But you love me," he said. "Always have."

"Not anymore. If I ever did."

"Sure you did."

She shook her head. "I don't know. Maybe I did. But that's past now."

"No one else can give you what I can," he said with a tint of anger sliding into his voice.

"I don't care about that," she replied. "Never did."

"Sure you did," he insisted. "Everyone does. Marrying me would be the best thing that ever happened to you. You know it, your father knew it, everyone knew it."

"Not everyone," she said, remembering. "Some warned me not to marry you, said you weren't good enough for me."

"Who said that?"

She blinked, realizing with a start what she'd just said. "It doesn't matter."

He grunted bitterly. "Maybe not, but me not good enough for you? Seems it's the other way around."

She stared at Trenton, pity now in her eyes. "That's one reason it never could've worked. You saw yourself as better than me. Yes, you tried to think differently, but deep down, you were just like your mother, your father. I was hired help to them, to you. You're like them, like your father." Her eyes blinked. She knew now she might as well get it all said. After all this time she had to tell Trenton what had happened to his father.

"The day your father died," she began, "he came to the cookhouse."

Trenton opened his mouth to interrupt, but she continued anyway. "You need to know he tried to . . . " And then she told him the story—all of it. How Mr. Tessier had pressed her for her favors, how she'd rejected him, how the two of them had fought, how he had slipped and killed himself.

Trenton listened quietly, his face not changing. When she'd finished, he simply said, "You should have told the sheriff. But I can forgive you for what happened. No reason it should keep us from marrying."

"I don't need your forgiveness," she said, bothered he'd seen it that way. "Except for keeping it hidden so long."

"The law could still come after you for this. If I pushed them to do it." She heard the threat in his voice.

"Of course I wouldn't set the law after my wife no matter how evil her crimes."

"I already said I couldn't marry you," she said flatly.

"You said for more than one reason. Is it because I'm a cripple?"

"No, that has nothing to do with it."

"Then what is it?"

Camellia hesitated, knowing if she admitted what she felt, it would change her life more than anything ever had. Yet how could she deny the secret in her heart? It was as certain as the ocean tide pulling in and out, as powerful as a storm that blew in from the south.

"I love somebody else."

"What?" He shook his head in disbelief.

"I love somebody else," she repeated, as much for her benefit as his.

"That's foolishness. You're throwing away everything."

"Maybe so, but I have to listen to my heart."

"You're not thinking straight."

"You're wrong. I'm thinking straight for the first time in forever."

"You mean this?"

"Yes."

His face grew hateful all at once. "Get out then!" he shouted. "I never want to see you again!"

"I don't want to be your enemy," she offered, hoping to ease the conflict. "We were friends once."

"I said leave me!"

Although grieved by his hurt, Camellia left the room. At the stairs, her feet began to move faster as she thought of where she was going. By the time she reached the porch she was running, rushing toward the one man she now knew she loved, the one man who made her feel like a man ought to make a woman feel, the one man with a gentle heart and kindly eyes and the spirit of the Lord coursing through his soul. She burst into laughter as she ran from the manse, her heart lighter than she'd felt in years.

Yes, she had a lot of questions she still had to answer, a lot of clouds still hanging over her head. What would the war do to The Oak? What would happen to the people there when the war came? What about Wallace Swanson and her mama in Richmond? Should she write them, go to meet them? What kind of marriage would her pa make with Mrs. Tessier? Would that succeed or fail?

So many questions, so much left to happen. But none of that mattered right now. What mattered was the one question that squeezed her heart more than any other, the one that would shape her life more than all the rest put together: Would Josh Cain live?

"Let him live, Lord," she prayed as she reached his house. "Let him live because I love him and want him to know that more than anything I've ever wanted in my whole life."

She ran in without knocking and hurried to his room. Beth sat by his bed. Camellia hugged the girl and told her she could take a break for a few minutes. When Beth had left, Camellia sat down by Josh and touched his cheek. "I love you. I want you to know that."

He didn't move. The breeze from the window played in her hair. She stood and moved to the window and looked out. Less than three miles away, the ocean rolled in and out. She took a deep breath and smelled the spring air, the hint of warmth already in it. She moved back to Josh's bed, sat beside him again. He'd said he loved her. Did he mean it, or was he out of his head from the bullet?

She saw a painting on the table by the bed and picked it up. The picture showed a man and a woman walking on the beach, their backs to the viewer, the sun going down behind them. The images were soft, the work of a gentle hand, the forms indistinct yet somehow still real. She remembered the painting she'd seen on the mantel the day she first went to Josh to talk about what had happened with Marshall Tessier. This wasn't it. When had he drawn this? Was it he and Anna, sketched years ago? Or was it Josh and her, something he'd done after Anna's death? She wondered who had found it and laid it out. Maybe Beth pulled it from some things he'd packed to take when they left The Oak.

She studied the picture and her heart warmed. Instead of feeling jealous that it might be Anna, she wanted to smile, to smile and cry at the same time because a man of such a sensitive heart had said he loved her. She turned back to Josh and held up the painting as if he could see it.

"I hope this is us," she whispered. "Me and you."

The breeze blew through again as Camellia studied Josh's face. "Me and you," she repeated, pointing to the picture. "On the beach on a Sunday as the sun goes down."

She took Josh's hands, squeezed lightly, and gazed at his face. Then, although she couldn't be certain, she thought she saw the touch of a smile.

About the Author

As a boy growing up in the red clay country of northwest South Carolina, Gary E. Parker quickly came to enjoy the folklore and history of his native state. One of his earliest memories is going to Charleston with his dad on a business trip and standing by the ocean, watching the ships come into the harbor. From that day Gary loved the smell of the salt air, the sound of the ocean's waves, and the stories of the men and women who lived and died in the coastal area.

Carrying that interest in Southern history with him to college, Gary majored in history at Furman University. Feeling called to ministry, he prepared at Southeastern Seminary, earning a masters degree, and at Baylor University, where he completed a doctorate of Philosophy of Religion, with an emphasis in historical theology.

After finishing his formal education, Gary began pastoral ministry, serving as senior pastor at the Warrenton Baptist Church in Warrenton, North Carolina, Grace Baptist in Sumter, South Carolina, First Baptist of Jefferson City, Missouri, and the First Baptist Church of Decatur, Georgia (where he currently serves).

In addition to pastoring a church, Gary obviously loves writing. His previous titles include four nonfiction works and twelve works of fiction. The fiction titles include five novels from Bethany House: *Highland Hopes*, *Highland Mercies*, and *Highland Grace* (the critically acclaimed Blue Ridge Legacy series), *The Ephesus Fragment*, and *Rumors of Peace*; four from Thomas Nelson: *A Capitol Offense*, *Dark Road to Daylight*, *Death Stalks a Holiday*, and *Beyond a Reasonable Doubt*; one from Victor: *Desert Water*; and three novellas from Cook Communications: *The Last Gift*, *A Shepherd's Cross*, and *The Wedding Dress*.

In addition to books, Gary has written extensively for Sunday school Bible study materials and national magazines.

361

Questions for Reflection

1. Camellia York is a young woman tempted to love a man who really isn't good for her. What about Trenton Tessier attracted her? How would marrying Trenton have affected her life? Are there times when you've been attracted to something that wasn't good for you? How did you respond?

2. Camellia finds comfort in her faith in spite of the fact that she can't get to church that much. How would it affect your faith if you didn't have the opportunity to share in a church family? How could having a church family have helped Camellia cope with the hardships she faced?

3. While defending herself, Camellia accidentally contributed to the death of another human being but didn't tell the whole truth about what had happened. How do you think you would have reacted in her situation? What did she do right, and what did she do wrong? Do you believe she committed a sin in what happened to Marshall Tessier? In the lie that followed? Why or why not?

4. Camellia struggled with the issue of slavery yet didn't know what, if anything, she could do about it. Are there cultural situations in your life that you know are wrong but don't know how to change? How can we improve race relations in our world?

5. Trenton Tessier is a spoiled, rich young man. How do you think he would have been different if he'd been born in a situation similar to Camellia's? How much do you believe our circumstances shape us and how much depends on our own personal choices?

6. Hampton York does a good thing in one minute and a bad thing in the next. Do you believe he's redeemable? Why or why not? Do you know people like him? What about them makes them attractive? What about them makes them so prone to temptation?

7. York at one point indicates that people don't become bad all at once. They slowly become that way as they make one small wrong choice after another. Do you agree with York or not? How do you believe people become "bad" people? How does a person change from making wrong choices to making right ones?

8. Several people have secrets in this story. How did those secrets affect their lives? What would have happened if they'd told their secrets earlier? What kind of secrets do you have? Do you need to tell someone about them? How will your life change if you reveal your secrets to someone else?

9. Josh Cain's faith is strong, yet he doesn't feel worthy to go to church. What made him feel unworthy? What trait of God did he seem to have forgotten? Have you ever felt unworthy of God? How can you get over this feeling? What does the Bible tell us about God's forgiveness of our sin?

READ THE HEART-POUNDING FIRST PAGES

OF THE SECOND BOOK OF THE

SOUTHERN TIDES TRILOGY

Fateful Journeys

BY

GARY E. PARKER

Chapter One

The Oak Plantation, May 1861

Dark still blanketed the South Carolina coastland on the morning that Trenton Tessier decided he had no choice but to take his revenge against the man who had stolen the woman he loved. His face soured by hours of drinking and a night without sleep, Tessier now slouched in a black leather chair by the stone fireplace in his second-floor bedroom.

"Josh Cain," he muttered, his tongue thick with the whiskey. "He took Camellia from me. I gave her a proposal of marriage, but she refused. It's Cain's fault. I will have my vengeance."

Trenton's brother, Calvin, younger by five years, sat in a matching chair across from him. "You're in no shape to avenge anything," said Calvin, gesturing toward the wooden peg that started at Trenton's right knee and ran to the floor. "You're barely a month past the day you lost . . . since you were shot."

Trenton took a sip from the silver flask he held and raised up slightly. A man of thin shoulders and short-cropped brown hair, he wore pleated, tan riding pants and a white shirt with a ruffle at the neck. He lifted one of the crutches that lay in his lap and aimed it at a rolltop desk across the room. "Hand me my pistols," he ordered. "Josh Cain stole what belongs to me. My honor is at stake."

"Your honor almost got you killed," Calvin replied.

"Better death than this!" Trenton pointed to his stump. "I'm a laughingstock! The fine Master Trenton Tessier, educated in the best schools the South can offer; heir to The Oak, finest plantation in the lowlands; a man of the highest social station—none of it matters now! Get me the pistols or get out!"

"You're drunk and crazy from not sleeping," argued the freckled Calvin, obviously trying to calm his brother's rage. "Cain is unconscious . . . in no shape to face you."

"I'm not worried about Cain's condition."

"You'd murder him?"

Trenton dropped his eyes, and his head cleared some. Could he go through with this? Had he sunk so low as to harm a man who couldn't defend himself? Part of him knew this was wrong; maybe he should let it pass.

Trenton took another sip of the whiskey and glanced down at his peg leg again. His eyes blazed as his resolve returned. "Cain deserves it, for what he did to me."

Calvin stood, moved over, and put a hand on Trenton's shoulder. "If you want to shoot somebody, it ought to be Hampton York," Calvin claimed. "He's the one who shot you in the leg."

Trenton glared at Calvin, who was the spitting image of their dead father. With his blocky legs and chest, wide hands and feet, thick jowls and thin hair, Calvin wasn't especially handsome. But he was powerful. If it came to a physical battle right now, Calvin could probably best him— a fact Trenton disliked immensely.

Striking like a mad snake, Trenton jerked Calvin's hand from his shoulder and bent his fingers backward. "You plan on challenging me on this?" Trenton growled.

Calvin's mouth twitched in pain. He eyed Trenton as if he wanted to kill him.

Trenton held his brother's fingers for another minute, then let them go. "Just get me the pistols," he said again.

Calvin stretched his fingers as Trenton took another drink from the flask. He wondered how much longer he could keep Calvin under his control. Every younger brother eventually tested the elder. Was this the time for him and Calvin?

Although his eyes stayed angry, Calvin finally eased across to the desk and pulled the pistols from the top drawer. Grunting with effort, Trenton stood, tucked the flask in his coat, arranged the crutches under his arms, and took the pistols. "Now hand me my coat," he instructed, arranging the pistols in his waistband.

Calvin stepped to a closet, removed a thigh-length black coat, and handed it to Trenton.

Now fully dressed, Trenton stood before the full-length mirror by his bed and stared at his stump. A set of pins held his pants leg in place in a neat fold just above the wooden peg. Underneath the pants the wound oozed a light but steady flow of foul discharge that required constant cleaning. Trenton ground his teeth against the weakness his leg caused him. He was a cripple!

Every night since the duel he'd prayed, as best as he knew how, that when he woke in the morning he'd find losing his leg all a terrible nightmare of pain and humiliation, unlike anything a man of his station ought to have to bear. But every morning when he opened his eyes and reached down, he found nothing but air where bone, blood, and skin should have been.

"How do you plan to get to Mr. Cain's house?" asked Calvin. "It's half a mile from the Manse."

"I'll walk," said Trenton.

"On crutches?"

"Josh Cain took Camellia from me. How far I have to walk to kill him is of little consequence," Trenton fired back.

When Calvin wiped his palms on his pants, Trenton stared closely at his brother. He saw fear in Calvin's eyes. "You have no part in this, so don't let it rest on your conscience."

"It's not my conscience I fear for . . . it's you."

Trenton patted Calvin's back. "Your concern touches me."

"Captain York will come after you when Cain is dead," Calvin said.

"I expect so."

"You want him to come, don't you?"

"Yes. He too owes me a debt that only his death will pay."

"Your duel with York followed the code. You took your shot but missed. Maybe you should accept that and leave things alone."

"York knew I had never dueled," Trenton claimed. "He took advantage of my inexperience."

"He let you have the first shot," argued Calvin.

"Okay!" snapped Trenton. "I missed! And I have cursed myself a thousand times for it. Then York shot me in the knee."

"Then you shot Josh Cain," said Calvin, his voice low and quiet, a hint of accusation in it.

"That was an accident and you know it! You gave me your pistol; I shot at York but hit Cain."

Trenton grabbed his flask and swilled down a full swallow, hoping the liquor would jolt him into action. No matter how much he hated Josh Cain, Trenton Tessier had never killed a man, so it would take some doing to follow through.

He glanced hurriedly around the room. His portrait, painted by one of the finest artists in Charleston, hung over his bed. A handwoven, multicolored Oriental rug lay at the bed's foot. A basin and pitcher of water sat on a nightstand by the bed. From the ceiling hung a chandelier, its sparkling glass shining from the light of many candles. Would all of this look different when he returned from killing Cain? So what if it did? None of it meant anything any more. Without Camellia, without his leg, without his honor, who cared what he possessed?

"Mother will not approve of this," said Calvin, interrupting Trenton's thoughts.

Trenton snickered at his brother's efforts to dissuade him. "The great Katherine Tessier!" He chuckled. "For years she paid little attention to me. Left my raising to a darky mammy while she spent her time in Charleston. Mother cared for nothing but her parties, her laudanum, her fine clothes, and fancy furnishings."

His voice dropped, and a hint of sadness edged in. "Only after Father's death, only after I became the heir of The Oak did she bother to get involved in my life. I care nothing about her approval."

"She loves you, Trenton."

Trenton laughed, but it held no joy. "If she loved me, she would never have accepted Hampton York's marriage proposal—forcing me to challenge him to a duel for his insult."

"She had no choice," said Calvin. "He has money she needs to keep

The Oak from the hands of the bankers."

"York is the overseer here! She might as well mate with a darky."

"Do you think killing Cain will end plans for the wedding? Is that what's pushing you?"

"It would be a bonus, yes. York stole his money from us."

"He says not."

"It doesn't matter."

"What will happen to The Oak if Mother doesn't marry York?"

"We're going to war, so who knows? Either way I don't need York to save The Oak. If Cain's death causes him to withdraw his proposal, then I'll have killed two birds with one stone." Trenton smiled at the notion and took a drink to celebrate it.

"Are you sure you want to do this?" asked Calvin, his voice halting.

Trenton lifted a crutch, pushed it hard against his brother's chest, and backed him up against the wall. Trenton's eyes narrowed, and a dark stare came into them—cold and unfeeling. "I know what you're doing," he hissed. "All these questions—slowing me down, hoping I'll change my mind. But I *am* the eldest son, cripple or not. *I* decide my destiny. Not you, not Mother. And you best not forget that."

Calvin's eyes met Trenton's for a few seconds, then broke away. "Forgive me," Calvin whispered, his eyes suddenly filled with tears. "But Cain is a helpless man. I see no honor in harming him."

Trenton eased the crutch to Calvin's chin and tipped it up so he could see into his brother's eyes. "I want you to understand," Trenton soothed. "I love Camellia, and I want her as my wife. But she says she loves Josh Cain. Of course she doesn't. How could she? But as long as he's alive, she won't come to me."

"I still think it's wrong."

Trenton lowered his crutch to the floor. "Who's to say what is wrong . . . and what is right? Cain will probably die anyway from the bullet I already put in him. I'm simply speeding up his passage."

Calvin wiped his eyes.

"I'll return soon," said Trenton.

"I wish you wouldn't do this."

Ignoring his brother, Trenton headed to the door. "I should return within the hour. Then it will be over."

"I expect it's just beginning," whispered Calvin.

Trenton took another drink and hobbled out, his chin set. In his heart, though, he figured Calvin had it right: What he did next would determine his fate—and that of everyone around him—for years to come.

Mending Places
—*Denise Hunter*

Meet Hanna Landin. Hanna put college on hold to help her grandmother run Higher Grounds, her family's failing mountain lodge, which soon will be closed if revenue can't be raised. Strange things are occurring at the lodge, and Hanna fears someone is trying to sabotage her family's business. When Hanna hires Micah Gallagher to be the lodge's mountain guide, a high-country adventure filled with love, intrigue, and romance ensues. Micah is forced to face the hidden places that haunt him, and Hanna must address her fears and determine if forgiveness can make way for love.

ISBN: 1-58229-358-9

Shoofly Pie
—Tim Downs

Get to know Kathryn Guilford, from a remote North Carolina county, and Nick Polchak—a.k.a. the Bug Man. When Kathryn receives news that her long-time friend and one-time suitor is dead, she refuses to accept the coroner's finding that his death was by his own hand. Although she has a pathological fear of insects, she turns in desperation to Polchak, a forensic entomologist, to help her learn the truth. Gold Medallion award–winning author Tim Downs takes you on a thrill ride as Kathryn confronts her darkest fears to unearth a decade-long conspiracy that threatens to turn her entire world upside down.

ISBN: 1-58229-308-2

HOWARD
Fiction

Betrayal in Paris
—Doris Elaine Fell

Get acquainted with twenty-seven-year-old Adrienne Winters, as Christy Award finalist Doris Elaine Fell weaves a tale of mystery and intrigue. Headstrong Ms. Winters is relentless in her pursuit to clear the names of her brother and father who were victims of a double betrayal on foreign soil. Travel along as Adrienne's adventure takes her from the streets of Paris to the hot sands of the Kuwaiti desert. Set on the backdrop of the September 11 Pentagon tragedy, Adrienne discovers a gentle romance as she sorts out her family's history and her faith in God.

ISBN: 1-58229-314-7

Sins of the Mother
—Patricia H. Rushford

You'll surely enjoy getting to know country music singer Shanna O'Brian, as award-winning author, speaker, and teacher Patricia Rushford draws you into a story of romance, mystery, and adventure. As dashed hopes are rekindled and a haunting past comes into the light of truth, you'll find yourself caught up in Shanna's complex world. And when the mysterious death of her mother turns Shanna's world upside down, you'll feel her conflicting emotions as she is forced to make sense of her life—despite her fledgling faith in herself, her God, and the man determined to reclaim her love.

ISBN: 1-58229-342-2

HOWARD
Fiction

Enjoyment Guarantee

If you are not totally satisfied with this book, simply return it to us along with your receipt, a statement of what you didn't like about the book, and your name and address within 60 days of purchase to Howard Publishing, 3117 North 7th Street, West Monroe, LA 71291-2227, and we will gladly reimburse you for the cost of the book.